# reverberation
## the novel

**vb holmes**

2012

Cover photo by Hillary Wittich
Cover design by Hillary and Michael Wittich
About the cover: The image represents the two shots which open the story and the resultant smoke generated by the early nineteenth century guns.

www.reverberationthenovel.com
http://vbreverb.wordpress.com/

*Reverberation:*
*an extended or continuing effect resulting from*
*an action or event.*

# Table of Contents

# *The Story Behind the Story*

Fact: I do not believe in ghosts.
Fact: I have seen one.
Fact: Three times.

I live in an old house in a historic village. The property is small, a little over an acre. It includes a wheelwright's shop, a blacksmith's forge and a fast-running stream. The house sits on the southwest corner of an early crossroad opposite an unrestored 18th-century inn and tavern. A Revolutionary War cemetery and its contemporary church are around the bend and up the hill. There is a strong sense of history in this narrow valley.

My buildings have been neglected for many years and are in need of repair. I help as walls are opened to allow access to electric wires and plumbing; bare-bones bathrooms and a primitive kitchen are replaced; closets and bookshelves are built. However, demolition reveals no secrets, unearths no souvenirs of past occupants. The only known memories are those which have been embedded by the current residents.

Time passes, and as I retire one night, I note the date: April 18, 1993. I awaken suddenly from a deep sleep. I immediately notice the lack of light coming in through the window which is opposite the foot of the bed. I turn to look at the two windows on the side wall. Moonbeams filter in through nearby tree branches and dapple the bedclothes. I return my glance to the east-facing window. The frame and panes are obliterated by what I perceive as, for lack of a better description, an undulating, opaque blob. I tell myself I am dreaming. I close my eyes and do not open them until morning when I have but a vague memory of the specter.

I throw myself into the transformation of my new home and forget about the apparent hallucination until the night of June 6, when I am again aroused from my slumber. This time, the apparition materializes on the wall beside my bed. I am alert and I make note of its particulars: two-dimensional; dense; impenetrable; stationary mass with agitated, quivering edges; approximately five feet in height, three feet in width; non-threatening. I date the big-box-home-goods-store receipt on which I have written my observations and place it on the bedside table. I wonder if I am having a brain glitch. Nevertheless, I turn out the light and fall into a dreamless sleep.

Upon awakening, I see the list. I pick it up, read the words and am relieved to find my intellect remains unimpaired. I discount the brain glitch. In the past, I have experienced what I call "receptions". These precognitive happenings have been of minor import and I have looked on them as electrical impulses received from a simpatico sender. My interaction with the amorphous mass is different. I am dealing with an intangible substance with unproven communication skills. I decide the house, with its presumed residue of aspirations, dreams, and disappointments, is the catalyst and I want to know more.

The exterior of the building yields the first clue. It is a three-story house with two front doors. Centered between four windows on the third floor, and over the space between the doors, is a datestone which reads: "W and P H, 1867". The inscription has piqued my curiosity in the past and now the possibility that the spirit of my opaque visitor is somehow connected to my home leads me to the local historical society.

Working backwards from the current date, I uncover the history of the old house. The two previous owners had rotated renters through the property (with one man temporarily housing his mistress there--my first possible troubled soul). Prior to the landlords, seemingly happy families were in residence, all but one utilizing the blacksmith shop for their livelihood. I trace the inhabitants back to 1849 when William and Phebe purchased the acre-and-a-quarter lot with its original log cabin. Following a fire, they replaced the charred remains with the current building (ergo, the datestone; also, the possibility of clandestine activity suggests another restless psyche).

Hopscotching over several short-term owners, I find the perfect candidate for my nebulous illusion: an itinerant blacksmith, a likeable ne'er-do-well who drank, fought and worked hard when he needed money. He married the daughter of a prosperous farmer and purchased the village smithy with the expectation of paying for it with his wife's inheritance. Newspaper articles and his personal confession tell the story of a man who overextended his credit, lost everything, and in desperation, committed a senseless murder. He was found guilty, sentenced to death on April 18, 1818, and hung on June 6, one-hundred-and-seventy-five years to the day before each of the two appearances of the mysterious mirage. I am fascinated.

I determine to write a biography of this ordinary early nineteenth-century man and his downfall. I have the outline of his life and anticipate an easy task of filling in the blanks which, with the exception of information on his early years, I am able to accomplish. I begin to write. Unfortunately, the story is boring and I choose not to offend his descendants by embellishing his tale. I am forced to abandon my original idea.

However, my inconsequential hero has staked a place in my consciousness so I retain the skeleton of his story, change names and descriptions and let my imagination run wild. I try to channel John Irving and take my thoughts past the outermost boundaries of reality and into the realm of incredulity. I question my ability to ignore convention and publicly acknowledge the extent of my mental creativity. I admit my cowardice as I cringe over my flights of fancy. I temper them and attack my new project with a little less enthusiasm and vigor.

I immerse myself in early nineteenth-century history and culture. My characters create themselves and take over my story. My hero charts his own path and leaves behind the simple man whose real-life story spawned his development. Minor auxiliary characters become viable players and influence the fate of my protagonist. At one point, I write a short segment in which he spends a single night in a utopian community. Never deigning to ask permission, my main man takes up residence.

Faced with a need for information on these idealistic organizations, I turn first to the local Free Love Valley, a loosely organized group of farmers and their wives who followed the dictates of Theophilus Ransom Gates and participated in bizarre sexual rituals and unconventional pairings. However, I want more than irresponsible sexual laxity so I read up on other mid-nineteenth century communes. There are many groups, religious and secular, whose members bonded together to create self-contained, economically autonomous, intellectually and philosophically compatible societies. They range from the hard-working, serious-minded residents of the Amana Colonies and the celibate Shakers, to the long-lived Oneida Community which combined the industriousness of the former with the radical religious philosophy and unorthodox moral code preached by John Humphrey Noyes. I end my research with the Transcendentalist residents of George Ripley's Brook Farm, as chronicled by Nathaniel Hawthorne. Although the ideas of Reverend Noyes establish themselves as the primary DNA in the intellectual genetic code of my imagined commune, my characters rebel against his dictum of controlled group marriage in favor of the unrestrained sexual freedom promulgated by Theophilus Gates. I find I am treading water in a previously unknown world of mid-nineteenth century social experimentation.

My days are spent in front of the computer. The phone goes unanswered; emails are ignored; appointments, missed. Invented characters replace flesh-and-blood family and friends. I soldier on. The blob is long forgotten, until one day, I recognize this is no longer simply a story. It is a reincarnation and I begin to wonder: "Of what?" Is my work motivated by the rebirth of long-dead individuals or is it a subconscious exploration of unresolved social issues and adulterated mores?

My subplots address present-day concerns which have passed forward through the history of life on earth: power struggles, torture, sex, discrimination have plagued humanity since the beginning of time, while the rationalization of sin has accompanied the civilization of man. I worry. Do these issues overshadow the storyline of my novel? I admit to the similarities between today and yesteryear and decide they have become primary stimuli to the development of my basic plot.

I explore the themes of vicious, slanderous, political campaigning; abuse of power by religious and secular father figures; social matters such as women's rights and abortion; racial, economic, physical and mental discrimination which dominate the headlines of our newspapers today. I plumb the same issues which existed almost two hundred years ago when Andrew Jackson battled John Quincy Adams for the Presidency of the United States; charismatic, radical preachers proselytized extreme philosophical and moral changes; lunatic asylums utilized tortuous cures, and nascent support groups formed to publicize injustices and promote equality. My characters respond to the challenges as I continue to work on my story. I wonder if the anonymous phantom really is the spirit of my ordinary man eternally trapped in time and if his essence will be transformed by the new life I am giving him.

The last months of 1993 pass, taking with them the next four years. I anticipate the dates of April 18 and June 6, 1998, as the one-hundred-and-eightieth anniversaries of the conviction and hanging approach. I am disappointed, yet relieved, when the undulating black form does not appear on the first date. I want to believe I am saving the wandering soul from purgatory by bringing change to his previous temporal manifestation.

On the evening of June 6, I handwrite the title and add my name to the final proof of my book. I sign and date the cover letter, place it on the corner of the desk and go to my bedroom. I pause in front of the wall where I last viewed my nocturnal visitor. Then, I walk to the east-facing window and glance down at the stream below, at the hemlocks which line the bank, the rocks which fill the creek bed. A breeze ruffles the fine-needled branches of the graceful evergreens and a leaf rides the wind toward the glass which separates us. I rub my eyes as I turn back to the wall.

I consciously stare at the empty space and concentrate with all my energy as I attempt to summon the spirit. Ever so slowly, the painted surface starts to vibrate. The vision begins as before, as an amorphous, opaque abstraction. This time, however, the undulating edges take on the outline of a man's body. A bit of color tinges the image and fills in the ill-defined shape. I watch as a broad-brimmed black hat materializes atop a featureless head. A faded green coat, ochre-colored nankeen pantaloons, coarse stockings and crude leather moccasins cover the pulsating apparition. I hold out my hand. For a brief moment, individualized characteristics fill in the facial blanks. I notice the mouth. It is twisted into a sardonic smile. The ghostly persona trembles and slowly fades. The encounter is over.

My positive thoughts of saving a troubled soul vanish when I realize what I have done. By rewriting the history of my hero, I have removed his tags. His biography has been overwritten and his original existence, deleted. By signing off on my manuscript, I may have saved my hero from purgatory, but at the same time, I have also condemned him to something much worse: I have consigned his immortal reality to oblivion.

I leave the bedroom, appalled by the knowledge that the mysterious phantasm has guided my work, and peripherally, my life, since I moved into this house. I fear the impact his altered saga will have on my own written and life stories. I am not an innately superstitious person, but as I approach my office, I cross my fingers for luck and chant aloud: "I do not believe in ghosts. I do not believe in ghosts. I do not…."

# *Preface*

*Reverberation, The Novel,* is a work of fiction which takes place a little more than forty years after the signing of the Constitution of the United States. The country's economy is primarily agrarian; however, industrialization is taking root in the cities. Westward expansion is stimulating the development of a national infrastructure and fueling debate about states' rights versus federalism. Large numbers of immigrants and free blacks are inflating the population and changing the demographics. The growth of a two-party system is altering the face of politics and political campaigning.

A philosophical shift prompts many Americans to actively support the abolition of slavery, the nascent suffragist movement, equal rights and free education for all. The traditional Calvinism of the early settlers is challenged by itinerant preachers who propagate evangelical Protestantism. In the extreme, religious and ideological prophets establish self-contained utopian communities based on the socialist tenet of shared property. Additionally, some advocate radical lifestyles such as celibacy, polygamy, group marriage and free love.

The end of the third decade of the nineteenth century is, indeed, a time of change and challenge. America underscores its growing transformation by sending Andrew Jackson, a rough, volatile, military hero from free-wheeling Tennessee to the White House to replace John Quincy Adams, a reserved, Harvard-educated diplomat from staid New England.

# Monday, August 18, 1828

The old musket recoiled against her shoulder as Esther stood firm and the ball stayed its course. Pain from the impact of the gunstock radiated across her chest and upper back; gray smoke from the ignition of the charge seared her eyes; the acrid smell of scorched gunpowder burned her nostrils.

It was, however, the accompanying sound that immobilized her. The deafening report reverberated around her. It penetrated her skull, numbed her brain, stamped her mind with its sinister implications. The amplified explosion culminated in mental shock waves which overrode the physical discomfort of the discharge.

The sound continued to assail Esther as it echoed off the gray stone house across the path, ricocheted off the towering façade of the adjacent wooden barn, beat at her from the woods which provided her shelter. The blast seemed to repeat itself, the clatter resonating once again, heightening her consciousness of her single shot, underscoring her unwelcome awareness of the malevolence of her deliberate act.

New sounds, coming from the direction of her target, steadied Esther. Voices, female voices, cried out. A sob, a broken plea for help vied with frightened whinnies and the muffled pounding of hooves striking the hard-packed earth.

She raised her eyes and looked at Squire Richard Holt, the man who had been in her sight. He sat straight in the saddle of his rearing horse.

"My shot," she said the words aloud. "It went wild." Esther's initial disappointment was replaced by an unexpected feeling of relief.

She stared at the squire as his horse flailed the air with its hooves before landing on the path in front of the imposing stone residence.

"No. My shot was true." She spoke in a whisper as she watched her victim grasp his shirt with his right hand and slump sideways in the saddle. A red stain spread across the white fabric and Esther winced as Richard Holt loosed his grip and relaxed his soiled fingers.

The roan reared again and the stricken man fell to the ground, one foot twisted in the stirrup. The horse, confused by the loss of its rider, returned to standing. It glanced down at the prostrate horseman and then bolted, dragging the limp body behind him.

Esther's chest tightened, bile rose in her throat. The scene swirled around her and then returned in sharp focus when she heard the sounds of someone running near her. Her uncharacteristic emotionalism evaporated and she was instantly on guard.

She turned her head and looked over her right shoulder. A scant fifty feet to her rear, she glimpsed the figure of her brother-in-law. A long gun clasped to his chest, he pushed through tall brush and struggled to run from the scene.

Esther was shocked to see James Daunt. A short time ago, the two of them had been sitting in her keeping room. She had intentionally kept her visitor well-supplied with rum as she outlined the plan she and her husband, Elias, had discussed before his arrival. Unfortunately, she had been overly generous with her spirits, and by the time she had finished explaining their scheme, James had collapsed, too drunk to comprehend her proposed conspiracy.

Seeing him behind her, and recalling the eerie echo of her solitary blast, Esther realized he must have, coherently or not, acted upon her proposition. Two separate shots had been fired at the squire. One had come from the musket she carried, the other from the firearm handled by James Daunt. At least one of those two shots had found its mark.

"Uncle! No! Uncle!"

"He was hit by lightning. I saw the flash. I heard the crack."

"No. He was shot. Look at his chest."

"Help! We need help!"

Esther returned her attention to the scene in front of the main house. The female voices belonged, not to adults, but to Richard Holt's two young wards, the daughters of his recently deceased younger brother.

The horse had ended its frightened flight and come to stand in front of the children. Squire Holt's foot was still held captive in the stirrup and Esther watched as the older girl labored to work it free. Her sister, hands covering the lower part of her face, stood staring at the bloodied, dirt-encrusted body of her guardian. Choking on soundless screams, she turned and ran to the house where she was finally able to cry out for help.

Esther's stomach heaved at the sight of the young girls and the mangled corpse of their uncle. Sharp pains, accompanied by nausea, surged through the trunk of her body. She folded her arms under her breasts and bent to relieve the torment. Only once before had she experienced such physical and mental discomfort. Then, as now, her anguish had been the result of a spontaneous act of indiscretion.

Her previous misstep had brought her unbearable shame; and a stranger for a husband. In order to cope with her disgrace, Esther Hicks Latch had fine-tuned her personal code of ethics until it was flexible enough to support her most controversial decisions. Following her moral transformation, she had rarely known guilt, felt remorse or allowed herself to doubt the validity of her final choices.

This time, things were different. The possible consequence of her assault on a living human being became a probability and threatened to undermine her resolve. In self defense, she closed her mind to the reality of her recent actions and concentrated, instead, on the need to arrive at her home before James Daunt. It would do no good if he found her, and his musket, missing.

James could barely see as he thrashed his way through the heavy undergrowth. Sweat layered his face, seeped into his eyes and blurred his vision. It filled the early lines and creases which belie the age of a young man who follows the blacksmith's trade. It dripped from his torso, his arms, his hands; it ran down the barrel of the unfamiliar gun he carried.

He pushed aside the grasping branches of the understory trees. He tore away the barbs of the wild-rose brambles which locked themselves into his hair, his unruly beard, his ochre-colored nankeen pantaloons, his faded green coat. He pulled himself free from the persistent thorns and struggled to put the grisly image of the horse and rider behind him.

A vine snaked across James' face and dropped around his neck. He tried to shake it loose. The supple creeper tightened in a strangulation hold. He stopped, grasped the invading tendrils and yanked the noose from his body. He tossed the insidious vine aside and charged on through the woods.

He was oblivious to the perspiration which continued to drench his hair, body and clothes. It filled his shoes and caused his feet to slip inside his crude leather moccasins. His progress was tortuous but James was driven by the primal need to keep moving, to flee from the incomprehensible circumstances resulting from his single discharge of another man's gun.

Roots grew along the surface of the ground and he was compelled to slow his pace. The trees thinned, and then multiplied, as he sloshed through ferns, skunk cabbage and watercress growing in a shallow steam.

Grasping at random twigs and low-hanging limbs for support, James stumbled into a small open area surrounded by tall pines. Slender blades of sunlight filtered through the seemingly impenetrable forest that faced him across the clearing. Unsure of the current time of day, he looked up to determine the position of the sun. The source of the fractured light was hidden by the dense trees above him making it impossible to verify whether it was middle or late afternoon.

An uprooted tree lay on its side, weeds growing between broken branches, moss melding with pungent fungi in the natural peat produced by the decaying giant. James staggered to the trunk, sank to the soft ground and leaned back in need of physical support. He had no idea why he had been opposite Richard Holt's house or why he was carrying Elias Latch's gun or why he had fired a shot at the Squire.

James tried to recreate the day's events. He remembered eating the noon meal at Hebe Balderston's tavern. He had a clear memory of riding from Hebe's to his brother-in-law's farm. He recalled Elias' wife, Esther, offering him rum while he waited for her husband to return from making the hay in a neighboring field.

He had been nervous when he arrived, and Esther's conversation further unsettled him. James had watched, without protest, as she continually refilled his glass. He remembered the drinking and some of the talking. Esther had discussed the money. It had been the prospect of his wife's inheritance that had prompted him to make irresponsible decisions in the past and he was certain that Esther's suggestion of forthcoming financial relief was behind his recent inexplicable behavior.

Esther Latch bent her long, thin body low to avoid detection as she followed the narrow deer path which paralleled the escape route of James Daunt. She watched the brush waver as he made his way toward the road. She quickened her pace and was about to pass him when she noticed that the foliage on her left had stopped moving. She paused, straightened and peered in the direction of James' retreat. He had turned away and was heading toward a thick stand of trees.

There was a break in the underbrush. Esther stepped off the path and crept to the opening. Shattered branches and trampled plant life marked the crude trail James had forged as he pushed his way into the leafy grove. She could see an exposed area where her sister's husband sat on the ground, his head in his hands, and Elias' flintlock at his feet.

Esther stared at James and frowned. The sight of his tortured figure reminded her of the reason she had fired at Richard Holt: the squire claimed to be the sole witness to her father's deathbed wish to leave his entire estate to her brother, Maris Evans Hicks.

She and Elias had discussed the unexpected declaration and decided that the squire, with his knowledge of the law and possible willingness to perjure himself, had aided Maris in a scheme to gain control of her father's holdings. Searching for a way to recoup Esther's rightful share, they had come to the conclusion that the oral will could not be probated if the squire was unable to validate the deceased's intentions in court. If he failed to appear at the hearing, they reasoned, the will would be declared null and void and the estate divided equally among Jacob Hicks' five children. Before they could confirm the veracity of their suppositions, Esther had learned Richard Holt was leaving the area for a month and would not return until the afternoon of the scheduled probate of her father's last will and testament.

In Esther's mind, James' presence at her door on the very day of Richard Holt's departure was an auspicious sign. Knowing of her brother-in-law's desperate need for money, she hoped to persuade him to perform the necessary deed that would prevent the squire's appearance in court. While pouring his third tankard of rum, she approached James, expecting him to embrace the opportunity to guarantee the inheritance of his wife, Margaret. She was taken aback when, in spite of his incoherent drunken state, James expressed incredulity that she would propose an act of murder.

When she broached the subject a second time, he managed to deliver, just before he lost consciousness, an outright refusal to slay Richard Holt. She was unprepared for the intensity of his response and her reaction was reflected in her face.

Esther Latch acknowledged her lack of physical beauty and made no attempt to soften her features. She wore her dull brown hair parted in the middle and pulled straight back. Thirty years of perceived disappointment had forged an inverted V between her heavy brows, and in concert with her naturally down-turned mouth, exaggerated her air of perpetual disapproval. Following James Daunt's collapse in a drunken stupor, she felt that look of disapproval develop into an expression of angry denunciation of the dissipated man in front of her. The furrow on her forehead deepened as the arc of her brows straightened and her vigilant dark eyes narrowed to a squint.

Concentration replaced condemnation as Esther accepted the fact that she was on her own. Elias was unavailable and there was no time to waste. In thirty days, the will would be probated; all of her father's money would be in the hands of her brother, and the squire's death would come too late. Without hesitation, she picked up her husband's flintlock. Then she spied the old musket standing in the opposite corner and she returned Elias' gun to its place. In spite of its extra weight and unpredictable reliability, Esther determined to use the musket because it belonged to James Daunt. She cast a cursory glance at the inert body of her brother-in-law who lay unconscious from drink, his arms and upper body spread-eagled on her keeping-room table. Then she had gathered the powder and shot and left the house.

Esther forced her thoughts to return to the present as an unbidden image of Richard Holt falling from his horse crossed her mind. In an attempt to deny her complicity, she suppressed the memories of her role in the planning and execution of the shooting and redirected her attention to James Daunt's current activities.

Confident that she was concealed behind the low-branching trees and tall brush, Esther watched as James struggled to his feet. His features were twisted in grief; tears channeled the sweat and grime which covered his face. Turning away, he stumbled into the trees on the far side of his resting place and began, again, to beat his way through the thick growth. His blows were ferocious as if intended to inflict the self-flagellation he, himself, deserved on the plant life that impeded his progress.

Esther was intent on gaining a lead on James as she swiftly retraced her steps. She stopped a few feet short of the deer path as an image of the clearing flashed before her eyes. There was Elias' gun, lying in front of the fallen tree where James had left it. The necessity of retrieving the flintlock before it was found, and perhaps, identified, overrode her need to pass her brother-in-law.

She spun around and ran back along the leaf- and rock-covered trail. Esther was oblivious to the noise of her approach as she hastened to the edge of the open area and determined that the gun was still there.

She quickly reached down, picked up Elias' flintlock and substituted the old musket she had fired at Richard Holt. Thinking its placement too obvious, she partially concealed it inside the rotting trunk. She left the end of the barrel exposed so it would be found. The secreted weapon, with its wooden ramrod and notched butt, was an antiquated relic of obscure origin. She knew of no others in the area. The owner of the musket would be readily known and suspicion would fall on James Daunt.

Satisfied with her actions, Esther shouldered her husband's flintlock, doubled back to the narrow deer path and hurried toward her home. In her haste, she failed to hear the crack of a broken twig and the soft thudding sounds of a rolling stone which was dislodged by an unseen observer who followed behind her.

James left the shelter of the glade and lurched through the woods looking for recognizable landmarks. He was relieved when he saw familiar creek banks in the distance. The stream would lead him to the two-room farmhouse where he had consumed too much drink and inadvertently fallen prey to his sister-in-law's scheme. It would also lead him to his horse which he had tethered in front of Elias' barn. He slowed his pace and tried to compose himself before crossing the rough farm road that lay between him and the creek.

A tired horse pulled a wagon filled with hay along the packed dirt lane. James recognized the driver as one of his former neighbors and he bent low in an attempt to conceal himself in the tall grass. He was in trouble and did not want to be noticed.

When he returned to standing, the road was empty. He crossed the open area and headed for the stream. At this point, the winding creek bed was deeply recessed with sharp embankments lining both sides. He scrambled down the steep slope and walked along the edge of the shallow water until he came to a ledge which was tucked under an outcropping of roots. The spot offered shelter and seclusion and he paused, knowing he still had to cross a second road before reaching the ten-acre Latch farm. He decided to wait until after dark as passersby would occasionally stop to water their horses and get the news of the day from Esther, a voracious collector and purveyor of local gossip.

James needed to clear his head, wash away the perspiration which clung to his face and body, and dry his clothes before he could risk facing others. He also needed to regain his bearings. Although sober at the moment, he was aware that a short time ago he had been very drunk and had fired a single shot at Squire Richard Holt.

He was certain he would be an early suspect. He had spent the previous evening drinking with his friends at Hebe Balderston's tavern, and at the height of the frivolity, he had spoken in jest about taking out his frustrations on Maris and the squire. The lads had picked up on the proposition and boisterously fantasized about the various retributions he could inflict on the two men who had confiscated his wife's inheritance. Other than the recreational thrill of conjuring up bizarre punishments, he and his friends had never seriously considered causing harm to anyone.

Now, less than a day later, and far from the camaraderie of Hebe's tavern, James stood alone: guilty of shooting a man and certain of imminent capture and eternal damnation.

He hung his sodden hat on a branch, took off his sweat-stained outer garments and spread them on a rock to dry. He shed his moccasins and waded into the stream. Leaning down, he submerged his head in the cool water. It flowed through his sandy-colored hair, floated his abundant whiskers and massaged his perspiration-drenched scalp. Then raising his head to breathe, he dropped to his knees and lowered his entire body into the soothing water. He turned onto his back and lay unmoving, his mind momentarily without thought. A vague awareness that he had been unable to pinpoint time since he had arrived at Esther's around noon momentarily threatened to interrupt his interlude.

James rotated his head slightly to the right and rested it on a smooth rock. He spread his arms and legs, inviting the slow-moving water to lull him into complacency. The trivial discomfort of the polished creek stones dissolved as he lay in a passive state, incapable of rational thought.

Esther hurried along the deer path. Her once sturdy leather shoes had been worn shapeless; the soles were thin and smooth. They allowed her feet to slide on loose dirt and low-growing foliage and made it difficult for her to move quickly on the rough trail. She no longer tried to follow James Daunt but was, instead, consumed by the need to reach her home as soon as possible.

The woods thinned, and an open field lay before her. A creek wandered through a deep crevice in the high terrain to her left and flowed toward her at ground level. She could see a narrow lane in the distance. It ran between her and the great road which bordered her farm. She stopped at the edge of the field and looked for signs that James had preceded her. She listened for sounds of his approach and heard nothing.

Glancing ahead and to her right, she saw a distant stand of pine trees that skirted the road and marked her property line. Angling off from the woods in which she stood, the pines ran the length of her neighbor's field and ended close to her home. She had two choices. She could travel along the edge of the woods to the refuge of the evergreen trees or she could expose herself when she passed through the open field, over the farm lane and onto the great road. The latter alternative was faster while the tree line offered shelter from prying eyes and the opportunity to cross both roads at a single spot. She chose to take the longer route.

Esther turned once again and looked to her left. Her eye caught a flash of movement in the trees by the creek. Foreign fingers of fear stabbed at her body as she strained to find the source of the distraction. Everything was still and her concern subsided. Satisfied that she was alone, Esther made her way along the periphery of the woods and entered the rows of pine trees. Once inside the protective covering of the narrow windbreak, she paused and stared back at the spot where she had seen the activity.

Slowly the brush at the edge of the woods parted and the figure of a young woman emerged. Facing Esther's tree line, the apparition stood, in full view, her hands anchored defiantly on her hips. Esther gasped. It was Sally Morley, the simple-minded girl who was rumored to frequent Hebe Balderston's tavern. With an impudent toss of her red hair, Sally flicked her skirt with her right hand, turned back to the woods and was gone.

The brief appearance of the unanticipated figure, and its abrupt disappearance, happened so quickly that Esther doubted she had seen anything. She continued to stare at the undergrowth as she searched for confirmation of Sally Morley's ghostly manifestation. Still grasses and bushes betrayed no trace of human disturbance, but Esther's confidence had been compromised. Her race for home assumed an added urgency.

Alternating frenzied sprints with short pauses to catch her breath, she reached the end of the tree line and turned toward the intersection which was her last obstacle. The two roads in front of her were empty, as was the neighbor's field where her husband had been working. She gathered up her skirt and petticoat and dashed across the junction. As she reached the far side of the crossroad, the smooth soles of her worn shoes slid on stones which had accumulated along the shoulder. She dropped Elias' gun as she lost her balance and fell into a shallow ditch.

Her hands hit the ground and she felt the loose gravel scrape the undersides of her fingers and cut into her palms. Her right knee landed on a rock and her neck twisted as the left side of her head hit the butt end of the flintlock. She cried out in pain.

Fearful of having been seen or heard, Esther cautiously turned over and sat up. She searched the area for bystanders. She was relieved to find she was alone and that there was no sign of the red-headed interloper. She tried to stand and was assailed by a sharp pain as her wounded knee collapsed. Unable to use her right leg for leverage, she leaned forward, carefully put her weight on both of her hands and used her left leg to push herself upright. She stood, balanced on one foot, and waited for the pain to stabilize. Then she bent over, and without taking a step, reached to retrieve Elias' firearm.

As she lowered her head and grasped the gunstock, another onslaught of pain exploded in the area of her left temple where she had impacted with the flintlock. It was so severe and unexpected that it knocked her off balance. This time, she fell headfirst into the ditch, striking her forehead on the same large stone which had injured her knee. Everything went black and she lay motionless in the gravel.

Esther slowly regained her faculties and she attempted to lift her head. The pain that had sent her reeling was compounded by a spasm in her neck which relayed stinging shock waves to her brain. She lay back on the ground.

Then, working around her useless right knee, she forced her body into a sitting position. She held her head upright and remained motionless for a few moments. She reached again for Elias' gun which had paralleled her body as she fell. She threw the flintlock onto the bank of the ditch and tried to bend her right knee. The pain in her leg increased, as did the torture in her head.

Esther shifted her position and tried to work her way out of the ditch. She used her uninjured leg and the low surface of the bank to push herself to standing. The throbbing in her head remained, but the neck spasm eased and the shock waves disappeared. She put her left hand to her forehead. Her hand was wet, and impatiently, she wiped it on her skirt. It was then that she noticed the blood. It came from the lacerations caused by her fall. It stained her palms, the gunstock, and streaked her clothing. The all-encompassing pain in her head and knee had obscured the minor discomfort of the abrasions.

This physical evidence of her absence from home added to her mounting number of problems, the most pressing of which was her desperate need to return, undetected, to the safety of her tiny farmhouse. However, before she could cross the newly-cleared field which lay between her and her destination, she had to stop the bleeding.

Esther lifted her skirt and found a spot on her petticoat where the stitches were loose. Deftly snapping the thread, she tore open a seam. Clenching the fabric between her teeth, she gnawed a break in the tightly woven cotton and tore away two strips which she bound around the wounds on her hands. Having stemmed the flow of blood, she tentatively put weight on her right leg. Shooting pains emanated from her knee and the joint buckled under her. She shifted her weight to her left leg and was able to regain her balance before falling to the ground.

Esther realized she was unable to walk without support. She searched the ditch for a stout branch to use as a staff. Finding nothing, she picked up the gun. It was too long. Barrel down, she angled it away from her body, placed the stock under her arm and took a step forward. The flintlock was an awkward solution complicated by the discomfort of the butt end of the gun tucked into her armpit

Again, she raised her skirt to address her simple petticoat. She drew the undergarment up and over her head and then wrapped the material around the gunstock. She used the drawstring to secure the cushion to her makeshift crutch. Esther placed the flintlock under her arm for a second time, located a low spot on the edge of the ditch and worked her way up to level ground. Time passed and her shadow grew long as she struggled across the field.

When she finally reached her house she collapsed on the lowest of the three wooden steps which led to the door. She noticed that James Daunt's horse remained tethered to the hitching post. Elias' bay, however, was not confined as usual in the paddock.

Still worried that James would find her outside of her home, Esther used her bound hands to lift her body and inch her way up the stairs. Once on the narrow landing, she grasped the crude railing and pulled herself to standing. The recognizable squeal of the iron hinges on the wooden door soothed her as she entered the keeping room and dragged herself to a table near the fireplace. The emotional and physical stress of her ordeal finally took its toll. She fell into the nearest chair, pushed aside the dishes from the noon meal, and laid the right side of her head on the smooth, worn surface of the old farm table which had passed through four previous generations of her family.

As the shock waves of pain returned, it occurred to her that, as far as she knew, she was the first member of the Hicks or Latch families to plan, and in all probability, commit a murder.

The gently coursing current which soothed James also cooled his body. He was cold. He rose, used his hands to wipe the dripping water from his puckered skin, climbed the stream bank and walked back to his shelter. He stretched out along the edge of a warm, flat, stone ledge. The intense afternoon rays of the late summer sun canted through the trees. His chilled body, already responding to the stored warmth of the rock shelf, welcomed the additional heat.

His undergarment dried on his back and he turned over. The concentrated assault of the sun's beams on the sensitive, heat-reddened skin of his face and arms, already victims of many hours spent in front of the blazing blacksmith's forge, prickled his nerve endings and kindled a vague life-affirming physical pleasure.

Again, he tried to relive the past few hours but his brain continued to rebel and he could call up only fragments of the day's

*13*

activities. The persistent undercurrent of guilt that had accompanied him throughout his frantic run to freedom dissipated, and he gave in to the mental indolence he had embraced throughout his adult years. He closed his eyes and encouraged the kaleidoscope of colors which patterned the insides of his eyelids. A comforting feeling of peace engulfed him as he returned to the somnolent state he had experienced in the creek.

"What're you doing here, James Daunt?"

The words filtered through the cotton in James' head and shocked him back to consciousness.

A female voice. It was familiar, slightly unsettling. It stirred exciting but worrisome sensations in James. He opened his eyes and sat up straight. Embarrassed to be discovered in his drawers, he crossed his arms over his stomach in an attempt to cover the trunk of his body. He looked around and saw no one.

A rustling sound above his head caused him to glance up. Disembodied bare feet and legs hung over the edge of the protective overhang. The dangling legs parted and a head, bursting with red curls, appeared between them. James stared at the upside-down, lightly-freckled face with taunting blue eyes. The mysterious intruder translated into Sally Morley, the strange girl who pleased the lads at Hebe Balderston's tavern.

The face vanished and the girlish figure of a slight young woman dropped to the ledge next to him. She turned and grinned suggestively as she looked him up and down.

"I been watching you, James Daunt," she said, placing her hands on her hips and slowly twisting her upper body from side to side. With an air of innate assurance, she tipped her head and looked seductively into his eyes.

"You're practically naked," she giggled.

With a knowing expression on her face, she pointed to his undergarment and said, "I know what's under there." She directed her gaze below his waist.

"I seen you naked, James Daunt." Shifting her eyes, she tilted her face towards his and slowly traced her upper lip with the tip of her tongue.

Still dazed, James stared at Sally Morley. In spite of his compromised situation, he experienced a shiver of pleasure as Sally's teasing manner assumed a level of intimacy.

"Sally," he said as his voice cracked. "Where'd you come from? Why are you here?"

She looked down at her feet and wiggled her bare toes. No longer the wanton tart, her vulnerability showed on her face.

"This is my place, James Daunt. You're the one who don't belong here. This is my secret hiding place, my thinking place." She turned her head away and then looked back at her toes.

"The boys. They don't know I come here. Nobody grabs at Sally here. Nobody teases Sally here." The serious look on her face vanished when she lowered her eyes and became the coy temptress once again.

"Are you going to grab at me, James Daunt?"

"No!" His answer was sharp and final. "Go away, Sally. I don't want to be bothered right now."

She stood still, as if evaluating the hurtful rejection. Then, replacing a petulant pout with tinkling laughter, she lifted her skirts to her waist. She danced a little jig and swirled her skirts provocatively.

"You used to like to grab at me." She cupped her breasts with her hands and slowly pushed them up while her hips swayed invitingly. "You used to do much more than that, James Daunt."

She grinned, and moving to the side of the ledge, twirled several times in place before pitching herself, dizzy and giddy, back to land next to him.

"Sally, I got problems," James said, as he inched away from her. "I got big problems and I got to think."

She reached over and placed her hand on his arm. He accepted her gesture of sympathy and they sat quietly for a moment.

James put his head in his hands. He could not concentrate. The remembered events of the afternoon, along with hints of the unknown, floated in his mind and fired up momentarily only to vanish in a flash like the lights of fireflies at dusk. He tried to catch and study some of the images, but they drifted from his grasp before he could bring them into sharp definition.

Sally brushed his arm with her fingers then moved her hand to his thigh. Looking down, she dragged her fingers across his body to touch him gently where she knew it pleased.

"No," he gasped, surprised that his physical being could respond to stimulation when he had such trouble.

"No, I don't have time for this, Sally."

However, his body was responding to her touch and she knew it. She continued to stroke him and the euphoria of the interlude in the creek returned once again. He allowed himself to fall into the abyss of sexual pleasure. Slowly, he reached out to pull Sally to him.

"Stay, Sally," he murmured, "Stay." His hands returned her advances and together they succumbed to the free-flowing passion of an uncomplicated, uncommitted sexual dalliance. He tried to contain himself but it was too late. He rolled onto Sally and they rose and fell in unison as their desires were jointly realized.

For James, release brought reality. Many events of the day were finally clear in his mind. He lay next to Sally trying as hard to repress the memories as he had previously tried to recall them. His reluctant acceptance of the enormity of his transgressions caused his chest to constrict, his breathing to accelerate, his knees to weaken. A feeling of undefined doom, physically as well as mentally, dominated his consciousness. Sally moved beside him, her arm crossing his abdomen. He felt no response to her presence and suddenly he was filled with revulsion. Horror accompanied his memory of the shooting of Richard Holt. Guilt and remorse tainted thoughts of his union with Sally.

When he and Margaret had married, James vowed to forsake the dissipation of his youth. Hard as he tried, he had been unable to overcome his predilection for rum. However, until today, he had successfully avoided fisticuffs and easy women. Now, within a few hours, he had shot a man in cold blood and had his way with the local whore.

His head finally clear, James became aware that his encounter with Sally presented a new problem. She could place him near Richard Holt's farm. She would remember he had been acting queer, lying near-naked in the water, his clothes spread out on the rocks.

Sally was a witness, questionable perhaps, to his whereabouts at the time of the shooting. She had also been a willing participant in his moral backslide. He was certain that Margaret would learn of his sexual indiscretion, as well as his attack on the squire, if Sally came forth and placed him near the Holt farm. His first thought was to swear the young woman to silence. Sally's reputation for being a bit slow would surely help to discredit any secrets she might divulge.

"You can't tell anyone we were here today." James pushed himself to a sitting position. "Do you understand that, Sally?" he asked, looking at her intently.

She stared at him. "You're ashamed of me, James Daunt. Just like all the others. They grab me and touch me all over. They have their way with me and brag to their friends. But they don't want to be seen with me outside of the tavern."

She turned away. "You, you were different, James Daunt. You said nice things to me when we was alone even if you did grab me in front of your friends. Sometimes you made fun of me, too, but there were times when you treated me good in front of people and didn't care what they thought. That made me feel special."

Guilt again. In the past, James had consorted publicly with Sally Morley, but in spite of his strong physical attraction to her, it was primarily to show off in front of his pals. They admired his lack of concern about the opinions of others. They credited him with more self-confidence than he deserved.

None of that mattered after he married Margaret. His wife's obvious, if not passionate, devotion made him feel important, as did his auspicious marriage into the influential Hicks family. His friends from Hebe Balderston's envied him his pretty bride and her well-fixed parents. At least they did until he developed money problems.

Sally got to her feet. "You changed, James Daunt, after you married that goody-goody Margaret Hicks. You're just like everyone else. Have your fun with Sally and throw her away." She was angry and James sought to appease her. He rose and stood next to her.

"That's not true, Sally. I still like you but I've got problems today and you can't tell anyone you've seen me here, do you understand?" His voice broke.

He took her face in his hands and looked into her eyes. "Please, Sally, say you understand and you won't tell anyone we were here together. Please," he repeated, desperation in his voice.

Her expression softened at his touch.

"Maybe I can help, James Daunt. I know what happened...." Her voice was serious. Then, seeing the impatient look on his face, she changed her tone. "I didn't do nothing wrong. I didn't do anything with you I don't do with all the boys."

An angry look passed over her face. She quickly smiled and replaced it with an invitation. "I just like doing it better with you than any of the others. Do you like doing it with me, James Daunt?"

"Of course, Sally. This time, though, you got to keep quiet about us being here today."

She appeared to think about what he was saying. "If it's important then I won't tell." Her serious expression turned bold and she added, "That is if you promise to make Sally happy again." She grinned suggestively, lifted her skirt and spread her legs.

James sighed with relief and frustration. "I promise, Sally, but later. I got to go now. Just remember, you never saw me today."

He leaned down and retrieved his clothes. He dressed with his back to her and when he turned she was gone.

James thought about Sally. In spite of her slapdash appearance and coarse manners, there was a faint, indescribable hint of mystery about her, an undefined intelligence which surfaced unexpectedly before being camouflaged by the unflappable confidence of a loose-moraled farm girl. She had left as surreptitiously as she had arrived and James wondered if the simple young woman who walked so silently was, perhaps, descended from the ancient Indians who were rumored to inhabit these woods.

He shook his head at the idea. Her delicate bone structure, red hair and fair skin belied that possibility. No, Sally Morley was not of Indian blood. Her mystique was, in all probability, a figment of his imagination.

Esther was exhausted and in pain. She remained in her chair, strangely comforted by the familiar feel of the old table top against her cheek and the potpourri of recognizable odors that emanated from the wood. She closed her eyes and allowed her mind to wander.

She and Elias had never thoroughly explored the logistics of assuring the squire's demise and she had thought no further of his death than its impact on the legitimacy of her father's will. Now, the reality of her actions took on added meaning as she accepted that she, as a woman, would suffer merciless derision and condemnation if incriminated, and the worst possible punishment if found guilty.

The pain in her head increased. Esther pressed her fingers to the base of her skull but felt no relief. She sat up and pushed her body back from the table. It was imperative that she move and crucial that she conceal her involvement in the shooting of Richard Holt.

She began by removing the crude cushion from Elias' gun, washing away the blood, and wiping the dirt from the outside and inside of the barrel. When she was certain everything was clean, she substituted a small chair for the support of the flintlock and leaned on it as she returned the latter to its place in the corner of the room. Each movement was unbearably painful; her temple throbbed and when she touched her knee she found it was swollen and hot to the touch.

Esther struggled back to the table, sat down and carefully removed the strips of fabric from her hands. She was relieved to see the bleeding had stopped. The wounds, which had seemed so serious when covered in blood, were little more than surface scratches caused by scraping her hands against the small stones. There were several insignificant pieces of gravel embedded under her skin. She removed them as easily as if they were ordinary wooden splinters.

The chair had proved to be an unwieldy crutch but it was Esther's best alternative. Holding onto its back, she pushed and dragged her way to the large stone fireplace that dominated the far side of the room. She balanced on her left leg as she swung her body around, picked a log from a recessed area in the wall and added it to the remnants of the noonday fire. A large iron pot, suspended from the end of a crane, hung over the glowing embers. It held an adequate amount of water for the preparation of the evening meal.

Esther worked her way to a corner cupboard and found a small tin box containing a bar of black soap. Although it was Friday and she always did laundry on Monday, she placed a small amount of the lye soap in the water and added another log to hasten the boiling.

Her head continued to ache and her leg and knee had gone numb by the time Esther shed her skirt and dropped it in the caldron. She found a knife on the table and reduced the tattered petticoat to random strips of cloth to be explained away as functional household rags. She added them, and the bloodied makeshift bandages, to the pot of heated water. There was just enough liquid to cover the telltale fabric.

Esther retrieved another skirt from the pile of mending next to her sewing basket and leaned heavily on the chair to maintain her balance as she slipped the wrinkled garment over her head. She checked the water to see if it had returned to boiling and glanced around the room. She was startled by a slight movement which was visible through the window.

Sally Morley? She was as worried about the young redheaded girl's brazen appearance as she was about James Daunt's possible awareness of her presence at the Holt farm. Why, she asked herself, would Sally be out there unless she knew something?

Perhaps, she reasoned, it could be James or Elias, or one of the neighbors in from making hay at the next farm. She reached for the chair and leaned on it. She dragged herself to the window but found no hint of human presence. The vision of Sally and her unanticipated appearance in the woods took on a new importance in Esther's mind. The possibility that the girl was spying on her became a conviction. She pushed the chair from the window to the door, opened it and called, "Sally. Are you out there, Sally? Come here, Sally."

There was no answer. She called again, and without venturing to the steps, she scanned the area. She appeared to be alone. She called again, and receiving no response, she returned to the keeping-room table. She turned the small chair around and seated herself. Her head pounded and her knee was burning, but her body parts commanded less of Esther's attention than the mysterious appearance of Sally Morley.

Her presence in the woods could simply be a coincidence, she reasoned, or, she shuddered apprehensively, the girl could have seen something incriminating for Esther. The latter alternative, in spite of Sally's lack of credibility, could present a serious threat.

Esther suppressed the ordinary clatter of farm life as she listened intently for the subtle sounds of crushed grass and broken twigs which would announce the presence of an unwanted intruder. Gradually, male voices, audible over the dull cadence of horses' hooves, infiltrated her state of compartmentalized concentration. Relaxing her focus, she identified Elias' high-pitched voice vibrating over those of neighboring farmers, John Willis, Jedidiah Worrell and Nehemiah Trimble.

"James' horse is here," Elias shouted triumphantly. "He is still in the area. He has to come through the woods to get here from the squire's farm. We'll find him."

She heard familiar sounds as he dismounted near the fence, hitched the bay to a post and hurried toward the house. The others urged their horses in the direction of the paddock.

"After I get my gun, we'll start searching the woods. Jedidiah, you find Maris Hicks and tell him that our no-good brother-in-law is a hunted man. A cold-blooded murderer." Elias was at the door.

Esther heard the references to James and her brother. She recognized the excitement in her husband's voice and rose from her chair. Aware that Elias and the three men in front of her barn already knew of Richard Holt's murder, she ignored her weakened condition and stepped toward the door without support. Her injured knee buckled under her weight and she cried out as she lurched forward, breaking her fall with her hands on the wooden table.

The door creaked open and Elias entered the room to find Esther pushing herself to standing, blood seeping from the scrapes on her hands. Startled, he stared at his wounded wife.

Dark hair streaked with gray accentuated the weathered skin which covered the sunken cheeks and sharply-defined nose of Esther's husband. Alert, yet bloodshot, brown eyes and thin lips completed the face of this man who daily worked the fields and carried his wares to market. He was small, a head shorter than Esther, wiry and strung taut, always ready to react when challenged or provoked.

"What happened?" he asked, uncharacteristically concerned.

Esther could not believe her luck. She had an explanation for the blood on her hands, her damaged knee and the unbearable ache in her head. Tears of relief, not pain, filled her eyes.

"When I heard you and the other men...." Again, Esther wiped her bloody hands on her skirt. This time, she ignored the stains as she began to tell her story.

"I started for the door to see what was happening. I tripped and hit my head." She pulled up her skirt, "Look, I have hurt my knee," she said.

Elias stared at her and frowned. "What are you saying, Esther?"

"I tripped. Look at my hands, my knee. And I've hurt my head."

"Stop talking funny, Esther," Elias was impatient. "I haven't got time for foolishness." He took a quick look at her knee, noted that it was not bleeding, and turned away.

"Don't look too bad to me," he said. He walked to the corner of the room and stood in front of his gun. "You move this?"

"No," she lied. "Why would I?" She hesitated, surprised by his accusatory tone. She had never touched his gun in the past although she would have taken it today if James' old musket had not been at hand.

"Stop it, Esther. You ain't making any sense. I don't know what you mean when you say funny things like that."

Esther was confused. She shook her head. "I just said I did not handle your gun. What is strange about that?"

Elias ignored her as he continued to look at his flintlock.

"It's been moved." Puzzled, he picked up the gun and inspected it. "Something's wrong." Visibly irritated, he cocked his head and stared accusingly at Esther. Then, he cradled the weapon under his arm and headed for the door.

"Squire Holt's been shot. Once. One shot to his chest."

One shot, Esther heard the words: one shot. Only one of the two balls had hit Richard Holt.

"Not dead yet but probably will be," Elias continued. "His nieces seen the villain with his gun in his hand. They say it was James

Daunt. They recognized his beard. Nobody else in the county has one as long or as full."

The girls had seen James. Esther paled as her stomach rebelled. She lowered her head as the blood rushed through her veins to empty with pounding finality into her throbbing temples, exaggerating even further the terrible pain she was suffering.

Had they seen her? This time both her knees gave way. She was able to catch the edge of the table and prevent herself from falling.

Elias looked at her suspiciously. "You all right?" he asked. Then he added, "Be careful, Esther. If James comes while we are gone, let him be. Jedidiah will be back shortly and he'll keep watch from the barn in case James comes back for his horse. You should be safe. And," he said as he moved to leave. "Stop talking funny."

The door creaked again when Elias opened it, this time to return to the search party.

Esther could hear the eager voices of the men as they vied for leadership in the hunt. She was sure Nehemiah Trimble was especially anxious to capture James Daunt and turn him over to the sheriff. Nehemiah had been sweet on her sister, Margaret, since he was a boy and had always assumed they would marry. He resented James Daunt for stealing her away from him. What, Esther wondered, would Nehemiah say if he knew that she had also fired at the squire and that it was possible no one would ever know whose shot had found the chest of Richard Holt.

Esther remained standing, buttressed by the table of her ancestors. If she, too, had been seen by the girls, the men would soon be coming back for her as well.

James left the ledge and traveled a short distance upstream. He needed a place of refuge until nightfall when he could retrieve his horse and be on his way. He stopped at the edge of a moss-covered rise that overlooked the water. Then he moved back from the stream to nest among high ferns which grew abundantly in a grove of tall trees. He lay down, and in spite of his hostile demons of inexorable remorse, he slept fitfully until dusk.

When James awoke, his brain was muddied by bizarre remnants of tormented hallucinations. Fragmented images of the blood-stained body of Squire Holt and the agonized faces of his horrified young wards mingled with the girls' screams and shouts and the shrill whinnying of his terrified horse. James' earlier feelings of guilt and regret intensified and he could find no relief from the oppressive hold they had over his mind and body.

His initial anguish was replaced by the interminable echo of his gunshot as it resounded over and over in his head. The relentless sound was accompanied by staccato flashes of memory: holding tight to Elias' flintlock; pouring in the powder; inserting the paper wadding and the ball; tamping them firm with the ramrod; cocking the hammer; aiming, and firing. Considering all the rum he had consumed, the process seemed too complicated for him to have completed successfully, yet he must have gone through the familiar routine without thought because he clearly recalled each individual step.

Oddly, he remembered nothing from the time he watched the squire fall until his surreal respite by the creek and his encounter with Sally. Panic permeated his body and he stood, desperately wanting to flee his gruesome memories and to shake the inescapable awareness that he had caused the death of a close friend and associate of Margaret's father.

Jacob Hicks was descended from four generations of prosperous farmers. His land holdings were extensive and his accumulated wealth, more than respectable. Upon his death, it had been expected that his estate would be divided five ways with Maris inheriting his father's large farm and Jacob's four daughters receiving smaller parcels of land in a nearby township. The money and personal goods were to have been split equally between his children.

The day after the passing of Jacob Hicks, Richard Holt had come forth with the news that he had witnessed the oral will of the dying man and that his friend had expressed the desire to leave his entire estate to his only living son, Maris Evans Hicks. Although the possibility of collusion between the newly-designated heir and Squire Holt was suspected, it could not be proved, and the impact of the revelation devastated the four women.

It was particularly bad news for James and Margaret. Several months earlier, Maris had approached James with an offer to sell him an acre of land with an existing log cabin and a blacksmith shop. Aware that his father-in-law was on his deathbed and that his wife anticipated a substantial inheritance, James agreed to buy the property. He signed a note and promised to satisfy the loan on Jacob Hicks' death. He took possession of the property and he and Margaret moved into the house and forge.

Located in a small village on a road between two thriving towns, James found the spot favorable for a smithy. A tavern and a village store were across the street and folks would leave their horses to be shod while they did their errands. James had more than enough business, but people were slow to pay. When his creditors, of whom there were now several, heard that the deathbed will had designated Maris as the sole inheritor, they filed judgments against James seeking immediate payment of his debts.

James turned to Maris for relief, but Margaret's brother, recognizing the opportunity James' financial straits presented, refused to help him. Maris repossessed the property and advertised the house and shop for sale. The other creditors, seeing the real estate notice in the newspaper, came to the forge, took all of James' tools and auctioned them off. He was thrown out of his home and business.

Margaret moved into a small house which her brother reluctantly provided for her and her unmarried sisters. Maris awarded each of the latter two a small monthly stipend to be paid from his father's estate but pointedly ignored Margaret's privation and adamantly refused his brother-in-law shelter.

When James finally found work in the shop of a competitor, part of his wages went toward the rent of a small room over his employer's forge. Between the rent, his meager expenses and the insignificant amount of money he was able to give his wife, James had little left for the payment of his remaining debts.

It was Elias who went to the courthouse, and in the names of Esther, Margaret and their two younger sisters, lodged a caveat against the probate of the oral will. Legal proceedings were begun to set aside the will based on the premise that Jacob Hicks was *in extremis* at the time he made testamentary disposition of his estate, and therefore, was incompetent to handle his affairs.

However, Elias told James the case would not come before the judge for at least six months. When James said he needed money immediately and could not wait that long, Elias replied that the oral will would be deemed invalid if the only witness, Richard Holt, could be prevented from testifying. James asked how they could stop him. Elias just smiled and ran his finger across his throat. James did not see the humor in his answer.

He had not seen Esther or her husband since the day of that conversation and it was only his desperate need for money that had driven him to visit the Latch farm. Now he was on the run, guilty of the attempted murder, or God forbid, the actual assassination of a man whose only publicly-known transgression was the questionable witnessing of the last will and testament of his close friend. James' guilt fueled his fear of the retribution which awaited him and he broke into a heavy sweat.

The bleeding had stopped before Elias left the house and Esther, still holding onto the table, needed to wash the residue of the new patch of blood from her hands.

Her right leg hung limp and offered no support. She leaned on the keeping-room table and dragged herself around to the crude bench on its far side. She sat down and slid across the smooth surface until she was close to a bucket of water which stood in the corner. She picked up a tin cup, filled it, poured it into a basin and washed away the remnants of her most recent accident.

Esther was well aware that her hands were a minor problem compared to the pain which pounded in her head and the relentless throbbing in her knee. She dropped a cloth into the cold water, retrieved it, wrung it out and tied it around her knee. It did nothing to relieve her discomfort. She needed a real crutch. She tried putting a broom under her arm but the bristles folded and the end of the broomstick, like Elias' gun, assailed the tender flesh of her armpit.

She returned to the wooden chair and leaned on it long enough to acknowledge that standing increased the pain. She turned the chair around, sat down, folded back her skirt and looked at her knee. It was swollen and her leg was red and hot.

She raised her wounded limb and rested her foot on the end of the long bench in front of her. The change in position helped a bit and she slid down in the chair and rested the base of her skull on its curved wooden back. The pressure eased the throbbing and she felt herself floating above the pain. Her brain told her the agony was still there, but she was detached from it. Her unreceptive intellect denied the horrendous headache, and in time, she felt nothing but a dull sensation of discomfort.

As she slowly slipped into delirium, Esther, who was rarely physically ill and had never experienced a debilitating injury, eagerly accepted the delusions which filled her mind. No stranger to self-deception, her previous forays into rewriting the truth were trivial compared to the story her semi-conscious mind concocted out of whole cloth. Her planned journey to the Holt farm to slay the squire conveniently took on the guise of a mission of mercy. She saw herself hurrying after James Daunt in an attempt to prevent him from carrying out an odious plot, solely of his own conception, to eliminate the man who had caused his wife to lose her inheritance.

The bothersome intimations of culpability and responsibility that lurked on the periphery of her mind subsided, and a nebulous feeling of complacency lulled Esther Hicks Latch as she willingly sank into unconsciousness.

"Margaret." The young woman called up to her sister on the second floor. "Maris is here. He wants to see you."

Margaret Daunt put down her sewing, stood, checked her reflection in the looking glass over her small storage chest, and came to the head of the steps.

Glancing down the open stairwell, she saw her brother huddled with her sisters, Hannah and Bettina, in the room below. Although Maris appeared to be calm, and was speaking quietly, the women were reacting emotionally to what he was saying. Hannah held her hands in front of her mouth and Bettina, with her arms crossed at her waist, was rocking back and forth.

Margaret's sisters were obviously shocked by Maris' revelation and they stared up at the pretty woman with the dark brown hair and eyes who watched them from above. Margaret started down the stairs, but stopped at the halfway point. She sensed that something was terribly wrong.

"It's not bad news about James, is it?" She searched the faces of her siblings as she completed her descent.

"I'm afraid it is, Margaret," Maris said, as he walked towards her. "And I'm afraid it's very bad news."

She stopped short of stepping from the final tread. She was alarmed by the ominous tone of her brother's voice and suddenly wanted to avoid hearing what he had come to say. She held her hand flat out in front of her in an attempt to cut short his message.

Maris was a slight man of average height and appearance. His straight brown hair was parted in the middle and combed flat to his head. Thin sideburns and a neatly trimmed beard covered a weak chin and prematurely wrinkled neck. His physical shortcomings had spawned an aggressive, overbearing personality which was in evidence as he watched for his sister's reaction to his words. He was well aware of Margaret's distress and prolonged her despair by turning and placing his hat on the rack to the left of him.

"Has he been hurt?" she asked.

"No," Maris said without emotion. "Squire Holt was shot today." He studied Margaret's face and watched her expression change from concern to relief and then to confusion.

"What does that have to do with James?" Margaret asked. "He hardly knows the man except as a friend of Father's. And," she added, "of yours."

"Richard Holt is dead. His nieces saw their uncle's murderer." Maris ignored Margaret's comment and continued to observe her closely.

"I still don't understand what Squire Holt's death has to do with James."

"The girls had a clear look at their uncle's killer, and...." Maris had a self-satisfied look on his face as he repeated, "and...," he paused again, "they say, without a doubt, his killer was James Daunt."

He rubbed his hands together then, catching himself, clasped them behind his back.

Margaret frowned. She heard the words but they made no sense to her. She turned away, searched for a chair, and then stumbled slightly as she lowered herself onto the one that stood behind her.

"How would the wards of Squire Holt know my husband?" Suspicion sharpened the tone of the pretty young woman's voice.

"James visited the farm several times to shoe the horses." Maris glanced over his shoulder at Hannah and Bettina before continuing. A smirk crossed his face as he returned his attention to Margaret.

"The girls remember him. And his musket was found on the Squire's property. It was hidden in a fallen tree trunk. Elias and Nehemiah are among the men who are out looking for James. Your husband left his horse in Elias' paddock and the men expect him to return to collect it. They plan to catch him there if they don't find him in the woods surrounding the Holt farm."

Margaret was stunned. James, a killer? It was impossible. It was true he was scrappy and had been in his share of fights before they had married, but James was not a murderer. And if he ever killed someone, it would be with his fists, not with a gun.

"No, Maris," Margaret stood and said with conviction, "What you say is false. James would never deliberately shoot another man. And he had no reason to kill Squire Holt."

"Yes he did," Maris declared. "He did it to prevent the squire from testifying to the validity of Father's will and thereby denying me the property that was rightfully left to me."

"No," Margaret gasped. "No. James would never do that."

In spite of her proclaimed faith in her husband, however, Margaret knew this accusation might be believed by some and would undoubtedly bring more troubles, and probably more debt. She tried to hide her discomfort but failed. Tears formed in her eyes. Life was not fair. They had enough problems without the implication of murder plaguing James.

Maris raised his hand in protest. "He was drunk, Margaret. How can you doubt the word of those innocent young girls who actually saw your husband shoot their guardian?" His face hardened and he backed away from his sister.

"This is your fault, you know. None of this would have happened if you hadn't married that lazy, good-for-nothing James Daunt. He has always been in trouble and the fact that he is a second cousin and related by blood, as well as marriage, makes this an even greater embarrassment for us.

"You have brought dishonor to our family, Margaret." He directed his attacks at her. "You allowed yourself to become involved with that man, and put yourself in a position where you would have to...."

He stopped short of reminding Margaret of her delicate condition at the time their father allowed the marriage to take place.

In truth, it was an unnecessary union. Margaret lost the baby three days after she and James married. There had been two more disappointments for her, both times resulting in relief for Maris and for his parents who, in spite of their ill-concealed preference for their pretty daughter, continued to express their disapproval of Margaret's reckless conduct and forced marriage.

"Do you realize the scandal James brings to our family?" Maris spat the words at her. "Now that he has murdered a defenseless man, we'll spend the rest of our lives battling the local gossips and rumor mongers. The disgrace of being related to a ruthless killer lasts longer than a lifetime of good works.

"Well," he snatched his hat from the rack, "I hope you're happy with what your wanton behavior has wrought."

He yanked the door open, banged it flat against the wall and stormed out of the house. Margaret watched him through the opening at the end of the hall. He mounted his horse, seated himself in the saddle and quickly rode off without a backward look.

She could not believe what Maris had told her.

James was not lazy. When he worked, he worked hard and well. His hinges and door handles were desired for their unique designs and careful craftsmanship. The inconsistency of his ambition, however, was one of his problems. Another was his carefree nature. He could easily be persuaded to drop what he was doing and join the lads in their carousing. James' friends spent most of their free time drinking and reveling at Hebe Balderston's tavern. She was sure her husband's womanizing days were behind him but she knew he had been unable to give up the drink.

The knowledge that he could be impaired by liquor was the only chip in her belief in James' innocence. She was not absolutely certain that he was incapable of harming someone when under the influence of rum. And, she shuddered, the combination of Squire Holt's scheduled testimony in support of her father's unexpected will, and James' well-known need for money, might convince people the girls spoke the truth, no matter what James might say in his defense.


James decided it was time to return to the farm, collect his horse and musket, beg some food and rum from Esther and leave the area. With luck, his sister-in-law would tell him the squire had survived the shot and was only slightly injured when dragged by his horse. The ache in his chest, however, verified his acknowledgement of the grave news that he feared awaited him.

He wondered if Elias was aware of Esther's scheme to shoot Richard Holt or if he knew that she had incited him to implement her plan. Elias certainly had the idea himself when he had answered James' query by mimicking the slitting of a man's throat. No matter, James reasoned, Esther would have to provide him with an alibi; he could name her as the one behind the plot. Unfortunately, he recognized the possibility that few would believe him. And, planning a murder is not the same as committing one.

James suddenly realized Elias' gun was missing. He searched the ferns and under the pine trees. He returned to the moss-covered rise and circled the area. The glow of late afternoon had dimmed to dusk and there was little light available as James examined his surroundings. He determined Elias' flintlock was not in the area. Knowing his brother-in-law would be inconsolable when he found James' musket resting in the corner where his prized weapon should stand, he decided to return to the ledge by the creek.

It was difficult for him to see as he climbed down the embankment and picked his way along the stream. The stones were slick and uneven in size and shape. He slipped and stumbled until he stopped, accepting the fact that he had little chance of locating the rock formation he sought.

Using his hands, James found a break in the brush, crawled up the bank and sat above the creek. He had need of a glass, or, better yet a bottle, of rum. His head was heavy and his brain dormant. He reviewed the probable consequences of his actions and they frightened him: if Squire Holt died, James would be hung; if Holt lived, he would be imprisoned for life. He did not want to experience either option.

The sound of men's voices interrupted James' thoughts. Looking over his shoulder, he saw the light of a half-dozen torches shining through the trees. He jumped up and began to run along the crest of the embankment. He tripped on roots and tough undergrowth but caught himself before he fell. He regained his footing and staggered forward in his attempt to escape.

"Here, James Daunt." A woman's voice startled him. "Come here. I can hide you good."

James stopped and peered into the darkness. He could not see the speaker but he recognized the suggestive tone of the voice and envisioned the seductive smile he knew accompanied the invitation.

"Sally?" James questioned, as the faint suggestion of a female figure appeared in front of him.

"You know it's me, James Daunt. I've come to take care of you." Her familiarity taunted him.

"Sally, I told you I got troubles. I got no time for you now." James tried to find his footing on the uneven surface of the bank.

"I know your troubles, I heard those men talking. They say you shot Squire Holt and that he is dead. Your friend," he heard Sally laugh softly, "and brother-in-law," she added scornfully, "Elias Latch, has got everybody fired up and they're looking to get you for murder. They're wantin' a hangin', James Daunt. Tonight."

James felt shock waves of fear travel from the base of his skull, down his spine and move forward to settle in his stomach. He tried to swallow the resulting effluence that clogged his throat.

"I meant it when I said I can hide you." This time he knew she was serious. "We got to leave now."

Sally took his hand and pulled him along with her. James was without a plan and he had nowhere to go, so he accepted Sally's lead and followed her into the woods.

She found a path which led through the trees and away from the stream. James could hear the men as they spread out to cover more ground. The voices grew faint as Sally guided him over unfamiliar territory.

"Quick, James Daunt, across the road, to the stand of trees." Sally ran ahead of him and he jumped back upon hearing a quiet snort.

"Hurry along," Sally was insistent and he started to run toward her voice. The outline of a horse and a small wagon materialized as he neared the spot where Sally waited.

"In the cart," she ordered. James climbed into the back of a well-used farm cart filled with loose hay.

"Cover yourself. We have a long night ahead of us."

He felt the wagon sway as Sally stepped up, slid onto the seat, readied herself, and snapped the reins. The cart moved forward. The horse's hooves made a familiar thudding sound as they hit the hard-packed earthen road. It was well after dark and people rarely traveled at this hour. James lay on his back and looked up at the heavens. The moon was full and the sky, clear.

Sally kept the horse at a walk and aside from the soft squeal of its wheels as they completed each go-around, the cart made little noise. He had no idea where she was taking him and he did not care. Perhaps, he thought, he would be able to get away. Perhaps he could leave this nightmare behind.

Briefly, he thought of Margaret. What had she heard? Would she think him guilty? Would she be implicated as an accomplice? James did not know the answers to his questions and he was not sure he wanted to know. He needed time to pull himself together, to formulate a plan. Sally was offering him a temporary respite and he accepted it.

He burrowed into the hay, leaving a small opening so he could breathe. After a while, he drove the memories of the day from his mind and replaced them with thoughts of his wife and the life that could have been. In spite of the hard wagon floor and the uneven surface of the farm road, he was able to will himself into a second deep sleep and briefly escape the unbelievable horror of his new reality.

Esther was still seated in the wooden chair when she heard the men return to the barn. The pain in her knee was severe; the ache in her head, near intolerable. She touched her knee and determined that the swelling had increased and the area continued to be hot.

"James Daunt's horse is still here," Elias called out. "We'll take turns standing watch and we'll get him when he comes for it."

The room was dark and Esther could see through the window that night had come.

Elias' footsteps sounded on the three wooden stairs leading to the keeping-room door. She heard the voices of the men who followed him.

She started, uncomfortably aware there was no candle to greet them and that lye soap and scraps of fabric filled the pot which should contain supper for her husband and the members of his search party. She tried to rise but was in too much pain to move. She remained with her head resting against the hard wood back of the chair. The pressure at the base of her skull helped dull the pain in her head. Unfortunately, it had no effect on her knee.

"Esther," Elias shouted. "Where are you? Why is it dark in here?" He paused and sniffed the air. "What's that smell?" She could tell he was irritated.

Esther drew a deep breath and recognized the odor. The water had boiled out of the pot which held the bloodied skirt and shredded petticoat. The stench of scorched fabric in the bottom of the caldron hung heavy in the room and would demand an explanation.

"I am...." she could not answer but Elias heard her muffled attempt.

"Where are you, Esther? Samuel, there is a candle on the shelf behind you. Light it," he ordered as he worked his way in her direction.

She saw the flame of the candle flare in the dark and Samuel Baker's face was illuminated. A doctor. Thank God.

# Tuesday, August 19, 1828

"We're here." James heard the words as they penetrated the periphery of his sleep-addled mind.

"Wake up, James Daunt." The voice, while modulated, was more insistent. He stirred, and then returned to his lethargy.

"Wake up." Another command. As he reluctantly abandoned the oblivion that accompanied his slumber, he determined that the speaker was Sally Morley. With recognition came remembrance. Ominous feelings hastened his awakening.

James heard the soft scuffle of departing footsteps as he opened his eyes to an early morning sun rising through a light mist. He waited for a moment and then sat up, numb from heavy sleep and stiff from the unforgiving boards of the vehicle which had carried him to this unknown place.

He was in a small valley covered by fields, the edges of which traced the lower contours of the surrounding gentle hills. James could see men tossing ears of corn into a horse-drawn wagon which moved along a path between the rows of vegetables. Grasses grew in an adjacent field and men were busy cutting and baling the crops to be used for hay. Tomato plants flourished in the plot closest to him; vines bearing hints of low-lying squash and pumpkins were nearby. Two women bent over the ground. One pulled weeds from the soil and the other plucked the ripe vegetables from the plants. The pleasant sounds of their voices, although muffled by distance, reassured him.

Sally was nowhere to be seen. She had left the horse and cart in front of a large stone barn. James could see bales of hay neatly stacked on the floor. He could hear, but not see, animals which were quartered nearby. A horse snorted, donkeys brayed, cows mooed. The barnyard sounds announced it was feeding time.

Cautiously, James slid to the end of the cart and attempted to pull himself over the side. The stiffness in his shoulders, arms and legs reminded him, first, of his flight, then of his transgression, and finally, of the immediate danger of being identified. He lay back on the hay-covered wagon bed. The pain in his chest returned, and with it, a renewal of self-reproach. He sat up as an inherent instinct for personal survival forced the negative thoughts from his brain. He looked over the side of the wagon, surveyed his surroundings and judged them free, for the moment, of serious threat.

He searched for additional people and saw a single woman standing over a washtub. She was middle-aged, with graying hair pulled straight back and secured in a knot. A nondescript figure, she looked tired and worn as she scrubbed her garment on a washboard, wrung it out and folded it over a line strung between two trees.

James noticed the other items on the line. Waists, pantaloons, an occasional skirt, all made of a single cloth, and all the same dull gray in color. Under her apron, the washerwoman wore a shirt and trousers of like material, and when James glanced back at the fields, he saw the workers of both sexes were similarly clad. The only difference between the apparel of the women and men was that the former wore their blouses outside their trousers while the men tucked their shirts in the waistbands.

Everyone was intent on the execution of his or her duties. No one appeared to have any interest in him or the little cart which had been abandoned in front of the barn.

A large, wooden building stood in the middle of a cleared area behind James. There were no trees to shade it, and even at this early hour, the shelter seemed vulnerable to the August heat. A door in the center of the building opened and two people walked out. One was Sally. She had exchanged her simple dimity dress for the same drab gray garments he had seen on the washerwoman and field hands.

Her companion was a tall, thin man whose height was accentuated by his ramrod carriage and formal black attire. His obvious self-satisfaction was betrayed by his haughty air and the arrogant elevation of his nose. James watched his expression soften as Sally took his arm. She ran her fingers down his forearm and entwined them with his.

She looked up at the pompous man and laughed. James heard the familiar invitation in her voice. He was immediately wary of this unknown recipient of Sally's overt familiarity who approached with such conceit and self-confidence. They stopped in front of the cart.

James pushed himself to standing, awkwardly climbed over the side and took four steps toward the couple. The man looked first at James; then at the cart; then at the hay which covered James' clothes, and then he frowned.

Sally watched his reaction and smiled up at him. James marveled at how her undisguised admiration for her escort was reinforced by her seductive smile. Only Sally, he thought, could do that. He watched as she gently pressed her body against his, unraveled her fingers and waved her hand in his direction.

"Reverend Goodenough," she said. "This is James Morley."

James started at the unfamiliar name. "Daun...." He began to correct Sally.

She quickly interrupted him. "Mr. Morley is my second cousin on my mother's side." She faced James, but directed her comment to the man beside her.

James grimaced at Sally's reference to her maternal parent. He thought of her solely as a girl of easy virtue. He could not imagine her as a member of a family, especially one in which both parents, like his, had been born with the same surname. Marriages between distant cousins were common, even encouraged, in his family. He and Margaret were second cousins, as were Maris and his wife, Delia, a homely woman with a sizeable inheritance.

Sally, obviously, was the product of two Morleys. He wondered if the older man who scrutinized him so closely considered him a hopeful suitor of Sally's. Or, perhaps, a competitor.

"James," she stressed his birth name. "I want to introduce you to the founder of Pleasant Valley Farm and our beloved leader, Reverend Thaddeus Goodenough."

Sally cast another admiring glance at the tall man beside her, then returned her eyes to James. The expression on her face became serious as she began to speak.

"When Reverend Goodenough was a young preacher, Mr. Morley, God, the Father, spoke to him in a dream. The Lord told him that if man unconditionally accepted him and his son, Jesus Christ, man would no longer have to live his life on earth under the threat of eternal damnation for his sins."

Unprepared for the words he was hearing, James stared at Sally. He thought he detected a hint of levity in her voice, but her face showed no trace of humor.

"The Bible says," Sally looked straight at James, "that Christ carried the sins of man with him to the cross and that our body of sins was destroyed when he was crucified."

The man of the cloth muttered to himself. "Stated in the Bible: One Peter, Chapter Two, verse twenty-four. And in Romans Six, verse six."

He raised his voice. "*'For then must he often have suffered since the foundation of the world; but now once in the end of the world hath he appeared to put away sin by the sacrifice of himself.'* Hebrews Nine, verse twenty-six."

"Reverend Goodenough preaches that after we, as individuals, are reborn with God in our hearts, we are incapable of sinning."

James was astounded. The words, as well as the inflection and confident delivery, were completely out of character for the supposedly slow-witted girl the lads at Hebe Balderston's called Sally of the Alley. He wondered why she was speaking this way.

The Reverend continued. "*'Whosoever is born of God doth not commit sin; for his seed remaineth in him: and he cannot sin, because he is born of God.'*" One John Three, verse nine.

"Man can be free from sin," Sally said. "On earth as well as for eternity." She smiled at James and then looked at Thaddeus Goodenough for confirmation.

The man in black stared defiantly at James as he continued to support his version of the word of the Lord with quotations from the Holy Bible. "*'But now being made free from sin, and become servants to God, ye have your fruit unto holiness, and in the end everlasting life.'* Romans Six, verse twenty-two."

"Thaddeus," the cleric winced slightly as Sally spoke his given name, "is truly blessed to have been chosen as a servant of God, as one to spread his sacred word. And we, the residents of the Pleasant Valley Farm community, are likewise blessed to have...," a touch of mischief tinged the glance she shot at the austere man as she identified him formally, "the Reverend Goodenough as our spiritual counselor.

"I think," Sally's tone of voice changed as she looked knowingly at James and continued, "in your current situation, Mr. Morley, you might find the teachings of the reverend most agreeable."

James was unable to take his eyes off Sally. The flirtatious glances, the suggestive laughter and body movements he had seen as she walked towards him, were familiar, but the words she now spoke were alien to the Sally he knew. How could someone be the local harlot and be without sin? And why would a man of God consort with a fallen woman or help a desperate fugitive?

Reverend Thaddeus Goodenough noted the bewildered look on James' face. He mistook it for an inability to comprehend Sally's words rather than recognizing it as a shocked reaction to the extraordinary demeanor of the young woman who uttered them.

"Sister Sarah speaks the truth, Mr. Morley." The preacher moved away from Sally and toward James. " *'Verily, verily, I say unto you, he that heareth my word, and believeth on him that sent me, hath everlasting life, and shall not come into condemnation, but is passed from death unto life.'* The Gospel according to St. John, Chapter Five, verse twenty-four.

"It follows, Mr. Morley, that here in the community, we are as one with Christ. Therefore, we are without sin and should not be subject to the censure of moral or legislated law. *'For sin shall not have dominion over you: for ye are not under the law, but under grace.'* Romans Six, verse fourteen."

"Is it true, Reverend, that once we achieve salvation, we will be forgiven acts committed before our conversion?" Sally asked.

"Of course, Sister Sarah. We give thanks to our Father," Thaddeus Goodenough bowed his head reflexively as he referenced the Lord, "'*who hath delivered us from the power of darkness, and hath translated us into the kingdom of his dear son: In whom we have redemption through his blood, even the forgiveness of sins:*' Colossians One, verses thirteen and fourteen."

"Forgiven by God alone? Or will our past sins be forgiven by civil law?" Sally's innocent questioning of the reverend seemed so guileless that James, himself, was momentarily taken in.

"We, in the community, consider ourselves to be above the laws of the unenlightened. We follow the words written in John Five, verse twenty-two: '*For the Father judgeth no man but hath committed all judgment unto the Son.*' We believe that when the saved sinner truly accepts God and the rewards man has been granted by the sacrifice of his only son, he becomes free from all sin, past, present or future."

Reverend Goodenough looked James in the eye. "Have you committed a sin, Mr. Morley?"

Unsettled by the direct question, and by the use of his unfamiliar new name, James struggled for an answer.

"Certainly not consciously, Reverend," Sally stated. "I would never have brought him here if he had deliberately sinned. In the past, my cousin has suffered from the curse of drink. He has, perhaps, acted incoherently while besotted. When he comes to know all that we follow here, I am quite certain he will find life in the community to his liking."

For just an instant, as she emphasized the word "all", the familiar Sally stood before James. She vanished just as quickly as she had appeared when she said, "I must show James to his room. I am sure he would like to get settled."

"Good day, Mr. Morley." The reverend bowed his head slightly as he dismissed James and turned to Sally. "I hope you have judged him rightly, Sister Sarah." The tall man took her hand.

"Until this afternoon," he spoke only to Sally. Then, his nose, no longer aloft but now held parallel to the ground, preceded him to the barn.

James said nothing. He looked questioningly at Sally who tossed her head and flashed her come-hither smile.

He heard her familiar taunting voice. "You passed the first test, James Daunt." She moved closer and pressed her body against his hip. "But if you choose to stay here, you got to remember you is James *Morley* and," with an exaggerated innocence, she grinned at him, "you *are* seeking salvation."

"What're you talking about, Sally? And what's happened to you? Why do you act so...so...different with him?" James pointed to the retreating figure. "I never heard you talk like that before. And," he said defiantly, "I have no interest in giving my life to God."

Sally ignored his last statement. "Come with me," she said. Then she laughed as she added, "Mr. Morley."

Sally's face became serious again and James could see she was back to her strange ways. He was not comfortable with the peculiar Sister Sarah.

When Esther returned to consciousness, she was lying on her back. Her right leg hurt and there was an excruciating ache on the left side of her head. Slowly, she raised her hand and felt the tender area. The pain increased at her touch and she withdrew her fingers. She hid them under the quilt which covered her as if their banishment would make the pain subside.

Esther stared at the ceiling, then lowered her eyes and clenched her teeth. She turned her head to the left. Sharp pains emanating from her temple shot through her skull and she sank back to her original position. In an effort to ease the discomfort, Esther put her hand on her forehead, and with an uncontrollable shiver, felt the heat of a fever sear her skin. On second thought, she was slightly comforted by the possibility that the fever might explain the muddle of thoughts clouding her brain.

The room was strange to her, but at the same time, it felt comfortable. She did not know why she was there and in such pain. Bewildered, alienated and alone, she felt threatened by the unknown.

Esther remained immobile, afraid to move her head. She cast her eyes left and right in search of a recognizable object which would identify her location. Although she saw nothing specific, she was certain she had been in this place before. She picked at the light quilt

*41*

and folded the edge toward her so the pattern was exposed. She closed her eyes and concentrated on a mental picture of the bedcover in her hand. She was relieved when happy thoughts temporarily dispelled the insecurity brought on by her confused state of mind. She saw herself, as a young girl, cutting squares from flour sacks and sewing them together. The quilt was part of her dowry, started long before she knew the identity of her true love or whether she would find the prince of her dreams.

As she lay motionless, Esther tried, unsuccessfully, to remember if she had married. She could not conjure up the image of a man in her life. She caressed the coarse material of the homely quilt and thought about the room in which she found herself. She willed the bedchamber to take shape in her mind. On her left, she easily envisioned a tall, narrow chest full of linens and items of clothing. Squeezed into the corner on her right, Esther visualized a trunk which she suspected held her personal belongings. The pictures were clear and she was sure they were correct. Her memory was returning.

Armed with the gift of partial recollection, she ascertained that she was in her bed, the bed she shared with Elias Latch, her husband. Not, perhaps, the man of her childhood dreams, but a partner who shared her ways and beliefs. She knew then that she and the bed were in the cramped sleeping room of his family's home.

She moved her right leg and involuntarily cried out. She was immediately reminded of the terrible pain she had experienced in the keeping room and her inability to walk without a crutch. She remembered Elias coming into the darkened room and relived her anxiety over the fact that she had not prepared dinner. She recalled her relief at seeing Samuel Baker, a doctor, who might be able to help.

Esther looked at the small window opposite the bed. The sun was shining. It was the clear light of early morning, quite unlike the remembered late afternoon shadows that had previously dimmed the keeping room to near darkness. She determined she had slept through the night and wondered how she had gotten to her bedchamber. The stairs from the lower floor were narrow, steep and winding. She had no memory of struggling up the stairs on her own or of having help as she negotiated her way to the tiny garret.

Esther could hear a discordant mix of voices, some coming from outside the house, some from the single room on the lower floor. Disembodied and distant, the voices were faint and indistinct yet they jarred her consciousness. She strained to hear what was being said. One voice predominated and was accompanied by the footfalls of a single climber on the winding stairs.

Elias, the man she now knew to be her husband, entered the room, and made his way to the end of her bed.

"How are you, Esther?" Elias asked, visibly uncomfortable at the sight of his incapacitated wife. "You sure gave me a scare last night, what with your funny talking and everything." He was not a demonstrative man and made no effort to touch her.

Esther tried to lift her head. A sharp pain in her temple caused her to return to her former prone position. She had a hazy remembrance of Elias admonishing her about her speech.

"You still hurt?" Elias responded to the pain that showed on Esther's face. "I thought you'd be better this morning."

Esther experienced a flash of resentment caused by her husband's seeming lack of compassion.

"Samuel Baker spent the night," he continued. "He's downstairs. The other men are outside getting ready to ride. We're going to search the woods for James Daunt. His horse is still here so he can't have gone too far. Squire Holt died, Esther, and his boys have put out a reward notice for James' capture. Our search party got much bigger when the word went out this morning." Elias shifted from one foot to another. "Everybody likes money; even some of James' cohorts have joined us in the hunt." Elias smiled slightly. He could not hide the pleasure he derived from the lack of loyalty of his brother-in-law's friends.

"You want me to have Samuel take a look at you before we ride?" He played with his hat which he held in front of him as if to ward off undefined evil spirits that might emanate from the body of his wife.

"I would like to see Samuel," Esther said haltingly.

"What'd you say, Esther?" Elias looked distressed. "Please don't talk that way," Elias pleaded.

"I want to see Samuel," Esther spoke firmly this time and started to raise her head, only to fall back in pain. "My head, Elias, it's hurting bad."

"I can't understand what you're saying, Esther. I'm gonna get him anyway. Maybe you'll talk straight with him. He is a doctor, you know." He spoke the last few words as if she needed reminding of Samuel Baker's professional status.

Elias walked to the head of the stairs and called down. "Samuel, Esther wants to see you." He waited until he heard the doctor's footsteps on the floor below and then he moved to the other side of the room.

The physician was tall and thin; his rough-hewn face was heavily lined from hours spent travelling from town to town in an open carriage under the country sun. He was a kind man who cared about his patients, most of whom were his personal friends. He was tired and panted slightly after his climb up the stairs.

"Morning, Esther." He came to stand next to the bed. "You had a bad night. How do you feel now?"

Esther thought for a moment before speaking.

"My head and knee hurt, Samuel." She waited for his reply, hoping he, unlike Elias, would understand what she was saying.

"Could you say that again, Esther?" Her confidence vanished as the doctor leaned closer. "Please repeat what you just said."

This time, she spoke slowly, carefully enunciating each word. "My head and knee hurt."

Samuel walked to the small window at the foot of her bed and stared out at the eager search party milling around below. He ran his fingers through his thinning hair.

"You have a pretty bad bruise on the side of your head." Samuel spoke, his back still to her. "It caused you a great deal of pain during the night. Is it still hurting, Esther?"

"Yes," she said emphatically.

Dr. Baker turned toward her, a surprised, but pleased, look on his face. "Good," he said. "This time I understood your answer."

She was relieved. She had spoken clearly and he understood her affirmative response.

"You appear to have sustained some rather serious injuries. Elias says you fell onto a table." Samuel Baker tapped nervously on the window sill as he considered his next statement. "These injuries are inconsistent with a routine fall." He looked closely at Esther. "It is important that I determine whether you had an accident or, perhaps, suffered a stroke which might have caused you to lose your balance."

"Dear Lord, no! Not a stroke," she whispered.

In spite of the heat of her fever, Esther shivered at the implications. Fragmented memories of her mother struggling to speak following a stroke momentarily broke through the cobwebs which snarled her brain.

"I couldn't hear you, Esther. Please speak up."

She closed her eyes and said nothing.

The doctor watched her for a moment before saying, "I assume you don't remember what happened yesterday. Am I correct?"

"Yes." She spoke the single word clearly and a smile crossed the doctor's face.

"Very good," he said. "Let me try another question. Please answer with a single 'yes' or 'no'. Do you think you could have fallen because you were lightheaded or dizzy?"

"I don't know." Realizing she had broken the single response rule again, Esther opened her eyes and pursed her lips.

Samuel Baker frowned as he said, "I will try one more question. Concentrate, Esther. Can you picture something on the floor that might have caused you to fall?"

She pulled her hands from under the quilt and clasped them tightly, wincing as the scrapes and scratches chafed at the contact. His suggestion had elicited a reaction: an undefined feeling, an amorphous memory. For lack of another direction, Esther closed her eyes and focused on the incessant pounding in her temple. The memory of her headlong pitch into the ditch materialized. She realized that her injuries had actually occurred when she slipped on the loose stones along the gully, rather than when she fell on the keeping room table. She could not remember why she had been on the road.

Again, Samuel asked if she had tripped over something. This time she answered with an insistent "Yes." The effort to make these simple responses intelligible was tiring, but in spite of her disoriented state of mind and faulty memory, she was aware that her answers were important.

"Well, that is good news." Samuel smiled. "Were you hurrying to do something before Elias came into the room?"

Images of her skirt and petticoat boiling on the stove flashed before her eyes. Fear associated with Elias or something Elias might know, inexplicably overwhelmed her. A vision of Sally Morley standing by the woods flickered briefly in front of her eyes. She tried to put the free-flowing memories in context but failed.

Samuel repeated his query.

Hurrying. That was a good reason for falling.

"Yes," she answered, hoping Samuel would stop questioning her. She closed her eyes. All she wanted to do was sleep. Her headache had worsened and she turned her body slightly in her bed to get some relief. In doing so, she inadvertently twisted her knee and cried out in pain.

"Are you all right, Esther?" Samuel asked.

"My knee, Samuel." She pointed to the quilt where it covered her leg. "I twisted it." The doctor did not bother to ask for clarification.

"Would you like me to look at your knee, Esther?"

"Yes," she answered, the tears forming in her eyes. She steeled herself and willed them to stop. Even in her weakened state, Esther Hicks Latch refused to cry.

The doctor lifted the quilt away from her knee and intentionally left the rest of her body covered. He gently rotated the swollen joint and his patient screamed in pain.

Samuel glanced over his shoulder. "Come take a look, Elias."

Esther's husband had been standing in the far corner of the room, twirling his hat on his finger, as he listened to the discouraging discourse between the physician and his wife. Reluctantly, he moved closer to the bed and looked down at Esther's knee.

"Appears pretty bad to me, Samuel. Is she going to get better?" The doctor gently touched the knee cap and Esther pulled away. She cried out as the pain shot up and down her leg.

"I'm sorry, Esther. I didn't intend to hurt you. Knees are troublesome under the best of circumstances and somehow, you managed to give yours a mighty whack. I won't be able to determine the extent of the damage until the swelling goes down, but," Sam Baker frowned, "it looks like you've probably shattered your knee cap."

He turned back to Elias. "She will have to remain in bed until the swelling goes down. If it goes down on its own, I won't have to bleed her."

Esther's stomach turned. Her mind conjured up reminiscences of the ugly worms that sucked the blood of her mother as she lay dying. In contrast to the elusiveness of recent memories, those associated with her mother's death were clear and true. Vivid pictures of leeches covering her mother's arms coursed through her brain and reignited her suspicion that the bleeding had hastened her mother's demise.

The horror she had experienced when viewing that barbaric treatment caused her to cry out. "Don't bleed me. Don't let him bleed me, Elias."

Esther jerked her head to the left to look at her husband as she pleaded. Then, in response to an agonizingly painful assault on her temple, she lay back, closed her eyes and tried to escape the misery she was enduring.

"Calm yourself, Esther," Samuel laid a hand on her arm as he guessed the cause of her agitation. "I don't want to bleed you anymore than you want me to do it. I will only resort to the leeches if the swelling doesn't subside or you develop an infection. You don't have a serious sore so let's hope neither situation occurs."

Elias was becoming impatient. He was as concerned about Esther's nonsensical words as he was about her wounds.

"Will she be able to talk right?" he asked curtly.

"I am not sure, Elias. I'm just a country doctor. I don't know much about malfunctions of the brain. I can patch the scratches on her hands, and if need be, I can splint or set her leg, but I don't know what's flummoxing her brain." Samuel Baker held his hand to his forehead and rubbed it thoughtfully. "Perhaps when that bump on her temple goes down she'll return to normal. I'm afraid we'll just have to wait, my friend."

Elias walked to the small window and looked out.

"Nehemiah and the boys are watching for James Daunt. He has to get his horse soon. Can't escape on foot. He'll have to come by, unless, of course, he steals one somewhere."

He started toward the door and paused by his wife's bedside.

"Samuel's with you, Esther. He's the one who knows the doctorin' business. Maybe he can fix your talkin'."

Elias left the room and the sounds of his footsteps on the winding stairs were followed by the closing of the keeping-room door. Then silence informed Esther that he was no longer in the house.

Sally touched James' hand as she guided him across the cart path. It ran along the edge of the fields, past the barn and ended at the big house. She seated herself under the one tree that provided shade from the August sun.

"What are you doing here, Sally?" James looked down at her. "Why do you sound so different? Talking about God and making up to a preacher." He was overwhelmed by the realization that he was speaking to the flippant young girl who had brought him to this place.

A flirtatious look and a bawdy grin restored the old Sally. "Don't you like me this way?" She patted the ground. "Sit down, James."

No longer the coquette, she said, "I will tell you all that you need to know for the moment." Startled by the abrupt changes in her personality, he followed her instruction and sat across from her. She uncharacteristically fussed with her hair and straightened her skirt.

"First, you should know that, if you are accepted into the community, you will be safe here." She paused.

"Safe from what, Sally? The sheriff? Elias and his posse? They aren't going to listen to what that minister says. I can't understand him and nobody from my world is going to see any sense in what he says."

James brushed his forehead with his hand. "And I didn't understand what you were saying either, Sally. I am not looking for salvation. I am not even sure I'm looking for a place to hide. I only want to know if Squire Holt is dead, then I'll know what is going to happen to me."

He lowered his head and shuddered. "I don't want to be hung, Sally, or go to jail. And at least one of those things is going to happen to me whether he is dead or not." James looked up. "I shot a man, Sally, and no preacher with his fancy words is going to lift that sin from my head or the law from my back."

Sally reached over and put her hand on James' shoulder.

"There's time, James, for you to decide what you want to do. Until then, this is a good, safe place for you to stay. Look around you. This is a farming community, just like the one where you've been living. It's different here, though." She was contemplative as if trying to decide whether to go on.

"We all have our chores. Men and women toil together in the fields; we share the weeding, plowing and planting of the crops. We all work in the barn, too," A breeze plucked a strand of hair from behind her ear and blew it across her face. She picked at it until she got a grip on the slender tormenter and tucked it back in place.

"Everyone takes his or her turn at milking the cows and caring for the animals. We have a potter's shed and a kiln where we make our household wares and we produce our own wooden barrels and tubs."

James was taken aback by Sally's words. He could not believe she was interested in cows and tubs and dishes, or that she had any pompous-sounding ideas about the way you did your work. He, like the rest of his friends, had always considered Sally to be empty-headed. Yet here she was, going on as if she knew about these things, and more importantly, as if she cared.

"We all do the household tasks like cooking, making butter, doing the laundry. The women do the fancy work like making small bags, hats, knitting as well. So far, we haven't gotten the men to try their hands at any of the delicate work." She laughed at the thought.

"It is usually the men who maintain the buildings and equipment. Both men and women take turns keeping the records and paying the bills, and we all participate in the scheduling and planning of activities and duties."

James was disconcerted by the change in Sally and overwhelmed by what she was saying. She did not sound like the fun-loving tease who eagerly gave herself to the neighborhood lads. She spoke like someone who was educated, organized, a thinking person.

James shook his head and dismissed that possibility. Yet, when he thought about it, he had to admit he did not know anything at all about Sally except that, he recollected with a slight smile, she knew how to please the boys.

She seemed to know everything about this farm, however, and the way she talked, he was pretty sure she understood the teachings of Reverend Goodenough. Even more astonishing to James, she seemed to know something about God. James had not thought about God since he was required to go to First Day School as a boy and he hadn't thought much about the Lord at the time.

"We grow and make everything we need and what we don't use, we sell in town," Sally continued speaking. "Self-sufficiency is one goal of the community. Another is the sharing of all we have and all we make. If you lived here, James, what is mine would be yours. And in the same spirit, what is yours would belong to me and to every other member of the community. More importantly, while we regard ourselves as individuals, we all belong to each other. We live in peace here, James, and work to honor our responsibilities to the community and to each other."

Sally smoothed her skirt. "I have given you much to think on, James. Try staying here for a few days. We do not have a resident blacksmith. We can use you. You'll have plenty of work to keep you busy. You have to understand, however, that we do not work for personal gain here. All monies go into a common coffer, and just as the fruits of our labor are shared, so, too, are the expenses."

She frowned slightly. "It might be nice, James, to live a life where you don't have to worry about how you're going to pay your creditors." James wondered if she knew of his money problems, and, if she did, how she had heard about them. But then, he guessed, everyone in the area knew of his financial woes.

An unexpected change came over the redheaded woman seated across from him. No longer serious, she smiled. The confident, knowing smile of the self-assured disciple of Reverend Thaddeus Goodenough was replaced by the seductive smile of the Sally of the Tavern, the Sally of the Ledge, the Sally of the Alley. She shifted her weight, threw back her shoulders, leaned against the tree and assumed a suggestive position which drew attention to her feminine attributes.

"I think you will find there are other doings here in addition to blacksmithing that will keep you busy, James Daunt Morley." She lowered her eyes and slowly untied the drawstring around the neck of her tunic. She dragged her finger over the fabric and the gathers at the neckline spread. The tunic dropped open and James could see the soft white flesh of a young woman's breasts.

He felt the familiar rush that Sally knew how to bring on in a man and he willingly succumbed to the physical thrill which flowed through his body. He was unprepared for an open invitation in this strange place from this unrecognizable Sally and he started to speak. She placed a finger over his lips and reached for his hand. She gently guided it inside the opening of her tunic and laid it over her breast. He felt her body firm to his touch and allowed himself to respond.

Unexpectedly stimulated by his tentative caressing of her breast, he did not want to stop. He had never touched a woman while sitting in a public place like this and he had never taken the time to be gentle or tender in his lovemaking simply because it brought him pleasure.

His physical reaction to the rhythmic repetition of the pattern of his fingers on her skin was heightened by the sense of danger inherent in the very real possibility that they were being observed. New sensations took James to a level of excitement he had never experienced in the past. He was on the brink of losing control when she removed his hand and raised it to her lips.

She kissed his palm and said, "Later."

Sally grinned wickedly and licked the ends of his fingers. "After you have settled yourself."

She arranged her tunic, tied the drawstring and stood. The encounter was over. He waited a moment before rising and then joined her. He carried his hat below his waist as they walked to the large white, wooden building at the end of the cart path.

*51*

Sally opened the door and motioned James inside. The washerwoman he had noticed earlier was standing off to the side. She glanced at him and then at Sally. Where Sally had been able to combine admiration and sexual provocation in one fleeting look, the visual manifestations of jealousy and love flashed in tandem with reproof and disappointment across the woman's face. Her eyes passed over James and came to rest on the red-haired girl who accompanied him through the entryway.

Sally, seeing the lone figure, frowned and tossed her head. She quickened her step, and left James and the woman behind as she headed down the hall. James hurried to catch up with Sally as she started to climb a steep set of stairs to the second floor. Halfway up, James stopped and looked back at the washerwoman. She was standing still, staring up at Sally. The older woman lowered her gaze slightly, looked questioningly at James and then turned away.

Samuel Baker had moved to the foot of Esther's bed and fiddled with his fingers until he heard Elias leave the house.

"I did not want to mention this in front of your husband." He looked down at the woman lying motionless in front of him. "Even though he was here last night and heard everything you said."

He glanced out the window to reassure himself that Elias had, indeed, joined his fellow huntsmen.

"Esther, you have been in a state." The doctor continued looking down at the men and their horses as he spoke. "While you were delirious, you mumbled a lot of unintelligible nonsense."

He turned around to face his patient. He ran his fingers over the smooth surface of the footboard.

"You seemed distressed, and most of the time, I could not understand you. However, at different times, you clearly cried out the words Holt and Morley." He paused. "You also mentioned," another pause, "the name of your brother-in-law, James Daunt."

He stared intently at the woman under the quilt.

Richard Holt. Sally Morley. James Daunt. The names reverberated in Esther's brain bringing with them total recall of yesterday's events. Like the echoing blast which followed her single shot from James Daunt's musket, the three names circled her brain with ruthless persistence, each, eventually, coming to rest atop its own personal cache of horrors.

"Oh, Lord, he knows." Her silent acknowledgement was accompanied by a facial expression of abject desperation she was unable to control. Esther took a deep breath, composed herself as best she could and slowly released the air from her lungs.

She glanced at Samuel Baker: country doctor, keeper of the physical, mental and emotional secrets of the local farm folk who trusted him. The look on his face told her, without a doubt, that he suspected she was, in some way, involved in the murder of Squire Holt. This knowledge brought with it the understanding that, in order to survive, she must keep her wits about her. She closed her eyes, and in so doing, temporarily denied the presence of the prying physician.

Samuel spoke, "Why are those people so important to you?"

Esther heard her companion's voice but ignored his words. She was concerned only with the necessity of formulating a plan and fabricating an alibi.

It occurred to her that, in spite of her pain and the unknown prognosis for the recovery of her speech and knee, the shock of Samuel's insinuations had restored her ability to think coherently. Now, she needed time and she needed privacy.

She opened her eyes, looked directly at the doctor and waved her hand in dismissal.

Taken aback by her unexpected response, Samuel Baker chose his words carefully to avoid further offending his patient.

"Esther, I should have waited before...." He stopped in mid-sentence as she repeated her imperious gesture of expulsion. Amazed, he watched as his confused, pain-ridden, pitiable patient transformed herself into a tenacious self-preservationist. Without raising her head, she had firmly, with a toss of a hand, overridden his disturbing query and confidently taken charge of the situation.

Esther's strong reaction to his deliberately provocative question convinced Samuel that she knew something about Squire Holt's demise. He refused to be unceremoniously discharged without further information.

53

"Esther," he decided on a direct approach, "your wounds are too severe to have been caused by a fall onto a table. To be blunt, I think you were outside when you fell. Small pieces of grit in the abrasions on your hands probably came from the road across the field."

He scrutinized her carefully as he spoke. "This observation leads me to ask if you remember why you might have been on the road yesterday."

She lay still with her eyes closed. Her breathing deepened but the veteran doctor was quite sure her sleep was a pretense. He put his hand on her shoulder and she did not move. Samuel had seen enough sleeping patients to know when they were exhausted and when they were perpetrating a ruse to avoid dealing with him. Esther was a typical example of the latter. He decided to let her continue with her deception.

There was a small stool, sized to fit under the bedstead. He pulled it out, grabbed hold of the bed post and grimaced when his bones creaked as he lowered himself onto the rush seat. He glanced over at Esther. Her eyelids quivered as she surreptitiously glimpsed him trying to get comfortable. He smiled at her and the fluttering stopped. He continued to study her face but the eyelids remained stationary.

Samuel Baker wondered why her reaction had been so strong and his curiosity, he admitted, was the reason he now sat patiently by her bedside as the morning slipped away. He and his charge dozed and finally slept while the good doctor awaited some answers.

James seated himself on a horsehair mattress which had been permanently depressed by the weight of many previous occupants. Sally had left him alone in a second-floor room. It was small: six feet across, ten feet in length. He knew the exact measurements as he had continuously paced the U-shaped space around the low, narrow bed while he waited for Sally to return.

There was no other furniture in the room; no chest or table, just four large nails pounded into a thick board attached to the wall on the left of the door. The crude pegs, obviously provided for hanging clothes, seemed unnecessary to James as he had only the garments he was wearing.

His stomach grumbled and he was acutely aware that he had not eaten since the noon meal he had taken the previous day at Hebe Balderston's tavern. That was before he had shot Squire Holt. That was before he had awakened on the bottom of a cart in this strange place. That was before he had lost control of his life and had come to be dependent on the red-haired chameleon now known as Sister Sarah.

James wanted to believe Sally had his best interests in mind when she brought him here. She had certainly taken a chance. They could have been caught while in the woods, or on the road. The odd Reverend Goodenough could have refused to take him in or, worse, could have turned him over to the sheriff. He realized that possibility still existed.

James heard footsteps coming in his direction. They were soft enough to belong to a woman, but unsure of his safety, he remained seated and waited to see if it was Sally.

"Good afternoon, James Morley." He jumped at the sound of the unfamiliar name, and at the same time, was relieved to see it was, indeed, Sally.

She noticed his reaction and frowned. "James, you must learn to answer to Morley. James Daunt is a hunted man who bears a very close resemblance to you," she observed wryly. "Using another man's name is a feeble attempt at disguise but it is the best you can do at the moment."

She stepped to the side of the bed. "I've brought some food. I'm afraid we missed the noon meal and I'm sure you are hungry. It has been a long time since either of us has eaten."

Sally carried a covered basket, some bed linen and a bundle of clothes in the same gray color as the garments James had seen drying on the line. She put her parcels down on the bed next to him.

"Sally, am I a prisoner?" James was worried. "Even though I'm a fugitive, I can't stay here if I have to remain cooped up in this room. I'm used to being outdoors and free to move around at will."

He turned to the lone window in search of a fresh breeze but the air outside was still and brought no relief.

Sally laughed. "No, James, you're free to come and go. Just remember, this is a working farm, and if you choose to stay here, you must be a productive member of our community." She handed him the clothes she had procured for him.

"We are all, men and women, outfitted similarly when we're working. I have brought these for you to put on while your own clothes are being washed in our laundry. If you decide to stay, you'll receive replacements each time you take these to be cleaned."

James thought of the strange washerwoman. "The woman I saw standing over the washtub, the one we passed when we entered this building, who is she, Sally?"

A guarded look crossed Sally's face and she was momentarily flustered by his question. Regaining her composure, she shrugged.

"One of the original members of the community, James. That's all. Just one of the old ones."

The way Sally emphasized *old*, the word assumed ambiguous overtones and highlighted the mysterious relationship James felt existed between the two women.

The sense of intrigue spread to Sally herself. A total stranger stood before him in this stark room, in this unknown location. James was aware that he was putting his life in the hands of a woman who, until this morning, he had considered a simple-minded whore. Now, recognizing her intellectual, if not sensual, transformation, he wondered if he, too, might have a chance to be more than a worthless bungler. If this community of Sally's had wrought miracles for her, perhaps he could change. Or was it too late for him? He would have to wait and see.

Sally picked up the basket and said, "Change your clothes, James. We'll eat outside and then I will take you to the old blacksmith's shop down by the barn. As I told you, we only have a visiting smith at the moment. There's a real need for you and your skills."

Sally left the room and closed the door behind her. James could hear her pacing the floor of the hall as he shed the shabby clothes he had worn since he left his employer's premises two days earlier. He slipped into the mandated trousers and shirt, both of which, like Sally's tunic, closed with a drawstring. Emulating the men he had seen in the fields, he tucked his shirt into the waist of his trousers before he went to the door.

James looked around the room. He wondered if this place really was safe, as Sally had said. Could he work here without worrying about his creditors stalking him? Would it be possible to make a new life for himself and…? He was about to include Margaret, but on reflection, doubted that she would want to take a chance on this new existence. James was also aware of the likelihood that his renewed physical attraction to Sally might be part of the impetus behind his consideration of Pleasant Valley Farm as a temporary refuge.

Then reality replaced speculation and he wondered, instead, how much time would pass before people learned he was an accused murderer, before the law would catch up with him. The now-familiar band around his chest tightened as the vision of Squire Holt falling from his horse filled his mind. He shook it off, stepped into the hall and followed Sally down the stairs and out into the heat of an August afternoon.

Sally led James back to the lone tree where they had lingered in the early morning. She opened the picnic basket and brought out a loaf of bread, a slab of cheese and a knife. She cut two slices of cheese and they each tore off a piece of bread. They spoke little and James, uncomfortable about their previous public intimacy, was relieved when Sally made no titillating overtures.

After they finished their simple meal, she smiled at James.

"Time to show you the blacksmith shop." She stood and held out her hand. He took it and allowed her to pull him to standing. They crossed the cart path and walked to the rear of the barn.

James was pleased to find that the blacksmith shop stood in the shadow of the larger building and was protected from the intense rays of the afternoon sun. Sally opened the door of the small, stone building and James could see the hearth on his left as he entered.

Bellows and tongs leaned against the wall. Remnants of the work of other smiths lay scattered on the floor and on a long bench which covered one side of the single room. An anvil sat atop a section of an enormous old tree trunk; chisels, hammers and assorted tools were stuffed into a nearby wooden box. Several horseshoes and door hinges stood out from the general clutter at the base of the anvil.

Without thinking, James started to pick through the debris. He found few items of worth other than the available equipment which he considered adequate. He reached for the tongs and was reminded of his own lost shop. Memories of his financial downfall reignited the vision of Richard Holt's fallen body being dragged by his horse. He looked over at Sally and the expression on her face told him she recognized his pain.

"Back to work, James," she said gently. "Time enough later to revisit the past." She looked out the window. "There is a need for your services here. You should stay until you clear your head."

"I don't understand why you are helping me, Sally. And why you seem so different today."

"You were nice to me, James. Even if you did," she placed her hands on her hips and thrust them forward, "grab at me in front of the other lads." She grinned suggestively then twirled around. When she came full circle and faced him again, the serious Sally had returned. "Finish straightening up, James, and we'll go to the dining room."

Sally watched James as he organized his tools and brushed away the waste from previous projects. She was surprised to see him examine the implements closely and group the best together on the bench. She had assumed he would be as carefree about his occupation as he seemed to be about his life. She wondered what else she would learn about the man she had rescued.

Sally waited patiently as James arranged the smithy to his liking, and when he had finished, she outlined the meal schedule. "We eat at prescribed times," she said. "Six o'clock for breakfast; twelve noon for dinner, and supper at five. There is little leeway. If you're hungry, you'll arrive on time; otherwise, you will go without."

Although it had only been a short time since they had eaten their bread and cheese, James welcomed the prospect of supper.

"I must admit, I'm still hungry, Sally."

She looked at him and grinned the familiar smile of Sally of the Alley. Then she gathered the fabric of her skirt in her fingertips

58

and raised the garment to her knees. She spread her legs, twisted her body back and forth and tilted her head.

James responded to her invitation and moved toward her.

Sally laughed and stepped aside. "Supper's about to be served, James Daunt. You'll have to wait until later for dessert." She brushed his body with her hand and said, "Hmmmm. I think you will find it to be a good dessert."

She dropped her skirt and resumed the more sedate stance of Sister Sarah.

"There is another regulation," Sally said, as she opened the door. "You must sit with the men while I join the women in their section. There are rules about fraternization, James, but on the whole, I think you'll find the attitudes of the residents most agreeable."

James was unsettled by the thought of sitting with unfamiliar men in this unknown environment.

"I don't have much to say to strangers, Sally," he said.

"Initially, you won't be expected to carry on a conversation. And we have a visitor who is going to speak after supper. You may be questioned about where you've come from; why you're here in our community; what you do, and where you're going, so you might think on those subjects." She laughed. "And don't forget that your name is James Morley and you are my second cousin on my mother's side."

Assorted answers swirled in James Daunt Morley's head as he followed Sally to the door of the dining room. By the time they had entered the room, he was convinced he would be in the hands of the law by supper's end.

It was late afternoon when Samuel Baker awoke from his fourth nap. His head rested on his shoulder, his mouth was open and dry, and his arms hung limply at his side. He was stiff and noted that, this time, his patient was actually asleep. He straightened and stretched his long limbs without leaving the stool.

He stared at Esther's still body and acknowledged that he probably knew more than anyone of the ups and downs of her life.

A boyhood friend of her father's, Samuel had been present at her birth. It was a difficult delivery and the doctor and minister had been called. Mother and baby survived, but memories of the life-and-death struggle tainted their relationship.

Esther was the second child, and the first of four daughters, born to the stern Jacob Hicks and his no-nonsense wife. Although Jacob, a wealthy landowner and farmer, was considered one of the most eligible bachelors in the county, his bride, Margaret Evans Maris, had looked on her marriage as a step down.

The Hicks and Maris families had arrived in the New World before the midpoint of the seventeenth century and had begun their lives as farmers. While the Hicks clan had prospered solely by investing in, and working, the land, the Maris family had produced doctors, lawyers, legislators and military heroes in addition to their agricultural endeavors.

At the time of her marriage, Margaret Maris had insisted on combining her surname with her birth name, thereby earning a reputation in the area as an uppity snob from the other side of the river. Margaretmaris Hicks was quite content to be considered an outsider by her neighbors and she made no effort to make new friends.

Samuel remembered that Esther was long, thin and plain at birth. By contrast, her three younger sisters were petite, feminine and pretty. The second-born girl, Margaret, proved to be especially attractive, both physically and socially. She had a quick, easy smile and a pleasant nature which overshadowed her intellectual shortcomings and perpetual aversion to accepting responsibility for her own, or family, duties. Esther, on the other hand, had a sharp mind and innate analytical skills which she used to keep herself apprised of the world around her; a world which included the personal activities of her neighbors. She was adept at utilizing that information for her own benefit and was always capable of conjuring up and executing a plan. At times, however, her abrasive personality inhibited her effectiveness as a successful manipulator.

As a young girl, Esther Hicks had set her cap for the personable James Daunt. His mother was Margaretmaris' first cousin, and as their children had been born a year and a half apart, the two mothers brought them together occasionally. James' father was a successful city doctor and Margaretmaris, deeming his offspring a desirable mate for her oldest daughter, secretly hoped they would be attracted to each other as adults.

Esther, who, unfortunately, retained her angular countenance and beanpole physique, favored the idea, while James, whose sandy hair, ruddy complexion and intense blue eyes complimented his roguish, carefree personality, had no interest in his distant cousin.

James had moved to the country after the death of his father. While he was never averse to a hard day's work when he needed money, he much preferred to cavort with the lads and patronize the lively ladies at Hebe Balderston's and other local taverns.

In deference to his mother, he reluctantly called on Esther from time to time. During one particularly tedious rendezvous, he caught sight of her younger sister, Margaret. Only fifteen years of age, she was too young for him to court but he determined to see her again. He increased the frequency of his visits to Esther.

Dr. Baker, recipient of Margaretmaris' confidences, recalled the story of Esther's infatuation and its consequence. One Saturday, after James and his friends had spent several hours at Hebe Balderston's, where the food was sparse and the draughts plentiful, an inebriated James rode to the Hicks farm.

Esther was in the kitchen preparing supper; Hannah, the youngest of the Hicks daughters, was confined to her sickbed with the sweats, and. the rest of the family was in town doing the weekly errands. Seeing James' defenses were down due to an abundance of drink, and knowing no one would return for at least an hour, Esther determined to set in motion an age-old plan to ensnare the object of her affections.

Shedding her apron, she escorted James into the front parlor which was occupied only on Sundays and holidays. She seated him on the down cushions of the claret-colored velvet divan. He leaned back, closed his eyes and stretched his legs in front of him. Still standing, Esther watched from across the room and feared he had fallen asleep.

Totally inexperienced, as well as unschooled, in the art of physical courtship, she hoped he would guess her intentions and take the initiative. Instead, he did not move and the eager neophyte assumed the role of aggressor.

Cautiously, she sat next to him and spoke his name. He did not respond. She moved closer and gently took his hand in hers. Her stomach was in knots as she vacillated between fear of being caught in a compromising situation and the thrill of physical contact with the man she loved.

She raised his hand to her lips and lightly brushed them against his skin as she breathed deeply of his smell. He did not reciprocate or, much to her relief, reject her as she carefully returned his hand to his lap. Emboldened by the knowledge that he was probably asleep, she leaned over and softly kissed his cheek. His eyes were still closed as he turned his face toward her.

Realizing no harm had come from her peck on the cheek, she determined to try again. Tight lipped and terrified, she kissed him full on the mouth. To her surprise, James, eyes still closed, raised his arms, grasped her shoulders and pulled her to him as he returned her advances.

Esther, with unfamiliar, overwhelming emotions raging through her, abandoned all inhibitions and rolled her body onto his. He raised her skirt and the two bodies became one.

Horrified by what she had precipitated, Esther pushed herself off James Daunt and ran to her room. She threw herself on the bed, covered her desecrated body, and sobbed uncontrollably, never knowing whether from shame or the aftermath of her surrender to unbridled passion.

James, now sober, rose from the divan, retrieved his cap, hastily put himself in order and fled from the house. The next morning, he enlisted in the army. Six months later, he was honorably discharged when his company disbanded.

Three months before his return, Esther and her mother visited Samuel Baker. The good doctor had a friend, Elias Latch, a bachelor who desired a wife. One week later, Esther and Elias, fifteen years her senior, were married. The baby was born six months later and lived for five days. As far as Samuel Baker knew, there had been no other pregnancies for Esther.

James Daunt never called at the Hicks home again but clandestine meetings with Esther's younger sister, Margaret, were disguised as seemingly accidental encounters in town, at socials and after church while the senior Hicks visited with the pastor and other parishioners.

Two years to the day after Esther's visit, Margaretmaris called on Samuel Baker with her second-born daughter. Another marriage was hastily arranged, this time with the baby's biological father as the groom.

Margaretmaris and Jacob Hicks never forgave James Daunt for his violation of their daughters but James rejoiced in his good fortune at winning the hand of the girl he had long desired.

As the sensitive doctor recalled the story of the moral downfall of his supine patient and her willing sister, empathy replaced the suspicion he had been harboring. He leaned over and straightened the quilt which covered the sleeping woman's body. He decided his questions could wait until Esther's speech returned. He left the side of the sick bed, descended the narrow stairs and entered the keeping room. He heard voices coming from the barn and knew Elias had returned.

The sun was nearing the earth's horizon line when Samuel Baker mounted his horse and set off for home. Elias and his posse were in a foul humor brought on by their unsuccessful efforts to find James Daunt. His disappearance frustrated the men. No one had seen the fugitive and his horse remained in Elias' paddock.

Samuel was convinced Esther Latch knew something about the shooting of the squire and he was also certain her speech impediment was real. She had been delirious when she had blurted out the slurred surnames of Holt, Morley and Daunt. She had uttered no other intelligible words that night and Samuel assumed the three names were of utmost importance to the disabled woman.

He wondered about her injuries and when, how and where she had come by them. He also wondered if, as he suspected, they were incurred in connection with, or as a result of Richard Holt's murder.

No one paid attention to James as he sat alone at the end of one of the long dining tables in the men's section. He kept his eyes on his plate and ate slowly to avoid any unnecessary contact with the others who chatted throughout the meal. When a gray-clad woman removed his plate, he averted his eyes and stared at the doorway on his left as if he was expecting a visitor.

After everyone had finished eating supper and the dishes had been cleared, Thaddeus Goodenough rose from his chair and silenced the room with a wave of his hand.

"We have a guest with us this evening." His voice was loud and firm as he addressed the tables of diners. "Our good friend, Reverend Maximillian Montague from Virginia, is here to spread the word about the American Colonization Society and its honorable endeavors to establish a colony of free Negroes in Africa."

"Welcome, Maximillian Montague." Individual greetings echoed around the room as the community received the Southern gentleman into their circle.

Reverend Montague was a small, trim man dressed in a tight-fitting, double-breasted coat made of rich midnight-blue wool. It topped a high-necked, white waistcoat and matching linen shirt. Fawn-colored trousers flared over his hips and thighs and narrowed as they descended to his ankles. Straps under his shiny black shoes held the pant legs tight and tidy as he moved to the center of the room. The ensemble was designed to emphasize his wasp-like waist and underline his patrician demeanor.

He stood for a moment, his right hand on his hip. A look of satisfaction crossed his face as he verified the positive impact of his appearance on his plain-clothed audience. Without changing his position, he surveyed the men and women who expectantly awaited his words.

"I have just returned from the great continent of Africa." Melodic tones of the South tinged his words. He continued to sweep the room with his eyes as the oohs and ahs of his audience confirmed the anticipated response.

"Six years ago, along with a contingent of our black brethren and three of my own kind, I sailed for Liberia. We survived the treacherous seas and tumultuous winds which buffeted our brave little ship and heralded our possible extinction." Maximillian took a breath and his silence underscored the danger of the undertaking.

"After many weeks of enduring debilitating conditions and overwhelming deprivation, we finally reached the promised land." There was a general shaking of heads as the assembled members envisioned the rough and perilous crossing and empathized with the frail dandy who spoke.

"When we landed on the shore, we were greeted by pitiable conditions. Dwindling supplies, disease, hostile natives and disheartened settlers threatened the realization of our dream for a new world." He scanned the room and was rewarded with sympathetic murmuring.

"During my time in Liberia, my compatriots and I lived through a malaria epidemic, built defense fortifications and quelled a native uprising." A master of timing, the little reverend allowed his listeners to absorb the travails of the resolute early emigrants to a foreign land.

"On the positive side, I am proud to say, we established a self-sustaining agricultural community and instituted profitable trade alliances. We made our new colony the economic and political center of the surrounding coastal areas." His audience brightened at the heartening news.

"And by the time we left, our intrepid immigrants, and those who followed, had claimed their lands, constructed homes and were leading productive lives."

He took out a handkerchief and delicately wiped his brow. It was hard to imagine this paragon of gentility involved in any kind of physically or emotionally demanding work. They loved him and they loved his story.

James turned and looked toward the women's section. Sally sat at the head of one of the tables and had a clear view of the preacher from Virginia. She was following every word, apparently captivated by his tale.

After a few additional anecdotes in which he presented himself as the central figure, Maximillian Montague came to the real purpose of his visit. He began to speak of the sorry plight of the free blacks in the United States and their imminent salvation by the American Colonization Society.

"Today, my friends, in our beautiful United States of America, free Negroes are no better off than their enslaved brothers. A deplorable racial history of devastating poverty, rampant rejection of Christian beliefs and ethics, unrestrained licentiousness and attendant personal debasement, condemns the majority of our free blacks to a lifetime of suppression." Two of the residents shook their heads in open disagreement while the others signaled their concurrence.

Seeking to please all listeners, the reverend added, "There are, of course, exceptions." He paused, looked over his temporary flock and decided to return to his original premise.

"However, many of these good folk find themselves barred from respectable professions which require a modicum of higher learning as they are unwilling or unable to pursue formal studies. Theoretically, all free men should be allowed entry into any enterprise. Unfortunately, the truth is that the color of the black man's skin bars him from social and economic advancement." He strode to the side of the room and pointed the index finger of his right hand toward the congregation.

"Look," he shook his finger and repeated himself. "Look to where you find the unemployed members of our colored population. Not in school or church or actively engaged in the search for an honest day's wages, but rather, in dens of iniquity with liquor, gaming and loose women.

"Desperate crimes," his voice rose, "occasioned by passion, poverty and rage, are committed by blacks and far outnumber those perpetrated by our white brethren. The end result of the privation suffered by so many of our Negro brothers is a life of squalor and moral dissolution, a life which ends in painful and debilitating disease of the body as well as the soul."

The reverend took a deep breath, retrieved his handkerchief, and again, dabbed at his forehead. Many of the residents shook their heads in sympathetic pity for these unfortunate, inferior human beings and sent silent thanks to God for giving them their pale complexions.

A woman sitting to the right of Sally impulsively jumped to her feet and demanded, "Tell us, Pastor, how we can help these poor, poor, miserable souls."

A slight tic appeared in the corner of Maximillian Montague's left eye. He knew he had them.

"Thank you, Sister," he smiled beneficently at the speaker who, somewhat sheepishly, resumed her seat.

"Thank you for asking that question. It is not fair to leave our dark-skinned brothers and sisters mired in their misery when a new life of hope and prosperity is available to them in the modern day Garden of Eden that is Liberia. Opportunity abounds along the coast where the waters of the St. Paul's River run free and the land is lush and fertile for farming. The town of Monrovia, named for the great statesman, James Monroe, has been established there and homes have been built on the high ground overlooking its natural harbor.

"At present, there is no official governor of the colony; however, the Reverend Jehudi Ashmun has been serving in that capacity and he is dedicated to establishing an American empire in Africa. To that end, he has acquired additional lands from the native tribes whose territories abut ours."

He took a few steps back so he could look everyone in the eye. "And while I was in the colony, we confirmed and established the 'Constitution, Government and Digest of the Laws of Liberia'." Maximillian projected an air of proprietary ownership as he spoke.

"Great progress has been made since our first courageous pioneers stepped foot on the continent of Africa. By moving to this new and unspoiled region, our immigrants are now able to see themselves as free men, no longer shackled by the prejudices and restraints which constrained them as members of a wretched and inferior race living in an inhospitable land. Many have come to our virgin colony with established professions; others have learned new skills, become traders or established farms which produce much needed food for our community. Just as idleness is not tolerated, land and home ownership are encouraged. And for every two acres appropriated to the settlers, a third lot is designated for public use. In just a few years, Liberia will truly be an American utopia on African soil."

Maximillian paused as his audience expressed appreciation for the opportunities awaiting the free black man. Then he drew a deep breath and took a chance. "The blessings conferred upon our disenfranchised brethren by the American Colonization Society are immeasurable: pride, prosperity, freedom from persecution, dignity, a sense of self-worth. Imagine the wondrous benefits for both the black and white races in America if all two-hundred and fifty thousand members of our free Negro populace were to be returned to the land of their forefathers to live and proliferate unfettered by the humiliation of an ancestry of bondage."

The Reverend Montague looked over his recent converts and saw varied reactions to his last statement. The majority smiled and nodded their heads at the wisdom of the Society's altruistic plan. However, some frowned as they privately acknowledged the Southern roots of the speaker and recognized the probable purpose of the proposal.

James glanced at Sally. The expression on her face was noncommittal. Her hands, however, were clasped and pulsating slightly as she almost imperceptibly opened and closed them.

He thought of Conshy Joe, the bent-over black boy who did odd jobs at Hebe Balderston's tavern. As far as James knew, he had arrived one night with the single name of Joe and claimed to have come from an unfamiliar area called Conshohocken. Hebe Balderston, a liberal Quaker in temperament and belief, privately suspected he was a runaway slave and provided him shelter. He worked for his daily fare and a spot in the hayloft at night. It was said she allowed him to keep any coins he might find on the floor after the heavy-drinking crowd dispersed. His rewards were thought to be few and far between but they allowed him a small measure of income which, it was rumored, he kept hidden in a tin box in the barn.

James wondered how Conshy Joe would feel about being relocated to a distant settlement in a strange and mysterious land.

He returned his attention to the speaker. Maximillian Montague, sensing resistance from his early adversaries was charging forward in an attempt to win them over. He looked at the dissidents as he continued.

"We deplore the horrendous state of our black brethren but understand it is foolhardy to ignore the future of the white race. We must remember that the contemporary slave owner is rarely the one who brought these refugees from a savage society to our nation. However, he is the one who exploits his miserable charges and fights to defend the egregious evil resulting from the monstrous dark stain of slavery which taints our otherwise fair land.

"Under the patronage of the slave-holder, the black population is able, even encouraged, to reproduce without restraint. At the present population increase of at least sixty thousand a year, their numbers will soon quadruple. Many white Americans fear that, encouraged by their majority, they will turn on their masters and rebel against the perceived brutality, inequity and persecution they have suffered, and that they will seek repayment for the cruelties they have endured.

"If this happens, a second revolution will be fought on our land, one which will be fueled by the fury of a subjugated people. Retribution will be their goal and the white man their target."

Maximillian Montague heard the gasps and moans which greeted his last utterance and was encouraged to amplify his views.

"Miscegenation will dilute the purity of the Caucasian race. Our lands will be laid to waste and wantonly burned along with our homes, churches and towns. Our people, men, women," he paused and took a deep breath, "and children, will be ravaged by rape and brutalization, martyred in their attempts to preserve the country their ancestors toiled without relief to build." The reverend's eyes flashed and his voice rose incrementally as he drove home his point.

"Confusion will reign; profligacy will flourish; debauchery, moral transgression and flagrant disregard for the law will overrun the land. This," he moved to the nearest table and brought his fist down on the corner causing the few remaining dishes to leap into the air before landing with a jarring finality. "This," he repeated as he emphasized each additional word, "cannot be allowed to happen."

The concerned residents cried out as they embraced his prophecy and endorsed his rejection. He returned to the center of the room, shook his head clear of oratorical passion and calmly continued his discourse.

"The American Colonization Society wants the best for all Americans. We aim to establish a grand new world in Liberia, one where our noble black brethren can do as our ancestors did: settle and own land, found and grow businesses, participate in government, educate their children, and live free from persecution. In other words, we intend to provide the free Negro with the means to achieve the American dream on his native soil."

Subtle beads of perspiration decorated the Southern gentleman's brow. He retrieved his damp handkerchief and delicately dabbed his forehead dry.

Taking advantage of the interruption, one of the skeptics stood and said, "Pardon me, Reverend Montague, but I am compelled to disagree with some of your assertions." The little man in the fine attire regretted his comfort break.

"Eleven years ago, approximately three thousand free black men attended a meeting in Philadelphia to discuss the American Colonization Society and the prospects of emigration and colonization in general. At that time, three prominent black religious leaders, Absalom Jones, Richard Allen and John Gloucester, favored the plans of the Society and spoke in support of the proposed emigration to Africa.

"In spite of the influence of these and other prominent black leaders, the men attending the meeting voted overwhelmingly to reject the effort to transplant the free blacks of America to an undeveloped, primordial land. They recognized that the free black population comprised the strongest opponents to slavery.

"The attendees resolved to remain in America where their ancestors had labored under the oppressive whip of the slave master and the debilitating onus of vassalage to clear the land and construct the buildings of our new country. These proud descendants of ill-used primitives, these early supporters of the concept of a racially-blind society, vowed to honor the sacrifices of their progenitors and to benefit from their sweat.

"Those men, Reverend Montague, understood the real reason which motivated many of the early advocates of the colonization movement: fear of a slave revolution instigated by free blacks. Many of the originators of this egregious repatriation were, like you, white men from the South. They were interested in protecting their enslaved property, not in the welfare of the Negro race. This incentive continues to exist today.

"The utopian society you so glowingly describe is, in actuality, riddled with accusations of racial bigotry; unjust government; quarrels between colonists and ACS agents; clashes between settlers and native Africans; disproportionate allotment of land and rations, and unrealized educational opportunities." The dissenter pointed to Maximillian.

"In other words, Reverend, what you are trying to sell these good people is a mirage, a deceptively disguised mass emigration plot to rid America of its free black people. The desired result is the continuation and protection of the tyrannical, slave-based society of your birthplace, the state of Virginia, and its collaborative neighbors in the decadent deep South."

Flicking a final confrontational glance in the direction of the evening's speaker, the challenger sat down.

Maximillian Montague was visibly shaken as he watched his audience swing from enthusiastic supporters to confused skeptics as they tried to sort through the conflicting information they had just heard.

"*'And I will gather the remnant of my flock out of all countries whither I have driven them, and will bring them again to their folds; and they shall be fruitful and increase.'* Jeremiah Twenty-three, verse three." The familiar voice of his fellow divine saved Reverend Montague from the dreaded curse of speechlessness and he stepped aside to allow Thaddeus Goodenough to speak.

"The Lord recognizes that the fate of our brown-skinned brethren is abysmal on our continent, that he has driven them here in error. Even if the opportunity presented itself to establish a colony in the western reaches of our land, the speed with which our white pioneers are moving to inhabit new territories would soon catch up with our free people of color.

"The white majority would bring with them their old prejudices. Injustices and persecution would again overwhelm the unfortunate sons of Africa. Prospects would evaporate and poverty, depravity and corruption would lead to sedition. Revolution would spread from the leafy banks of the Potomac to the arid sands of the Gulf of Mexico.

"No, the alternatives to the American Colonization Society's plan are unacceptable. The Lord knows Africa is the fold from whence the ill-fated black man was plucked. He was taken under duress to a strange, and for him, cruel land and he now deserves to be returned to his native homeland with dignity.

"As the Reverend Montague has so eloquently elucidated, Liberia is the Garden of Eden for the former Negro slave. Using skills he has honed here in America, he, his family and fellow colonists will have futures full of opportunity, peace and prosperity. Yes, Liberia is the answer to our brown-skinned brother's dream of freedom and happiness."

Thaddeus Goodenough turned to the grateful little man.

"Now is the time for Reverend Montague to explain how we can materially help the Society to realize its benevolent dream of repatriation for all free men of color and the resultant cleansing of the collective conscience of the white men who once owned them."

The revered leader of Pleasant Valley Farm took his seat and looked expectantly at his colleague from the South.

Buoyed by the renewed attention of the assemblage, Maximillian assumed a serious, businesslike stance and began to sell.

"Our glorious Society is supported by federal and state grants as well as by private donations. This money, however, is hardly enough to pay for the passage of our emigrants, the expenses incurred by the colony upon their arrival, the costs of land purchases and development necessary for the growth of the settlement. We need financial support from other sources as well.

"We recognize that those who hear our story have great empathy for the free black man who faces such a bleak future in our country. We also know that few can afford to give us large amounts of money. Our solution is to offer this exquisitely designed document...." Thaddeus Goodenough rose from his chair and handed a piece of parchment to his fellow pastor.

"Thank you, Reverend Goodenough." Maximillian Montague held the paper high so all could see.

"This exquisitely-wrought document officially confirms that the owner is a member for life of the American Colonization Society. This handsome certificate, designed to grace the wall of every home, is a testament to the character, compassionate sensibilities and unbounded generosity of the man or woman whose name it bears. At a cost of only thirty dollars, this certificate of life membership is most appropriately priced for gifts to family members, beloved ministers, teachers and friends." Enthusiastic heads bobbed their approval.

"We appreciate any help you can give us. As you have heard, the rewards for Liberian immigrants are innumerable." Maximillian held the certificate in both his hands and displayed it in front of his chest.

"The rewards for your generosity," he pushed the parchment forward, "are this tangible proof of your liberality and the knowledge that you are a step closer to a seat on the right hand of God in heaven."

His confident demeanor restored, the little minister bowed slightly to the members of the community and then walked over to join his sponsor. The audience clapped and murmured praise of the two men of God for espousing such a wonderful cause.

James watched as the outspoken objector rose, and shaking his head in disbelief, left the room. His companion remained but did not participate in the congratulatory response of the group.

Out of the corner of his eye, James caught a glimpse of Sally. Responding to a signal from Reverend Goodenough, she left her seat and joined the two preachers as they exited the room. James, unsure of his next move, remained at the table.

The other diners lingered to discuss the purchase of life memberships in the American Colonization Society. Although James was determined to avoid any involvement in conversation, he was fascinated by the level of interest in Maximillian's proposal.

To a woman, the feminine contingent was in favor of supporting the Society's work. Their sympathies lay with the enterprising black emigrants and their expectations of new and rewarding lives in their ancestral lands on the African continent.

The men spoke of their personal support for the liberation of the black race. James, however, suspected that many of the avowed good intentions were tainted by the awareness that the free black man performed tasks less expensively than his white counterpart. The resettlement of these low-paid competitors would ensure the unchallenged perpetuation of established wages for their Caucasian friends and relatives.

The dialogue ended with unanimous declarations of approval of the Society and its dynamic spokesman from Virginia. Everyone was more than satisfied that they had a worthy cause to champion and they bristled with the sanctity of their newly-adopted altruistic endeavor.

The women were the first to leave the dining room. James waited until all the men had risen before he pushed his chair back and stood. He watched as each man selected a lantern from a table near the large stone fireplace, picked a piece of tinder from a basket, touched it to the fire, lit the candle inside and left the room. James took the last one, completed the routine and followed the line of men down the hall and up the stairs to the quarters on the second floor.

The late summer sun was setting and the light in the hallway was dim. Uncertain of the location of his room, James peered through the doorways on his left. After three tries, he spied his unmade bed. He slipped from the dwindling procession, entered the empty room and closed the door behind him. He sat on the lumpy horsehair mattress, relieved to have made it through the meal without serious scrutiny.

He waited for Sally to come to him but time passed, and although he heard women's footsteps amongst the men's, none stopped at his door. James looked around the dimly-lit room and noticed a simple Betty lamp which hung on the wall beside the bed. He opened the lantern from the dining room, removed the candle and used its flame to light the wick.

The room brightened and his first impulse was to blow out the candle. He decided against it as he was uneasy in his current lodgings and wanted to leave a light burning while he slept. The oil in the lamp burned openly in its metal bowl while the candle was enclosed by a pierced iron casing. He extinguished the lamp and placed the lantern in the corner near the door.

The bedding Sally had delivered remained neatly folded on the bed. James removed a sheet, opened it and spread it over the mattress. The smell of fresh linen evoked memories of spring breezes and moist air rising off the slow-moving stream running next to his little log cabin. Images of Margaret and those early days of their marriage when he was filled with the prospect of a good life with his pretty, young wife ran through his head.

It had been months since he and Margaret had left the house; he to hunker down in his competitor's barn, she to live on Maris' charity. They had abandoned their dreams on the pebbles of that gentle stream. They had left them to flow, unimpeded, into the nearby river and be dispersed forever as they were swept out to sea. James cringed at the unfamiliar romanticism of his last thought and briefly feared these eccentric surroundings might be affecting his manhood.

His current circumstances, he had to admit, were the result of the way he lived; he rarely planned ahead, seldom sought to control his options. His decisions, large and small, were consistently based on whims, and he assumed little responsibility for the direction of his life. Even his purchase of the forge had been thrust upon him. Maris had offered to sell it to him and he had agreed to the terms without giving consideration to the tenuous source of his money or his ability to sustain the business. It had been, he admitted, a foolish folly with disastrous consequences.

James sat on the edge of his partially-made bed, and for the first time in years, thought back over his life. He had trouble remembering his birth date until he recalled his mother telling him that it had been very cold that day and that he had arrived shortly before midnight on December 31, 1799. His father, a doctor, was thrilled to learn his first-born was a son. In an exuberant moment, he had named his child James George Washington Daunt, in honor of himself and of the great American hero who had recently passed away. The newborn was a son of privilege and his father vowed to treat him appropriately.

James spent his early years as a student at the Academy where he learned to read, write and recite prose and poetry before his peers. The hours consumed by the forced memorization of Noah Webster's *American Spelling Book* were counterbalanced by the more interesting scholastic activities that filled the rest of his day. He had particularly enjoyed reading *Aesop's Fables*, Roman history, and stories from Greek mythology. Homer's *Odyssey* introduced him to the adventures of Telemachus and his search for his father. He was spared the study of arithmetic as mathematical exercises were postponed until the student's brain was judged mature enough to comprehend the challenge of numbers. He was intellectually curious, a quick learner and was considered an accomplished student who would go on to study at the university.

Of average height, he developed broad shoulders and a full chest as he passed his twelfth year. His stride took on a swagger which was exaggerated by his slightly bowed legs. Subconsciously, he bent his elbows and clenched his fists as he moved through the rooms of the Academy. By the middle of his thirteenth year, his early physical development and assertive mannerisms had attracted the attention of the older boys and he was often challenged to defend himself with his fists. At first, he lost to the experienced contenders and returned home in bloodied defeat. His father, having faced the same confrontations during his school years, said nothing and hoped his son would learn from the experience.

In spite of his aggressive carriage, James was more interested in books than fighting. He lacked an instinctive aptitude for self-defense. Rebuffed by his intellectual father when he asked for guidance, he turned to the stable man for instruction. Horace Johnson, a large burly man with callused hands, taught James the questionable art of street fighting. The third time James used the rough means employed in the back alleys down by the docks to get the better of one of his hostile schoolmates, his father was called upon to treat the wounded challenger. The headmaster took the doctor aside and announced that James was no longer welcome at the Academy.

Ashamed that his son would resort to such crude methods to win a fight, and embarrassed by his expulsion, the senior Daunt apprenticed James to a blacksmith who allowed him to live in a small room above the forge. The naive doctor had little understanding of the circumstances to which he was condemning his son. Fighting became a way of life for James and his survival in a world ruled by fisticuffs and tempers inflamed by the intense heat of the blacksmith's forge, depended on the denial of his background.

He took to drink, began to speak in the vernacular of the taverns he frequented and hid behind the façade of a carefree, fun-loving reprobate. After a while, he found he liked the role he had created and surrendered himself to a life of decadent irresponsibility.

James continued to languish in this state after the death of his father and his unplanned departure from the city which was necessitated by a visit from the constable seeking repayment of several debts. He traveled to the country where an acquaintance provided him with a room. He avoided steady employment but being a proficient smith, was able to earn enough to pay his expenses. It was only after he married Margaret that he had tried, albeit briefly and unsuccessfully, to change.

The remembrance of his financial difficulties returned James to the present. He cleared his mind and finished putting his bed together. He removed his worn moccasins, rough stockings and gray muslin trousers.

Wearing only the community-issued shirt, he stretched his body on the bed and tried to stop thinking about the unreal experiences he had lived through during the last day and a half. He pushed aside the accompanying guilt and fear and concentrated on the hope that, somehow, he would be able to build a new life for himself; one without the horror his drunkenness had wrought.

Deep in his conscious mind, he recognized the fact that, if he stayed at Pleasant Valley Farm, his new life would, in all probability, include a new woman. Guilt feelings accompanied his speculation that she would be Sally. Both excited and confused by his growing attraction to the woman he had once considered no more than a casual plaything, he tried to mesh the reality of his past life with his manufactured dreams of an altered existence. The effort caused his head to ache and eventually, he escaped into the deep sleep of a physically and emotionally exhausted man.

The hand which touched his body was rough but the stroke was gentle, comforting, reassuring. Devoid of the promise of forbidden pleasures, this was the touch of a loving mother calming her sick or frightened child. At times, barely pressing on his flesh, the hand softly explored his body, delicately fondling his sensitive areas, lightly massaging his tired and tense neck and shoulders, always returning to quietly stimulate his desires.

Half-awake, James rolled toward the compassionate lover who lay next to him. Deftly, the intruder slipped her body under his. She stroked his back with one hand as she silently guided him to her. Peace and contentment replaced the expected flash of passion as she gently removed his body before he lost control.

She held him tenderly as she caressed the hollow between his shoulder blades, his buttocks, the backs of his legs. Completely relaxed, he drifted back to sleep without ever having fully awakened.

# Wednesday, August 20, 1828

"It's five o'clock, James Morley."

The sound of a woman's voice jolted James out of the comfortable cocoon his mind had spun. The room was dark and the sudden interruption of his deep sleep left him groggy. He struggled to acclimate himself to his surroundings. The dim outline of the person who had addressed him by the unfamiliar name materialized as she moved closer to the bed.

"I trust you slept well?" It was Sally. Her voice, taunting, hinting of unspoken possibilities, was easily recognizable. He marveled at the way she turned a simple statement into a provocative question.

He thought about the candle he had left burning and wondered whether it had gone out by itself or if it had been intentionally extinguished. Vague impressions of the mysterious nighttime encounter came to him as he looked up at Sally. Her question implied she was aware of something out of the ordinary.

James was certain his visitor had not been Sally. The woman's hands, while experienced in the art of lovemaking, were coarse, her demeanor, gentle and patient. Sally had soft hands and she certainly was not patient. Her sexuality was blatant; her skills, immeasurable, and her wiles, irresistible. She elicited immediate response to her overtures. No, his unanticipated partner had not been Sally.

"Someone came to me during the night...." He hesitated, waiting for her reaction.

"I know, James Morley. On my recommendation, Reverend Goodenough deemed you acceptable to the community. Last night he agreed to waive our usual waiting period, and as a result, he allowed your initiation."

"My initiation? Into what?" James was bewildered.

"Yesterday, I told you that, here, we work together for the good of the community and that we share everything. That extends to our male and female relationships. There are no married couples here, James. Every woman belongs to every man and vice versa. A woman is as free to go to any man as a man is to choose his partner for the night. Monogamous attachments are discouraged, although friendships between members of the opposite sexes flourish. Many times, men and women who are attracted to each other emotionally and intellectually are ill-suited for sexual intimacies. Here, they are free to turn to others to satisfy their appetites. No man or woman need go unfulfilled."

"*'For in the resurrection they neither marry, nor are given in marriage, but are as the angels of God in heaven.'* Matthew Twenty-two, verse thirty." The unexpected appearance of Reverend Goodenough caused James to pull the sheet up to his neck.

"Matthew tells the parable of a man who died leaving his wife childless. His brother then married the widow. That man died and left the widow to the next brother. There were seven brothers, and by the time the woman was deceased, she'd had them all as she survived each of the seven. The question remained: whose wife she would be in the resurrection? And Jesus answered that she would be no man's wife as in the resurrection there would be no marriage. Thus it follows that for all of God's children who, like the members of our community, have already been saved here on earth, the sacrament of marriage, which will be obliterated at the time of the resurrection, is a mortal conceit, an unnecessary hindrance in the human pursuit of happiness.

"God, Mr. Morley," the pastor continued, "created the pleasures of the marriage bed for both men and women to enjoy equally. At Pleasant Valley Farm, the coming together of members of the opposite sex for the sheer enjoyment of physical gratification is encouraged, if not mandated. It is a core tenet of our ideology.

"However, the freedom to pursue the fulfillment of these desires comes with responsibility. We do not welcome children here. We are a communal society and we depend on all members being productive. Children are distractions for our contributing female members, therefore, a woman who finds herself with child, must leave the community." Thaddeus Goodenough paused, ostensibly to allow James to think about what he had just said.

James was aware that he was clad solely in his community shirt. He remained under the bedclothes and tried to comprehend what he was hearing. The words went against all he had been taught by his parents, by his teachers at the Academy, by the men of God who preached in the houses of worship he had occasionally visited. However, he understood full well the personal benefits of the preacher's Biblical interpretations and the prospect of the quasi-sanctified redemption which accompanied it. He was intrigued by the possibilities, but wary.

While James had, in the past, been promiscuous to a fault, he ultimately believed in the institution of marriage. The idea that women, the same as men, could come and go to whomever they wished, whenever they desired, was beyond his imagination. He thought of Sally and her antics with the lads in town. He now understood why she was free with her sexual favors; her religious mentor preached unrestrained physical satisfaction and Sally was a willing and dedicated practitioner.

James realized he had never heard the word "love".

The divine looked James in the eye as he continued. "There are constraints that come with the privilege of multiple relationships. The woman must monitor her menses to ensure she is not fertile at the time of copulation. And the man," Thaddeus paused again, "must practice *coitus interruptus*".

The Reverend Goodenough realized that James had not understood his last comment and he stated bluntly: "The withdrawal of the man before he achieves climax."

James jerked his head toward Sally who stood quietly behind the preacher. Her face showed no emotion. He turned back to stare at Thaddeus in disbelief. He tried to maintain an impartial expression,

*81*

but it was too late and his reaction to Thaddeus' words had registered with the speaker.

"You must be able to accept our ways, Mr. Morley, if you are to stay here." He looked down on James. "You must be willing to learn and profess our beliefs. And you must take the pledge."

"Pledge?" James queried.

"We have a requirement that each new acolyte pledge to dedicate his or her life to the personal achievement of salvation here on earth. We do not believe God meant for us to wait for life after death to achieve the state of absolute purification. As Sister Sarah and I explained yesterday, when we unequivocally receive God into our hearts, he forgives us our sins and we are free to live the rest of our lives without the onus of sin to circumscribe our actions. Our beliefs allow us a great deal of latitude when making our everyday and lifelong decisions."

James was stunned by the preacher's revolutionary dialogue and he did not know how to answer. He thought for a moment then asked, "When do I have to take this pledge?"

Knowing that his commitment would give him time in his flight from the law, he was tempted to take the oath. The James Daunt of two days ago would have done so without a second thought. The new James Morley, a man in need of a rewritten past, a man who faced an uncharted future, needed to clear his head and think things over before committing to a way of life so foreign to him.

"We do not expect you to join us without thought, James," Sally said. "You will know your mind when the time is right and we will be waiting to accept you."

Without so much as a change in stance, the old Sally returned. "And now, get up and get dressed." She smiled her wicked grin as she said the last two words.

James was relieved when he saw that her face held the invitation he needed and he relaxed as she said, "We'll be off to breakfast and then to work."

The second night after the shooting had passed with no news from, or about, James. It was early morning and Margaret stood on the porch of Maris' small house. She looked down the road, foolishly hoping her husband would appear on horseback, laughing with his friends and cleared of all suspicion.

She could hear Hannah and Bettina cleaning up from breakfast. They spoke of the day's schedule, what they needed to buy during their weekly visit to town, what they were going to wear. Margaret knew they would not ask her to accompany them. She also knew they, as the sisters-in-law of a suspected killer, were apprehensive about their own reception by the townspeople. It was bad enough that the three Hicks sisters were penniless and living on the charity of their brother, but this, the possible mortal transgression of her husband, would further sully their reputations.

Margaret heard Hannah suggest they cancel their trip but Bettina pointed out that their larder, never overflowing, demanded replenishment. Margaret was glad they decided to go as she hoped they would bring back some news, good or bad, that was free of Maris' vindictive hatred of James.

James followed Sally into the dining room. He noticed that most of the residents were gathered around a large slate which stood in the corner of the dining room. Sally joined the group and James edged in beside her. She pointed to his name. *James Morley* was listed under the heading of *Field Work.*

"What does that mean, Sally? I thought I would be working as a blacksmith here."

"We take turns with chores, James. Every day there's a new schedule. That way, no one has to do a distasteful job more than one day in a row. You will probably be assigned to the blacksmith shop more often than not, but today you are needed to work in the fields. Most of us will be there as we are bringing in the corn. As the saying goes: 'Many hands make light work'. Now, you will have to sit with the men. Breakfast is about to be served."

James saw three residents around his age sitting at the end of a long table. He walked over and sat down. Making no attempt to disguise their curiosity, the men looked him over and then all three glanced in Sally's direction.

"You know Sister Sarah?" A man with a black beard asked curtly.

"She is my…." James hesitated, trying to remember what Sally had told the Reverend Goodenough. "She is my cousin. On her mother's side."

"Oh." He thought he detected a sigh of relief as the man acknowledged his answer. "She keeps her own company," he grinned, "if you know what I mean."

James frowned, confused by the man's comment.

"We can't just drop in on her like we can with the other women. Sister Sarah doesn't welcome uninvited company." He looked hard at James. "You come from town?"

Again, James hesitated. He had not formulated the story of his life and he was afraid to say something he might regret. He turned to the man next to him.

"Do we always eat at the same time?" It was an unnecessary question but it ended the probe of his personal life.

"Yes."

"Oh."

A woman dressed in the short tunic and trousers of the community appeared with a plate of eggs and a piece of bread. Relieved, he looked down, picked up a fork and began to eat.

"We don't eat meat here." The man with the black beard volunteered the information.

James answered without looking up. "This is plenty for me."

"No liquor or tobacco, either."

"That's fine."

"You look like a drinking man to me." The man kept on speaking. "Red face. Always a clue."

"I'm a blacksmith." James had used that excuse before and was glad to have it come so easily. The conversation was over. He finished his meal and rose from the table.

"I've been assigned to work in the fields." He looked around the room and could not find Sally.

The third man, who had not spoken, motioned to James. "Follow me."

James took a last look at the man with the black beard and realized that the assumption of a new identity was going to be a constant challenge.

His first day as a contributing member of the community passed quickly and James was tired when he sat down at the supper table. The faces of the men around him were familiar now, and although he was a bit more comfortable in their company, he was anxious to return to his room where he could relax. As he pushed his chair back, the voice of Thaddeus Goodenough broke into the constant murmur of genial conversation.

"We were all moved by Reverend Montague's account of the plight of our black brethren." Thaddeus turned a full circle and included all of the residents in his address.

"After some discussion, it was decided the community could afford to buy four of the Society's certificates for a total of one-hundred-and-twenty-dollars. They will be used as gifts for those townspeople who have been so helpful to us during the past year."

Again, the preacher turned to include everyone as he asked, "Does anyone disagree with this decision?"

The support for the humanitarian purchase was unanimous.

James searched the room for the man who had expressed his displeasure the night before. He was not present in the dining room and James could not recall having seen him at breakfast or lunch. And he was quite sure he had been absent from the fields during the day's work session.

# *Early September, 1828*

The days passed and James became more comfortable at Pleasant Valley. He was surprised to find men and women alike were encouraged to seek knowledge as part of their daily routines. Everyone read. The residents were as familiar with current news and international gossip as they were with contemporary literary writings and the classics. Without hesitation, they shared informed opinions on an ever-changing variety of subjects.

Meal times were considered prime opportunities for provocative discussions with those seated at the same dining table. More formal sessions after the evening supper found guest speakers or residents presenting articulate lectures on current events, history, science and the arts. One evening, there was a spirited discussion of the supernatural. Particularly inflammatory debates centered on the upcoming presidential campaign of Andrew Jackson. Members of the community appeared to be equally split in their support of Jackson and the incumbent, John Quincy Adams.

Sally lent James a copy of James Fenimore Cooper's *The Last of the Mohicans* which he reluctantly began to read at night. In the past, he would have been too busy gallivanting with the boys to even look at a book. At Pleasant Valley, things were different. He was captivated by the story, and one night after he had finished reading, he asked Sally a question.

"Would you be lying here with me if I was a man of color…red or black?"

"What are you talking about, James?"

"I was thinking about the book you gave me."

James paused. "About Cora and Uncas. About a white woman falling in love with a red-skinned man."

Sally raised her body up from the bed and supported herself on one elbow. "You surprise me, James Daunt. What happened to the country bumpkin I rescued in the woods? I see the glimmer of an intellect lurking in your head."

"Don't poke fun at me, Sally. It got me thinking about…things." James was embarrassed and Sally, seeing his discomfort, thought for a moment before she commented on his observation.

"Cora was not innately biased against those of another race. She spoke out against using the color of a man's skin and his different manners as negative judgment criteria. Her liberal attitude made the relationship possible." Sally looked expectantly at James, encouraging him to move forward with the discussion.

"Yet," James pointed out, "she was willing to die rather than become the wife of the Indian, Magua."

"He was an unkempt, evil-spirited villain," Sally countered. "Uncas on the other hand, was graceful, dignified and beautiful in his countenance. His character embodied the good and natural which is found in native peoples."

James spoke hesitantly. "I wonder if the thought of mixing dark and light blood would have been repulsive to me if Alice, with her yellow hair, fair skin and delicate nature had been attracted to the majestic heathen instead of the dark-haired, dark-complected Cora."

"It is possible. Cora is a quadroon. Her blood was already diluted by the heritage of her mother who was half white and half black." Sally paused. "It is interesting that the author chose to match the pure-blooded descendent of red-skinned chieftains with a woman of mixed blood. Perhaps he was faced with the dilemma you just mentioned."

Sally lay back on the bed and said, "James, a love story is a love story and there is a romantic aura which surrounds the affection of any pure-hearted white woman for a mysterious noble savage."

"And for us, Sally? Do you think there is a romantic aura around us?"

Sally laughed and rolled on to him. "Romance, James? Are we capable of romantic love? I don't know. But I do know that I would lay with you no matter what your color."

James, inspired by the enjoyment he had found in reading, regularly availed himself of the community's supply of reading material in the library. He looked forward to the hours he spent reading by the light of the single oil lamp as he awaited Sally's arrival.

One evening, after supper, Reverend Goodenough overheard James ask Sally how she reconciled the dictates of God and his disciples with her own personal creed of self-determination.

On hearing James' question, Thaddeus stopped and spoke sharply. "In spite of my teachings, Sister Sarah follows her own rules and," he added sarcastically, "sometimes I think she believes that *'every man makes a god of his own desire....'*"

Before he could state its source as was his wont, James correctly credited it to Virgil. Thaddeus Goodenough's head snapped around and he challenged his companion.

"How do you know that quotation?"

James hesitated as he debated whether to reveal information about his past. "I studied at the Academy," he said. The surprised look on the reverend's face attested to the value he placed on a respectable education. "We were required to read translations of Virgil and Homer, among others."

Thaddeus frowned, and then looked away. Indecision was visible on his face as he considered questioning James further about his background. The arrival of a community member seeking advice cut the conversation short and saved James from the possibility of a full-blown inquisition.

In violation of a community rule which prohibited visitors from remaining in their hosts' rooms following romantic encounters, Sally rolled over and settled comfortably beside James. She raised her head and gently rubbed her face in his beard.

"I love the scratchy feel of your hair on my skin. It makes me…." She did not finish the sentence. Although the light was dim, he could tell she was smiling at him as she twirled her finger in his wiry beard.

"Do you think you could be content here, James Morley?" The question was straightforward even though it was tempered by Sally's suggestive, bantering tone. He turned on his side, and looked at the dim outline of his bed partner in the dark room.

"You know I am happy just being with you, Sally." He did, indeed, desire to remain with the unpredictable redhead who lay next to him.

"Can you accept our ways, James? I see you struggling with some of our convictions."

"I can't admit to a lot of what Reverend Goodenough proclaims is the truth and the word of God, however, I want to be with you and this is your life. But," he turned his head away, "I'm married. Someday I will have to face up to my responsibilities to Margaret."

James closed his eyes. He was ashamed to acknowledge that he rarely thought of the wife he had coveted and shamelessly won by taking advantage of her trusting nature.

"I have much to be sorry for in my past, Sally. Some of my actions are regrettable; others, unforgiveable."

The vision of Squire Holt falling from his horse brought old feelings of guilt and remorse which welled up in his chest and tightened around his heart. He tried to shake the threat of discovery which constantly undermined his prospect of a prolonged stay in the community.

"I don't know that I will be able to remain here." Sadness and regret augmented his feelings of self-reproach as he realized what his life could have been if he had made other choices. He turned back to face Sally.

"I am grateful to you and to the reverend and the community for taking me in." He shook his head clear as he drove the doomsday thoughts from his mind.

"Before coming here, I was besotted from drink. I had forgotten how to use my mind for anything but survival. Now, I see the many benefits of your cooperative life, and while I do not think I will ever be able to justify some of the reverend's doctrines, I'll do my best to fit in, Sally. If," he said, turning away from her, "I continue to have the opportunity."

Then James rolled onto his back and his serious expression faded as he laughed away his doubts. "It will have to be on my terms which," he added, "I must work out by myself."

He lay still for a moment. Then, lightheartedly he said, "Don't forget, Sister Sarah, you have broken a few of the rules yourself. What would happen if Thaddeus Goodenough found out about your escapades with the lads from Hebe's?"

"He knows who I am, James. He will never admit it, not even to himself, but he knows. He followed me one day. I was not aware he was there until he intentionally allowed me to see him when I was with one of the boys. The look on his face broke my heart." James could tell from the sound of her voice that there were tears in her eyes.

"Sally, I've seen you with him. Is he your lover?"

She turned back to him. "He has been. Just once. He was the one who initiated me. I always knew he loved me in a nurturing, protective way. I was too young and too naïve to recognize the signs when his platonic love evolved into carnal desire for my body.

"When I received my menses, I overheard him discussing my initiation. When I realized what he was talking about, I prayed it would be Thaddeus who would come to me."

Sally paused and took a deep breath before continuing. "I knew my body was ready for, and in need of, physical gratification. I went to the reverend for counseling. He was shocked to see me and hear my pleas. I fled in embarrassment. He knew then that it was time for him to fulfill his duties. He failed, however, to realize the consequences of his uncontrollable lust and how it might impact me, his only child."

James heard the last three words and realized how difficult it must have been for Sally, growing up as the sole child in a community of adults.

"At first, he was gentle. He took his time, explaining every touch of his fingers, every emotion he hoped to arouse in me. He spoke of God's word and the true happiness which comes with communal love of one another and of God the Father.

"He told me that no man belonged to one woman and no woman to one man and that God had ordained him, Thaddeus Goodenough, to spread his word. He said it was his duty to his Savior to introduce each of the women in his flock to the physical joys which accompany the earthly love of God. He explained that this exaltation of the Heavenly Father was achieved by the coming together of man and woman just as Adam and Eve had come to know one another in the beginning.

"He stroked my arm and kissed my hair, the same as he had done when I was a young child. But this time, it was different. As he spoke, his touch became more intimate. I was bewildered, and for all his quiet reassurance and my eager anticipation, I was uncomfortable being alone and unclothed with a man, even though nudity is discreetly accepted in the community.

"Thaddeus preaches that, following the crucifixion of Jesus, the Romans parted his garments among them and left him naked on the cross. Thaddeus believes that Christ's sacrifice and the public display of his mortal remains purified the human body and transformed it into a sacred vessel for the sanctified soul of the saved believer. Thus, the sinless man should wear his nudity with pride as his body is a tangible symbol of his salvation. While Thaddeus theoretically glorifies the unclothed human body, he discourages public nakedness except during rare celebrations.

"Although I was aware of Thaddeus' revelations, I had never, since I was a young child, undressed in front of another person. The strangeness of my situation was magnified by the overwhelming emotions I was experiencing and I became frightened.

"He sensed my discomfort and calmed me as he spoke, again, of God and God's will. When he saw I was relaxed, he very gently came to me and consummated our union. Then he lost all control, James. He changed from caring, sympathetic teacher to self-absorbed, frantic lover. He ravaged my body. He was out of control and could not help himself." Sally pulled away from James and sat up. She wiped her eyes.

"Afterward, he was ashamed and humiliated. He thrust me aside and apologized over and over. I felt such empathy that I opened my arms to console him. He misunderstood my gesture and came to me again.

"This time, however, I found myself welcoming his body. I cared not about his overwrought emotions and sought only to heighten my own satisfaction. By morning, I was exhausted physically, emotionally, mentally, but I craved more. That is when, James, I came to realize, at a very young age, that I was, indeed, my father's daughter. For when I am consumed, passion replaces reason and later, reason justifies passion.

"When Thaddeus Goodenough realized what he had unleashed, he grabbed his clothes, bolted from my bed and rushed from the room. Filled with contrition, he spent weeks in his study redefining the sin of copulating with those of your own blood. Eventually, he declared there was no sin if no seed had been spilled." She smiled cynically. "Before he reached that conclusion, he mentally rewrote his memory of that night."

The tears returned, but they fell softly as tears of compassion rather than distress.

"Unfortunately, it was early morning when my father left and there were people in the hall who saw him racing from my room. While he was able to create a new doctrine for the members of our community, he was unable to make peace with himself or his God."

"Your father?" James gasped, the reality of Sally's revelations finally coming clear. "Your biological father?" He had assumed she had been referring to the reverend as her spiritual father not the man who had sired her.

When Sally did not answer, James paused then asked, quietly, "You were intimate with your own father?"

"It is the way here, James. All initiations, even mine, are performed by my parents."

"Your parents? Your mother is here?" Sally had spoken calmly as she revealed her family secrets. "Who is she? Have I met her?"

Even as he questioned her, he remembered the woman with the calloused hands who had so gently made love to him on his first night in the community. He had not thought about the smell of lye soap, the mélange of odors from the kitchen, which accompanied his previously unidentified lover. The washerwoman. The washerwoman was Sally's mother and his previously unknown bed partner.

"My mother has been with him for many years. She truly loves him. I was conceived in a fever when my father was studying to be a minister. He would have been expelled if it was known he had sired a child out of wedlock. Shamefully, he sent her away to face her disgrace alone.

"After ordination, Thaddeus rejected assignment to a single pulpit and chose, instead, to travel the countryside as he developed and preached his own interpretation of the word of God. He was," Sally paused, "and continues to be," she paused again, "a charismatic speaker, and while some who heard him were sorely offended, others willingly embraced his teachings. One of his converts gifted Thaddeus with this land on the condition that he build a community where his unorthodox teachings could be practiced with impunity. His followers rejoiced and eagerly joined him.

"My parents were reunited when my father started Pleasant Valley Farm. My mother came here, unannounced, and brought me, his illegitimate daughter. The guilt he had nurtured since his original transgression reached a climax with our arrival and he has been possessed by it ever since. In his own way, he tried to make it up to my mother when he decreed that she be the one to initiate our male novitiates. She once said she derives satisfaction from the pleasures she brings to the young men but finds little for herself." Sally put her head in her hands.

"Her pain is intensified by Thaddeus' lusting after me. Although he has never again come to me, my very presence amplifies his shame and makes it even more difficult for him to mollify the self-reproach he feels every time he sees my mother. He regards her presence here as his penance and as God's daily reminder of his moral degradation.

"I look as my mother did then and his early passion for her was transferred to me. His advocacy of sexual gratification through multiple relationships and his rejection of the sacrament of marriage were born from his attempts to justify his moral turpitude." Sally wiped her eyes again.

"He is a tortured man, James. He knows he has sinned, not only with my mother but with me, the fruit of his seed, the consequence of his lust. We deal with our demons in our own ways: my father seeks to guarantee salvation through his personal reinterpretation of the word of God; my mother, through her endurance of his emotional and verbal abuse, and I?" Sally paused again. "I exult in my earthly pleasures while I can with no thought to the future. Can you accept this, James?"

Even in the dark, he could tell Sally had turned back to him. Instinctively, he put his arms around her and pulled her close. He stroked her hair and her body relaxed. Slowly, her hands began to move down his body and her advances increased in intensity. He responded, his passion fueled by the bizarre insight he now had into the personal history of his loved one. And he did love Sally. Physically and intellectually, Pleasant Valley Sally stimulated him in ways he had never known were possible.

Their coupling was overwhelmingly intense and mutually fierce. Eventually, they separated and lay exhausted beside one another. Then they slept.

It was still dark when Sally heard someone enter the room. The intruder stopped in front of the clothes board with its empty nails and faced away from the bed.

Recognizing the outline of the silhouetted figure, Sally eased her body from under the covers and stepped behind the open door. She waited until the woman drew back the bedclothes, climbed onto the mattress and turned towards James. Then Sally retrieved her clothes from the floor, slipped around the door and slowly pulled it to the jam. She looked at the handle. It was bare; she had forgotten to add the customary ribbon or handkerchief to alert the others that James had a visitor.

Sally was surprised by her mother's presence. She had assumed the older woman only visited the men's dormitory for initiations. She did not want her to know she was once again competing with her daughter for the attention of the same man.

James abandoned his deep sleep as he responded to the touch of the woman next to him.

"Sally," he murmured as he reached out for her.

The stroking stopped and his lover turned away. She left his bed, dressed and crept quietly from the room.

James never opened his eyes; there was no need. His nose informed him of the identity of his caller.

# *Friday, September 12, 1828*

"How long has it been, Elias? How long since I got laid up?"

Esther asked her husband questions which she knew would go unanswered. Elias ignored her and continued his early-morning vigil at the window.

James Daunt's horse remained tied to the post where it had stood for more than three weeks. He kept a sharp eye on the animal when he was in the fields, in the barn, in the house. When the horse was out of his line of sight, he listened for sounds coming from the area where it was hitched. He rarely left the farm for fear of missing the opportunity to capture the fugitive. The apprehension of James Daunt had become an obsession for Elias Latch and it dominated his waking hours.

"Going out to the barn." Elias left the room without so much as a glance at his bedridden wife.

Tears of frustration came to Esther's eyes as she thought of the life she had led since she had taken aim at Squire Holt. The fall in the ditch had crippled her right leg and robbed her of intelligible speech. Her mind, however, remained intact. There were days when she wished it, too, had been impaired as the frustration of being unable to communicate was unbearable.

"He's one of Andrew Jackson's 'Hurrah Boys.'"

The man sitting next to James at the midday meal held his hand over his mouth as he pointed to the colorfully-clad visitor at the end of the table.

"He's just come from a rally where he and his cohorts planted a Hickory Pole. Now he's on his way to the city where he is organizing a presidential campaign rally for Jackson with a militia turnout and barbeque."

"Why is he here?" James asked Tom Yarnall, a contemporary with whom he had become friendly.

"Come to spread the word about Ole Hickory, I suspect. And to drop a few nasty rumors about John Quincy Adams as well." Tom laughed.

The visitor heard the mumbling and looked up from his meal.

Tom, embarrassed that he had been overheard, directed a question to the stranger. "Is it true you've come from a Jackson rally?"

"Yes, my friend. I have. A very impressive turnout we had, I might add." He speared several green beans and put them in his mouth. He pushed them aside with his tongue before he continued.

"It was a grand event. One of the boys found a magnificent hickory tree in the forest outside of town. Over eighty feet in height, with a straight-as-an-arrow trunk. Took three days to fell it, trim the branches, peel the bark and haul it to the town square.

"Folks came from miles around, the strongest men aiding in the raising of the pole. Planted it right in front of the mayor's house, we did. Everyone gathered around and shouted as we got it up." He looked directly at Tom and then fixed his eyes on each of the men at the table.

"The good Presbyterian ladies from the church sewed a splendid flame-red flag with the words 'Jackson and Respect' cut out of gold cloth. It was so big that when the wind blew it full out, you could read it from almost any spot in town." The stranger smiled with pride.

"We were organized. Circulated handbills announcing our rally all over the county. General Jackson's popularity was borne out by the hundreds of citizens who came to cheer the planting of the pole. Speeches were given by the mayor and prominent citizens in support of Jackson's character and heroic leadership. It was a memorable day indeed." He smiled again before putting a forkful of potatoes in his mouth.

"You Jackson men?" He finished chewing as he surveyed the diners seated at the table and awaited their answers.

The community residents remained silent.

Finally, the stranger said, "I am."

He lowered his fork. "And for good reason. I know Andrew Jackson is the right man to hold the office of president of the United States. He's a man of, and for, the people. Born in a log cabin he was, and raised on the frontier. Andrew Jackson knows, firsthand, the hardships of the common man. He will fight for equal rights for all us ordinary folk and lash out against the special privileges enjoyed by the rich."

The visitor flicked a glance around the room, and noting the uniform gray clothing of the community, deduced that he had not spoken out of turn when he denigrated the wealthy.

The Jacksonian was a man who, above all, relished the opportunity to address an audience, and secondly, to sell his message. He spoke in carefully modulated tones as he began to deliver his memorized campaign patter.

"General Jackson is respected for his high morals, his bravery, his leadership on the battlefield, his support of moderate tariffs to protect our commerce," he took a breath, "his promotion of internal infrastructure and western expansion, his belief in limited federal government and his support of the sovereignty of individual states." He paused, took a breath, and then added, "as long as they respect their bond within the Union, that is."

The campaigner's words flowed flawlessly as, with practice, he had mastered the art of elocution.

"The general's views are opposed to those of John Quincy Adams who supports high tariffs, wants to expand the scope of the federal government and advocates the use of federal rather than state monies to build local roads, canals and public institutions of learning. Mr. Adams even wants to construct," he spat the words out, his voice, mocking and spiked with derision, "*'a lighthouse of the sky'*."

The stranger paused for effect before raising his eyes in mock disbelief as he enunciated each word. "That's an *astronomical observatory,* like the ones they've been building in Europe so people can observe," a sneer accentuated the look of disdain on his face, '*the phenomena of the heavens'.*"

He scanned the blank faces in front of him as he continued. "This tomfoolery is typical of the frivolous endeavors on which Mr. Adams proposes to spend our federal government's money. We must stop this senseless spending which benefits the wealthy and the privileged classes and ignores the needs of the common man in whom General Jackson believes without reservation."

Tom Yarnall drummed his fingers on the table. "This man is misrepresenting the goals of John Quincy Adams," he muttered, choosing to keep his comments for James' ears only. "The president does, indeed, have a plan for a federal internal improvement system. It will tie together all the economies: industrial, commercial, agricultural, as well as the various regions of our country, North, South, East, West, with the aim of promoting unity and prosperity on our shores. An approach of this magnitude would fail, if as advocated by Andrew Jackson, it depended solely on coordination and implementation by the individual states."

Tom held his hand to his face to block his words from the others at the table. "President Adams also supports tariffs for the protection of our national interests." He frowned. "This plan is not popular with everyone, particularly the slave owners and cotton growers in the South, but it is necessary to reduce our dependency on foreign goods and to allow for the success of our economic development. Under Mr. Adams' administration, we have enjoyed a sound economy and the national debt has been significantly reduced.

"No," Tom shook his head as he continued. "The ideas expounded by John Quincy Adams are not the frivolous dalliance of a man of privilege as the Hurrah Boy implies." He resumed the tap-tapping of his fingers on the table.

"While President Adams has been involved with diplomacy since he was his father's secretary at the age of thirteen, Andrew Jackson has little experience as a legislator," Tom sighed. "He was elected to the United States Senate twice, and both times he resigned before the end of his term. He is savvy, however. He is said to have recognized that, as a senator, he would have to vote on certain sensitive issues which might have alienated some of his supporters in his run for president. Supposedly, he resigned to avoid taking a stand."

"Why don't you speak out?" James whispered.

"I am no debater," Tom turned away. "I'll leave that to someone else."

The Jacksonian, aware of the competing conversation, shot an irritated look in the direction of James and his companion. Registering his displeasure, he continued, his voice rising as he sought to override the distraction.

"In contrast to the aristocratic Mr. Adams, Andrew Jackson is beloved by the people, and by rights, should have won the last election."

The visitor paused, noted that his audience had increased, then waited for a reaction to his last statement. The men at James' table remained silent but all of them, their curiosity roused, were focused on the visitor, intent on hearing his words.

James glanced around the room and saw other faces turned toward the speaker.

"Four years ago, during the election of 1824, when General Jackson ran against John Quincy Adams, Henry Clay and William Harris Crawford, Andrew Jackson received the largest number of popular and electoral votes.

"He was cheated out of the presidency when, it is said, John Quincy Adams negotiated a corrupt bargain with Henry Clay, one of the four men competing for the office. In return for his support, Mr. Adams awarded Mr. Clay the coveted position of Secretary of State."

"It is not that simple," Ethan McGreevy, the man seated on James' left, interjected. "Our Constitution requires a presidential candidate to secure more than fifty percent of the electoral votes in order to win an election and none of the four candidates garnered the required one-hundred-and-thirty-one votes. Mr. Clay certainly could have influenced the disposition of the votes he received but he did not have the power to award them outright to Mr. Adams. The individual states control their electoral votes."

Surprised by the unexpected outburst, James and his table mates turned to stare at the normally taciturn man who had just spoken with such certainty. Ethan, uncomfortable with the attention, reached in his pocket and brought out a handkerchief. He self-consciously wiped his brow and cleared his throat. Then he took a deep breath before continuing.

"Sir," he looked across the table at the stranger. "The Twelfth Amendment to our Constitution states that the House of Representatives must decide the final outcome of a presidential election when a majority is not achieved."

"How do you know that, Ethan?" Tom asked, with an astonished look on his face. "I didn't know you had that kind of learning."

Ethan's neck reddened as a flush worked its way up to his face. "I read for the law before I came here," he answered quietly.

Undeterred, the Jacksonian picked up where he left off. "Mr. Adams never would have won without the support of...."

"Henry Clay's ideas for America's future," Ethan interrupted, his delivery stronger this time, "were closer to those of Mr. Adams than to those of General Jackson. Moreover, Mr. Clay did not think the General's military prowess, which was the basis of his popular appeal, or his volatile temperament, qualified him to be president. Mr. Clay simply supported the man he felt was the better suited for the position."

"What you say is true, Ethan," Tom spoke up. "I have heard stories of Jackson's legendary outbursts and impetuous decisions. It is said that he has a violent and uncontrolled temper...."

"Balderdash. Andrew Jackson is bold, daring and courageous. His acuity, his dedication to duty, his unshakeable self-confidence and his bravery spring from a firmness of virtue which has sustained him well in his years of service to his beloved country.

"You speak, my good fellows," the stranger faced Ethan and Tom as he attempted to negate their comments, "with little knowledge of the accomplishments of our," he paused, and then emphasized each word as he continued, *"Hero of New Orleans."* He fairly puffed up with pride. "Andrew Jackson's victory at New Orleans...."

The visitor stood and looked around the room. Noting that he had everyone's attention, he repeated his statement in a loud, authoritative voice. "Andrew Jackson's victory at New Orleans was, without doubt, one of America's greatest military feats"

The Hurrah Boy loomed tall, empowered by his ability to captivate. His personal glory, however, was cut short when Ethan rose from his seat, and with quiet determination, challenged his stance.

"I will not discount the national pride my countrymen have in General Jackson's victory during the battle of New Orleans but I, like my friend," he pointed to Tom, "have heard reports of his arrogance and the wanton disregard of the law that he has displayed throughout his military career. In 1814, Andrew Jackson ignored existing civil authority when he took control of New Orleans and placed the city under martial law. He declared that anyone found on the streets after nine o'clock in the evening would be apprehended as a spy.

"During this time, your Old Hickory had a non-military American citizen, a Louisiana state senator, one Louis Louaillier, arrested for," Ethan's sarcasm matched the stranger's as he spoke, "writing, and causing to be published, an *essay*." His emphasis on the final word was so derogatory in tone that the visitor was taken aback.

"This essay criticized the general for banishing the French soldiers, the ones who had gallantly fought for New Orleans, from the city. It also denounced the general's refusal to remove the onus of martial law after the battle had been won and the troops had been allowed to return. Andrew Jackson had Louaillier charged with writing willful and corrupt libel, inciting mutiny and being a spy. The last mentioned charge, by the way, carries the death sentence."

Ethan waited a moment for a reply from the Jacksonian and when none came, he continued.

"Mr. Louaillier's lawyer filed a writ of habeas corpus which was signed by a Judge Hall. Instead of honoring the legal document and surrendering Louaillier to civil authority, Andrew Jackson had the judge thrown in jail with the defendant. They were joined, I might add, by the district attorney who was arrested for trying to extricate the judge.

"The general then ordered Mr. Louaillier to be tried by a court martial. Louaillier argued that, as a member of the Louisiana legislature, he was exempt from military service, and therefore, beyond the reach of martial law and that he had the right to claim a trial in civil court.

"Accepting his argument, and recognizing that it was highly improbable that the senator from Louisiana would publish his views in a widely-circulated newspaper if he was acting as a spy against the United States, the members of the court martial acquitted him.

"Andrew Jackson set aside the verdict, ordered Louaillier back to prison and banished Judge Hall from New Orleans. All of this took place after the British, defeated in battle, had retreated from the city and rumors of the war's end were rampant. The General's rejection of the civil rights of these citizens and his refusal to sanction the findings of Louaillier's court martial are examples of Old Hickory's blatant abuse of power."

"Ethan," Tom spoke up. "Wasn't Andrew Jackson brought to task for his behavior?"

"Yes. After receipt of official word of the signing of the Treaty of Ghent, martial law was lifted, Louis Louaillier was released and Judge Hall returned from exile. A few days later, the judge ordered Andrew Jackson to answer charges of contempt of court, and following a well-prepared defense, the general managed to get off with a fine of $1,000."

"The people," the Hurrah Boy interrupted Ethan to defend his candidate, "were there to support their hero. They cheered him on with shouts and enthusiastic applause before he spoke in his defense. They surrounded him joyously after he was dismissed.

"By the by," the stranger added, "I know a little law myself. The Articles of War state that a commanding officer may appoint a general court martial when necessary and Andrew Jackson, not the civilian courts, was in charge of maintaining order in New Orleans. He was within his rights to act as he did to maintain the peace."

Ethan clenched his fists as he spoke. "Your hero, out of pique, court-martialed a citizen, refused to accept his acquittal, imprisoned him and expelled a judge who was following the law."

Ethan took a deep breath and was about to resume his seat when he snapped, "And how can you accept Andrew Jackson's 1818 court martial of Robert Ambrister and Alexander Arbuthnot, two

British civilians accused of inciting and abetting the Indians during the Seminole War? The members of the military court sentenced them both to death. Ambrister's case, however, was reconsidered, and on a second vote, his sentence reduced to fifty lashes and a year at hard labor."

Ethan shifted his weight.

"Unhappy with the reduced punishment, Andrew Jackson overruled Ambrister's sentence and both men were executed the following day: Arbuthnot, also charged as a spy, was hanged by the neck; Ambrister suffered death by gunshot. If you do, indeed, know your military law, my friend, you are aware that when a man is sentenced to death by a court martial, the entire proceedings must be transmitted to the Secretary of War, who will pass them on to the president for his approval or disapproval before the sentence is carried out. Your 'Hero of New Orleans' ignored that stipulation.

"His actions in this situation were questioned as well. In 1819, a Senate report condemned the executions as an unnecessary act of severity on the part of the general and a departure from the humane treatment of prisoners which is inherent to our national character.

"No," Ethan said as he moved away from the table. "Andrew Jackson may have great love for his country but he is an arrogant, violent man who has little regard for the law and less for the value of human life."

Ethan headed for the door. "He will not get my vote and," he glanced around the room, "from the looks of things, there are others here who agree with me."

Some of the men in the dining room had risen from their seats and were following Ethan from the room. James remained in his chair.

While he listened to the impassioned debate, James regretted the years he had spent drifting through life relying on his fists instead of his brain. He had never voted for the president of his country. He knew nothing about the current election beyond what he had heard since coming to the community. Aware of his shortcomings, he longed for the knowledge and the confidence to form his own opinions and to participate in the daily deliberations which swirled around him.

# *Monday, September 22, 1828*

James was surprised to find he was alone in the library as it was the usual after-supper destination for a dozen or so residents. He rifled through the newspapers which lay on the long table in the center of the room and chose a recent copy of the *American Gazette and Literary Review*. He sat on one of the straight, wooden chairs, opened the paper and spread it on the table. The light was dim and he lit a candle.

He scanned the front page and began to read. He was engrossed in an article when he heard someone enter the room. He waited until he had reached the end before looking up. Sally stood opposite him, on the other side of the library table. The candlelight illuminated her body while her head and arms were in shadow. James reflexively closed his eyes at the sight of her. When he opened them, he tried to focus on her face. She was smiling. He lowered his gaze. She was naked.

James was thunderstruck as she backed away from the table and stood, fully exposed, in front of him. The shock of seeing her in her natural state had taken him so by surprise that he was unable to speak. In spite of all his sexual exploits, James had never actually looked at a woman's nude body.

Shock gave way to involuntary fascination and James stared at the base of her neck, the subtle curves of her collar bones, the soft mounds of her breasts, the delicate protrusion of her navel, the graceful contour of her torso which narrowed at her waist and expanded to outline the tops of her hips. He averted his eyes and looked no further. It was too much. He was unprepared for this erotic revelation of the mysteries of womanhood.

James stared down at the newspaper as images of Sally's sexual attributes obscured the type. Although he longed to go to her, he tempered his desire to explore her newly revealed stimuli. He knew if he so much as touched her he would lose control.

James kept his eyes down as he swallowed hard and asked, "Why are you...?" He was unable to say the word "naked".

"Ah do believe you have nevah seen a nekid lady, James Daunt." Sally mimicked the accent of a woman from the South as she called him by his given name and teased him about his distress.

James regained his composure as he sought to override her mockery with indignation. "What are you doing here like...that?"

"Tonight is the autumnal equinox." Sally spoke conversationally, as if she were seated at tea with the ladies.

"Twice a year, in March and September, day and night are of near equal length. On those two days, we at Pleasant Valley reaffirm our belief in the equality of all human beings, be they man or woman, strong or invalid, wise or fool, Christian or heathen, black or white.

"While we vigorously promote intellectual achievement and enthusiastically applaud the conscientious development of the talents of each of our members, we recognize that not all people are born with like capabilities and tolerances.

"Therefore, James, from sundown until midnight of the equinox, we put away our worldly goods and shed our clothing in a symbolic renunciation of our uniqueness and we celebrate the equality of all men under God. The Book of Job tells us that we were naked when we came out of our mothers' wombs and we will be naked when we return. And thus we will be on judgment day."

James continued to stare at the pages of the newspaper in front of him. He could not believe that he was listening to Biblical references coming from the mouth of a provocative nude woman standing on public view in the community library.

"For the next four hours, we will gather by the side of the river and celebrate our similarities and the love of humanity which unites us all. We will end our observance at midnight when we enter the water, attempt to cleanse ourselves of personal vanity and avarice, and renew our pledges to honor the godly values and precepts of Thaddeus Goodenough and the community.

"Now...." Sally leaned over the table. "You must go to your room and get ready for the evening's activities."

"I cannot do that, Sally." James kept his eyes averted. "I will not bare my body in front of other people."

Sally did not speak for a moment. James raised his eyes and saw that she was, once again, standing upright. His gaze locked on her body. He studied each sensuous line, curve and volume and allowed himself to fill with her beauty. Embarrassed, he pulled his shirt down and covered his vulnerability.

Sally noticed his discomfort. Instead of taunting him, as he expected, she spoke in a low tone.

"I understand, James. Our ways are not for everyone and this celebration is one of our rituals. I will tell the reverend you are sick." She turned away. "I hope he will accept it as truth."

James watched her walk to the door. The rhythmic swaying of her hips beat on his brain and caused him more physical pain. As he struggled to contain himself, he had to admit that, although the erotic revelation of Sally Morley's earthy pulchritude had been overwhelming, the once-irresistible lure of her sexual mystique had been somewhat diluted.

After a while, he picked up a copy of Washington Irving's *Rip Van Winkle* and returned to his room. The din of distant drumming and chanting kept him awake and he read the first three chapters before falling asleep fully clothed.

The warmth and smell of a strange woman's body awakened him. It was neither Sally nor the washerwoman. James could hear the ritual sounds of the celebrants in the distance and became aware of the touch of her fingers. In spite of the primal vibrations emanating from the drums in the background, he did not respond to the woman's approach. She sensed his unspoken rejection and left his bed. The door clicked closed as he returned to an uneasy sleep.

# *Wednesday, September 24, 1828*

It was still dark when Sally stretched her body next to James. Fall had come to Pleasant Valley and dawn arrived later each day. During the past five weeks, she had spent every night but one, the night of James' initiation, in the bed of her lover.

James' emotional confusion caused by seeing her naked had passed and the thrill of their lovemaking had increased with frequency. There were times during the day when an all-consuming need to touch his body drove Sally to abandon her chores and race to the blacksmith's shop.

James had only to look at her as she burst through the door and the desire which lay dormant when the two were separated, flamed into reality. They would come together on the dirt floor of the forge, she breathless from her run, he red-hot from the fire and dripping with perspiration. Their chests, pressed hard against each other, would adhere and they would laugh when they finally pulled apart. Sally would leave the smithy bathed in the odors of male sweat and sexual consummation. Although she never admitted it, the danger of discovery accentuated the excitement and heightened her pleasure during these clandestine trysts.

She turned toward the dimly lit body of James Daunt and traced his chin with her forefinger. She had never stayed with one partner before, and other than the night of her first taste of carnal delight, had never felt such passion. Her cravings, once random and easily satisfied, now centered on this one man.

Attracted by his Scotch-Irish looks and devil-may-care personality, Sally had desired James the first time she had seen him. Before his marriage, he had been a willing partner, even though, she thought sadly, he had always returned to his friends, leaving her alone, still wanting him.

She rolled onto her back, reluctant to accept that her early sexual attraction had grown into a mature love for James Daunt. She was haunted by the fear of living like her mother, whose passion for Thaddeus Goodenough had brought her years of humiliation and degradation.

Sally pitied her mother knowing she would always be shunned by the father of her child. Thaddeus never criticized her to her face but could be heard proclaiming the potatoes were watery and the carrots scorched when she was assigned to the kitchen. His shirts came back gray, his socks, unmatched, only when her mother was working in the laundry.

Over time, Sally, who had considered her mother a competitor for her father's attention, came to realize she was not a threat. It was devastating shame that drove Thaddeus Goodenough. He had debased the one woman whose love and devotion he had selfishly accepted, then ruthlessly spurned, only to compound his transgression by lusting after the issue of his sin.

On the night of her first menses, Thaddeus had come to her mother's room. The young Sally had listened at the door. Now, several years later, as she lay by James Daunt, she remembered the words Thaddeus had spoken when he told her mother he would be the one to consummate their daughter's initiation.

"It is my duty," he said. "Just as it would be yours if we had a son. You are the only one sanctified by our God to teach our male initiates how to satisfy a woman and experience gratification without ejaculation."

"But we do not have a son," her mother protested. "Not that it would make a difference. Sarah is your daughter. What you propose is against the word of God Almighty."

"No," Thaddeus shook his head. "When Lot went into the cave with his two daughters, '...*the firstborn said unto the younger, Our father is old, and there is not a man in the earth to come in unto us after the manner of all the earth: Come, let us make our father drink wine, and we will lie with him, that we may preserve seed of our father. And they made their father drink wine that night: and the firstborn went in, and lay with her father....And it came to pass on the morrow, that the firstborn said unto the younger, Behold, I lay yesternight with my father: let us make him drink wine this night also; and go thou in, and lie with him, that we may preserve seed of our father. And they made their father drink wine that night also: and the younger arose, and lay with him....Thus were both the daughters of Lot with child by their father.'* Genesis, Chapter Nineteen, verses 31 through 36."

"You left out '...*and he perceived not when she lay down, nor when she arose.*' I, too, know some Biblical verses and Lot's daughters deceived him. He was under the influence of the wine and knew not what he was doing when he lay with his children. His actions were reflexive, your intentions are premeditated."

"God approved the unions," Thaddeus bristled. "The son of the firstborn daughter became the father of the Moabites and the son of the younger sired the children of Ammon. If God had damned the coming together of Lot and his daughters, he would not have allowed their progeny to survive and propagate our peoples."

Sally heard Thaddeus' footsteps as he paced back and forth in the small room.

"It is my destiny...," he paused before continuing, "to be the one who introduces each of our new initiates to the joys of sexual fulfillment as she crosses the threshold of womanhood. At the same time, I have the responsibility to teach each and every novice how to help her partner through withdrawal before his seed is spilled."

The morning following her initiation, Sally remembered Thaddeus Goodenough's self-righteous sounding pronouncement. She was aware that he had broken a cardinal rule of the community, not once, but every time he had come to her that night.

Sally wondered how many times Thaddeus had been in full passion with her mother. At least once, she knew, on the occasion of her conception. She hoped the same consequences did not await her and she fervently prayed that Thaddeus had not left her with child. Even at her young age, she was sure she would be unable to bear the thought of sharing her father's carnal love with a daughter of her making. She did not allow herself to think about her mother.

Over the years, Sally had tried to lure her father back to her bed. She had nurtured his hunger by pressing her hip against his, carelessly touching his knee with her fingers, casually guiding his hand to the skin of her neck, allowing her breast to rest on his arm. He had never discouraged her attentions and she had continued her assault on his sensibilities. She knew there were times when he could not speak, his emotions so overwhelmed him. She wondered whether she brought this added torment down on him because she loved him and wanted his attention. Or was it because she hated him for introducing her to the sublime ecstasy she had experienced that night of her first awakening and then denying her need for more.

Memories of the demise of her virginity brought with them the old familiar stirrings. Sally tried to bury the remembrances but they persisted in haunting her. Her rekindled thirst for random titillation stimulated her juices and her cravings increased. Tingling with excitement, she looked over at James, asleep on his side and made a decision.

Carefully, she slid off the bed, picked up her dress, stockings and shoes and slowly opened the door. She knew that, if she hurried, she could hitch the small cart to one of the horses and be at Hebe's before the lads started filtering in for their late afternoon draughts.

Sally hastened down the hall and away from the room she shared with James. Without warning, she gagged. The bitter sting of bile seared her throat and informed her that she was about to lose the contents of her stomach. She covered her mouth with her hand and broke into a cold sweat. Panic overtook her as she raced down the stairs, burst through the door and crossed the cart path.

Sally was shaking by the time she reached the lone tree which stood at the edge of the field. She regurgitated again and again until the remaining fluids had run dry and her throat was raw. The nausea persisted and her stomach heaved in a futile attempt to cast out that which was no longer there.

She folded her hands across her stomach and told herself it could not be true. But she knew it was. It had been six weeks since her last menses. Her breasts were tender and a persistent ache in her lower back had started two days ago.

When the retching subsided, she pulled herself together and walked slowly to the rooms she shared with her mother.

"I saw you through the window, Sarah." Her mother was waiting for her. "How long have you known?"

"I tried to wish it away, but as of today, I am sure." Sally sat on the edge of the bed. "When I awoke this morning, I had the old urges...." Unexpectedly, she felt herself blush. "I wanted to return to Hebe's, to be free again, to cast off the emotions I feel for James. I thought it was a good sign, that I was myself again, that I was not carrying...."

"Your wayward ways were bound to catch up with you, Sarah." Sadness rather than recrimination colored the words.

"I thought I was barren after...." Sally did not complete her sentence, but her mother knew her daughter referred to her early introduction to the ways of men and women. She understood that Sally's dissolute behavior outside the community was driven by her need to override her father's night of passionate transgression and her mother's apparent acceptance of his impropriety. It was her futile attempt to minimize the sin of incest by diluting it with her indiscriminate reception of the intimacies of many men—none of whom, her mother admitted, would have been suitable in the eyes of the reverend. No man would ever receive the blessing of her daughter's aberrant first lover.

The older woman recognized that, in spite of her past indiscretions, Sally had finally found a man whom she was capable of loving. She was happy and had carelessly satisfied her desires. She had lain with him nightly instead of planning the timing of their coupling. She had been caught and now had to suffer the consequences of bearing the child of a married man.

"I am going to Hebe's." Sally stated her intentions without emotion.

"Not now," her mother protested. "Not now that you are...," she took a deep breath, "with child." She had said the words aloud. It was now an indisputable fact, both for Sally and the woman who loved, feared and envied her more, at times, than she could bear.

"I am going to see Hebe, not the boys. I do not think I can change," Sally said with genuine regret, "and she is the only person who might know what I can do about this unfortunate situation."

She did not have to explain further. Her mother knew what her daughter was contemplating. "It is God's will that you conceived, Sarah." She bowed her head.

"I cannot change who or what I am," Sally said, a sadness born of her acceptance of reality present in her voice. "And I know I cannot bear this child."

Her mother laid her hand on Sally's shoulder and said, "I have paid dearly for my fall from grace, Sarah, but I still believe in God and God's word as written in the Bible. '*I know that, whatsoever God doeth, it shall be forever: nothing can be put to it, nor any thing taken from it: God doeth it, that men should fear before him*'." After all these years of listening to Thaddeus Goodenough, she could not help adding, "Ecclesiastes Three, verse fourteen."

She paused before stating her judgment. "You will be committing murder, Sarah, if you force this child from your body."

The long-suffering woman thought of the day, many years ago, when her own mother had quoted that verse to her and how it had impacted her own life-altering decision. She said nothing more.

James turned over and threw his arm across the bed. Drowsy from a full night's sleep, he drifted off again. Slowly, he awakened to the realization that Sally was not by his side. He looked out of the window and saw the last traces of the moon fade as the early morning sun began to color the gray-blue sky.

He estimated the time to be around six o'clock. He was late in rising and wondered why Sally hadn't roused him when she left his bed. James pulled himself to sitting, then reluctantly, to standing. He dressed and headed to the blacksmith's shop. Once there, he laid the charcoal in the bed of the forge and readied his tools in anticipation of

*113*

a busy day. He returned to the main house in time for breakfast and searched the dining room as he entered. Sally, who had a healthy appetite and never missed a meal, was not there. He wondered again about her absence.

James, choosing to sit alone, ate slowly as he kept an eye out for Sally's entrance. She did not appear before he returned to the smithy.

The heat of the late September day had raised the temperature in the building and James was relieved to know that eight blanks of butterfly hinges awaited his preparation. He postponed stoking the fire in the forge, and instead, he punched the necessary holes in one of the blanks. After he had completed punching the remaining seven pieces, he put them aside, prepared for his afternoon's work and left the forge.

James walked back to the main house and returned to the dining room for the noontime meal. He scanned the room searching for Sally. He could not find her. Hoping to hear some news of her whereabouts, he looked for some of the men he had come to know. Their tables were full and James, uneasy and insecure about sitting with strangers, seriously considered returning to the forge. Recognizing, however, that he would not have the opportunity to eat until the six o'clock supper, he sat down at a table with two unfamiliar men, neither of whom looked up when he joined them.

Following the example of his dinner partners, James kept his eyes riveted on his plate of food. He finished the main course, passed up dessert, rose and left the room without having uttered a word. For the first time, he realized how much he had come to depend on Sally's presence for his confidence. He hurried back to the security of the forge and the distraction of his work.

James stoked the fire and examined his hinges. He had added a decorative curve to the simple form and was pleased to see how its outline echoed the shape of a delicate butterfly wing. He recalled the first time Sally had noticed that he personalized his creations. He had initially been embarrassed but her enthusiasm encouraged him. He explained how easy it was for him to add a serpentine twist to the end of a strap hinge, a decorative curl to the end of a door bolt. She had looked at the other items he had made since coming to the community and her glowing praise had reinforced his pride in his designs. He realized his newfound creativity was only possible in a place like Pleasant Valley Farm where the demands were small and the schedules were lax.

James' concern about Sally's absence increased as the afternoon passed. He finished rolling and assembling the hinges and then returned to his room before going to the dining hall for supper.

The members of the community always washed up and changed their clothing before the evening meal. Other than the second set of trousers and spare shirt Sally had found for him, James had only the clothes he had arrived in to substitute for his community-issued uniform. As cleanliness was an accepted attribute of the residents, he made sure his meager wardrobe made frequent trips to the laundry.

Hearing a noise in the hall, he reached over and opened his door. An older man who worked in the barn nodded as he passed on his way to his room. Disappointed that the passerby wasn't Sally, James stepped into the hall, closed the door behind him and headed for the dining room.

He entered the large hall and a young man waved him over to his table. Relieved to be included with known comrades, he made his way across the room and joined the three men he had toiled with the day he had been assigned to work in the fields. As he pulled out his chair and sat opposite his acquaintances, James glanced in the direction of the women's tables. Several of the younger ladies had their heads together and appeared to be engaged in a serious conversation.

James spent the mealtime listening to light chatter about the heat, the crops being harvested and the imminent arrival of fall. He admitted to his worry when Sally did not appear during the evening supper.

It was early evening when Sally arrived at Hebe Balderston's tavern. Instead of taking the cart, she had chosen one of the horses and ridden hard hoping the long ride would terminate her problem. There were no signs of change in her condition when she pulled up in front of the tavern and hitched her horse to the rail.

She recognized some of the other horses and knew the boys had already gathered. A deep sadness surged through her as she thought of James and the bond he shared with his friends. Without a miracle, he would never again know the luxury of their company.

Sally straightened her skirt and shifted her weight as she removed the thin sash from her waist and allowed her gray community shirt to hang loose. The soft folds disguised her slightly distended breasts. They were sensitive to the touch. She shuddered at the prospect of the boys coming close and putting their rough hands on her body. Then she thought of James and wondered how he would feel if he knew why she was here.

She entered the tavern, and one by one, the lads noticed her, hooted and called out to announce her arrival.

"I'm first," Elijah Darby stated as he walked toward Sally.

"Not tonight, Elijah," she said. "I am here to see Hebe." Elijah, stopped by her tone of voice, acknowledged the difference in Sally.

She held herself straight and had a no-nonsense air about her. She did not tease and thrust her hips forward or offer her breasts for a quick fondle. Instead, she walked straight to the corner of the room where the bar was located and asked, "Where might I find Hebe?"

Taken aback by her take-charge attitude, the man standing behind the cage-like enclosure which housed the tavern's liquor supplies retorted, "What makes you think Hebe Balderston is going to come out and speak to a trollop like you, Sally Morley?"

"I'll find her myself, thank you." Sally marched past the bar to a door at the rear of the room. She knocked and opened it in one movement. The door banged against the black boy, Conshy Joe, who was sweeping the floor.

"I'm sorry, Joseph," she murmured, as she closed the door behind her. "I did not see you there." The young man barely raised his eyes as he glanced in her direction. Without breaking the rhythm of his stroke, he continued with his chore.

Hebe Balderston sat behind a desk covered with papers. She wore spectacles which she removed as Sally approached. It took a moment for her eyes to adjust from the close scrutiny of numbers to the distant figure of the intruder standing in the doorway.

"What are you doing in my office, Sally Morley?" Hebe's voice was terse but her expression was puzzled. She could see the difference in Sally's dress and in her carriage. Her eyes narrowed as she said, "You've changed."

"Hebe, I've come to you because I have a problem that I cannot resolve by myself." Hebe's reception of Sally's statement came as a surprise.

"You got yourself in trouble."

Sally frowned. She had needlessly wondered how she would explain her situation to Hebe and was relieved to find the woman knew without being told.

"It's in your face." Hebe looked her up and down. "And in your body. It's written all over you, Sally Morley. You've been coming here for a long time, and as far as I know, this is the first time you've had a problem. What happened? And who is the father?"

"I cannot tell you that, Hebe. But I also can't allow this situation to continue. Can you help me?"

"I keep my own counsel when it comes to people's problems, Sally. Too many ways to bring trouble on yourself when you interfere in the lives of others." She picked up her spectacles, hooked them over her ears and returned to the figures on her desk.

Sally glanced away as she felt tears come into her eyes. She willed them to stop. "Do you know anyone else who can help me?"

Hebe looked at the young woman who stood in front of her. This Sally resembled the familiar one in facial features only. Gone was the unbuttoned bodice, the tucked-up skirt. Gone was the seductive tease who frequented the alley behind her tavern. Instead, a confident, though distressed, young woman, dressed in practical, gray garb, regained her composure as she asked the question.

Hebe narrowed her eyes, pursed her lips and stated, "The father is James Daunt."

Sally started, shocked by Hebe's powers of perception. The truth of the older woman's assumption showed on Sally's face and she looked away.

"Perhaps," she tried to cover her emotions and aggressively said, "Perhaps I don't know the answer. There have been so many."

117

"You know, Sally Morley, and I won't help you unless you tell me the name of the father of your baby." Hebe Balderston was certain James Daunt was the man responsible for Sally's predicament, and for some unknown reason, she wanted it confirmed.

Sally turned to leave.

Hebe realized she would not get an answer. She thought for a moment and then asked, "Do you know where the creek flows near Elias Latch's farm?"

"Yes," Sally answered warily. She recalled the day she had taunted Esther Latch after she had raced away from the scene of Richard Holt's murder. She remembered, too, following the creek back to the ledge where, so many times in the past, she had sought refuge from her demons. She recalled her joy at finding James Daunt stretched out, exhausted, on the flat stones. She often wondered if she should have told him then that she had witnessed the shooting. Once he agreed to come to Pleasant Valley Farm, she had been afraid she would lose him if he knew about Esther's shot. She had decided to tell him if he was captured.

"...follow it south," Hebe had started talking while Sally was thinking of the past, "...from the Latch farm. You will pass one ledge surrounded by pine trees on your left. Keep going until you come to a second ledge which sits over a tangle of roots. This is where you'll meet...." Sally gasped.

Hebe had just described the exact spot where she and James had come together the day of Squire Holt's death. Was this a good omen or one of warning?

"What's wrong, Sally Morley?"

"Nothing, Hebe. I was simply thinking about something. Please," she took a deep breath, "finish what you were saying."

Hebe squinted nearsightedly at the young woman and frowned as suspicion alternated with a grudging approval.

"You sure have changed, Sally Morley. Everything about you is different." Hebe raised her eyebrows at the mature young woman with serious, intelligent eyes, who resided in the body of the shameless, simple nymph who had wantonly frolicked with the boys on prior visits to the tavern.

"Are you sure you want to go through with this? The woman I speak of is an old Indian. She's versed in witchcraft, not doctorin'. Even though others have gone to her you must be aware that you would be taking a chance following her ways."

"I have no choice." Sally seemed to falter for a moment then she shook her head up and down. The familiar strumpet of the past reappeared as Sally thrust her hips forward, spread her legs and placed her hands under her breasts.

"How can I keep your lads happy if I am with child, Hebe? It is to your advantage to get me out of this predicament. Tell me how to find your witch doctor and I'll soon be back to my old self again."

Hebe was conflicted. She knew Sally pleased the boys in the tavern when she was in attendance but she much preferred the young woman's new persona. In any case, the illegitimate child of a married murderer would benefit no one.

"You can't go now, it's almost dark. I've got a room in the back by the kitchen where you can stay the night. No charge." Knowing the old Sally would have no money for a room, she assigned her the cook's quarters. Cook was visiting family for three days and would never know her room had been commandeered to shelter the whore of Hebe's tavern.

Sally had not considered the need for money when she left Pleasant Valley. She had spent the nights of her previous visits on the ledge or in someone's barn. The thought of Hebe's offering her a bed brought the tears back to her eyes. She moved behind the proprietress' chair and put her arms around the shoulders of the seated woman.

Hebe shook her off. "None of that. I don't get personally involved with my customers. It doesn't pay." She looked over the rims of her glasses and Sally knew she was referring to the free lodging.

"Tomorrow you can go to the ledge and wait. She will know you're coming. And," Hebe's eyes twinkled with rare humor, "she'll recognize you. She seen you there with James Daunt," her expression darkened, "the day he shot the squire."

James watched as the women who had drawn kitchen duty for the evening began to clear the tables. He was very worried about Sally and could not decide whether to return to his room or wait for her in the dining room. His attention was diverted by the figure of Lemuel Buckwalter as he strode to the center of the room.

"Tonight we are convening at the request of several of our members. There has been talk of formulating a written declaration of the goals and doctrines to which we adhere in our community.

"The learned originator of our tenets, Reverend Goodenough," the speaker turned and bowed slightly in the direction of Thaddeus, "has written numerous pamphlets and delivered many an informal sermon in parks, lecture halls and private homes."

He continued speaking as he turned back to his audience.

"It has been suggested, however, that we need a formal written treatise, based, of course, on Reverend Goodenough's proclamations. This will help to legitimize our existence as a valid intellectual and social movement and can also be used for the edification of our current and future neophytes. It will serve, as well, as a reference for our active residents."

Several of the older members and all of the newcomers nodded their heads solemnly as they signaled their endorsement of the speaker's message. James glanced at Thaddeus and recognized the scowl of disapproval which crossed his face. It was obvious to James that this meeting had not been called at the reverend's instigation.

Lemuel carried on with his discourse. "Those who seek information on, and membership in, our community are usually drawn by the intellectual stimulation and companionship of philosophical sympathizers. On the whole, they are already supportive of our open-minded views on abolitionism and the equality of men and women. It is our sexual liberalism with which some are slightly uncomfortable."

There was a general shifting of bodies as the speaker touched on the delicate subject.

"The seminal issues which are the most difficult to understand are our rejection of the sacrament of marriage; our encouragement of intimate, but uncommitted, relationships between unmarried partners, and our acceptance of public nudity."

The representative was interrupted when he stopped to take a deep breath.

"Please explain why you do not consider public, um, exposure a violation of the natural laws of decency." James could not help smiling at the speaker's apparent inability to utter aloud the words *nudity* or *nakedness*.

Lemuel thought for a moment before responding.

"We do not walk on public streets in a state of undress nor do we wantonly reveal ourselves as we go about our normal daily routines in the community. However, we do have certain celebrations and rituals which involve the exposure of the human body." James cringed at the remembrance of his refusal to participate in the commemoration of the equinox.

"And in the evening, after we have retired from community activities, there are no restrictions placed upon a person's choice of dress," Lemuel reddened slightly, "or lack thereof.

"Nakedness is not synonymous with lewdness or indecency here at Pleasant Valley. It is," he paused as he searched for the correct words of clarification. "It is, instead, utilized as a challenge." He sighed in relief as he honed his explanation.

"Casual encounters between unclothed members of both sexes render the sexual attributes of the human body mundane."

James recalled his initial reaction to seeing Sally's nude body and the temporary diminution of her mystique. He smiled to himself as he allowed that, contrary to Lemuel's proclamations, their lovemaking since that night had become even more exciting than in the past.

The memory caused him to worry even more about Sally. There had been no mention of her absence and he was afraid to ask questions which might arouse suspicions, and perhaps, cause problems. He determined to wait until the morning before approaching her mother.

"The resulting ordinariness," Lemuel was still speaking, "challenges an individual to seek stimulation from an appreciation of a partner's intellect as well as from the temptation of his or her naked flesh."

There was an obvious shuffling of feet and moving around on the hard wooden chairs. Several of the younger men exchanged charged glances with young ladies who blushed as, embarrassed by the knowledge of their own interests, they stifled their giggles. More experienced older men tried to hide their disbelief of the speaker's naiveté while several bright, but physically unattractive, women who had joined the community in search of an ideological home, glanced expectantly around the room.

Unable to contain himself, Thaddeus Goodenough leapt from his chair and roared with indignation. *"'And they were both naked, the man and his wife, and were not ashamed.'* Genesis Two, verse twenty-five."

He stopped and gained control of himself. *"'Were not ashamed',"* he repeated in an attempt to achieve a conversational tone.

"In the beginning," the preacher modulated his voice although a faint quiver crept into his self-conscious monotone, *"'God created man in his own image.'"* He paused. He could not help himself. He was unable to speak, even in anger, without pretentiously identifying each Biblical passage, "Genesis One, verse twenty-seven."

Thaddeus Goodenough continued. "Man has always come naked into this world. Nudity is the natural state of mankind and was not considered an aberration by the Creator. The original sin of Adam and Eve brought forth the curse that causes us to cover our bodies in shame and hide our physical beauty.

"After Adam and Eve had eaten the forbidden fruit, *'the eyes of them both were opened and they knew that they were naked; and they sewed fig leaves together, and made themselves aprons'.* When God confronted them, Adam said, *'I was afraid because I was naked.'* To which God replied, *'Who told thee that thou wast naked?'* Genesis Three, verses seven, ten and eleven.

"It is indisputable," the reverend continued, "that the Lord was pleased with man as he had originally created him and intended him to glory in his nakedness. *'And God saw every thing that he had made, and, behold, it was very good.'* Genesis One, verse thirty-one. He did not mean for Adam and Eve to eat the fruit, behold their nakedness, and classify it as evil.

"The point is," Thaddeus Goodenough jabbed the air with his finger, "we all acknowledge that God is the perfect being, and that he made a perfect man in his image. From the rib of this perfect man, he created a perfect woman and planned for them to rejoice in the splendor of their divine beauty."

He scanned his flock before continuing.

"Our esteemed brother has just declared that the acceptance of nudity in our community renders mundane and ordinary the physical beauty of the re-creation of God's likeness in human form. And Mr. Buckwalter intimates that one would be emasculated by monotonous, routine exposure to the naked human form and would, therefore, succumb to intellectual motivation rather than physical provocation as the stimulus for copulation.

"It appears he sees repetitive subjection to the unadorned human body as synonymous with the elimination of the ecstasy, the rapture, the passion, the ultimate thrill which accompanies the divine coming together of a man and woman who physically lust after one another."

The reverend was visibly perspiring and violently thumping the table as he expounded his rebuttal. Realizing he had gone too far, and perhaps, revealed too much about himself, he announced, "This dialogue is over. I will be glad to meet with those of you who are interested in formalizing our goals and doctrines, but accomplishment of a project of this magnitude is too complex to put up for general discussion. Good night."

A small female voice broke into the momentary silence that followed Thaddeus' tirade. "Can we please discuss relationships between unmarried men and women? I have so many questions."

"Madame," the preacher spoke harshly without turning to see who had spoken. "If you are seriously questioning one of our basic philosophical principles, you do not belong in our community and I suggest you pack your things and leave."

With that, a tiny middle-aged woman burst into tears when she looked across the room at the man who had been her husband before they came to Pleasant Valley Farm. At the same time, the Reverend Thaddeus Goodenough strode from the room, conscious that his authority had been challenged and he had not escaped unscathed.

# *Thursday, September 25, 1828*

James spent a sleepless night alternating between worrying about Sally's safety and being angry with her for disappearing without a word. The possibility that she had returned to Hebe Balderston's tavern crossed his mind, but now that he had come to know Sister Sarah, he could barely remember the old Sally of the Alley. He did not think she would seek out her old haunts.

James also could not imagine returning to his former life. The contrast between the drunken camaraderie he had enjoyed at Hebe's and the intellectual solidarity he found in the stimulating conversations, the planned evening programs, the library with its volumes of classic and contemporary writings, the order of the daily chores at Pleasant Valley, was immeasurable.

He surprised himself with the admission that he much preferred his current sober, productive life. He wondered what his life would have been if he had not been expelled from the Academy and thrown into the life of a blacksmith. Would he have continued his learning and become a doctor like his father or embraced the word of God like the Reverends Goodenough and Montague?

James had no doubt the preachers had convinced themselves of the righteousness of their beliefs and their dedication to their followers, but he was not sure either was true to the word of God.

Thaddeus Goodenough rewrote the laws of morality to justify his own behavior and led his followers to abandon their virtue and embrace his heretical dictates. Maximillian Montague lured disheartened and potentially rebellious free blacks to the primitive land of their forefathers with the interests of Southern slaveholders as his impetus.

Were these the paths God had chosen for his disciples? In spite of the novelty and excitement of rogue interpretations of the Bible and social mores, James was certain these theologians were consciously, or unconsciously, primarily motivated by personal desires, rather than the word of the Lord.

He thought of Margaret and was unable to picture her in this environment. James had seen only her pretty face and winning ways when he pursued her. It still puzzled him that she had returned his favors. It had been, perhaps, the prospect of his reformation that had fueled her attraction to him. It was, however, Sally who had offered him solace, then shelter, then hope. And finally, purpose. She was the woman who changed his life from one of chaos and degradation to one of stability and growth.

James arose determined to find Sally. He was reluctant to seek out her mother as he had been shocked by the older woman's second visit to his bed. He had overtly avoided any contact with his unbidden lover. He could not turn to Thaddeus Goodenough as he was unsure of the extent of his knowledge of their relationship.

James decided to go to the office where Sally oversaw the domestic expenditures. Needing an excuse, he asked about the procedures for ordering iron for the forge. He was politely informed that Reverend Goodenough handled all material purchases for the community.

He thanked the woman who helped him and then casually asked, "Is Sister Sarah here?"

The woman blushed and looked away.

"No," she answered, without volunteering any additional information.

"Do you know when she will be here?"

Her eyes still averted, the woman in gray community clothing said, "She's away." He noticed her evasive behavior and wondered if the entire community was aware of his fraternization with Sally.

He thanked his informant for a second time and walked to the early morning meal.

James hesitated before he entered the dining room. One of the two strangers with whom he had shared a table during the previous day's noon meal was talking with Thaddeus Goodenough. The man held a sheet of paper in his hand and was pointing to something written on it. There was a deep frown on the preacher's face as he took the paper from the stranger. James stepped back and listened from the far side of the entryway.

He could hear Thaddeus' voice as the two men moved from the center of the room and came toward the door.

"I do not believe you. The man you are referring to is named James Morley, not James Daunt. He came here with the highest recommendation. In fact, he is a cousin of one of our most respected community members. Here, take your handbill. You are mistaken."

James began to perspire heavily. He looked at the main door then back at the entrance to the dining room. There was no way he could exit the building without being detected. He turned, and without knowing where he was going, hurried down the hallway to his left.

As he passed the laundry, the door opened and the washerwoman beckoned to him. He paused, and then followed her into the heat-filled room.

"Wait," she commanded and she held up her hand to stop him. "I have to get something."

She hurried to a far corner, disappeared behind three large drying racks which were covered with wet items of clothing.

Several of the women glanced at him, and then quickly looked away, embarrassed that he had caught them satisfying their curiosity. James knew that men worked in the laundry on Saturday mornings, and as this was Wednesday, he was out of place. In an effort to appear at ease, he surveyed the room.

A fire burned vigorously in a large stone fireplace which stood between two open windows. Several flat irons rested on a piece of metal in front of the flames. A woman bent over, wrapped a heavy woolen pad around the handle of one, picked it up and carried it across the room. She set it on a metal stand which rested on a large board balanced on the backs of two chairs. She shook her hand to relieve the burning discomfort of the hot handle.

James, concerned when his guide did not reappear, impatiently shifted his weight from one foot to the other. He could not believe he was standing in the middle of the laundry room watching women at work when he had possibly been discovered by the law.

Sally's mother finally rematerialized. She waved him to her, and as he came close, she quietly said, "You must leave immediately."

She took his hand and led him around an odd-looking apparatus which held a large flat stone-filled box resting atop two wooden rollers which were partially covered by a white sheet. As James tried to pass, he knocked into a short, plump woman. She looked up at him, stifled a comment and then resumed pulling on a rope which moved the box back and forth over the rollers.

"What is that?" He had no time for questions but, nevertheless, was puzzled by the function of the device.

"A mangle. It presses flat linens," the washerwoman answered. She gave no further explanation, but instead, hurried him along.

James could see an open door at the end of the room. The older woman ushered him through it and guided him into a secluded courtyard. Several vats of boiling water, suspended from horizontal poles which rested on iron tripods, were heating over fast-burning fires. Four women rubbed and pounded the items of clothing as they came out of the copper pots. The high temperature in the laundry room had exaggerated the stress James was experiencing and his heart began to pound. Now, assaulted by both the humidity of an unseasonably hot September day and the heat from the steaming cauldrons, he was forced to stop. He put his hand to his head.

"No time for curiosity or coddling yourself," his companion admonished him. "Those men you ate with yesterday were sent here by the family of Squire Holt. They are not yet sure that you are the man they seek, James Daunt." He was startled by her knowledge of his real name. "But they intend to find out. There's a sizeable reward on your head so they will continue looking for you. And," she said, "you can rest assured, they won't stop until they capture you.

"You will need a horse. Come, he's not a pretty one, nor a young one, but no one will miss him." She led him to a field close to the road.

An old horse stood in the pasture. "I have a bridle but you will have to do without a saddle. Be gentle with Old Caesar and be aware that if you push him too hard, he will stop in mid-stride and start to sneeze. Otherwise, he is still reasonably sure-footed and able to follow the trails in the woods. Stay on them if you can, you will be safer if you stay out of sight." She hesitated and looked at him with compassion.

"Sister Sarah...." She corrected herself. "Sally...is at Hebe Balderston's." She stopped and watched his reaction. He tried to disguise his dismay but it was obvious she recognized his pain.

He hid his face as he started to put the bridle on the horse.

"I'm sorry, but that's the way it is. And that's the way she is, James Daunt. She won't change. Go back to your wife if she will have you. Sarah will not settle down. At least not for the present."

James looked up and saw her flick her hand toward the woods. "Now go. I don't know if you will be able to escape the search parties. Notices offering a reward for your arrest are still posted in the area and there are many who would like to be the ones to bring you to justice. The description of you is an accurate one and I am afraid it will be difficult for you to disguise yourself."

She turned her back to him, lifted her skirt and handed him two parcels she had tucked into the top of her petticoat. The first contained a black hat made of soft felt.

"One of the reverend's...?"

The washerwoman looked away without answering. James put it on and pulled it down over his brow. It covered his forehead and shaded his face.

The second packet held a black shirt and had, in one of the pockets, a steel razor with a tortoise-shell handle and matching comb.

"Put this over your work clothes, James Daunt. There were no trousers in the laundry this morning but the shirt is long and will help to cover you. Not many people know our clothing but the two men who are looking for you do, so tuck your pants legs into your stockings. That may help as long as they don't get too close."

She scrutinized his beard. "Use the razor if you choose. You will have to shave yourself without a looking glass. Ridding yourself of the beard would alter your appearance, and if you do return to your wife, the comb may come in handy for sprucing up before you approach her." Sadness tinged the small smile which crossed her face.

James tried not to show the disappointment he felt at hearing her reference to his possible reunion with Margaret. He desperately wanted to see Sally but the hurt precipitated by her return to the lads at Hebe's overrode his desire.

James looked away and then followed the first part of the washerwoman's instructions. He donned the shirt. The addition of another piece of clothing added to the heat but he was grateful for her help. He forced the pants legs into his knee-high stockings, mounted the feeble horse and turned it toward the northwest. He looked down at the second woman who had tried to rescue him and felt a tenderness grow in his chest.

He smiled and said, "Thank you," as he leaned down to gently touch her face with his fingers. "Thank you for everything."

She blushed and looked away. "Godspeed, James Daunt. And the blessings of the Lord to guide you on your journey."

James pressed Old Caesar into a slow trot and left Pleasant Valley Farm. He turned to wave to the washerwoman but she had already picked up her skirts and was running back to the laundry.

He felt regret, interspersed with guilt, that he had never bothered to learn her given name.

James did not know how much time he had before the two men discovered he was no longer at Pleasant Valley. He hoped they would be temporarily detained by Thaddeus Goodenough's denial that he was the man in the handbill.

He was afraid to return to his former lodgings above the blacksmith's shop. The city, to the east, was the place of his birth and youth and an obvious refuge. It was an impractical choice, however, as the roadways were heavily traveled making it difficult to avoid detection if word of a reward had been widely circulated. He decided to go north as he had no known connections in that direction.

He urged Old Caesar onto a path which followed the perimeter of the community's property. Its existence was partially hidden by a stand of trees, and although its packed surface had been worn smooth by many Saturday shopping trips to the neighboring village, it was rarely used during the week.

As he neared the edge of town, James veered off to the west and circled around on an old cow path. He followed it until the village was far behind him and he saw a dirt crossroad ahead. He pulled Old Caesar to a stop. He had to make a decision.

James needed a destination. He had left the dining room without eating and he was hungry. More importantly, he had no money. He felt confident he could make enough to feed himself by doing day chores, but he needed to find a place where he would be safe. A place where there would be no posters, no men in the employ of Squire Holt's family.

When he had left the army, he had visited the home of one of the men in his company, a fellow blacksmith who lived on a large farm upcountry. James could not remember a village, or even a store, in the area. His friend travelled between farms performing his services as they were needed. Perhaps he had need of a helping hand.

The sun was on the ascent, signaling midmorning, and his belly was grumbling. He ignored his hunger and set about initiating his next move. Glancing again at the sun, he reaffirmed his original decision to head north. He flicked the reins, turned right at the junction of the two lanes and gave Old Caesar his head while he tried to work out a plan.

James had settled into his new life at Pleasant Valley Farm, and in that utopian environment, had been able to suppress memories of his past and to avoid thoughts of his future. Now on the run again, he realized how foolish he had been to assume he was safe in the community. He had come to believe that Sally could protect him from the outside world but wondered, in retrospect, if she would have had any more influence than her mother when it came to harboring an assassin.

He was angry with Sally for returning to her old ways, and at the same time, he was struck by the physical pain the thought of her brought to his chest, the sadness that accompanied his anguish. It was true, her uninhibited sexual prowess had intrigued him at first, but as time went on, it was her intelligence and intuitive nature that stimulated him and made her the centerpiece of his reformation.

James thought about the love he had allowed himself to give to Sally. It was a love founded on trust; a trust forged that day in the woods when he put his life in her hands; a trust she violated when she left him to cavort with the lads. Now, bristling from hurt, he chastised himself for committing so completely to the relationship.

Attempting to regain his self-respect, James turned his thoughts to Margaret and remembered the washerwoman's advice to go back to his wife. Impulsively, he pulled the old horse to a halt. Margaret. For the first time since his encounter with Sally on the rocks next to the creek, James missed his wife. He refused to acknowledge the suspicion that his reborn attraction to her was motivated by his need to purge Sally from his life. Instead, he mentally molded his nascent longing for her into an illusion of desire. Hoping to eradicate the hurt Sally had inflicted on him, he elected to take a chance and go south to Margaret. Months had passed, and as he had now been spotted northwest of the scene of his crime, he reasoned that folks would expect him to continue fleeing in that direction.

James did not know how long it would take to reach the farm where his wife lived with her sisters. His horse was old and he would have to negotiate rough paths and overgrown fields to avoid detection. Before changing direction, he dismounted and led Old Caesar to drink from a small stream which ran through the trees bordering the north-south road. Afterwards, he tied his horse to a low-hanging branch, dipped his hands into the water and splashed it on his face and neck. He caught a glimpse of his reflection in the rippling water and considered using the washerwoman's razor.

Sally's words, "I love the scratchy feel of your hair on my skin," resonated in his head and the pain of her betrayal girdled his chest. He thrust his face into the stream. The cold water settled him. He shook his head, stood, and appreciated the cooling effect of the water as it dripped off his hair and stained his two shirts. His hunger returned and he searched for berries near the bank of the stream. Finding nothing, he stirred Old Caesar, and remaining on foot, led him back into the sun. An Indian summer heat was upon the fading fields and James chose to walk alongside his aged mount as he knew the old horse would suffer with a rider on his back. He passed the edge of the community lands before the farmers returned from the noon meal.

When Thaddeus Goodenough realized Sally and James were both missing from the community, he went to the laundry.

"Did they leave together?" He saw no reason to identify the individuals he sought.

Sally's mother was hanging wash on a line which was strung between two trees. There was a breeze, and in spite of his inner turmoil, the smell of freshly washed linens pleased the reverend's sensibilities.

"No. Sarah's gone back to her old haunts and James left to avoid capture by the two men who came here looking for him."

"How long have you known that he is James Daunt and not James Morley?"

"Not long. I, of course, knew he was not related to my family but it wasn't until Sally slipped one day and I recognized his name from the gossip I hear."

"Why didn't you tell me?"

"I didn't want to hurt her."

"Does she love him?"

"As much as she can, I suppose."

"They will find him, you know."

"Yes."

"Was...." He hesitated before asking the question that had been on his mind since he read the advertisement for James Daunt's capture. "Was she involved?"

"Only in bringing him here. Not in his crime."

"I see." Thaddeus Goodenough turned and left the laundry. His shoulders were hunched and his head bowed. Tears came to the woman's eyes as she felt his despair.

James' progress was slow and the sun's rays were hot. As the day slipped away, however, the heat was tempered by the cool fall breezes which commonly arose on a late September afternoon. Still drenched in sweat from the hours he had spent on unsheltered farm paths, James stopped under a single tree which grew next to a field of corn.

He tied Old Caesar to one of the limbs and shed the two shirts he had been wearing. The coarse gray blouse of sturdy, close-woven fabric had trapped his perspiration in its durable threads, while the shirt Sally's mother had given him was of light-weight muslin and more forgiving. Unfortunately, its black color absorbed the heat and added to his discomfort. He hung the two shirts and his hat on the tree.

The last time James had spread his clothes out to dry, was the worst day of his life. At the same time, it was the beginning of the happiest, most positive time he had ever experienced. He had to admit that, in addition to Sally, he was going to miss the community. He liked the people. Quite improbably, he realized he would also miss little things like the etchings which hung on the walls of the dining room and down the long halls of the main building. They were depictions of European cities, classical ruins and famous paintings, some of which he recognized from his days at the Academy when Mr. Thomason lectured on the necessity of a gentleman having knowledge of great art. The stately art enthusiast believed all of his students would have the opportunity to study abroad and he assiduously prepared them for the day they sailed from America to immerse themselves in the grandeur of the great European cities. In truth, many of his pupils were the sons of craftsmen who began their apprenticeships long before they were old enough to visit the fatherlands of their sires.

Life at Pleasant Valley Farm had reintroduced James to the rewards of higher learning. Again, he berated himself for sliding onto the indolent path he had so apathetically followed since being removed from the Academy. His mental breast-beating ended when the memory of Squire Holt falling from his horse supplanted his lesser transgressions and he forced them all from his mind.

He touched his still damp shirts. The black one was almost dry but his work shirt was still too wet to wear. He planned to travel through the night and did not want clammy material sticking to his back. He rotated the shirts toward the sun before he sat down under the shady side of the tree. His horse had been watered at their last stop, and during their walk, had frequently munched on available grass to calm his belly. James, unfortunately, had not been able to find his next meal and hunger pains assailed his stomach.

Early in his flight, he had passed fields ripe with squash but had not picked one for fear of being seen. He regretted his decision as he glanced over at the stalks of corn in the nearby field. He did not relish eating uncooked corn but it would have to do.

He leaned back against the tree and reflected on the many times he had turned to sleep as an escape; he marveled at the fact that he had not dozed once since his arrival at Pleasant Valley. There was too much to do in a day and he derived great pleasure from his varied activities.

Now, however, he was simply marking time until he could continue on his journey. Reverting to his old ways, James stretched out on the hard earth, closed his eyes and slept.

Esther pulled the bedclothes up around her neck and lay very still. A flock of migrating geese flew overhead and their honking told her they were landing in the fields. There was plenty for them to eat. Every year, remnants of harvested wheat and corn drew the hungry travelers to the ground. Soon, as one body, they would lift off and continue their flight south.

She heard the sounds of a large wagon as it approached on its return from the market. The farmer was going home early.

"He's had a good day," she thought, as she listened to the empty wagon bounce along, jerking side to side, without a heavy load to steady the wheels when they hit the bumps and potholes. The everyday sound of the passing wagon comforted Esther. It summoned memories of a normal life; one that she knew was gone forever.

A puff of cool air crossed her face. It reminded her of the winter to come and her body chilled at the thought. She resented the breeze which continued to drift over her chest and legs. She wanted to close the window and stop the unwelcome onslaught.

Esther rarely left her bed except to relieve herself, and as the chamber pot sat nearby, she had no need to walk without support. She could draw the curtains together without leaving the bed but the top of the sash was beyond her reach.

Esther dropped her legs over the side of the bed and stretched her feet to the floor. She held onto the bedpost and pulled herself to standing. She stood for a moment then let loose her hold and took a step. Her knee buckled and she cried out as she fell to the floor.

"Esther? Esther, you all right?" She heard Elias call to her.

"I've fallen." She shouted as loud as she could but her verbal appeal was thin, muffled even to her ears.

"Can't understand you. I'm coming up." She heard him stop in midstride. A horse whinnied outside the window. "Keep alert, Esther. I think something's moving over by Daunt's horse."

Esther knew that, in spite of Elias' perpetual preoccupation with the capture of his brother-in-law, help was on the way. She lay unmoving on the floor and did not even attempt to muster the strength to stand on her own. She felt completely dependent on Elias for her survival in this new reality she had been forced to accept.

"What you doing on my land?"

Visions of Sally had dominated James' dream but the words which awakened him were not the taunting, sexually-charged challenge of the woman in his reverie. Rather, what James heard was an accusation spit out in a crusty male voice, hoarse from tobacco, threatening in intent.

James sat up in a panic. Leaning over him was a massive man. The lower part of his face was covered by a long, sandy-colored beard. A full head of like-hued hair hung low on his forehead and joined with extraordinarily heavy bright red eyebrows which partially obscured pale blue eyes. He had an over-developed torso and arms so powerful the veins appeared to strain from exertion even though his hands hung free at his side.

"I've been on a long trip." James spoke defensively. "My horse is old. I'm giving him a rest." James struggled to his feet, suddenly conscious of his bare chest.

"It's hot and my shirts are wet." He pointed to the shirts on the tree. "I'm allowing them to dry."

The man stared at him through half-closed eyes.

"Your name James Daunt?"

The shock of his words caused James to stagger backwards. As he regained his balance, he said, "James Morley." He tried to recover, "My name is James Morley. You startled me. I was well asleep and dreaming when you woke me."

"You fit the description on the handbill." The man walked around him. "Clothes are different but you look like me. And it says you be a blacksmith just like me."

James stared in disbelief. He did, indeed, look like the man who confronted him. They were both of the same height and coloring; both had the brawny body and red face of a blacksmith. However, the man who stood in front of him carried a third again more bulk. James was intimidated by his size.

"Two men. They came by yesterday. Tried to take me to jail for killin' someone. I told 'em I weren't gonna lose a day's work. Refused to go." He laughed. "They left when I picked one of 'em off the ground and hung him from the ceiling of the barn. On a meat hook." His smile vanished and a frown united his enormous shaggy eyebrows.

"They'll be back if they don't find the murderer." He stared hard at James. "You'd do just as good. If I was to turn you in, it'd keep 'em away from me." He started to move closer.

The truth of what was happening struck James and he reacted quickly. He grabbed at the black shirt, yanked it off the tree limb and jumped sideways to avoid his attacker. He turned and ran back to the path he had been following. He gambled on the fact that the man's weight would slow him and he could outrun him. He was right about the weight, but he had forgotten about Old Caesar. As James raced away, he could hear the horse's hooves gaining on him. He heard the man shouting, "Faster, you old nag, faster."

James pushed himself even harder. He could smell the aged horse's rancid breath as his adversary closed in on him. Then, all of a sudden, the horse sneezed. James heard the man curse as Old Caesar came to an abrupt stop and sneezed a second time. The massive body of the blacksmith flew over the horse's lowered head and crashed onto the path. James stopped running and looked back. Old Caesar stood over the motionless man and sneezed again. The exhausted horse raised his eyes, glanced at James, and with a gentle toss of his head and a final snort, slowly collapsed on top of his abusive rider.

Cautiously, James approached the bodies and knelt down. He put his hand on the neck of the horse. There was no pulse. Warily, he touched the blacksmith. Again, there was no sign of life. He had no idea where the man lived, if he had a family or whether someone would miss him. He had a momentary bout of guilt. This was the second man who had died as a result of his actions. The guilt did not last, however. James realized that if the blacksmith had survived when he fell from Old Caesar, he, inevitably, would have taken him prisoner and he would now be on his way to incarceration in the county jail.

It occurred to James that this was a genuine stroke of luck. If, indeed, the men searching for him thought the dead blacksmith was James Daunt, he might, for the moment, be in the clear. He retraced his steps, retrieved his community shirt and black hat from the tree and walked over to the field where the corn stalks grew high. He picked three ears, shucked them, hid the husks in amongst the crop and bit into the raw kernels. They were tough but it had been almost twenty-four hours since he had eaten and he was famished.

The nights were the hardest times for Margaret. After supper, Hannah and Bettina sat on the porch or in the parlor and did handwork or read aloud to each other. She was not invited to join them. During the day, her sisters were forced to speak to her. There were chores to be done and meals to be shared. Occasionally, they forgot she was an outcast and the three of them chatted and laughed together as they had in the past. When the early autumn sun set, however, and the house was dark, Margaret sat alone and wondered what had happened to James and what would happen to her.

Few neighbors continued to call and when they did, Margaret was relegated to the kitchen or bedroom. Except when the visitor was Nehemiah Trimble. He always asked for Margaret, and when he was in the parlor, her spinster siblings, each with an eye out for an unattached male, relented and included her in the festivities.

# *Friday, September 26, 1828*

With the loss of Old Caesar, James was forced to continue his trip entirely on foot. Night came and clouds drifted across the sky, intermittently blocking the moonlight and rendering night travel arduous and unpredictable.

Deep ruts, debris, large and small stones made walking in the dark challenging. Many times during the night, he stumbled or lost his balance when he stepped on a wayward object in, or alongside, the road. There was little traffic, and with no other adventurers on foot, James was able to stay on the main roads. The few times travelers passed by, the sounds of their horses' hooves and carriage wheels gave advance warning and he was able to throw himself onto the ground or grope through the underbrush for concealment. He was quite sure he had not been detected.

The early morning sky changed from black to gray and James recognized familiar territory. As he neared his destination, he acknowledged the increased danger of capture which confronted him.

He pulled his hat low over his eyes. He was acquainted with many of the farmers and knew they would be up and out in their barns before dawn and in the fields by sunup. Most of the land had been cleared for cultivation by these hardworking men, and healthy trees were at a minimum. Without woods, he had nowhere to hide. His only hope was to reach Margaret before he was seen.

When he came to the familiar bend in the road near Maris' tenant house, James turned right and cut across a narrow meadow. A small barn which harbored the lone cow and single horse his brother-in-law provided for his dependent sisters lay ahead of him. Glancing around, he saw no signs of life, and in an effort to avoid detection, he hunched low and began to sprint toward the shelter.

Daily, Margaret rose before the sun. As the only member of the household without a means of support, she was resigned to rising early in order to perform some of the menial chores her siblings assigned her in exchange for her room and board. She had been the pampered favorite in her childhood home and recognized the satisfaction her comeuppance brought to her siblings. Innate friction, born of youthful jealousies, was intensified by the infamous disgrace of her husband and it pervaded the daily relations between Margaret and her sisters.

The situation was compounded by the fact that Margaret was not a naturally resourceful woman and chores frequently had to be explained each time they were assigned. She was a slow starter and easily distracted and there were times when Bettina and Hannah gave up and did the work themselves as getting their sister to complete a job was simply too difficult a task. Her spotty performance led to further frustration and resulted in additional resentment. Life in the small house was stressful.

As Margaret's previously easy-going disposition began to sour, she layered her disappointment onto memories of her life with James. She came to accept that her marriage had been a mistake and she should have considered Nehemiah Trimble's proposal even though she had already given herself to James.

This particular morning, she chose to dress by the faint light which came in the window. She dropped her petticoat over her undergarment and covered it with a loose-fitting smock which she tied close to her body with the strings of her muslin apron.

Something caught her eye as she bent to slip her shoes onto her feet. She straightened and peered out the window. A man, his face obscured by a large, wide-brimmed, black hat, was running across the meadow toward the barn.

Margaret's heart pounded in her chest. "James," she uttered his name aloud. A familiar thrill, brought on by the remembrance of her fun-loving husband, coursed through her body and erased all thoughts of life with the reliable, but dull, Nehemiah.

Was it possible? When she first learned of his flight, she had wholeheartedly believed in James' innocence and prayed for his return. Now, with so many people convinced of his guilt, she feared for his safety.

Her next thought was of the negative impact his return would have on her life: If caught, his trial would command the attention of the county for a long time to come. Whether he was proved innocent or not, she would never escape the disgrace of being married to a suspected murderer. She pushed the pessimistic possibilities aside as the reality of James' return supplanted her doubts. He was here and she could not wait to go to him.

Her first chores of the day were to milk the cow and gather the eggs from the henhouse. Fortunately, the cow was in the barn and she could start there. Her sisters rarely rose before she returned from doing her chores and she was particularly quiet as she moved around her room. She was certain Bettina and Hannah would raise an alarm if they learned James was on the property. She did not want to lose her husband to the sheriff because of her carelessness.

Margaret finished putting on her shoes, tiptoed across the room, opened her door and approached the stairs.

Hannah, unable to sleep, had risen while it was still dark. She could hear Margaret moving around in the next room. Instead of dressing and proceeding to the kitchen as was her wont, she had lingered by the window and watched as the black sky of a sporadically moonless night gave way to the reluctant arrival of dawn. Clouds, which obliterated the first pale rays of early morning light, broke apart and allowed narrow ribbons of subtle pastel colors to emerge. Reluctant harbingers of a dreary day, the dark clouds soon reunited, and once again, obscured the glow of sunrise.

Dawn made Hannah sad. She was still young and would like to marry but did not want an old man like Esther's husband, Elias, or a ne'er-do-well like James Daunt. She actively nourished her hopes of finding the perfect mate and dawn brought with it the awareness she was able to sidestep during her nocturnal musings: The years were passing and the unmarried male population was dwindling.

As she continued to stare at the changing sky, Hannah noticed a movement in the field. She leaned forward and concentrated on the sight of a running figure in a broad-brimmed, black hat. She initially thought it was Maris and wondered why he was on foot. Then she had taken a closer look. The gait and bearing were familiar. She was certain that the man in her view was her brother-in-law, James Daunt, and the furtive sounds of Margaret's cautious exit from her room indicated that she, too, was aware of his arrival.

Bettina was awakened by the soft sounds of Margaret's tiptoed footsteps on the stairs. She raised her head and listened closely as she noticed a difference in her sister's tread. It was softer, more considerate than usual. She resented Margaret's ingrained insensitivity and credited it to the advantage of having an attractive face.

Bettina, who had been pretty as a child, had come to resemble both Esther and Margaret in maturity. She had Esther's harsh countenance, but where her oldest sister's features were sharp-edged and angular, Bettina's were soft like Margaret's. The combination made her appear weak and ineffectual. Over the years, she had developed a personality which conformed to her appearance and people rarely paid much attention to her.

She had a curious nature, however, and as a result, she remained alert, relaxing only after she heard the faint grating sound of the wrought-iron bolt as it was pulled open on the door at the bottom of the stairs. Then she returned to her bed, satisfied that the morning milking was the impetus behind her sister's odd behavior.

James was relieved when he reached the barn. Cautiously, he pushed on the weathered, wooden door, slipped through the opening and slowly pulled the door shut. Once inside the barn, he climbed the ladder to the small loft and collapsed on a pile of loose hay.

He lay back, closed his eyes and tried to think of ways to contact Margaret but he could not hold a thought. He had been walking for a good part of the last twenty-four hours. The stress of his journey and the lack of rest caught up with him and he immediately fell into a deep sleep.

Trembling with excitement, Margaret entered the cluttered space of the barn where various pieces of farm equipment and a small cart vied for interior space. Two stalls and bales of hay lined the outside walls. A single horse looked up and followed her with its eyes as she neared its enclosure. It whinnied softly. She casually stroked its nose as she moved on to the lactating cow. She opened the gate, placed a bucket in the corner of the stall next to the milking stool and walked out, closing the gate behind her. The cow, anxious to be relieved of her morning production, mooed. Margaret ignored her.

She stood at the foot of the ladder which led to the loft and listened intently. She was relieved to hear sounds of snoring. She placed her foot on the first rung and began her ascent. She poked her head through the hole in the floor and looked at the sleeping man whose breathing had increased to a loud wheeze followed by short gasps for breath. She had heard James make similar noises when he was exhausted from work, or she thought dismally, worn out after a long night at Hebe Balderston's.

She pulled herself up into the loft and thanked the Lord for the smell of sweat rather than rum.

*James bit into a glossy piece of taffy he picked from the wooden bowl on Esther's table. He relished the rich, sweet flavor of molasses as he sunk his teeth into the chewy delicacy. His fingers were greasy; they were coated with butter and he reached for another glob of the sticky confection. He worked it into a malleable slab. He found a knife and cut the taffy into small pieces. He was hungry. He popped a second piece, then a third, into his mouth before he had finished the first.*

*There was a door to his right and he heard voices behind it. Men's voices. He did not understand what they were saying but the tone of their conversation was threatening. He looked down and realized he was clad only in his worn cotton underdrawers and tattered boots.*

*His trousers were on the back of a chair. He eased his way over to the chair and sat down. He started to draw the woolen garment over his heavy leather boots. The pant legs were too narrow and he struggled to remove the boots. They became tangled in his trousers and he tore at the fabric to free his feet which were now bound together by his pants.*

*He chewed furiously on the taffy. It expanded and filled his mouth. He forced his jaw open, reached in and pulled on the substance. It no longer tasted like molasses. It was dry and grainy, like chalk. The more he pulled, the more his mouth filled. His teeth became embedded in the mass. It hardened and he could not open his mouth.*

*His hands were covered with taffy which stuck to the trousers as he pulled at them. He was trapped. He sat, alone, bare-chested, in his knee-length drawers, with his hands and feet bound by the legs of his woolen pants.*

*The door opened and a voice said, "James. It is you."*

He threw his left leg to the side of his bed of hay and jerked himself out of his nightmare to look into the familiar face of his wife as she whispered, "James. It actually is you."

"Margaret," he gasped. His heart was pounding while his teeth and lower part of his face throbbed from the intensity of his jaw-clenching hallucination.

"Margaret," he repeated, this time with relief as he realized there were no men behind her and the voices had been part of his terrifying dream.

His wife leaned down and brushed his hair from his forehead. She traced the outline of his face with her finger and smoothed his cheeks with the back of her hand. She knelt beside him, laid her head on his chest and cautiously curled her body next to his. She jumped slightly when she felt her breasts touch his arm and delicately pulled back. She cared deeply for James but had never recovered from the shock of their first coupling.

Throughout their clandestine courtship, James had curtailed his overtures. He had stroked her arm and caressed her hair. He had kissed her lightly and spoken of his love with sincerity. One day, he had tentatively fondled her breasts. She had pulled back then, as she did now, but having been introduced to erotic pleasure, she ultimately relaxed and waited for his hand to return. She had closed her eyes and allowed herself to be lulled into a euphoric state which increased in intensity as his hand moved to explore other parts of her body. Before she knew what was occurring, he had gently urged her back on the grass and lowered his body onto hers. She had experienced an uncontrollable emotional response to his passionate release but at the same time, was repulsed by the physical intimacy of their union. After he left her side, Margaret vowed she would never permit a man to get that close to her again.

That was before she and her mother visited Dr. Samuel Baker. That was before her unplanned marriage of convenience. That was before she realized that, in spite of her inherent dread of the intimacy of the marriage bed, she really did love James Daunt. That was before the loss of her babies, the loss of her home, the humiliation of Maris' charity, the filing of murder charges against James, the embarrassment of his flight which seemed to prove his guilt. That was before she had become enslaved to her vindictive siblings.

Hannah glanced at Bettina's door as she exited her room. There were no signs that her sister had risen and Hannah, treading carefully, made her way down the stairs and out of the house. She walked through the scraggly grass to the barn door. She slowly pushed on it and squeezed through the narrow opening she created.

The cow heard her and mooed a second protest. Hannah stopped and stood still. There was no other noise in the barn. She moved to the base of the ladder which led to the loft. She cocked her head and listened. She could just make out the whispered conversation being carried on in the loft above her.

"Where have you been?" Margaret asked.

"At a farm." James answered without further explanation.

Hannah heard enough to confirm her suspicions that the man in the barn was, indeed, her brother-in-law. Gambling that the reunited lovers were engrossed in each other and oblivious to her activities, she went to the stall which held the solitary horse.

She cautiously picked the bridle off the wall, opened the half-door and went inside. She slipped the reins over the horse's head, put the bit between his lips, and pulled the bridle up and over his ears. Praying he wouldn't balk or neigh, she led him out onto the hard-packed floor and to the back of the barn. Hannah opened the rear door, and with the horse in tow, left the building. She looked over her shoulder to make sure James and Margaret had not heard her, then she shot a quick glance at the house to see if Bettina was in sight.

Assured she had not been detected, Hannah hurried to the road where she stopped by a sawed-off tree trunk. She ascertained that no one was in the area before she self-consciously raised her skirts to her waist and clambered onto the decomposing remnant. She balanced on her left leg and swung her right leg over the bare back of the horse. She clasped his neck and pulled herself into a seated position. She urged him into a walk and left the farm behind her. As soon as she was out of hearing distance, she accelerated him into a gallop.

Still smarting from the injustice of Maris' theft of her father's estate, Hannah headed for Esther's home. There was a reward on James Daunt's head and she intended to get a part of it for herself. She knew she could not capture her brother-in-law without help and decided that, if she had to share the money, Esther and Elias would be more grateful than Maris.

"Where have you been?" Margaret asked the question again.

"At a farm upcountry." James repeated his answer and added a vague reference to the location of the farm.

"We don't know anyone who lives upcountry," Margaret mused. "Why did you go there?"

James, immediately sorry that he had hinted at the location of his refuge, tried to think of an acceptable explanation. He closed his eyes; he was too tired to be clever.

He waited a moment and then said, "I will tell you the whole story when I sort it out, Margaret. Actually," he decided to lie. "I was visiting another blacksmith, a man I knew when I was in the army."

"What is going to happen to you, James?" Margaret raised her head and stared at her husband.

Still unsettled by his nightmare, and defenseless against his wife's probing, James continued to hide behind his tightly sealed eyelids.

"I don't know, Margaret, I do not know."

He sighed, stretched his arm and moved it under her raised head. He bent his elbow and let his hand fall softly alongside her breast. He pretended not to notice as she shuddered at his touch. He was used to that kind of response from the pretty woman who lay next to him.

James thought of Sally and how different she was from Margaret. Where James had forced himself to be cautious in his lovemaking with Margaret, Sally relished his aggressive approach and responded with exciting propositions of her own. A union with her was exhilarating, provocative, stimulating, and contrasted sharply with the tentative, dispassionate response his overtures elicited from Margaret.

He opened his eyes, looked at his wife and wondered why he had gambled so heavily to revisit his old life.

Then he remembered Sally's defection and admitted to the spite which had fueled his return.

Sally sat astride her horse as he carefully picked his way along the rough path bordering the bank of the creek. When she reached the familiar grouping of large rocks which surrounded her ledge, she dismounted and tied him to a tree. She stepped over the loose stones and fallen branches which had accumulated around the site and climbed down to the flat, stone shelf which overlooked the water. The sun had warmed the rock and as she sat, arms holding her knees close to her chest, she welcomed its heat. She closed her eyes and memories of her visits to this special spot crowded each other and vied for her favor.

James was the only man she had known on the ledge. Her other visits had been solitary, spent in thought. She had been here when she first admitted to herself that some of Thaddeus' actions contradicted, rather than reinforced, the word of the Lord which he so readily championed. In this same spot, she had questioned, and later denied, the existence of God. Over time, she had constructed and embraced a convoluted moral code that allowed her to roam from Pleasant Valley in search of physical gratification and emancipation from the psychological detritus of her youth. She developed a strong sense of personal independence as it was no longer necessary to justify her actions to a higher power or fear an afterlife in purgatory.

Sally jumped as her reverie was interrupted by the unannounced arrival of Hebe Balderston's problem solver.

"You seek the wisdom of a healer." The Indian woman's statement was presented as a fact not a question.

"Yes," Sally struggled to her feet. "I think so. Yes." She spoke hesitantly as she evaluated the blanket-wrapped woman who stood on the rock above her. "I need help with a," Sally flushed as she searched for an acceptable definition, "personal problem."

The stranger, who had appeared monumental in size as she imperially commanded Sally's attention from above, proved to be small in stature when she stood on the ledge.

Her wizened face was marked by a myriad of deep furrows, v-shaped between her eyebrows and bow-shaped on either side of her mouth. They fanned out from the corners of her heavy-lidded eyes and crisscrossed her forehead and cheeks. Her resemblance to an ancient tortoise summoned its mythical association with great wisdom. Sally alternated between trust in Hebe's recommendation and misgivings about the advice of a native witch doctor.

"Sit." The woman lowered herself onto the ledge and indicated the spot where Sally was to take a seat.

"You have baby growing in belly." Again, a statement. "You want to rid body of baby."

"Yes." Sally's cheeks felt the heat of embarrassment or humiliation. She was not sure which emotion had inflamed her face.

"I have herbs," the woman said.

Sally had heard wild stories of women who had taken herbs to rid themselves of a pregnancy. Some of the remedies had brought death to the prospective mother, others disfigurement or mental retardation to the child. She shook her head negatively.

"My herbs are safe."

The woman put her hand on Sally's and held it still. The heat from the gnarled fingers warmed and soothed her skin. Sally felt herself relax. She began to trust the mysterious native spiritualist.

The old woman removed her hand, reached under her blanket and brought forth three small soiled leather bags, each tied with a length of gut.

The calming effect of the woman's touch subsided and Sally's stomach turned at the sight of the sacs. Despite the philosophical freedom she had gained with her banishment of the reinterpreted god of her father and her rejection of traditional Christian lore, she instinctively feared the ingestion of a pagan concoction.

"Is safe. Not only for Indian women. Many white women come to me."

Sally swallowed hard and asked, "What must I do?"

"I mix tea for you," the shaman said. "Then you drink."

"Now? Here?" Sally looked around her.

This place, which had brought her solace during times of trouble, and great pleasure when she had lain with James Daunt, now took on a sinister air. She had no doubts about her decision to terminate the pregnancy. She had, however, serious fears concerning the consumption of an unwashed seer's poison.

"No need to wait. You drink now and come back tomorrow. Eat nothing. You take potion instead of food. Come again third day and you be rid of problem."

Sally thought for a moment then said, "I must return to my home before I take your medicine. I will come again in three days."

"As you wish. Cannot wait too long. I not give tea to woman who waits too long."

Sally scrambled up the side of the rock to the top of the bank. She looked back. The woman sat motionless on the ledge, her arms raised to the sky, her head bent back, her eyes closed. Sally could hear the chanting start as she mounted her horse and headed back to the road which ran past Elias Latch's farm.

"What's going to happen to you, James?" It was the third time Margaret had posed the question and the third time James had responded with "I do not know." He had forgotten her annoying habit of asking the same question over and over

In the past, he had resorted to making up simple answers but there were times when that would not do and the questioning would continue. The queries were rarely of consequence although this particular question was very important and he really did not know what he was going to do next.

"Margaret," James said as he removed his arm from under her head, "I have not eaten since the day before yesterday. Can you get me some food?"

"I don't know," Margaret spoke slowly. "Maris gives us little money, and since your disappearance, I've had nothing to offer toward the expenses." She instantly regretted reminding James of their unfortunate circumstances and vowed not to let him know the sisters limited her access to the pantry.

"Each day, we parcel out our food so I will have to be careful," she lied. Then she brightened. "It's my job to milk the cow and gather the eggs. I can get you milk, and as long as the hens are not off their feed, I can save out one or two eggs to mix in with it.

"It's Bettina's job to prepare the noon meal," she continued. "If I offer to help I may be able to get some bread, and" she smiled, "perhaps, a bit more." She kissed him lightly on the cheek, stood, smoothed her skirt and looked down at him.

"It's good to have you here, James. I have worried so."

She climbed down the ladder and James realized the closest he had come to lovemaking had been a casual hand laid next to her breast. Which, he thought ruefully, she had immediately rejected.

Margaret retrieved her milk pail and set about relieving the unhappy cow. When she finished, she picked up a small bottle which she found in a corner outside the stall. It looked clean so she filled it half-way with fresh milk and placed it next to the lower rung of the ladder.

Afraid that she would soon be missed, Margaret ran to the henhouse. She collected the eggs and wrapped them in her apron.

She hurried back to the barn where she broke two eggs into the bottle. She shook the mixture until the yolks and whites had blended with the milk. She carried the bottle up to the loft, placed it next to her dozing husband and immediately descended the ladder. She gathered her milk and eggs, left the barn and walked toward the house.

Bettina, wondering about Margaret's strange behavior, kept glancing out of her window. She noted her sister's trips between the henhouse and the barn. Her curiosity faded, however, when she saw Margaret returning to the house. Satisfied that things were back to normal, Bettina tiptoed into the hall and past Hannah's bedroom on her way to the kitchen. She never noticed that the door was slightly ajar and the room was empty.

Hannah slid from the bare back of Maris' conciliatory gift horse and tied the reins to a fence rail in front of Esther's farmhouse. An aged, sway-backed stallion was tethered to the hitching post. It contrasted sharply with Elias' proud bay which was standing free in the paddock. Taking a second look, she recognized the sad, old horse as the one belonging to James Daunt. Hannah wondered why it was not behind the fence with the bay and suspected the crafty mind of Elias Latch had positioned it there as an attractive lure for his fugitive brother-in-law.

She mounted the three steps to the small landing and knocked on the door of the house. There was no answer and no sound of nearby footsteps. She knocked again and looked up at the single window on the second floor. It was slightly open at the bottom. There was no movement, no verbal acknowledgement of her presence.

She took a step back and called, "Esther. Esther, are you there? It's me, Hannah. I need to see Elias. It is important."

Hannah heard a muffled grunt. She had not seen Esther since shortly after her accident and had forgotten the flawed speech which rendered unintelligible the single-word response of her older sister.

"Elias' horse is here. Is he?" Hannah called up to the window. "Is he in the field? May I wait inside?"

There was no answer.

"Esther, I'm coming in." Hannah pressed down on the latch and cautiously pushed her way into the room.

She was shocked by what she saw. The unswept floor was covered with bits of hay brought in from the barn and clumps of dried mud from the barren areas which surrounded it. Once pristine flat surfaces were obscured by debris and dust. Work clothes hung on the backs of chairs; a few dishes and cooking utensils soiled by leftover food lay on the table. The unmistakable smell of rotting animal and vegetable matter was overwhelming.

Something was terribly wrong. Hannah wondered how long it had been since Esther had seen the kitchen and how Elias could ignore the filth. She was tempted to turn back, to run, to let someone else discover the reason for the abominable conditions. Concern for Esther, combined with morbid curiosity, motivated her to step through the clutter and head for the narrow stairs which led to the upper floor. The cramped stairwell was too narrow for a handrail so she dragged her palm along the wall in order to keep her balance during the steep climb.

"Esther?" she queried, when she reached the top step.

The bedroom was in the same unkempt condition as the kitchen and the offensive odor was even stronger. The acrid tang of urine blended with the terminal stench of decay and burned her nostrils.

The curtains of one window were completely closed while those on the side window gapped open at the bottom allowing in a small shaft of light. Grimy bedclothes covered one side of a heavily-spotted mattress and lay in a high heap which stretched full length from the top to the bottom of the bed. Linens and a few pieces of clothing dangled from the corners of half-closed drawers in a tall, narrow chest which had been squeezed into a corner. Assorted additional items were scattered next to a small, open trunk.

The pile of bedclothes moved and Hannah watched as a withered arm reached over and pulled tight the curtains of the side window. The dimly-lit room faded to near darkness.

"Esther?" she asked again. "It's too dark. I can't see and I can't breathe. I have to open the window and pull back the curtains."

Hannah walked past the foot of the bed and the smell increased. She covered her nose with her hand and reached to open the window. She tripped over something on the floor, flung out her arm to stop her fall and accidentally pulled the rod and curtain from the wall.

"What is this?" she asked, as the light fell on a large bundle resting against the toe of her shoe. She wiped her eyes in an attempt to clarify what lay before her. She made out worn boots, a pair of overalls, a faded blue shirt, and she gasped, the grotesque death mask of a man who had died in excruciating pain.

Her hands flew to her mouth when she saw the dark brownish-red stain which surrounded the handle of a large knife that pierced the front of the man's shirt. Hannah recoiled as she identified the body as that of Elias Latch, husband of Esther, the woman who lay stationary and uncommunicative under the filthy pile of linens.

The bedclothes moved again and Hannah jumped back. She stared, horrified, as her sister pushed away the coverings. Always sharp-featured, Esther's face was now bone-thin. Her eyes were submerged deep in sooted sockets; her complexion, a dark shade of ash; her skin, coarse and leathery; her lips, dry and brown. Her pitiful appearance bespoke the physical and mental deterioration she had endured.

She was a tortured, desecrated old hag whose nightdress, Hannah saw, was stained with the same brownish-red substance that covered the prostrate body of her deceased husband. Esther pointed to Elias' corpse and then stabbed her finger at the door while she shouted nonsensical syllables in a broken, hoarse voice.

Terrified, Hannah turned and ran from the room. Desperate gibberish, uttered with human inflections, followed her down the stairs and out the door. Incomprehensible tirades coming from the bedroom window assaulted her ears as she untied her horse, leapt onto his back and whipped him into a gallop.

She bore right when she reached the country road in front of Elias' house and headed away from the reality of Esther's disintegration. She beat wildly on the back of her bewildered mount until she realized she had no idea where she was headed or to whom she could turn. She pulled up and tried to clear her mind. James Daunt and the coveted reward were, for the moment, the furthest things from her mind.

Instead, she was overwhelmed by the probability that two members of her family might be murderers. She had no choice but to go to Maris. He and Bettina were the only ones left and Bettina would be of no help. Hannah did not want to go for the sheriff as her concern for Esther and her ghastly predicament was overshadowed by her own selfish desire to ward off the shame of another scandal.

The unspeakable horror of the bedroom scene spurred her to prod her horse into a canter and then to a gallop. She continued west until she reached the intersection with the Great Road. She turned to the left and headed south.

It had been early morning when she had slipped into the barn and verified it was, indeed, James Daunt who was in the loft with Margaret. It had taken about an hour to ride to Elias' farm. Still unable to believe what she had seen, she had no way of determining how much time she had spent in her brother-in-law's house.

The sun was nearing its noon position in the sky and Hannah prayed Maris would be at home eating his midday meal.

In spite of her feeble condition, Esther raised her body to a seated position. She had a mission and was determined to complete it. She sat quietly for a moment while she garnered the strength to push her legs over the right side of the bed. She grasped the bedpost with both hands and tried to put weight on her injured leg. She felt no pain, only a numb sensation as it gave way. Without thinking, she shifted her weight to her left leg. She was weak but the leg held true. She grasped the footboard and dragged herself, hand over hand, along the worn wooden support. Slowly, she made her way to Elias who lay feet first in front of her on the floor.

The sight of her husband's bloodied decaying body made her retch, but an obsessive desire to remove him from the room fed her resolve. Still holding on to the footboard, she leaned down, grasped his right foot and pulled. His body refused to move. Terrified by the probable consequences of Hannah's unexpected appearance, Esther was driven by the need to leave the house and to take Elias with her.

Her husband's corpse was stiff with rigor mortis and was impossible to budge while she was holding onto the bed. She loosened her grip and carefully lowered herself to her good knee. She reached forward and jerked on Elias' lifeless foot.

Laboring from a kneeling position, weight on her left knee, right leg dangling uselessly to the side, she painstakingly began to maneuver the dead man's remains into the center of the room. She backed away then yanked on his foot, repeating this effort, inch by inch, until she had moved him to the top of the stairway. Relying on the superhuman strength that comes from desperation, she pushed the rigid body down the steps. Slowly, she turned around, and still using only her left knee, backed down the stairs.

Esther reached the bottom of the narrow steps where her wasted physique proved to be an asset as she slid past Elias and dragged herself, once again, to the soles of his feet. She looked from the landing to the door on the far side of the keeping room; the distance between the two seemed interminable. Committed to completing her mission, she thanked God Elias was lean and the house was small.

Continuing her one-legged crawl, she pulled her husband's body to the door, only to find Hannah had slammed it tight when she left. Esther grasped the latch from her kneeling position, but did not have the strength to release it.

She reached for the small chair she had trusted so many weeks ago when she first struggled to cope with her injury and used it to pull herself to standing. She managed to trip the bolt and unlock the door. She dropped back to the floor. She was exhausted and obliged to rest before she tugged Elias across the threshold. She stopped again before she pushed his body to the edge of the landing where she left it.

Esther reached back through the doorway and grabbed the leg of the chair. It fell through the opening and she bounced it down the three steps to the ground. She followed it down the stairs and used the chair to pull herself to standing.

The barn lay on the other side of the paddock. Oblivious to the bruises on her left knee and the pain in her arms and shoulders, she leaned on the chair and laboriously hauled herself across the dirt. Esther had abandoned all reason. She was consumed by the need to bring the horse and wagon to the landing, collect Elias's body and drive away from the horror she fervently hoped she could leave behind.

Hannah was shaking as she stood on the front porch of the home Maris had inherited from her father. She did not know how he would react to her news. He had a terrible temper and the object of his wrath was, more often than not, the person at hand rather than the deserving party. She momentarily regretted her decision to bypass the sheriff. Then, admitting again to the added humiliation another scandal would bring, she tried to pull herself together.

Still trembling, she opened the door without knocking. She entered into the front parlor and crossed the small landing at the foot of the stairs which led to the second floor. She could hear the voices of the field hands who ate the midday meal with Maris and his wife, Delia. She hung back before entering the large keeping room.

"The fields are just about done, Mr. Hicks." The transient's voice was unfamiliar to Hannah although she immediately recognized the monotone of the next speaker.

"We'll be finished with the corn by day's end." Nehemiah Trimble wheezed as he spoke.

"Tomorrow will be our final day," Maris said. "We'll settle up after we bring in the last of the crops."

Silence followed Maris' pronouncement. For some of the men, his words meant the end of summer employment; for others, his message freed them to return to their own farms and finish their chores before fall turned to winter.

Hannah shuddered as the gruesome scene in Esther's bedroom supplanted the everyday farm talk of the men seated at the table. Straightening her shoulders, she stepped into the room. One of the workers saw her out of the corner of his eye and paused his fork before it reached his mouth. Others saw him hesitate and turned to find out what had caught his attention.

Maris and Delia, their eyes fixed on their plates, continued eating.

"Maris," Hannah stopped and took a deep breath. "It is most important I speak with you." Her voice broke as she spoke.

Her brother looked up, irritation replacing surprise as he identified her. Delia looked confused and she turned to her husband for guidance.

Hannah tried again, her voice muted by tension. "It's terribly important that I speak with you."

"What are you doing in my house, Hannah?" She realized it was her unannounced presence in his keeping room, rather than curiosity about the reason behind her journey, that had caught his attention.

"It is personal, Maris." She could barely speak she was so distressed. "You must...," she hesitated and then repeated her words. "You must listen to what I have to say." This time she was insistent.

"How dare you?" Maris' temper flared. Then he closed his mouth, stood and excused himself to his wife. He walked over to where Hannah waited. He took hold of her elbow, steered her out of the room and into the parlor.

"Wait here until I finish my meal." He glared at Hannah and returned to his dinner.

Hannah had not been in the front parlor since Maris had banished his two youngest sisters from their family home after the death of their father. It looked the same as she remembered.

She took a deep breath and absorbed the odor of pine which still lingered. For a brief moment, the horrors of the present were replaced by sweet memories of the past.

Hannah could still see her mother as she stuffed small cushions with pine needles before sewing them closed. As a special treat, she allowed her last-born child to place them on the overstuffed furniture where they kept the stale smell of an unused room at bay. It had been years since her mother died; her sister-in-law must have replenished the pillows.

The red velvet divan was still under the window to her left. Two green slipper chairs sat on either side of the fireplace and a tattered arm chair covered in faded brocade faced them. The old high chest, which had come from England with her pioneering ancestors, occupied the place of honor on the wall which faced the front door. Her father's desk still stood opposite the fireplace, positioned so the radiating warmth from the glowing logs soothed his bones on cold nights.

She had always loved this room. Although the children were forbidden to enter the parlor unless invited by their parents, Hannah had delighted in the hours she spent surreptitiously hiding behind the couch to escape the torment of her older siblings.

She blushed as she recalled leaving her sickbed and escaping to her sanctuary the day Esther brought James Daunt to the sofa. Mortified by her unexpected introduction to the carnal ways of men and women, she never told a soul what she had seen and heard that day. Years passed before she connected Esther's visit to Dr. Baker, or, for that matter, her oldest sister's subsequent rush to the altar, with the shenanigans on the divan.

Hannah tore herself from the past as Maris' footsteps resounded on the pine floor of the small hallway. Her ears pounded to the beat of her heart as he marched to her side and grasped her arm.

"What's this about?" He hissed. He squeezed her hard before releasing his grip.

"Stop, Maris." Her old fear of her brother and his uncontrolled rage returned and she desperately looked over at her former hiding place. He watched her and mocked her innate desire to avoid confrontation.

"You're no longer a child, Hannah, and there's no room for a grown woman behind the sofa."

Her head snapped around. How had he known of the coveted shelter of her youth?

"What is so important that you sneak into my home, interrupt my meal and disrupt the harvest?"

"It's Esther. And Elias." Her voice shook as her distrust of Maris superseded the urgency of her message. She took a deep breath and tried to calm the pounding in her head and chest.

"Sit down, Maris. This is a very serious problem and difficult to discuss when you are bullying me."

"I am not bullying you." Maris spoke firmly as he reluctantly moved to the couch. He sat down at the same time Hannah lowered her body onto the adjacent cushion.

Her anxiety, fed by her proximity to Maris, caused her to hyperventilate as she started at the beginning.

"In the first place," she paused to take another deep breath, "James Daunt has returned. He's hiding in the loft of our barn."

The shocked look which passed over her brother's face caused her to gasp for breath. She started to shake again and clasped her hands together before she resumed her revelation.

"Margaret knows he's there and is helping him."

Maris leapt to his feet and started to leave the room. "I'll gather the men. We have to ride immediately before he moves on."

"Maris! Wait!"

The commanding tone of Hannah's voice startled her as well as her brother.

No longer shaking, Hannah took charge of the conversation. "There is more. I have just come from Elias' house. I went there to alert him to James' return...."

Maris paled as he broke into her dialogue. "Why did you go to Elias? Why didn't you come to me?"

Knowing firsthand of Maris' greed, Hannah realized his anger had returned and he was thinking about the likelihood of Elias claiming the reward before he could get to James.

She ignored his outburst and said bluntly, "Elias is dead. Esther killed him. She has lost her mind, Maris. She was just lying in her bed when I got there. Then she sat up and...." Tears came to Hannah's eyes.

"She was covered in blood. Lots of blood." Hannah started to shake again. "Just like Elias. There was so much blood. The bedding, the mattress, everything was covered with dried blood." She began to cry.

Still planning the seizure of James Daunt, Maris barely reacted to her grisly news. "You bleed mighty bad when you are stabbed in the heart," he said dispassionately.

Hannah continued. "Then she started to make those sounds, Maris. The ones you cannot understand. But this time, they were desperate. I think she was trying to tell me something but I was so scared. I just ran out of there and came here. Maris, it was horrible."

158

Her brother rubbed his knuckles. He was oblivious to Hannah's misery as he mulled over her message.

His dilemma was not caused by Hannah's discovery of the body of Elias or the knowledge of James Daunt's return. Rather it was the order in which he should prioritize his handling of these events that concerned him.

If, indeed, James Daunt was in the barn with Margaret, his capture should be the first item on the list. James might leave or someone else might spot the fugitive and beat him to the reward if he were detained by the discovery of Elias' body and the investigation of his mad wife. However, upon reflection, he realized it was imperative that he be the one to initiate action concerning the bizarre happenings at Elias Latch's farm. He knew he should also be the one to monitor the information made available to the sheriff.

The choice was a difficult one but he finally decided the chances of an outsider coming on Elias' body were slim. He ignored Hannah and returned to the keeping room to enlist the help of two of his men as he initiated the quest to capture James Daunt.

Hannah heard Maris order Nehemiah Trimble and Will Fieger to ride with him. She knew she should follow them and be there when they confronted James. If she waited here, Maris might take all the credit for the capture, but she no longer cared about the reward. She regretted she had been the one to expose her sisters' complicities in criminal acts and did not have the heart to hurt them further or to benefit from their misfortunes.

She sank down on one of the slipper chairs next to the fireplace. She was relieved now that Maris had taken responsibility for both James and Esther, but at the same time, she was distressed by the ramifications of the two upcoming arrests. She was sad for Esther and could only see jail or incarceration in an insane asylum as just punishment for her violent deed. She prayed she would not be hung, a fate Hannah felt certain was planned for James Daunt.

She pressed her hand against her forehead in an attempt to ward off an oncoming headache. It would be a long time, if ever, before the scandalous news of the moral degradation of the Hicks family faded into obscurity.

As she sat in the parlor of her youth, Hannah remembered her Quaker-educated mother sitting by the fire and reading aloud from Shakespeare. One of her oft-repeated quotations came to mind: "*When sorrows come, they come not single spies, but in battalions.*" How true, she thought, how very true.

She and Bettina had already felt the sting of derision when they went to town. The first incident occurred when the dispute over Maris' inheritance became known; the second, as word spread of James Daunt's shooting of Squire Holt. What would it be like when Elias' stabbing death was attributed to Esther? How could they possibly survive more humiliation?

Hannah stared impassively at the red velvet couch. She noticed that the luxuriant plush finish of the velvet covering was worn bare in spots; the armrests were soiled; the left cushion was torn, and one back leg had been replaced by a crudely carved block of unfinished wood. Her long-standing totem of elegance had fallen to the nadir of disrepair.

An overpowering feeling of sadness tightened Hannah's chest and a long-suppressed image of James Daunt on that unforgettable day erupted from deep in her memory. She had been behind the divan when Esther led James into the parlor and settled him on the down-filled cushions. Afraid of being detected in her illicit hideout, eight-year-old Hannah had squeezed between the legs of the couch and tucked herself under the far end of the seating area. That was where she had been sequestered when Esther lost her virginity to the inebriated young man who was destined to become the husband of her prettier younger sister.

After Esther fled the room in tears, James Daunt staggered to his feet. He stood with his back to Hannah and she could only see to his waist when she looked up from her secret spot on the floor. Suddenly, he reversed his position, faced the couch and leaned down to retrieve something from the pillow. That was when she noticed his trousers gaped open in the front.

At first, discomfited by his partial state of undress, she averted her eyes. Then, curiosity got the best of her and she glanced up again. This time, she noticed that the most private parts of a man's anatomy were fully exposed. Hannah stared at James Daunt's pubic area, fascinated, yet appalled by her shameless behavior. James returned to standing and looked toward the door as he buttoned his trousers. He seemed to assure himself that no one had observed his spontaneous indiscretion with Esther. Then he turned and fairly ran from the room. After he left, Hannah had curled her body into a ball and tried very hard to forget all that she had seen and heard.

Hannah had never admitted to herself how indelibly that image of James Daunt was imprinted on the back alleys of her mind and how profound the impact of that subconscious memory had been on her life. As a young woman of courting age, she was confident she would meet her true love, marry and live happily ever after. She was prettier than many of the girls in the area and she always tried to be pleasant when speaking with the boys who came calling.

The year Hannah turned eighteen, she had been particularly smitten with a young man from town who, at times, brought flowers and wrote her heartfelt, if somewhat clumsy, love letters. He arrived one afternoon dressed in his Sunday best and carrying roses. She was certain this was the day he was going to ask for her hand in marriage. He spoke awkwardly of his feelings and mentioned he would like to speak to her father. He had not formally asked her to marry him when, quite unexpectedly, he pulled her to him and kissed her full on the mouth.

She was completely taken by surprise, and as his lips pressed hard on hers, the dreaded image of James Daunt's dangling token of manhood flashed before her eyes. She pulled back as stomach acid rose in her throat. She tried, unsuccessfully, to free herself from his embrace as she vomited all over his new clothes.

Aghast, her shocked suitor shoved her away. He stared down at his contaminated garments, looked up with revulsion at the miserable Hannah, retrieved his roses and escaped forever from the threat of matrimony.

During the preparation of the midday meal, Margaret managed to put aside a slab of bread and two small pieces of meat for James. Hannah had not yet joined them and Bettina had gone to her room to see if she was ailing. Neither of the sisters thought it odd when Bettina reported that Hannah was not in the house as she was apt to start and finish her work day in the garden.

Hannah was a true farmer's daughter, and it was said, had been born with dirt under her fingernails. That was not exactly true, as the youngest girl in the Hicks family was fastidious about her appearance and careful to guard the purity of her hands even when planting and weeding. Her sisters envied her this ability, but in spite of trying, they were never able to emulate her meticulous ways.

Bettina became impatient as time passed. Irritated by Hannah's tardy attendance at mealtime, she left the kitchen and settled herself on the front porch. Margaret, seeking an excuse to return to James, followed. She seated herself on the bench which faced the barn and then jumped to her feet.

"Oh dear," Margaret exclaimed. "I think I left the gate to Bessie's stall ajar."

She ran down the front steps and across the grass to the barn. Once inside, she stopped short and looked into the horse's stall. It was empty. She remembered petting his nose when she first entered the barn early in the morning but had no memory of seeing him when she milked the cow. She had been in such a hurry to get to the henhouse she had not noticed whether the horse was there or not.

How long had he been missing? And, she groaned, how long had Hannah been gone? And why had she left and where had she ridden?

Margaret quickly ascended the ladder and shook James awake.

"You must leave," she commanded.

Taken aback by Margaret's tone, James sat up.

"Hannah's missing and our horse is gone. I am sure it's not a coincidence. She must have seen you, James. She has left to get help. Please," she begged, "Please leave."

James stood. He was still groggy and had nowhere to go for refuge. He deeply regretted returning to Margaret. He had been foolish and careless and genuinely hoped he had not put her in jeopardy. Now he was physically on the run again and this race was liable to be lost.

"Where can I hide?"

"I don't know, James. I just know you're not safe here. The woods behind the house are not deep but they are dense. You may find shelter there. I don't know. I just don't want to lose you again. There's been talk of a hanging, James. Please go now."

James thought of the razor the washerwoman had given him and regretted not having used it. Shaving off his beard would have dramatically changed his appearance, but if Margaret was right and Hannah had sounded an alert, it was too late. He had missed his opportunity.

He put his foot on the top rung and Margaret leaned over and kissed him on the cheek. For this, he thought bitterly, he would probably pay with his life.

He backed down the ladder and turned to face the barn door. It stood open and Bettina, flintlock on her shoulder, had him fixed in her sight.

"Margaret." Bettina glanced up at her sister before she addressed James. "I thought she was acting foolish today. Now I know why. Don't you move, James Daunt. I never liked you before and I don't like you now. I have no compunctions about shooting you between the eyes and saving all of us the disgrace of a public trial."

Maris, Nehemiah and Will pushed their horses hard as they rode to the farm which sheltered James Daunt. They were relieved to reach the fork where the rough road to the tenant house veered off to the right. Maris raised his hand and brought his small posse to a halt.

"We will proceed at a walk from here," he declared. "No point in alerting James before we are in place."

He jumped off his horse and picked up a long stick. He drew a rectangle in the dirt then added three small circles. "Here are the spots where we will take up our positions."

He drew three arrows. "This," he pointed to one of the long sides of the four-sided figure, "is the main barn door. I will enter here. Nehemiah, you watch the rear door, here," he moved the stick. "Will," he waved at the third man in the party, "you stay behind me and cover my back."

Maris remounted his horse and followed the lane to the right.

"We can tie our horses to the fence by the road. There are no windows in the loft so, unless James is brazen enough to go into the house and show himself to my sisters, he should be a sitting duck." He smiled. "Simple for us to pluck." He was pleased with the thought of an easy capture.

"What if he has a gun?" Nehemiah Trimble was not a brave man and feared the worst.

"His old musket was found in the woods near the squire's farm, and to my knowledge, there are no arms in the house. Anyway, I would venture a guess that, by now, he is tired of running and ready to give himself up. Why else would he have returned?"

Maris reached over and patted Nehemiah's shoulder. "Don't worry. Except when he's full of spirits, James Daunt is not a violent man. It's the drink that makes him foolhardy."

Maris began to regret having asked his neighbor to accompany him. He had chosen the itinerant worker, Will Fieger, for his size and the competence he had shown in the fields. He had picked Nehemiah Trimble because he knew the naïve, young man still begrudged the fact that James Daunt, an outsider, had stolen Margaret's affections.

Arriving in front of the barn, the men tied their horses to the fence posts as Maris had dictated, and three abreast, they walked toward the barn where Hannah had indicated James Daunt was hiding. They passed the paddock and assumed their places: Maris and Will by the heavy wooden doors which led into the center of the barn; Nehemiah at the left of the second entrance.

Cautiously, Maris opened the door and listened. Hearing nothing, he poked his head inside and looked around. There was silence, no sign of activity.

He signaled to Will that he was going inside. Slowly, he crossed the threshold, stepped onto the straw-covered floor and waited a moment before walking to the bottom of the ladder. Once there, he stopped, looked up and was relieved to see that James was not waiting at the top of the stairs. Stepping to the side, he readied his flintlock and pointed it up to the loft.

"I know you're there, James Daunt," he shouted. "Come over to the ladder before I start shooting through the floor."

There was no response. Maris repeated his demand. Still no response. He stepped back, out of the line of fire, and looked over his shoulder at his compatriot in the doorway.

"Come here, Will," he said. "I'm going to start shooting."

"Don't bother, Maris," Margaret pushed in front of Will and entered the barn.

"Bettina has James tied up in the kitchen and she has no intention of letting him out of her sight. You can forget the reward, Maris," Margaret said bitterly, "Bettina plans to claim it for herself." She could not believe her brother and sister were both after the reward for the capture of her husband.

"Bettina?" Maris shook his head. He could not picture the taciturn old maid who spent most of her life in the kitchen playing the role of vigilante.

"How...?" He shook his head. "How did she capture James?" He stared at Margaret who returned his look without flinching.

"She took the flintlock from over the fireplace," Maris started. He had forgotten the old gun that was mounted on the wall.

Margaret continued, "She had some shot hidden away in a tin can. She loaded the gun, positioned herself in the center of the barn door and waited for James to come down the ladder. Because of me," she teared up, "it was easy."

"What does she plan to do with him now that she's captured him?" Maris was thinking fast. "She won't be able to hold onto him once she tries to move him. He will overpower her or find some other way to break loose." He paced back and forth on the barn floor. "She is going to need me, Margaret, to help her get him to the sheriff."

Margaret interrupted Maris. "She said to tell you that you may get away with falsifying Father's wishes when it comes to the disposition of his property, but she is not going to let you steal the reward money from her. She's got a gun, Maris, and she intends to use it on you, or on James or," she paused, "on me if I stand in her way."

"How is she going to get James to jail without help?"

"She plans to wait until Hannah returns with the horse. Then, she's going to hitch up the cart, bind him to the seat and drive him to the sheriff's office."

Maris turned to his sister. "Why are you out here in the barn, Margaret?" He narrowed his eyes. "You must want something from me."

Several possibilities passed through Maris' mind. He quickly assessed each option before saying, "Now that we all know James is here, he is going to be captured one way or another. I'll make a deal with you, Margaret. You help me get James away from Bettina and I will split the reward money with you. Your share should cover the costs of James' defense."

"You are despicable, Maris. You would do anything for money: cheat your sisters; turn in your brother-in-law; even shoot him, I would guess. I have seen the reward notices. They say 'dead or alive'. We all know it's easier to bring in a dead man than a live one." She turned away in disgust.

"James is safer with Bettina than he would ever be with you. It is time for you to leave well enough alone, Maris. If James has to be turned in for money, let Bettina collect it. She, like all of your sisters," he could hear the derision in her voice, "needs money. You don't.

"Besides which, Bettina has enough shot to hold you off, Maris, let's not...."

The sound of horses' hooves broke into their exchange.

"Mr. Hicks," Will called out from his place by the barn door. "It's the sheriff and," he peered in the direction of the commotion, "it looks like he's got a posse with him."

"I guess Bettina wins, Margaret. Either way, you and your precious James Daunt lose." Maris smiled as he walked from the barn to greet the lawman. Margaret followed. Deep despair accompanied the knowledge that her brief reunion with James was at an end.

"Afternoon, Mrs. Daunt, Maris." The sheriff tipped his hat to Margaret and nodded to her brother.

"Afternoon, Cyrus," Maris wanted to hear what the sheriff had to say before offering any information.

"Man who looks a lot like James Daunt got himself killed yesterday. Lady who claims to be his wife found him out in the field. We've just come from there. He was lying under a dead horse. Crushed to death."

He looked at Maris, then at Margaret. Brother and sister exchanged glances, their own thoughts racing toward formulation in their brains.

Maris avoided Margaret's eyes as he said, "It's not James. He's here. We've got him in the kitchen. Bettina has tied him up and is holding a gun on him."

Margaret, seeing the possibility of a last-minute reprieve vanish, spoke up.

"Bettina captured him by herself, Sheriff. Maris arrived after she had discovered James in the barn and after she had taken him to the kitchen where she bound him to a chair. Maris had nothing to do with James' apprehension."

Tears formed in her eyes and she turned away. At that moment, she converted all the disappointment James' actions had brought her into hatred for her greedy, callous brother. She blamed him and his abduction of her inheritance for the loss of her home and of James' business; for her dependence on his pitiful largesse; for the subservient position she had been relegated to by her poverty, and most of all, for James' desperate assault on Squire Holt and its subsequent consequences.

She wiped away the tears and preceded the group to the kitchen where, if necessary, she could protect James and Bettina from the wiles of her scheming brother.

There were no problems. The sheriff verified that the prisoner was, indeed, James Daunt, and then he commandeered a horse belonging to one of his men. A visibly unhappy Maris Hicks helped harness it to the small cart that stood in the barn.

Still under Bettina's watchful eye, and still safely at the end of her gun, James was brought from the house and placed on the seat next to the deputy who had surrendered his horse. Margaret tried to touch her husband's arm before he climbed onto the cart but was forbidden contact with the fugitive. Bettina, intent on preserving her right to the reward, insisted on riding along with the men. She had to sit, legs straight out, in the bed of the cart but she did not complain. Her flintlock at the ready, she preferred being behind, rather than beside the prisoner. With the sheriff leading the way and the posse bringing up the rear, the party embarked on the ride to the county jail. As she walked back to the house, Margaret realized she had not given James his pilfered meal of meat and bread.

Maris watched as the sheriff's party rode down the dirt path and turned onto the crude road which led to the east. They would soon bear south and pass his farm on their way to the county seat. He had not chosen to accompany the triumphant troop but had sent Nehemiah Trimble and Will Fieger back with them so they could return to work in the fields.

He glanced at Margaret as she slowly walked to the house after James' departure with his armed guards. He felt no pity. She had gotten herself into this situation and now she had to live with it. Unfortunately, he thought, so did he, as the ramifications of James Daunt's guilt would impact the reputation of the entire Hicks family.

He turned his thoughts to his next challenge. Repulsed by the prospect of confronting Esther and the corpse of her husband, Maris briefly considered waiting until morning before going to his sister's home. He knew, however, he did not have that option. Hannah would talk, and she would let on that he was aware of Elias' murder. His lack of action might cause him to be suspected of complicity.

With a shake of his head, he acknowledged his poor judgment. He should have told the sheriff about the state of affairs at the Latch farm; he should have asked Nehemiah and Will to accompany him when he confronted Esther. If his sister-in-law was out of control or, God forbid, violent, he was going to be on his own, without anyone to help or serve as witness. His next thought was of the rumors that would circulate if others saw the murder scene before he had a chance to evaluate its present state, and he was satisfied with his decision to go alone.

Maris walked to the fence where his horse awaited him. He untied the reins, mounted easily, and traced the path the preceding group had taken.

When he reached the Great Road, he turned north instead of south and headed for Elias' farm. He was surprised that he was calm in the face of his disappointment over losing the reward for the capture of James Daunt and his awareness of what lay before him when he reached his next destination.

Arriving at his sister's home, Maris chose to tether his horse behind the barn rather than in the paddock where it could be seen from the road. As a precaution, he collected his flintlock and tucked it under his arm. He avoided the customary entrance and entered the single room through a narrow, low door in the rear. The first thing he noticed was the smell. It was much worse than he remembered.

Rancid odors of decay intermingled with the dry, flat scent of layered dust and dirt, painfully assaulted his nostrils. He had anticipated the stench of neglect and the general disarray of a household in crisis, but Hannah had not prepared him for the intolerable acrid stink which pervaded the room. He reached for the kerchief he wore around his neck and pulled it up to cover his nose.

Maris walked to the stairs and began his ascent. In spite of the filtering effect of the bandanna, he could not avoid the increased odors emanating from the bedroom. Cautiously, he peered into the tiny room. The bed, with its bare mattress and pile of soiled linen, was the first thing he saw; Esther was not on it. Then he noticed the blood stains. They were everywhere: on the bed, on the floor, on the wall.

He looked around the room. The four-poster bed stood three feet above the floor. He noticed the end of a loaf of bread. Was that what Esther had been eating? Maris leaned down and stared between the legs. His view was unobstructed and he could see that the rough pine boards on the far side were marred by an oval-shaped, reddish-brown stain.

"Elias' body was there," he thought. "Where is it now? And where is Esther?"

Again, he searched the room with his eyes. There were no hiding places save the small trunk next to the bed. It was highly improbable that either Esther or Elias' body would fit in there. He had to see for himself so he walked past the bed, stepped to his left, and holding the kerchief tight to his face, raised the lid. A few small trinkets, mementos of another time, covered the disheveled bed linens inside. He lifted the top sheet and confirmed the trunk had not been used for any other purpose.

Hannah had mentioned a knife, or, a shiver ran down his right arm, had she? He remembered his comment about the amount of blood spilled when a man was stabbed in the heart. He could not recall his sister's exact words; just her remark about a lot of blood.

Standing next to the incriminating discoloration, his stomach turned as he stared at the spot where he assumed Elias Latch's dead body had lain. Swallowing hard, he turned to leave the bedroom. In his haste, he almost missed seeing the path that cut through the dust which lightly covered the floor.

Maris frowned as he considered the probability that someone else had come to the house after Hannah left. Although Elias was small and wiry, he had a sturdy physique. Esther was far too debilitated to pull his dead weight across the room. A third person must have taken Esther and Elias' body from the house. Who? And why? He had no answers. Maris followed the trail down the stairs and through the keeping room. It ended at the door. Outside, the small landing had been blown clean by the wind and the path vanished.

Maris did not believe Esther could have moved Elias without help. The last time he had seen her, her leg had not healed properly and she had been reduced to skin and bones. As far as he knew, she had not walked since her accident and spent most of her time in bed. If she had managed to move her husband's body on her own, there was only one place she could have taken it. To the barn.

Maris left the house and walked to the paddock. He noticed James Daunt's horse had not been moved. It did not raise its head and he wondered when it had last eaten. Elias' horse, he noted with alarm, was no longer behind the fence. He increased his speed as he neared the barn. Upon entering the building, he immediately checked the stalls. Elias' horse was missing. Moving quickly, he searched for the farm cart. It, too, was missing. Esther, Elias' body, and perhaps, an accomplice had to be in that cart. He had no idea where they might be headed.

Lacking direction, Maris decided to return to his home. He wanted to talk to Hannah before going after the sheriff. Fortunately, this was Hannah's story, not his. He would not have to admit he had been to the Latch farm or that he knew Esther and Elias were missing.

He had only to report the hysterical narrative of a woman who, he realized, would be even more upset when she learned she was not getting part of the reward for the capture of James Daunt.

For a very brief moment, he allowed himself to feel a twinge of sympathy for Margaret. Three of her four siblings were willing to sell her husband's freedom for reward money and the fourth would, most likely, have been just as culpable if she had been able.

Then Maris recalled the resentment he had always felt toward the pretty, spoiled, favored daughter, and his pity turned to callous disdain. He had never recovered from the disgust he felt when he learned of Margaret's eager acquiescence to the seduction of a no-good ne'er-do-well like James Daunt. Her moral disgrace, while shielded from the public eye by her hasty marriage and the loss of the baby, had served her right and her financial downfall was the just dessert for a foolish, irresponsible hussy.

James Daunt's hands were tied behind his back and he swayed precariously on the narrow seat of the cart as its wheels caught in the ruts of the road. He was certain the deputy was intentionally guiding the vehicle into the potholes and ditches dotting the well-used dirt road. James wondered whether the driver was trying to torment him or to rid the vigilant Bettina of her weapon.

He was disheartened by his capture and tried to blame Sally for his predicament but admitted it was his own foolish decision, not hers, that brought him back to Margaret. He could have gone north, or returned to Pleasant Valley in the hope that the representatives of Squire Holt's family had been unable to convince the Reverend Goodenough that James Morley was actually James Daunt.

The driver hit a deep hole and his vehicle temporarily pitched out of control. James could hear Bettina yell as she fell backwards. The gun clattered as it flew out of her hands and landed on the wagon bed. The driver pulled his horse to a stop.

James slid from his seat, dropped to the ground and began to run toward the open field on his right. When the deputy jumped from his seat, Bettina grabbed her gun and climbed over the side of the cart. She faced the fleeing man and aimed the rifle at his head.

*171*

"Stop, James Daunt. I got you in my sight." Bettina's voice rang out over the deputy's cries as he struggled to regain control over the frightened horse. Used to carrying a single rider rather than pulling a wagon, the horse balked at its unfamiliar harness and rough handling and then reared.

Running hard, James was stopped short by a shot which passed so close to his ear that he could feel the air it displaced. He stood still. He had nowhere to go; the field was endless and offered no physical protection as far as he could see. He thought of letting Bettina end his odyssey with her next shot but his will to live was too strong. He turned and walked back to the cart.

"Get in," Bettina ordered. "You...." Her next comment was cut off by the sound of pounding hooves and the appearance of a galloping horse with a farm wagon bouncing behind.

As it neared, they could see the horse, wild-eyed and foaming at the mouth. A runaway, it was in a near frenzy. The driver, seeing there was no room to pass without going off the road, attempted to pull on the reins. The horse received the feeble message and gratefully slowed as the deputy lunged for its bridle and brought it to a halt.

"Are you insane?" Bettina shouted when she realized how close she had been to being trampled. "What do you think you are doing?" She turned her gun on the driver and gasped.

"Esther!"

The exhausted woman, weakened to the point of total collapse, lost consciousness and slumped sideways on the seat.

The deputy looked for James Daunt. Wearied by the prospect of being on the run again, James had climbed back onto the seat of Bettina's cart and turned his life over to the vagaries of Fate.

When Maris rode up the lane which led to his home, he saw the small cart he provided for his sisters. James Daunt and the deputy remained ensconced on the seat. As before, Bettina was in the back, legs stretched in front of her, flintlock at the ready. The three remained in place and did not turn as he pulled closer.

A second horse and wagon stood nearby. Several members of the sheriff's posse stood at a distance from the larger vehicle. They quickly glanced his way, then, with nods of recognition, turned back to their vigilance.

One man, a checkered kerchief to his nose, choked when he ventured close to the wagon. Maris recognized it and knew it contained the body of Elias Latch.

He did not, however, see Esther.

Without approaching the men, Maris called out. "That Elias Latch's wagon?"

The men nodded without speaking.

The man with the kerchief backed away and rejoined the posse.

Maris dismounted, led his horse to the rail, tied it firmly to a post and started walking toward the large farm cart.

"Don't go there, Maris," one of the men called out to him. "Elias is dead. Got a knife in his heart. Body's in the back there and the smell is bad."

Maris had not anticipated Esther's presence at his home and he did not know how to react. Should he be surprised? Shocked? Unbelieving? Appropriate questions formed in his head. How? When? Why was the body here?

He did not want to admit he had been to the Latch farm. He could not, however, pretend ignorance. Hannah had surely told people about the situation with Esther and Elias and that she had turned to him for help.

The deputy saved him.

"We were on our way to jail," he said, "when Esther Latch tried to pass us on the road. She was driving crazy and almost ran us down. Tommy, here," he pointed to one of the other deputies, "he caught the bridle of her horse. Brought him to a stop."

The deputy looked at his friends and then back at Maris.

"She's mad, Maris. Stark, raving mad. Her hands and clothes are covered in dried blood and it sure looks like she's the one who killed Elias. The sheriff took her in the house and he and the womenfolk are with her now. We've sent for Sam Baker. Hopefully, he'll come soon."

Maris tried to look concerned. "Who's with her? Delia?"

The man nodded, "And your sister, Hannah."

"Can Esther speak? Can she tell you what happened?"

"She only makes these wild sounds and waves her hands. No one can understand her. Personally, I think she's crazy, Maris. I'm sorry, but your sister is just plain crazy."

"I'll go to see her. Maybe I can help." Maris strode to the door of his home and entered into the parlor.

Delia had covered the divan with an old quilt before she allowed the men to lay Esther's unconscious, blood-stained body on it. Now, she and Hannah were standing watch from a safe distance. The sheriff was balanced awkwardly on the edge of one of the slipper chairs, poised to leap to their rescue if necessary.

"I have just returned from your place, Hannah...." Maris began establishing his story by avoiding any discussion of his second stop. "The men tell me Elias' body is in his wagon out front. They say Esther brought him here."

Esther's eyes flew open at the sound of her brother's voice and she attempted to sit up. The sheriff leapt to his feet, his hand on his gun. Hannah and Delia jumped aside.

Esther fell back on the couch and let loose an unintelligible harangue which was accompanied by feeble hand signals. She pointed in the direction of her brother and tried to emphasize her pathetic thrusts with more grunts and weak, high-pitched shrieks.

Maris stepped back in horror. Fearing that her incriminations would be taken seriously, he recoiled at her accusations.

Seeing her husband's discomfort, Delia moved to Maris' side. "Don't worry, dear," she stroked his arm. "She has been doing this to all of us since she got here."

Her words calmed him and he regained his composure.

The deputy who had stopped Esther's horse burst into the room. "Sam's here. We filled him in as best we could. He's coming in now." He slammed the door behind him as he left.

Maris reopened it. He could see the doctor hurrying up the walk and stepped aside as Samuel Baker entered the parlor.

Esther recognized the familiar figure of the doctor. She sighed as her body eased into the down cushions.

"Put the gun away, Sheriff." Samuel Baker took charge as he looked from the lawman to the family members.

He nodded his greetings. "Afternoon, Hannah, Delia, Maris."

Samuel stared at his patient and said, "Afternoon, Esther." He glanced at the attending group and asked, "What is going on here?"

Without waiting for an answer, he returned his attention to the woman on the couch. Esther took it upon herself to reply to his question and resumed making her incoherent sounds.

"Not now, Esther. Save yourself.

"Maris, you take the women out of here. All of you, go to another room. I want to speak to Esther in private. Sheriff, that applies to you as well. I want to be alone with my patient."

"She is out of control, Doc. I don't think you are safe in here." The sheriff stood his ground.

"I'll be fine," Sam said, "but Esther will not be, unless you all move along."

Reluctantly, the three family members and the representative of the law took their leave of the room.

"And I do not want anyone listening at the door."

As Samuel threw out his order, Maris stopped in the doorway and said, "I would like a word with you."

The doctor hesitated then stepped into the hall.

"Please close the door," Maris spoke quietly. "I don't want Esther to hear what I have to say." Samuel pulled the door shut.

"Esther's been sick ever since the accident, Samuel. She has been getting worse as time passes. She is...," his voice cracked. "She is quite mad, you know. And she needs help. I hear there is a hospital in the city which takes good care of lunatics. Perhaps, Samuel, you can arrange for her to go there."

Samuel Baker was unprepared for Maris' request. He knew little of the insane ward at the asylum, however he had heard other doctors talk of patients' treatment. Some of the stories were horrific; one had ended with a miracle cure. Unfortunately, as he remembered it, the patient had died several days after being pronounced sane.

Esther presented a unique problem. She was physically incapacitated as well as unbalanced. She could not live alone. If she

175

had, indeed, stabbed Elias, she was also a possible danger to her sisters and to Maris and his wife if they took her in. She had no children, and as this solution was Maris' idea, the doctor assumed he would take responsibility for his sister's supervision.

It was not a good option but one which must be considered if he confirmed that she was severely deranged.

"I will do my best to evaluate her condition, Maris, and we can talk about this later."

Samuel Baker was upset by the conversation he just had with Maris Hicks. He took a moment to reflect before he returned to the room where his patient lay rigid on the divan.

Esther was fully covered by her nightdress which lay loose on her emaciated frame. He could see the outline of one leg stretched taut while the other lay limp and deformed as a result of her bizarre accident. She held her arms stiffly at her side. Stress, grief and fear alternated as the emotions distorted her gaunt features and accentuated their severity.

Samuel walked over to Esther and gently lifted her hand. It was shaking.

"Esther, it sounds like you have a passel of troubles."

She began to protest but he stopped her.

"In the past weeks, we have not made much progress in getting you to talk but now, it is extremely important that we be able to communicate. Try very hard to answer me, Esther. Nod your head 'yes' or 'no'."

The doctor spoke slowly and enunciated each word. "Did you kill Elias?"

She shook her head violently back and forth and stabbed the air with her finger as she pointed toward the door.

Samuel looked over his shoulder. The door remained closed. "I have seen his body. It is still in the wagon." He looked at the woman opposite him. "He has been dead for a while, Esther. Days. Why didn't you try to get help? Wave out your window? Anything to get attention."

Esther stared ahead. Then, very slowly, she began to speak. She concentrated on every syllable.

"The day it happened, I tried to close the window on the far side of the bed. When I put my feet on the floor, I stumbled and collapsed in a heap. Elias heard me fall and started to come up the stairs to help me.

"He was halfway there when I heard the outside door open and I recognized Maris' voice. He came into the keeping room and began to yell at Elias for trying to overturn my father's will in court. Elias kept climbing and when he reached the top step, Maris caught up to him. He threatened my husband but Elias said he would keep fighting as the will wasn't fair." Esther stopped and took a breath. She was excited and animated. Dr. Baker decided to let her finish without interruption.

"That's when Maris pulled out a knife and placed it against Elias' chest. I think he just wanted to threaten him, but Elias struggled. Maris got angry and thrust the blade into him. Then he pushed Elias away, ran down the stairs and out the door.

"Before he left, he looked over at the bed but never saw me on the floor. The bed is high, Samuel, and I could see under it. I saw everything. Elias staggered over to where I was, tried to pull me up but was too badly wounded. He fell on top of my leg and died. A long time passed before I could work my leg out from under his body."

Esther pointed to her leg. Samuel followed her finger and noted that the exposed area was patterned with faint purple, yellow and brown relics of bruising.

"It took all my strength to get back on the bed. Afterwards, I was too exhausted and too scared to move." Esther continued making her sounds as Samuel stared at her damaged appendage. "I just lay there and prayed Maris would not return."

Esther looked intently at the doctor. The distressed woman prayed again, this time hoping that the doctor had concentrated on her words and that she had been able to get her message across. His expression told her she had been unsuccessful.

"I know you're trying, Esther. And I feel, whatever it is you have to say, it's important. But, unfortunately, I still cannot understand a word you're saying."

Esther's hopes plummeted.

Samuel pulled on his ear and spoke softly to himself. "If only Jacob Hicks hadn't been so dead set against girls having schooling. If only you'd taught yourself to write as well as do numbers."

Sam could hear the sheriff's footsteps as he paced back and forth outside of the door. There was no reason for him to wait any longer. Esther was too weak to run and there was no place for an invalid in the jail. She would have to be released in the custody of her brother as her sisters did not have the financial wherewithal to care for her.

He opened the door and passed on his opinion. Grateful to be freed of the responsibility, the lawman left the house and strode past the wagon where his deputy, James Daunt and Bettina Hicks sat waiting for the resumption of their trip. He stopped in front of Will Fieger and Nehemiah Trimble.

"Some day for the law, gentlemen. A spinster lady single-handedly captures her brother-in-law, who is a cold-blooded assassin, and her sister comes riding up in a wagon with her murdered husband's body hanging out the back. Old Jacob Hicks would turn over in his grave if he knew what was going on here."

He turned to the remaining members of the posse and said, "Mount up, boys. We gotta get the prisoner to jail."

Sally stopped at Hebe Balderston's tavern for an early supper. She ate quickly and was relieved to note the paucity of diners and the absence of the proprietress. She was about to leave when the door opened and two of the lads, Nathaniel Pusey and John Heep, entered the room.

"They found him." John glanced around, recognized Sally and addressed his news to her. "They caught James Daunt."

Sally felt her knees buckle as she heard the words of the man by the doorway. She grasped the edge of the table and leaned on it for support. Her heart was pounding and she felt faint.

"What's the matter, Sally? You got a liking for James Daunt?" Nathaniel laughed.

She straightened, placed her hands on her hips, thrust her pelvis forward and faced the two men she had known in the alley.

"They caught James Daunt?" She swiveled her hips in one direction and her shoulders in another. "I been trying to do that for years." She smiled her wicked grin and licked her lips. "Where is he?"

"We were with the posse and we took him to Maris Hicks' place. Probably on his way to the county jailhouse by now." Nathaniel Holmes looked Sally up and down. "I didn't know you favored him, Sal."

She smiled again. "I favor all you boys, Nathaniel. You know that." She twirled around and pulled the long gray community shirt up over the top of the trousers she wore. She tied the ends together so the skin above her waist showed.

Surprisingly, neither Nathaniel nor John noticed the exposed flesh.

"You got on pantaloons, Sally." The lads were astonished. Women did not wear men's clothing at Hebe's. They stared at the trousers in disbelief.

"I had some hard riding to do," Sally spun around again and fingered the top of her trousers to draw the young men's eyes to her waist. "These seemed better than a skirt." She reached to her right knee and drew the fabric above her ankle. She twisted it provocatively and the men made appreciative comments.

"What is going to happen to James?" Sally continued to tease with her ankle as she asked the question.

"They'll hang him, I guess." John answered, looking down at the floor.

"I thought he was your friend. You don't seem too upset by the news."

"We tried to find him," Nathaniel aimed his words at Sally. "No one knew where he was. Then we rode with the posse hoping we could get to him first. Now it's too late. He shot a man, Sally. He was seen. They'll hang him for sure and there is nothing we can do."

The knowledge that his friends thought James would be found guilty and sentenced to death stayed with Sally as she collected her horse and set out on her long trip back to Pleasant Valley. She had to admit that she had erred by not telling James about Esther's presence at Squire Holt's. It had been foolish folly to believe he would not be

*179*

found and now she desperately hoped she could right the wrong she had done when she kept her silence.

Sally was exhausted, physically and emotionally. The strain of the journey in her condition and the mental anguish she was experiencing were taking their toll. She located a stand of trees off to the side of the road, found an opening and entered the shallow woods. She dismounted and tied her horse to a tree.

She found a bed of moss, curled up and fell asleep.

An alarmed whinny, the sounds of horses' hooves and men's voices filtered through disturbed dreams and awakened her.

"Look! There's a horse over there. In the trees."

"Stop! Ezra, you check it out."

"Can't tell if anyone's around."

"Hey," Sally looked up into the face of one of the men she'd seen at Hebe's. "It's Sally of the Alley."

The members of the posse started hooting.

"Hey, Sally, what are you doing here?"

"Who's the lucky one, Sally?"

"Can we stop for a while, Sheriff? Take a little Sally break?"

Sally sat up and looked over at the wagon which stood by the side of the road. She could tell that James was the prize passenger.

He was sitting on the seat next to the driver. She saw the ropes on his wrists, the cord which bound him to the seat, and the woman who sat behind him with her gun pointed directly at his back. He did not look at her but stared straight ahead.

"What are you doing with James Daunt?" She directed her question to Ezra but spoke loud enough for all to hear.

"Taking him to jail for the murder of Squire Holt. You hear about that, Sally? At Hebe's?"

"Yes," she said quietly. "I did hear about it." She raised her voice. "I also heard someone else was shooting at the squire."

She saw James glance in her direction.

"Where'd you hear that foolishness, Sally?" The sheriff guided his horse over to where she stood.

"Around." Sally hung her head. She did not know how much to say to the sheriff. She could not prove Esther was there. It was just her word, and she knew, no one except James, would pay attention to what she said.

"Enough." The sheriff motioned his posse forward as he turned his back on Sally. "You have said enough. Don't you go getting anyone else involved in this. James Daunt is the killer and we have him in custody. You go on home, wherever that is, and don't bother your head over things you don't know anything about."

The sheriff rode to the front of the party and joined his men as they resumed their journey. James never glanced her way again. Sally watched as he was driven out of sight. Then she began to cry.

Samuel Baker paced back and forth then stopped next to the couch.

"We will have to go back to the 'yes' and 'no' answers, Esther. We had some success before so let's try again. You were in the bedroom. Was Elias in the room with you before…," Samuel searched for a way to soften his question. "Before the accident?"

Esther thought for a moment. Did Samuel mean all day or just prior to Elias' encounter with Maris?

She shook her head from side to side.

"All right. Your answer is 'no'." Samuel understood her negative response.

"Did you summon him to the bedroom?"

"Yes, I fell. I needed help."

Samuel frowned. "Esther, please remember. I cannot understand what you say."

Esther clasped her hands tightly and pressed her lips together.

"Did you call him because you were angry with him?"

"No!" She tried to lift her head as she cried out in frustration. "I wasn't the one who stabbed Elias. It was Maris."

"You said 'Maris'." The doctor emphasized her brother's name. "Was Maris there?"

She shook her head up and down, relieved that he finally understood Maris was involved.

"When was Maris at your home? Was it the day Elias was stabbed?"

She nodded her head affirmatively and smiled.

Samuel Baker was shocked to notice that, since he had last seen her, Esther had lost her front teeth.

He changed the emphasis of his questioning.

"Esther, you have lost some teeth. How did that happen? Did Elias have anything to do with the loss of your teeth?"

Esther reviewed what had happened. She had wanted to go downstairs. Elias had been supporting her when she lost her grip on his arm and fell against the door frame at the head of the steps. She had broken the top four teeth in the front of her mouth.

Her lips had become terribly swollen and the pain from the shattered teeth had been so bad that, a few days later, Elias had rubbed her gums with alcohol and pulled them out. The relief she had experienced after the raw nerves had been removed far outweighed the pain of the extractions.

She moved her head up and down.

"Elias was responsible for the loss of your teeth?"

Again, she confirmed his assumption.

"Hmm." Samuel Baker's fingers landed on his earlobe and he pulled hard.

"Did Elias get angry with you when you couldn't communicate with him?"

Esther stumbled over the word "communicate". Deciding Samuel was asking her if Elias got angry when she was unable to talk to him, she had to answer "yes". Elias did get annoyed with her, but he was a good husband, a better one, she had to admit, after she became an invalid. He tried to accommodate her injuries and worked hard at being patient.

She shook her head affirmatively and clarified her answer. "Yes, but only because he wanted me to be normal again. He loved me, Samuel. I know that now. I didn't know that before." Tears came to her eyes.

Samuel Baker noticed the tears and misread them as indicators of the unbearable misery of a badly mistreated woman. He concluded that Elias had been beating his maimed and speech-impaired wife out of exasperation and contempt. It was understandable that she would retaliate in the only way she could, by stabbing him with a knife, a weapon she could obtain and conceal on her body.

The doctor retrieved his medical bag which contained a meager supply of potions and extracted a small bottle.

"Open your mouth, Esther. This will help you to relax."

Her hands still shaking, Esther swallowed the liquid which he carefully poured into her mouth. He stood by her until she became drowsy then he went to the door.

"Esther, I am going to get Maris now. Do not be afraid. I will make sure you never go to jail for Elias' murder." He looked back at Esther. "In my heart I know you were justified in your actions."

He was confident no judge would convict a decent but totally insane woman of first degree murder. No, he would follow Maris' suggestion and make sure Esther Hicks Latch got medical help as a patient in the asylum rather than see her languish behind prison bars.

Dr. Baker never noticed the look of horror and disbelief which crossed the face of his patient before she drifted into a drug-induced stupor brought on by the laudanum she had unknowingly consumed.

He also never recalled the single intelligible word she had uttered: "Maris," or Esther's acknowledgement that her brother had been in the Latch home the day of the stabbing.

The bright light of day had dimmed to dusk and the sun was setting when the sheriff and his party reached the county seat. As they turned onto the main street, they could see a large group of people, many carrying torches, milling around in front of the courthouse. The word of James' capture had travelled fast and the local folk had come to view the accused murderer.

"General Jackson is respected for his high morals, his bravery, his leadership...."

James' head snapped up when he heard the familiar words. As they neared the jail, he stared hard at the man in the red-white-and-blue top hat who stood on a makeshift speaker's platform in front of him. It was the Hurrah Boy. The Jacksonian was bellowing out his election spiel to the crowds of onlookers who had gathered to catch a glimpse of James Daunt as he was escorted to the adjacent jailhouse.

"A vote for Andrew Jackson is a vote for the common man. Vote out the elite John Quincy Adams with his Yankee learning and Northern loyalties. Vote in the brave, honorable defender of our country, our Hero of New Orleans, Andrew Jackson."

"Tell us about the bodies in the six coffins." A raucous heckler thrust his fist in the air as he shouted down the campaigner. "Tell us about the half-dozen loyal soldiers who Andrew Jackson had shot as deserters because they left their regiment when their contracts expired."

"Yes, and tell us about Jackson's wife, Rachel, the adulteress." Another voice, another disruption.

"Tell us how Jackson carried her away and how they lived in sin while she was still married to another man." Another protester.

"Andrew Jackson's mother was a common prostitute and he is the illegitimate son of a mulatto."

Men and women, alike, shouted accusations at the Jackson advocate who maintained his composure while he waited for the crowd to settle down. Noting the ineffectiveness of the verbal assaults, critics and supporters, alike, returned to their vigil, unaware that James Daunt sat in a nearby cart.

The Jacksonian jumped into the void left by the retreating Adams supporters.

"Andrew Jackson is a gentleman." He shouted his rebuttals. "The general refuses to sanction attacks on members of the feminine persuasion. He defends the weaker sex from slanderers like you with the same vigor that he defended New Orleans against the British." His tone became conspiratorial.

"He would never suggest that Abigail Adams approached the wedding altar, not as a virginal bride, but as a woman, like her mother before her, knowledgeable of the ways of the man at her side. No, Andrew Jackson would never condone talk like that."

The crowd turned back to the Hurrah Boy, some expressing their disbelief, others nodding their assent. He basked in their attention.

"It is also said, but not by the honorable general, that John Quincy Adams procured young American girls for the czar of Russia.

This is known by all of Washington, but never discussed in the presence of Andrew Jackson or his virtuous and pious wife who was mercifully rescued from an abusive and destructive relationship."

"Andrew Jackson stands for war," the original heckler shouted out. "John Quincy Adams has kept our nation at peace; our economy sound, and under his administration, our national debt has been significantly reduced."

"Andrew Jackson can't be president." A new voice, a very loud one, took command of the protesters. "He was born in Tennessee before it became a state."

The dissenter stood on the back of a wagon and spoke with authority. "The Constitution says you have to be a citizen of the United States at the time of the signing of the Constitution to be eligible to run for the presidency. Tennessee did not become a state until 1796, nine years after the adoption of the Constitution. Andrew Jackson can't be president."

"I heard he was born in Ireland."

"No, he was born on the high seas before his parents reached America."

"He was born out of wedlock in the Southwest Territory."

"This is preposterous." The mayor mounted the makeshift platform and stood next to the Jacksonian.

"I don't agree with everything this stranger has to say but I do know that Andrew Jackson was born in South Carolina, which is one of our original thirteen states. He has every right to run for president of the United States, so stop this slanderous folderol you people are spreading about both of the candidates."

A low murmur from those assembled in front of the jail interrupted the mayor's angry censure of the crowd.

"There he is. There's the murderer!" The alarm was sounded and the original heckler pushed his way through the group standing around the political advocate and climbed onto the platform.

"Murderer! The Lord will smite you down without mercy! Infamy awaits you at the end of a rope!"

The heckler tried to arouse the people who had gathered outside the prison. They ignored him as they recognized James Daunt and moved toward him. They stared hard at the suspected killer; the expressions of some became accusatory as their curiosity was satisfied. Others turned their backs and whispered among themselves or pointed fingers in his direction as they relived the scandal of his financial and moral downfall.

The sheriff pulled the cart in front of the jail. James glanced over at the Hurrah Boy who was staring back at him. A frown, a flicker of recognition followed by a look of uncertainty, crossed the normally unruffled face of the professional campaigner as he recognized his table mate from Pleasant Valley Farm. A smile replaced his confusion and he saluted James.

"Good luck and God be with you," he shouted. Then, without missing a beat, he cried out, "A vote for Andrew Jackson is a vote for an honest, law-abiding citizen...."

## Saturday, September 27, 1828

Sally travelled through the night and reached Pleasant Valley Farm by mid-morning. Upon her arrival, she tied her horse to one of the posts and went in search of her mother. She began in the main building and finding her rooms empty, she went to the laundry.

Her mother looked up and raised her eyebrows when she spotted her daughter. Sally shook her head in answer to the unspoken query about the results of her visit with Hebe and pointed to the hall. She preceded her mother to a small room at the end of the building and immediately asked what she knew of James Daunt.

The news of his arrest and the resultant unmasking of James Morley had not yet become public knowledge in the community. Her mother, however, was able to tell her of his escape on Old Caesar. She had seen James head north when he left and mentioned it to Sally. She also disclosed the fact that James was aware she had gone to Hebe Balderston's.

Sally was dismayed to learn of her mother's revelation and she experienced the old feelings of resentment toward her parent. She shook them off as she admitted to the positive change in their relationship and how much she appreciated having a confidante at this time.

Her thoughts returned to James and his probable assumption that she had reverted to her old ways and was seeking gratification from the lads at the tavern. She knew he had not gone north but rather south to Hebe's, or she sighed, to Margaret's. Either destination would have been perilous for James and had, obviously, ended in the loss of his freedom.

"Sarah, there's a woman here...," her mother stopped speaking as the door opened and two laundresses entered with their arms full of sheets. Sally's mother reached for the women's bundles and began storing them on the shelves behind her. Seeing she was back at work, Sally left the room and returned to care for her horse.

She had not eaten since she left Hebe Balderston's and she was hungry. She had just enough time before the noon meal to feed and water her horse. She removed the bridle, put on a halter and re-tied her weary mount to the post before she headed to the dining room.

Thoughts of James, and speculation about his fate, persisted, and no matter how hard she tried to suppress it, the probability of his death by hanging circulated through her brain with relentless clarity. Reminders of her time with James were everywhere: the fields, the blacksmith shop, the residence, the dining room. All held evocative associations which brought her mind back to the man whom she had last seen bound to the seat of a farm cart.

At first, she tried to stem the painful longings his image stirred in her body. Pausing under the lone tree where she and James had lounged the morning of his arrival, she found she did not want the desires to subside. As long as she hurt, she felt he was with her.

New sensations, however, demanded her attention: fullness in her breasts; a taut, nervous tension in her abdomen; a recurring feeling of nausea. She had temporarily forgotten about her problem and now that James was a prisoner, the need for a solution to her impending motherhood assumed a new immediacy. The reality of her condition tempered her preoccupation with her reverie and Sally abandoned the euphoria of her memories. She left the shelter of the tree and finished her walk to the dining room. She glanced around the women's section as she entered. She noticed four of the younger residents seated together and chose to join them.

"You missed our guest last night." A fair-complected, blonde-haired woman patted the seat next to her and Sally sat down.

"Lucy McDougal from New York." The name was familiar but Sally could not recall where she had heard it.

The speaker continued, "Sarah, you, especially, would have enjoyed Mrs. McDougal's talk. She spoke about the *Declaration of Independence* and how it guarantees the rights of men to be equal and how that equality should apply to women as well."

A second diner jumped in: "She went on to say women have historically been suppressed by male-propagated myths which claim we are the weaker sex." She frowned. "Men do not take into consideration the fact that we, and our married sisters, milk the cows, carry the water, hoist the logs that keep the fires going...."

"Yes." A third participant interrupted. "Men ignore the physical demands of our everyday lives. They envision us as living comfortably, and ignorantly, within the confines of a home where our time is spent performing our duties as the mothers of children and caretakers of husbands rather than as independent women who, if we so choose, are capable of living alone and caring for ourselves."

"Too much education corrupts our delicate minds, they say." The blonde woman pointed to her temple as she picked up the conversation. "And our emotions," she moved her hand to her heart, "render us ineffective as leaders.

"Lucy McDougal accused our...," she emphasized the next two words as she continued, "male leaders," she paused again, "of endeavoring to keep us clear of political and religious involvement. She said they counsel us to abandon any attempt to become the intellectual and influential equals of our masculine protectors."

"Of course," Sally thought. She recalled reading of Lucy McDougal and her inflammatory ideas. At any other time, she would have welcomed a discussion on the subjugation of her sex, but today she had too many other things on her mind. She ate quickly, ignoring her four companions as they revisited the radical ideas of the outspoken visitor to Pleasant Valley.

"Do you remember how she complimented Reverend Goodenough?" The mention of her father's name brought Sally's attention back to the conversation.

"She congratulated him for his advocacy of men and women sharing the same chores and receiving like rewards. She championed his belief in freeing the sexes from the harness of traditional marriage

189

and the shame of spinster- and bachelorhood. She cheered his revolutionary permissiveness toward the coupling of unmarried partners and," she raised her hands to the ceiling in celebratory praise, "his advocacy of the prevention of unnecessary propagation of our race.

"Then, Sister Sarah...." The young blonde woman looked over her shoulder as she lowered her voice and directed her comments to Sally. "She said that while we have achieved a foothold on the ladder to equality, we must go further. We must fight to get the vote; strive for a voice in the formulation of our laws; demand the right to own property and to receive equal wages when we are forced to provide a living for our families."

Another of her companions reached across the table and took Sally's hand. "She also said," she dropped her voice to a whisper, "that women should have the right to choose whether to bear a child." She lowered her voice even further. "After, as well as before, conception...."

Sally's head jerked up and she looked at the speaker. "What did she say about that?"

"After she finished speaking, she told us...." With a sweep of her hand, the blonde woman broke in and indicated that her three tablemates were also recipients of Lucy's revelation. "She told us that she, and others with similar views, had learned the secrets of the foreign women and that she, like her liberal-thinking sisters, is able to provide help to those in need."

Sally leaned back and tried to keep her voice calm.

"Where has this Lucy McDougal gone?"

"Don't you know? She's still here. Your mother said she could stay in your room for as long as she likes."

Sally took a deep breath, slowed her eating and thought about this new development as she finished her meal. The terrible news of James Daunt's capture had been accompanied by the realization that her personal problem may well be resolved.

When Esther awoke she was confused and she was cold. The room was unfamiliar; her head ached, and she was too weak to move.

Staring at the ceiling, she tried to remember how she came to be in this unknown place. Fleeting memories of a spacious room with large windows and two grand staircases rising high above her outstretched body competed with images of Samuel Baker and her dreaded brother standing by her side. She could not hold onto a concrete thought; everything was vague and disassociated. She closed her eyes and drifted back into a safe state of unreality.

"How are you, my dear?" The words, spoken in a strange voice, brought Esther out of her trance.

"Wha...t?" Esther whispered.

She opened her eyes and tried to focus on the wall across from her bed. Shadows formed ominous patterns on the dingy surface as they advanced and retreated with cadenced precision. She tried to capture a single image but each assumed a new form before she could anchor a specific one in her consciousness. Defeated, she turned her head to look at the speaker.

"Who...who...?" Esther found it difficult to formulate a coherent thought. "Who are you?" She forced out the question.

"Ah, those curious sounds again. Are you unable to talk, my dear? Are you a mute? Deaf as well as dumb?" A strange unkempt woman, dressed in a soiled, faded garment, leaned close and put her ear next to Esther's mouth.

"Try again, my dear."

Esther turned her face away. The rancid smell of the intruder's stringy hair, filthy clothes and unwashed body roiled her stomach.

She tried to lift her arms, to push against the woman's torso, but she could not move them. She tried again, this time sensing the iron bands which bound her wrists to the bed. She tried to raise her legs but came to realize each foot was shackled to a corner of the bedstead. There was a band across her chest binding her solidly in place. Although she lacked sufficient strength, Esther tried to pull against her manacles. She attempted to raise her hips off the bed, to break free from the restraints.

She cried out for help and began calling for Elias, forgetting that she had last seen her husband's decaying body lying stiff and bloodied in the bed of his farm wagon.

"Please stop." The alien voice spoke again, this time with the urgency of a command. "They will come for you if you make a fuss."

The woman put her hand on Esther's arm. "As weak as you are, my dear, you put up a struggle last night when they brought you here. That's why they put you in irons. If you create a disturbance again, they will do terrible things to make you stop. You cannot misbehave in here, my dear. No. You certainly cannot misbehave." Sadness tinged the woman's voice as she tried to calm the new arrival.

"Where am I? This is not my home. What am I doing here? I don't belong here." Esther was exhausted emotionally, physically and mentally. She stopped fighting and appealed to the woman.

"Help me. Please help me," she whispered as she looked into her face. There was compassion and caring in her visitor's eyes and Esther began to sob.

"Dear," the woman started to speak but instead backed to the door and stood quietly as she listened for sounds of someone coming in response to Esther's outbursts. Satisfied they had not been heard, she padded back to the bed.

"You have to be very careful in here." Her eyes became furtive and she looked over her shoulder. "If you cause a commotion they will take you to The Room."

Esther trembled at the tone of the woman's voice. Fear had replaced her samaritan's kindly countenance.

"The way to survive in here...." Esther interrupted the woman before she could finish.

"Where is 'here'? I don't know where I am."

"I cannot understand what you are saying. You must listen to what I have to say if you...."

The sound of a door opening, then closing and a bolt being thrown, restored the fear in the eyes of the stranger and caused her to stop speaking. She stepped to the entrance, cautiously peered around the corner, then slipped through the doorway and was gone. Esther was left alone, frightened by the irons which bound her limbs and alarmed by the warning the woman had been unable to complete.

Another door was unlocked and opened. Cries born of pain, anguish and despair punctuated an incoherent babble of vocal protestations and monologues delivered to an unseen audience. She desperately wished her surreptitious visitor would return. The squeals of opening doors, and the dull thuds as they closed, intensified as unknown beings approached down the hall. She closed her eyes and pretended to sleep.

Her door, which had been open, clanged shut. She could hear a conversation but the words were indistinct and impossible to make out. The speakers moved on to the next room and fresh sounds of a miserable human being assaulted Esther's ears. She was terrified.

New voices could be heard in what she assumed was a corridor. She was aware that her senses, which had been confused and dull when she had awakened, had sharpened. She could pick out individual speech patterns and she recognized the voice of Samuel Baker. Her spirits rose. He was the last person she had seen. He would help her. Then she remembered: Elias was dead and the doctor thought she had killed him.

For the first time, she acknowledged the probability that no one, not even her sympathetic visitor, would ever understand what she was saying. She also knew that, without intelligible speech, her chances of convincing anyone of her innocence, and of Maris' guilt, were nonexistent.

Sally hurried from the dining room and made her way to the two small rooms she shared with her mother. They were next to each other and each had its own separate entrance into the hall. The rooms could also be accessed from one to the other by an interior door, the only such room arrangement at Pleasant Valley.

She knocked softly on her mother's door. "Are you there?"

"Come in." Her mother opened the door. She was wearing her one good dress and Sally noticed a tray with two plates on the end of the bed. The residue of the midday meal could be seen on one of the dishes, no food remained on the other.

"I tried to tell you earlier, Sarah, Lucy McDougal is staying in your room. At the moment, we have no available lodging in the community and I did not know when you would return. If you're planning to stay, you can sleep on the floor in my room."

"May I speak with her?" Sally had no interest in the sleeping arrangements. She was only concerned with the noted speaker's possible knowledge of pregnancy terminations.

"She's resting. I cannot disturb her now."

"I must talk to her. I think she can help me."

Her mother nodded her head. "She has spoken of her familiarity with female problems. You must remember, she is not a midwife or a doctor, Sarah."

"I couldn't trust Hebe's heathen shaman so I left before taking her potion." She glanced at the dishes then turned to her mother. "You seem to know this woman. Would you suggest I follow Lucy McDougal's instructions?"

"It is a serious decision, Sarah. There is the question of your health as well as the possibility of your child surviving with permanent physical damage. I cannot advise you on this matter and I do not know what your father would say. If it were anyone but you, he would forbid the taking of any action and insist that you leave the community. However, you are his daughter and he does not always apply the same rules to you."

There was a knock on the door between the two rooms.

Sally's mother opened it and the stately figure of a middle-aged woman filled the doorway. Her hair was parted in the center and an abundance of wiry tendrils sprang away from her face and created an aura of energetic rebellion.

Her high-waisted cotton dress was of sensible fabric and cut to emphasize her capacious bosom. She was taller than most women and had a commanding presence. She walked through the door and extended her hand to Sally.

"Sister Sarah?" Sally nodded. "I am Lucy McDougal. Your mother has spoken of you and your spirit."

"The women are agog over your presence here...." Sally paused. She did not know how to address the woman in front of her.

Sensing her discomfort, Lucy McDougal said, "You may call me Miss Lucy. That is how I am known to my intimates."

She walked to the bed and sat on the edge. "It would be nice if you had a chair or two in here," she mused.

"An extra chair would be considered a vanity in the community," Sally's mother said as she walked around to the other side of the bed. "We could go into the dining room if you would be more comfortable, but word would quickly spread that you were there. If you prefer your privacy, you will have to content yourself with a seat on the bed."

Sally noticed her mother's defense of the reverend's dictum even though it obviously discomfited her guest.

"I am fine. I rather admire your dedication to the values of Pleasant Valley Farm, even though some of them do not make sense to me." Lucy McDougal turned to Sally. "You are looking robust, my dear."

Sally reddened as she suspected her mother's guest was inquiring about her condition.

"I have heard it said that you know the secrets of the foreign women who aid in solving a woman's problems."

Lucy McDougal looked steadily at Sally and said, "I believe that a woman should have sovereignty over her body and that she, and she alone, should decide whether, and when, it is appropriate to bear a child."

Sally was startled by Lucy McDougal's revolutionary convictions. She wondered how, or if, the reformer succeeded in overriding husbands' wishes and preachers' Bible-based procreation exhortations to have her voice heard in the male-dominated world in which she lived. At the moment, however, that question was of little concern to Sally.

"If," she began hesitantly. "If the child is already growing...."

"A delicate situation," Miss Lucy interrupted. "If the mother has experienced quickening, nothing can be done."

"Quickening?" Sally queried.

"If movement has been detected, it is too late. However, if there has been no activity, there are methods which can be utilized to alleviate the problem."

"Methods?"

"There are special potions I can mix to bring on a woman's menses, and implements, that I do not recommend under any circumstances, which can be used to end the problem. And then, there is the most common and acceptable remedy: a long, hard ride on horseback."

"That won't work for me," Sally said sadly. "I've ridden over seventy miles these last two days and I have no sign of relief."

"There are dangers when you drink the potions."

"My mother has already warned me," Sally interjected. "I am willing to take the chance. I am not in a position to bear a child, Mrs. McDougal." She chose to use a formal address instead of the more familiar one suggested by the well-known advocate for oppressed women.

Miss Lucy looked over at Sally's mother for confirmation. Unable to interpret the older woman's expression, she directed her attention back to Sally.

"I recommend a tea brewed from the leaves of the pennyroyal plant, dried blue cohosh and tansy. To this, I add a tablespoon of yeast which seems to increase its chance of success."

She surveyed Sally through half-closed eyes. "The tea must be very hot when you drink it and it is necessary to take this three times a day for a week. If you do not have results at the end of that time, it is imperative you stop taking the remedy as too much of it will cause permanent harm to you and the baby you would still be carrying."

She walked over to Sally and placed her hands on her shoulders. "You will probably be nauseous. Do not worry unless it becomes so severe that you are retching uncontrollably. Then you must stop the cure. If your toes and fingers become numb or you experience dizziness or extreme perspiration or you begin to bleed from your eyes, ears, nose or mouth, you must cease the ingestion of the pennyroyal tea.

"The choice you are faced with cannot be made capriciously. There are women who have not exercised caution or used common sense and they have suffered excruciatingly painful deaths."

Lucy McDougal stepped back and looked over at Sally's mother as she awaited the younger woman's response.

Sally walked to the window and stared out toward the barn. Her horse was still tied to the post. Several thoughts went through her mind as she looked down at him. Then, after a moment, she turned to face the two women.

"I have not yet stabled the horse. I want to ride for a bit and when I return, I will start taking your potion, Miss Lucy. I have," she added, "no choice."

Sally left the room and went to the fence where her horse was tied. She replaced the halter with a bridle but did not saddle the horse. She flung herself on his back and slowly headed out into the fields. The crops had long been picked and the remaining plants had withered and died.

She rode at a leisurely pace until she was far enough from the community to escape the watchful eyes of her mother and Lucy McDougal. Then she gave her horse his head. She pressed him into a gallop and intentionally allowed herself to physically experience the shock of each impact of his pounding hooves on the unforgiving earth. Abandoning herself to the discomfort of the ride, she demanded even more speed.

A fence marked the end of the community's fields and she guided her horse straight for it. She felt a shiver run down his back just before he took to the air. His front legs cleared the fence but she heard the clatter of his back hooves as they hit the top rail. She felt his legs give way as he landed. She tried to grasp his neck but his head dropped down as he pitched forward and she slid off to the side. She landed next to a pile of hay which, in a flash of insight, she realized had spooked the horse.

Everything swirled around her and she started to lose consciousness. As the darkness enveloped her, Sally Morley felt the blood begin to flow and knew she no longer had a need to partake of Lucy McDougal's noxious brew.

The door opened and Dr. Samuel Baker, the man she considered her friend, walked in. Following behind him was the person she feared most in this world: her brother, Maris Evans Hicks.

Esther closed her eyes and pretended to sleep.

"As her only close male relative, I am in a position to commit her, Samuel." Maris spoke in a clipped, efficient tone.

"I have the application, signed and dated by me. And I have the payment in advance for her board. All I need now is a certificate signed by you stating that she is, indeed, insane and is a candidate for confinement here. And you know as well as I do that, for an honorable woman like Esther to stab her husband, she would have to be mad. Totally mad."

Esther's eyes flew open. Samuel Baker was staring down at her, genuine despair showing in his face as he surveyed her bound body. He placed his hand on her shoulder and said, "I had no idea, Esther, I had no idea."

Maris pushed his way between Samuel and his sister.

"Esther, this is the best place for you." His voice, brusque at first, softened as he made his case.

"You need help, Esther. They have the latest cures for lunacy here. The doctors can make you well. That's what we all want.... " His uncomfortable attempt to assume the role of sympathetic caregiver was unconvincing.

"We all want to see you get well." Maris bowed his head, "I am sure you appreciate the sacrifice Delia and I are making to provide for your rehabilitation. We are doing it from the goodness of our hearts. After all, you are my sister, Esther."

The good doctor walked behind Maris and reclaimed his place by the side of the bed. He stroked Esther's hands. He gently massaged her ankles where the shackles had rubbed her thin skin raw. His eyes were sad and his demeanor, dejected.

"I am so sorry, Esther. I had no idea." His shoulders sagged as he turned away and left the room. Maris stayed behind.

"Esther, you will get the best care here. I am committing you and paying in advance for thirteen weeks of board. We will see how you are doing at the end of that time."

As if afraid she would rise up and stop him, Maris held his hand, palm down, over Esther's body. Without touching her, he abruptly turned to follow Samuel Baker.

The footsteps of the two men sounded like gunshots to Esther's ears as she heard them walk away, leaving her alone in what she now knew to be a madhouse. She had heard of lunatics and insane asylums and everything she had heard was frightening. She still had enough reasoning power to recognize that Maris had convinced Samuel and the people in this building that she was mad.

For the first time since her fall into the ditch, she could see clearly through the veil of depression which had descended over her. She knew she would need every ounce of strength she could muster to weather this challenge, and more importantly, she must have all of her wits about her. Unfortunately, she had few reserves left and her fighting instinct faded. In spite of her aversion to weakness, the tears came, and this time, she was incapable of preventing them.

Samuel Baker sat next to Maris on the wagon seat. His face was calm but his thoughts were in turmoil. He could not escape the vision of Esther Latch, her body literally in irons, condemned to live in unspeakable misery in the basement of a lunatic asylum. He had to accept a share of the responsibility for her imprisonment as he had signed her commitment papers.

Samuel could not look at his traveling companion. He suspected Maris Hicks had been born mean and he should have been on his guard. Less than a year after the birth of Margaret, Margaretmaris bore a second son, Josiah. The two children, sweet-natured and fair of countenance, grew more attractive as time passed. Their parents clearly favored the pair and gifted them with special treats which their sisters resented and their jealous older brother routinely confiscated. Samuel knew of Maris' mischief as there were times when his open hostility manifested itself in physical injury and the doctor was called.

One day, when Josiah was eight years old, he and Margaret were playing beside a neighbor's pond. Maris came upon them and sent his sister home. A short time later, Maris ran to a nearby farmhouse and cried out that Josiah had fallen into the water. The farmer raced to save the lad but it was too late. He brought the boy's body to Samuel who noticed that there was a bruise on the side of Josiah's head. He could prove nothing but had been wary of Maris Hicks ever since. Today, the good doctor was certain his suspicions were justified and that he must try to find alternate care for Esther.

# *November and December, 1828*

The days passed, and Esther saw only the attendant who released her manacles at midday so she could relieve herself before eating a simple meal of tea, salted meat, cold potato and one slice of hard, dry, bread. She was too weak to chew her food and subsisted on the tea and bread which she softened by dipping it into the liquid. The overall deprivation forced her to adjust to the strict regimen imposed on her bodily functions. Where she had been eerily emaciated when she arrived at the insane asylum, she was now a grotesque caricature.

Esther had not been allowed off the bed or out of the room since her incarceration. The physical act of dragging Elias' body from the bedroom to the barn had taken extraordinary effort fueled by irrational fear and desperation. Her subsequent internment sealed her slide into total physical dissipation. She developed sores from the base of her neck to the backs of her knees. The skin under her restraints remained raw, and ugly black flies regularly attacked the open wounds. Horrified at first, she no longer noticed them as they circled her body before landing to feast on her infected flesh.

There was a barred window high on the outside wall, and when she had the strength to turn her head, she could see the ankles and lower legs of people who passed by on their way to the neighboring outdoor market. Shortly after her arrival, Esther overheard an attendant tell a visitor they were in the section of the main hospital building where the truly insane patients were housed.

She became immune to the constant din of senseless prattle punctuated by the screams and yells of periodically agitated, protesting inmates. Sometimes, when sleep claimed all the occupants of her ward and there was silence, she waited, nerves on edge, for something to set them off again. Those nights she slept little. Other times, she dozed off and on, waking only when a disturbance occurred outside her door or the attendant prodded her with his stick.

When she first arrived, she tried to keep track of time, but the days blended into nights and back into days and after a while she lost count. She had not seen her mysterious caller since that original encounter and sometimes questioned her existence.

One day, however, she awoke to: "My dear, are you all right?"

The voice was familiar; however, Esther did not recognize the woman who stood in the doorway. Her hair was clean and coifed; her dress, fashionable and pristine; she smelled of rose-scented perfume.

As feeble as she was, Esther recoiled from her visitor, aware that she was now the only one who offended.

"My son came to see me today. They cleaned me up and put me in a comfortable room upstairs. There were large windows that overlooked trees and flowers and a small pond. I was to pretend it was my private quarters." Esther had not noticed her cultured accent when she had first appeared in her cell. "I did as I was told." Her mysterious caller leaned against the wall.

"They do not realize that my son has no interest in whether I am cared for or not. He had me legally declared unsound of mind and committed here so he could take over my affairs. I was quite wealthy, you know." She looked at Esther. "I was. And I am not crazy. At least I wasn't before I came here."

The woman seemed a different person now that she was presentable and Esther was embarrassed by her own pitiful condition. Although she had been bathed and dressed in rough, but clean, clothes on her arrival, she had received no personal care since that day. In fact, she had come to fear any attention or attempt to restore her sanity. She heard the screams of recalcitrant patients who were subjected to various treatments and had come to associate the word "cure" with torture and persecution.

The woman, showing signs of exhaustion, approached the bed. "Do you mind if I sit?"

Esther nodded her head slightly. Her body and the chains holding her prisoner left little room on the meager mattress and the woman had to perch precariously on the edge of the frame.

"Are you able to speak yet?" Esther shook her head.

"I am sorry. Have you been dumb since birth?"

Esther paused before answering; the act of moving her head exhausted her.

"An accident?" The woman asked the question before Esther could answer.

"I had a bad time after I visited you," she continued. "One of the attendants caught me out of my dungeon and threatened to report me. He blackmailed me until I had depleted the small amount of money my son left me when he brought me here. Then he reported me. He and four others took me to The Room. They said I had been scheduled for a cure." Her hands were tightly clasped in her lap and she rocked back and forth.

"There was a doctor in the room, and although I felt he genuinely believed he was there to administer medical aid, I knew better. I knew the attendants had lied and told exaggerated tales of my lack of cooperation." She looked down at the floor.

"My son pays them, you know, to try to drive me insane. And I think they are succeeding." She glanced toward the door.

"When they took me to The Room, they removed my clothes...." Tears formed in the corners of her eyes and trickled down her cheeks. "Then each held one of my limbs and pulled hard while the fifth climbed on a chair and poured buckets of cold water on my face.

"I could not breathe when the water hit me from such a height. I was suffocating and I was frightened. I cried out for mercy but they kept replenishing the buckets. The doctor finally stopped them when I lost my senses. Later, they returned me to my bed and left me without any clothing or covering for two days." The strain of the ordeal showed on her face and in her bearing as she slumped forward and held her head in her hands.

"Sometimes I think the doctors and their minions are the lunatics and we, the patients, are the sane ones. It has taken me all this time to get the courage to visit you again. Now, to tell the truth, I don't care. I know, from what I learned today, that my son has finally been granted complete control over my affairs. He will never allow me to leave this place so I have nothing to lose." She raised her head. "I want the attendants to see me roaming the corridor. I welcome their cruelty. It will hasten my demise and save me from committing the mortal sin of taking my own life."

Esther tried to move her hand to touch the woman's arm but she was too weak to lift the shackles that held her in place.

The woman noticed her attempt and covered Esther's hand with her own. After a moment, she stood up and looked down at the bed.

"Now you know what awaits you in The Room. You should also know that there is a good chance your brother has put you here for the same reason my son committed me. For money." She sighed. "The reason I visited you when you first arrived is that I recognized your name. My son is your brother's lawyer and he is handling your brother's defense of your father's will." She reached down and stroked Esther's face.

"Don't you think it's odd that you are still strapped to your bed even though you have caused no trouble since the night you arrived? And I'll wager you have never had a doctor visit you. Am I correct?"

Esther closed her eyes. She had convinced herself she was here because Samuel Baker made the erroneous assumption that she had killed Elias in a fit of rage. There had always been the hope that he would return, recognize the truth and she would be freed. Now that she knew Maris was the only one behind her incarceration, and that he had, in all probability, assured everyone that she was insane, she was certain she would never leave the asylum.

Maris' stabbing of Elias had probably been unplanned. The threat, however, had been real. When the situation had gotten out of hand, Maris must have realized the beneficial ramifications of the circumstances. He could eliminate two of the people who challenged the legality of his father's will: Elias, who filed the suit against him; and Esther, the instigator behind that challenge and one of the beneficiaries of an equitable distribution of Jacob Hicks' property.

The capture of James Daunt, and his upcoming trial for the murder of Richard Holt, assured Maris of an easy attainment of their father's estate. Margaret, Bettina and Hannah were temperamentally incapable of standing up to him without additional support. And if Bettina had received the reward money, they would have enough to live on and would probably settle out of court. Maris will win, she thought, and she really did not care as she, like her furtive friend, no longer had anything to gain.

Her last comfort, sleep, overtook her and she escaped into the mental vacuum she had come to depend on for survival.

The vibrant red, rust and gold highlights of early autumn were replaced by the dull brown of a barren fall. As November passed, however, the ground brightened under a thick covering of white as snow fell on Pleasant Valley Farm.

Anticipating a long confinement, the community unanimously embraced the idea of opening a public-access store in the spring and set about making items for sale. Daylight hours found some of the women sewing muslin morning caps which they personalized with delicate tatting on the borders. Others wove straw bonnets with deep brims to shelter ladies' faces from the sun. Embroidered handkerchiefs, scarves and purses were scheduled to join the hats on storeroom shelves.

The men regretted the loss of James Daunt and his blacksmithing skills as they had counted on his decorative utilitarian items. They searched for alternative products and decided to use his forge for blowing glass. They soon learned an open fire did not produce enough heat to mix and soften the necessary raw material.

A glassmaker was summoned to the farm and the inexperienced residents began planning the construction of two simple barn-like structures, each of which would house a furnace. One would be used to heat the glass to two thousand degrees so it could be formed; and the second, would be kept at eight hundred degrees to allow the completed objects to cool gradually and avoid cracking.

As production could not commence until the buildings were completed and the novices had learned the glassmaking business, it was decided that, for the first summer, the shop would feature only the ladies' handicrafts. Given the sole accountability for the success of their initial retail venture, the female members of the community spent every available moment creating their wares.

During this time, Sally was confined to her bed and she missed the hustle and bustle of converting part of the agrarian complex into a rudimentary manufacturing facility. Her fall from the horse had left her with a number of ugly bruises and minor scrapes and cuts, but she had escaped without any broken bones. However, her bleeding persisted long after the bruising faded and the wounds healed. She grew weak and had little spirit to fight the will of her mother who insisted she stay in her bed while the older woman slept on the floor.

Lucy McDougal remained in Sally's room, seemingly unaware of the inconvenience she caused by her presence. She enjoyed the intellectual stimulation of the community almost as much as the personal admiration she received, and while the food was plain, it was well-prepared and the portions generous. As an acknowledged guest of the reverend, she had no responsibilities and found the life most agreeable for a widow in well-concealed financial straits.

Lucy was the first one to be consulted about Sally's female indisposition and she recommended garlic as an anticoagulant. She also advocated a cup of hot tea three times a day which she brewed and served herself

Unbeknownst to Sally's mother who kept a constant vigil over her daughter's sick bed, Lucy added a diluted dose of the herbs used in the toxic brew she had recommended as a solution to Sally's original problem. They did their job and the light flow of blood continued. Instead of improving, Sally's poor health continued. She became nauseous and suffered abdominal cramping and debilitating headaches. With no doctor in residence in the community, Sally's mother was anxious to keep the herbalist at hand while her daughter's health floundered. As a result, Lucy was assured a place at the table as long as she was able to deter Sally's return to wellbeing.

Esther awakened as her door slammed against the wall. Two men, one very tall and one extraordinarily short, charged into her room. They unlocked the irons holding her arms to her sides, her ankles to the foot of the bed, her torso flat to the meager mattress. They threw the restraints aside and the short man put his hands under her arms and pulled her up. Then, with a grunt, he released his grip and Esther's legs collapsed, leaving her in a heap on the dirty floor.

The tall man reached down and hauled her dead weight upright. He put one arm around her back, pressed her body to his and ran his other hand over her breasts. He turned away, spit on the floor and muttered, "Nothing there. You take her." He pushed her limp body toward his companion who scrambled to catch her as she collapsed a second time.

"What did you expect she would be like after a month in chains?" The short man gave her chest a cursory check, agreed with the assessment, flung her over his shoulder and walked through the door into the corridor. Although she was bent at the waist, he was so undersized that her fingers dragged on the floor as they moved along.

"Where are you taking me?" Esther asked weakly, without trying to raise her hands.

"None of you nuts makes any sense. I don't know why they keep you alive." Her transporter carried her to the end of the hallway and opened the door to a pitch-black room. He dropped her body into a high-backed wooden chair as his companion lit an oil lamp.

Esther heard a low groan coming from the far corner of the room. She turned her head, and as her eyes adjusted to the dim light, she could see the outline of a human form slumped in a seat. The chair was suspended from a beam by four ropes and it moved slowly in a circular motion as the cables unwound on their own accord. A stool, surrounded by four large buckets stood nearby. Esther needed no confirmation. She was in The Room.

"Give him a couple of twists while I get started on her."

The tall man responded by halting the chair. He grasped the handle of a large gear and turned it away from him. Ropes led to more gears on the top of the beam which accelerated the circular motion of the chair. Its semi-conscious occupant moaned as the speed increased.

"Stop," he mumbled, "can't take it any longer. Stop." His body fell forward and bounced off the cords which held him in place.

The tall man was laughing as he increased his turning and the chair reached a dizzying speed. The victim's body began to jerk this way and that but the operator continued to turn the gear at a frenetic pace. Esther looked away as the sight of the diabolical whirligig in action made her faint. The suspicion that she was the next occupant of the chair caused her to gag.

"Them doctors say you gotta stop all that blood rushing to your brain," he shouted. "Relax, mate, this is supposed to cure you." Laughing even harder, he cranked the gear faster and faster. He was out of control, possessed by his power to torment the already broken man in the swing.

"Get over here." The short man barked the order to his cohort as he pushed Esther's head back into a wooden box lined with linen padding. It surrounded her head on three sides and the enclosure prevented her from moving it forward, backward, or side to side. He pressed her body close against the back of the chair and pulled a leather band tight across her chest and upper arms. He then secured another strap over her stomach, restricting any movement of her torso. Additional leather bands secured her wrists to the arms of the chair and her feet to wooden platforms which extended beyond its legs.

Esther struggled feebly against her shackles. They stayed true.

"You ain't goin' nowhere," the short man said with a smile. "Not even to relieve yourself." He reached behind the chair and brought out a pan and flashed it in front of her face.

"Stool-pan," he said gleefully. "You're in the Restraining Chair and it's nailed to the floor. Supposed to 'eliminate any visual stimulation'." His sarcastic quotation of the doctors' explanation was followed by a quick hoot of laughter.

"You don't get to look at anything but that wall over there. This is supposed to cure you but I tell you, if you are not totally mad already, you will be by the time they let you out of this chair."

Esther heard the tall man give the gear one last twist before he left to join his companion.

"Doctor will be here in a few minutes."

Esther's spirits lifted and she raised her eyes. The tall attendant noticed the hint of hope in her glance and laughed contemptuously.

"Don't get your hopes up. You're about to receive the cure." He pointed to the unconscious figure still rotating in the swinging chair. "Just like him." He laughed again and the two men left the room.

The sound of the ropes rubbing against each other as they wound down almost drowned out the low moaning of the other occupant of the room. Esther was aware that she should be afraid of what lay before her, but after weeks spent strapped to a bed and now, inextricably bound to a chair, she realized she was too weak physically and spiritually to care. She closed her eyes and willed herself into a self-induced trance.

Luck turned against Lucy McDougal when she depleted her supply of herbs and was unable to replenish them at the nearby country store. As soon as Lucy ceased doctoring the tea, Sally began to improve. The nausea, cramping and headaches stopped almost immediately and the bleeding slowed and disappeared within the next few days.

Initially, the coincidence of her improvement and the discontinuation of Lucy's brew went unnoticed by Sally and her mother. However, as she regained her physical health, Sally's mental state stabilized as well and she began to suspect Lucy of medical subterfuge.

Although she was originally tempted to report her misgivings to her mother, Sally decided to confront the perpetrator of the plot. Knowing Lucy spent her mornings reading or writing in her room, Sally knocked on the door and opened it before receiving a response.

"I must speak with you," she said to the woman who looked up from the book she was reading.

"You're out of bed," Lucy was surprised, but she recovered quickly. "I am pleased."

"Yes. My headaches and nausea seem to have disappeared overnight and my female problem has been cured. My strength grows each day and my head is completely clear."

Sally looked down at the respected lecturer who busied herself marking her place in the book.

"I'll come straight to the point, Mrs. McDougal. I think you have been poisoning me." She watched the woman's reaction to her words. Although her features remained inscrutable, the color drained from Lucy's face.

"It is difficult for me to imagine the motive behind your actions. I can only guess you believed my continued illness," Sally trembled slightly at the thought, "would allow you to stay here indefinitely without the constraints that come with accepting our conventions."

She walked to the window. "That is not going to happen. I want you to leave this afternoon or I will inform both my mother and Reverend Goodenough of your duplicity."

Lucy was stunned. "They won't believe you," she said confidently. "I will tell them your accusations are unfounded, the ranting of a still-incapacitated convalescent."

"You underestimate my position in the community, Mrs. McDougal. If I were you, I would pack my bags and be gone before my mother returns from her morning chores."

Sally faced the seated woman. "You have a well-earned reputation as an influential reformer. I have read your discourses on abolition and the subjugation of women. They are compatible with the convictions we hold here. We, too, believe that no man has the right to own another; that each person, black or white, male or female, should have the right to pursue the profession of his choosing and to receive equal compensation; that everyone, rich or poor, should have the right to an education, to own property, to vote, to hold office. Free-thinking people espouse your views and you are accepted in many social and intellectual circles throughout our country and abroad. You must continue to pursue your calling."

Lucy slumped back in her chair and confessed. "I have depleted my funds. I have nowhere to go."

"Unfortunately, you have overstepped your bounds while you've been with us. Besides which, you do not belong here. We are a self-contained society, and while we welcome visitors and encourage the exchange of ideas, we have limited exposure to outsiders. You need a wide audience and...," Sally looked accusingly at Lucy, "I fear your mission has been seriously compromised by the complacency you have embraced since coming to Pleasant Valley. You need to be out in the world, not cloistered on a farm surrounded by fields instead of people."

Sally eyed her up and down and announced, "I have no doubt that you will land on your feet. You are a resourceful woman who has parlayed your intellect, social skills and eloquence into a position of influence and respect. You will have no trouble charming your way into your next refuge."

Sally smiled ruefully. "Don't let your dark side re-emerge, Lucy McDougal. I believed in you. I was ready to take your venomous swill, a lesser dose of which, I suspect, is what you fed me when I was sick. I do not believe you meant me permanent harm so I am willing to take a chance and let you go. I hope I am right and you will not lose your way again and inflict harm on another unsuspecting victim."

She walked to the door. "I will arrange for someone to drive you into town. The stage stops there. You will have to hurry if you want to be on this afternoon's run. If you are late, you will have the cost of a night's lodging as you are no longer welcome here."

Sally went back to her mother's room and closed the door behind her. She was still weak and the exertion of her confrontation left her exhausted. She sat on the edge of the bed and held her head in her hands.

The realization that the woman in the next room had willingly jeopardized her health for her own gain seemed preposterous, yet under the circumstances, it was plausible. Sally hoped she had made the right decision in sending Lucy on her way. The thought of reporting her to the sheriff brought feelings of despair as she was reminded of James and his arrest.

During the past few weeks, Sally had suffered grotesque nightmares about James Daunt. At the same time, her befuddled mind had not been capable of concrete contemplation about him or his circumstances.

Now that she was on her way to recovery, the reality of his situation settled in and her chest ached with the knowledge that he had little chance of escaping the hangman's noose. She tried to shake the feeling of doom as she rose from the bed and headed to the stable to find someone to drive Lucy McDougal to the depot.

"Wake up, Mrs. Latch."

Esther slowly rose to a conscious state as the familiar sound of her surname triggered a positive reaction in her brain. This was the first time since she had been admitted to the institution that anyone had addressed her by name.

A man, dressed in the dark coat of a professional gentleman, stood in front of her. Seeing her eyes were open, he leaned down and brought his face directly in front of the box which surrounded her head.

"I am Doctor Paxton," He smiled into the box. Through half-closed eyes, Esther discerned the look of insincerity which accompanied his self-introduction.

"I am here to help you get well." The doctor withdrew from her view and she could hear him rummaging around behind the chair.

"Here you are, my darlings." He returned to confront her and held out a pottery jar whose top edge was decorated with small perforations. An iron clasp secured the lid.

Even in her debilitated state, Esther recognized the dreaded leech jar.

"No," she whimpered. "No. Not the leeches."

The doctor did not bother to mention that he could not understand her protestations. Instead, he smiled again and opened the jar.

He gently swung one of the leeches back and forth in front of her face. "These are my pretties, my helpers," he said, broadening his smile. "They will make you well. They will suck all the poison out of your brain, and before long, you will be fine. You would like that, wouldn't you, Mrs. Latch?" He dropped the leech back into the jar and moved to the side of the chair.

Esther winced as the sting of a knife cut a small incision in her left arm. She sensed the warmth of the blood as it oozed from her vein. She felt the touch of the doctor's index finger as he rubbed it over the wounded area and watched as his bloody finger entered the box which held her head. She closed her eyes as he smeared the blood on her forehead. He gathered an additional supply on the tips of his fingers and rubbed them on her temples. He finished by wiping them clean on the area around her mouth.

"You are too weak for me to bleed you by opening your veins so I must use the leeches." The doctor spoke as he straightened and moved away from the chair. "The blood I daubed on your head will draw them to the critical areas and the sweet little creatures will happily do my work for me."

He vanished again only to reappear with his dreadful jar. He opened it and brought out several leaches. He took a moment to admire them. Esther fainted.

The doctor did not notice his patient's comatose state. "You will be all right, Mrs. Latch," he said, after he finished placing a sufficient number of the repulsive worms on her face. "I'll come back in the morning to check on you."

Dr. Paxton picked a handkerchief from the drawer of a small chest and wiped his hands. He returned the leech jar to its resting place, reached in and extracted a single worm. He placed it across the fingers he used to smear Esther's blood. The leech did not bite him so he replaced it in the jar.

"Good, no blood left on my fingers."

He walked over to the man in the swing, searched for a pulse and then stepped back.

"I must have someone remove the body," he muttered. "In a few days, I will need the Rotating Chair for Mrs. Latch."

Dr. Paxton extinguished the lamp, closed the door and left the room.

At the exact same moment the light was snuffed out, so, too, was the life of Esther Hicks Latch. Physical debilitation and sheer terror had proved too much for the formerly tough farm wife and she was spared forever from the leeches and the Rotating Chair.

Her last thought was of the eternal damnation to which she was sure the Lord had condemned her. She had no fear. Hell could not possibly be worse than the life she had been living since she had aimed James Daunt's musket at Richard Holt and pulled the trigger.

# Saturday, February 14, 1829

James Daunt's trial was scheduled to begin on the third Monday in February.

The Reverend Thaddeus Goodenough planned to visit the prisoner the day before he went to court and to stay in the county seat throughout the trial. When Sally heard of her father's preparations, she asked to join him. At her mother's request, he refused. Sally prevailed and he gave his consent.

This would be her first trip away from Pleasant Valley since James' apprehension, the resolution of her personal problem and her discovery of Lucy McDougal's lethal tea. She would have preferred to make the trip alone but Thaddeus was determined to minister to James before his trial and provide support during his ordeal. She did not look forward to the two-day ride and the winter conditions foretold a particularly slow and grueling journey.

Sally rose long before sunrise and found Thaddeus had readied the horses and hitched them to the farm wagon by the time she reached the paddock. It was a raw dawn that broke on the horizon and spread across the gray sky as they travelled south. The reverend planned to drive thirty miles to Hebe Balderston's and spend the night before undertaking the additional twelve miles the next morning. Sally, however, wanted to keep secret her association with the tavern. She talked him into stopping at the Sign of the Ship which was halfway between the community and the county seat. As it was a particularly cold day, he agreed, for the scarves and blankets in which they had wrapped themselves failed to stave off the chill of the frosty air.

Snow was on the fields and ice filled the holes in the dirt road. Their trip was slow at first as the horses were hampered by the difficulty of negotiating the frozen wagon wheel tracks. As the sun rose in the sky, the ice softened and the horses adopted an easy pace.

Father and daughter stopped at a public house to warm themselves and eat their noonday meal. Sally dreaded leaving the warmth of the fire but she was anxious to complete the trip and get settled in time to see James before he faced the judge and jury.

The second leg of their journey was uneventful. They reached the Sign of the Ship tavern in late afternoon and secured accommodations. The temperature had discouraged travelers and they each had a room to themselves, a rare occurrence, indeed. Many times a man was required to share a room, and sometimes a bed, with strangers. Women, too, would have to share their lodgings when an inn was crowded.

They had rarely spoken during their time together in the wagon and they each chose to eat alone huddled next to the fireplaces in their separate rooms. The hardships of the trip had exhausted Sally, and in spite of maintaining a well-stoked fire, she was cold. She remained fully dressed, removing only her shoes before crawling under the quilts stacked on her bed. She immediately fell into a deep sleep and the nightmares she had suffered during her recovery returned.

*James' body was swinging from the end of a hangman's rope. She carried a large knife and stood in the back of the crowd of sightseers. She began pushing her way through the mob so she could climb the gallows and cut the rope to release him before the noose tightened all the way. People were shouting at him, calling him "murderer", "villain", "scoundrel", and they closed in on each other to prevent her from reaching the gibbet. Desperately, she slashed out with her knife as hands grabbed at her body. She tried to scream but she made no sound.*

Sally had come to know when she was having a nightmare and tried to pull herself out of her deeply troubled sleep. The hands touching her body were softer now, no longer aggressively pulling at her, now caressing and soothing her. Gradually, she awakened and when she finally opened her eyes, the reverend was standing over her, gently stroking her shoulder and smoothing her hair.

"I heard you cry out and came to see if you were all right." He moved back from her bedside. "I wanted to comfort you."

Sally turned her head away and stared at the wall.

"I will leave now that your dreams have stopped." He turned and walked to the door. "I only wanted to help you." He opened the door and left the room.

Sally started to cry. She sobbed uncontrollably as the memories of that first night flooded her mind. She recalled the years spent seeking her father's attention, trying to entice him back into her bed so she could, once again, satisfy his, and she had to admit, her own desires.

When she finally stopped crying, she did not know whether the aggressive hands in her dream had been real or imagined. She did know, however, that it no longer mattered. Her father was no longer the most important man in her life. A married man slated to hang for murder had supplanted the reverend and she finally acknowledged that her attraction to James was much deeper than carnal lust.

# *Sunday, February 15, 1829*

Thaddeus Goodenough was able to secure space in the inn across the street from the jail. He and Sally were squeezed into two separate rooms which they shared with other outsiders. In addition to prosecution and defense witnesses, the town was filled with lawyers, writers and curious spectators. With one day to go before the trial, rooms were at a premium.

The prosecution had summoned thirty-six men and women willing to testify to the petty misdemeanors, degenerate nature and murderous inclinations of James Daunt. Their primary witnesses were, of course, the two young nieces of Squire Holt who saw the defendant standing at the edge of the woods just before their uncle fell.

The defense had only the endorsements of six lads from Hebe's. James had not revealed his whereabouts during the time he was on the run so no character witnesses had been called forth from Pleasant Valley Farm.

As Sally followed Thaddeus out of the inn and across the street, she looked at the gray stone building which sat to the left of the courthouse. An attractive three-story house with paned glass windows anchored the corner of two well-used roads. When she had first seen it from the wagon, Sally had been encouraged by the civility of James' imprisonment. She was later told by the proprietress of the inn that what she described was the sheriff's home. The jail was the attached two-storied, windowless building made of square-cut stone which abutted it and extended out the back.

She and the reverend entered the grim prison through a solid wooden door which opened onto the main street. They were stopped by a large man who carried a pistol. He aimed it at the visitors.

"I'm the sheriff of this town and nobody is allowed in here until after the trial. Go to the courthouse in the morning if you want to see the murderer."

"I am the Reverend Thaddeus Goodenough and this is my daughter, Sarah. We have come to spiritually support James Daunt as he faces his fate at the hands of the court."

Sally could see that her father's commanding voice and dignified bearing impressed the man who stopped them. "And," he continued, "I am under the impression that Mr. Daunt has not yet been convicted and is innocent until proven guilty."

The big man hesitated and then relaxed the hand which held the pistol letting it fall to his side.

Thaddeus gently pushed Sally past the sheriff and toward the door at the rear of the reception area.

"Stop!"

The sheriff raised his pistol and leveled it at the reverend. "I can't let anyone go back there. There's been talk of a lynchin' in town and it is my job to make sure that doesn't happen."

Sally froze. She did not believe in miracles and knew the chances of James being set free were scant but the thought of strangers forcing their way into the jail and dragging him into the street before…. She stared at the sheriff and he saw the horror on her face.

"We're not going to let that happen, Miss." He narrowed his eyes and looked from Sally to her father. "You relatives?"

"No. I am Mr. Daunt's religious and philosophical counselor. I have come to ease his mind during this time of tribulation."

"He's got a preacher," the sheriff growled. "Reverend Godfrey has been here every day for over a month. Taking notes, he is. He's going to publish James Daunt's confession."

Sally glanced at the regal man standing next to her. He had gone pale.

"His confession?" The reverend faltered for a moment before he regained his composure. "I am sure there has been a mistake. I am his confessor for secular as well as spiritual matters. I have a duty to speak with the unfortunate member of my community." Thaddeus raised his nose and glared down at the sheriff.

"Is this the way to the dungeon where you are holding James Daunt?" Sally allowed herself to be guided by Thaddeus' hand on her shoulder as they moved down the hall. The sheriff did not answer but he stepped aside to let them pass.

They followed the wood planking which was used as flooring and came to two heavy wooden doors which fronted side-by-side cells. Sally stopped and peered through the barred opening of the first cubicle. A stranger lay on a cot. He twisted his neck around so he could look at the visitors, then turned back to stare at the wall. She moved to the second cell and involuntarily gasped.

James was there. He sat, with his head in his hands, on a small cot covered by a bare mattress.

She was shocked to see his wrists and ankles encased in shackles. The chains were locked to a hook anchored to the floor. The fetters appeared long enough to allow him to stand straight but too short for him to walk any further than a few feet from his bed.

"The chains…?" Sally whispered.

The sheriff heard her and muttered his apologies. "Sorry, Miss. Squire Holt's brother is a friend of the mayor. He insisted Daunt be chained and his movements restrained. Can't do anything about it." He averted his eyes.

Thaddeus cleared his throat but James did not look up.

"James," he said. "Sister Sarah and I have come to counsel you before your trial tomorrow."

James started at the mention of Sally's community name. He stared first at Thaddeus Goodenough and then at Sally. He struggled to his feet.

She was dressed as Sister Sarah. A plain black wool cape covered the gray woolen work clothes of Pleasant Valley. Her trousers, which she wore for warmth as well as convention, were masked by a gathered skirt of the same fabric. A black woolen bonnet with a deep brim obscured her face from anyone who was not standing directly in front of her. The shapeless skirt and head covering were required attire for women when they represented the community in public. Thaddeus had declared that the conservative dress helped to offset the whispered rumors of bizarre behavior which titillated the good folk of Pleasant Valley's neighboring areas.

"Missus," a voice from the adjoining cell broke the awkward silence. Sally moved back to the first door and looked directly at the speaker. He had risen and was standing by his cot.

"You look like somebody I seen before."

Sally recognized him as an infrequent visitor to Hebe's. She had teased him once, playing to the pleasure of the other boys at the bar.

"I don't know you," Sally said dispassionately. "I am sorry."

Confused, the man shook his head and sat down on his cot. Sally returned to James and her father.

Thaddeus spoke. "I am here to console and guide you through your hour of need, James. *'But the Comforter, which is the Holy Ghost, whom the Father will send in my name, he shall teach you all things, and bring all things to your remembrance....'* John Fourteen, verse twenty-six.

"I, as a mortal representative of the Comforter, will bring you solace through the word of the Lord, and perhaps, I can help you remember or clarify something that will aid in your defense."

"Nothing can help me now," James said. "I am guilty and I will be sentenced to hang." He looked long and hard at Sally, as for a brief moment, he recaptured the life they had together. Then he returned his attention to Thaddeus Goodenough.

"A local preacher, Solomon Godfrey, has been here every day, and in spite of his endeavors, he has not been able to bring me to the Lord. I am, and always will be, a skeptic." James glanced away.

"I sinned in the eyes of the law as well as in the eyes of your God when I shot the squire. For a brief time, however, I thought your God might have forgiven me when Sal..., Sister Sarah introduced me to Pleasant Valley."

James looked away before he resumed speaking. "Reverend Godfrey has tried to make me believe that, instead of embracing the Lord, repenting and changing my ways when you rescued me, Sally, I compounded my sins by immersing myself in the reading of profane books and the acceptance of blasphemous ideas."

"What are you saying, James?" Sally was stunned by his rote repetition of another man's words.

"I have thought long and hard on his words and I know that I cannot accept Reverend Godfrey's condemnation of the intellectual awakening I experienced in the community and I cannot accept the existence of his all-powerful God." He directed his attention to Thaddeus. "Your fellow divine tried to comfort me by reading from the Book of Job...."

"*'Naked came I out of my mother's womb,'* " Thaddeus Goodenough interrupted James' dialogue. "*'And naked shall I return thither: The Lord gave and the Lord hath taken away....'* Job One, verse twenty-one." The preacher cleared his throat.

"It is true, James, in the time you were with us, the Lord granted you opportunities which, it seems, came too late for you to fully cultivate. He, however, has not abandoned you; rather, you have abandoned him. You reject him now when you need him most, in this, your hour of need."

"I have not believed in God since I was a boy," James confessed, "and I cannot turn to him now."

"*'Behold, I stand at the door, and knock: if any man hear my voice, and open the door, I will come in to him, and will sup with him, and he with me.'* " The Reverend spoke with conviction.

"*'To him that overcometh will I grant to sit with me in my throne, even as I also overcame, and am set down with my Father in his throne.'* Revelations Three, verses twenty and twenty-one.

"God awaits the sinner and glorifies in his redemption, James. But you must believe in order to be saved. There is no better time than the present to open your heart and let him in."

James shook his head. "I tried. I tried to accept your belief that a state of sinlessness can be achieved by those who give their lives to God," James shook his head, "but I cannot turn to your God now. I would be false to you, and to myself, if I were to pretend to have faith when my mind cannot grasp the concept of a supreme being. I can accept the limitless space of the sky above me and the vastness of the earth beneath my feet but I cannot conceive of a being, tangible or not, that can be all things to all men, in all places at all times, a judge, an advisor, a comforter, a disciplinarian."

"Yes, it is difficult to embrace the Almighty for the first time. Just remember, '...*with men this is impossible, but with God all things are possible.*' Matthew Nineteen, verse twenty-six." Thaddeus drummed his fingers on one of the bars as he continued speaking. "It is faith, faith in the word of God, which allows you to accept the incomprehensible."

James looked down at his hands. "Even with the daily guidance of Reverend Godfrey, who professes to care for my soul, I have been unable to find that faith. He has convinced me, however, that by allowing him to write the story of my life, I can leave behind an image of myself as a penitent human being."

"Nonsense," Thaddeus began pacing back and forth in front of the door to James' cell. He angrily addressed the prisoner. " *'Beware of false prophets, which come to you in sheep's clothing, but inwardly they are ravening wolves.'* Matthew Seven, verse fifteen."

Thaddeus stopped his prowling and stood in front of the barred window.

"The Reverend Godfrey comes not to save your soul or relieve your anguish; he comes instead to line his pockets with the profits from the sale of your confession. The sheriff spoke of his exploitation of your tragic circumstances."

"It does not matter. He has promised to give some of the money to Margaret and my.... " James stopped speaking and stared at the floor.

"Does the sheriff allow the Reverend Godfrey access to your cell, James?" Thaddeus asked.

"Yes. He comes for one hour each day."

"I must speak to the sheriff." Thaddeus turned and hurried down the hall.

Sally leaned close to the bars and spoke softly.

"James, listen to me." The seriousness of what she was about to say was evident in her voice. "I want to testify in your defense." Sally slipped her hand through the bars of his cell. James reached for her but the chains around his wrists and ankles locked him into his limited space.

"I can honestly say I was with you that day, James. I can supply you with an alibi."

James raised his hands to his head.

"I cannot let you, Sally." He lowered his hands and said softly, "I cannot let Margaret know about you." He took a deep breath. "Reverend Godfrey has agreed to keep our relationship a secret." He looked away. "Margaret must continue to believe in me. She is," he paused, and then continued miserably, "She is with child."

As his words permeated her brain, a shock wave fanned out from the base of her skull; it traveled across her shoulders, pulsed down her spine, vibrated through her arms and legs and set her entire body afire with an undefined emotion.

"How long...?" Her chest constricted. "Did you know....?"

"No," James interrupted her. "Margaret did not realize she was in a family way until after I was arrested. She doesn't know when the baby will be born." He rubbed his forehead. "She only told me a few days ago." He looked away and murmured, "Honestly, Sally, I cannot remember the last time I was with her."

He returned his hands to his head and massaged his temples. "The child of a murderer. Margaret is carrying the child of a murderer. That is why I agreed to the publication of the pamphlet."

James looked back at her and Sally could see despair in his eyes. The realization that she, too, had been with child, his child, overwhelmed her. Although she had never wanted to have a baby, particularly one born out of wedlock, she had to admit it was envy that consumed her at the moment. She was terribly jealous of this woman who would bear James Daunt's child, this woman whom she had never met, who would have a tangible part of him forever.

Sally felt tears come to her eyes and moved to the side as she wiped them away. She composed herself, cast off the romanticized notion of motherhood, accepted the fact she had no desire to raise a child, and returned to promote her offer of help.

"I never told you this, James. I was unrealistically hoping you would never be found and would be able to start a new life at Pleasant

Valley." The tone of Sally's voice caught James' attention and he took a step forward.

"I was there when the shots were fired at Squire Holt." Surprised by her words, James backed away and sat on the cot.

"I was waiting for...," Sally caught herself before admitting she had been waiting for Richard Holt's youngest son.

"I was walking nearby when I heard the first shot. Then, an instant later, I heard a second shot which came from the opposite direction."

James looked straight ahead, a frown on his face. "I only fired one shot, Sally."

"I know. The first one was fired by Esther Latch." Sally looked at the man behind bars who stared back at her in disbelief. "Richard Holt was killed by a single shot, James. Only one ball reached its target and that shot could have just as easily been Esther's as yours. You may not have been the one who murdered the squire."

"I don't understand...." James rubbed the skin between his eyebrows in an attempt to erase the frown that deepened as he tried to remember what happened that day. "Esther was there?" He turned his head from side to side as he assimilated this new information.

"I've been told my gun was found near the squire's house, however, I am certain I was carrying Elias' gun when I ran away after I...." He could not bring himself to admit to firing a gun at another human being.

He shook his head. "I don't know why I had Elias' flintlock instead of my musket. I only know that I could not find it when I was hiding in the woods."

James tried to reconstruct the scene in the Latch keeping room. "I have no recollection of Esther being in the room when I awakened. Perhaps...," he thought for a moment. "Perhaps she had already left and had taken my gun with her."

"Yes." Sally interrupted James. "That could have happened." She was excited about the revelation and her voice rose. "I heard the shots and then I saw you. I followed you to the clearing. I noticed the flintlock lying on the ground when you left." Sally took a breath. "I was about to go after you when I heard someone coming through the brush. It was Esther. I saw her trade the gun she carried for the one you had left behind. She placed your musket inside the hollow of the tree trunk where you had been sitting. I didn't understand why she made the exchange until later, when I heard it was your gun that was found in the clearing."

Sally looked away. "I thought it strange that she would leave her gun behind. I would have taken the musket if I had known it was yours." She did not mention that she had then taken Esther's path and deliberately exposed herself at the edge of the woods so the older woman would know she had been seen.

"I always liked you, James Daunt, and I liked being with you." For a split second, as she said his name, a playful, come-hither smile lit up her face. It vanished as she cast her eyes down and said, "I did not care deeply for you then as I do now."

James shook his head. "It's too late for us, Sally. I am a condemned man. I have a wife who is carrying my child and I don't know how that child will ever be able to live down the curse of having a murderer for a father." He looked straight into her eyes.

"You cannot testify for me, Sally. It would come out that I have been with you. I tried, Sally, I tried to be faithful to my marriage vows and that is how I want to be remembered. As a faithful husband. For my child's sake.

"Sally." He stood and reached for her. Again, she pushed her hand through the bars. They were still too far apart to touch. James looked down as he dropped his arm to his side.

"Our days together were the happiest days of my life...." The pain on his face was heartbreaking. "However, I cannot have 'adulterer' added to the name of the father of my unborn child."

The name stung, but Sally knew it was true. Their relationship was adulterous and the consequences of it becoming known outside the community would assure his conviction by the jury.

"I would not have to mention that I saw you by the stream. I could introduce the possibility that there was another shot and that it, rather than yours, might have been the fatal one."

"The verdict has already been decided by the public No one would believe you. The prosecutor would destroy you on the stand."

Sally moved back from the door when she heard footsteps resounding through the dungeon.

Thaddeus Goodenough returned with the sheriff who carried a large brass ring with two identical-looking keys. He inserted one into the lock on James' cell. He twisted it, jiggled it and then withdrew it from the keyhole.

"You'd think after ten years I could tell the difference," he muttered as he pushed the second key in the lock. The door opened.

Sally entered the cell and walked over to the cot. She wanted to touch James even though it would be unacceptable behavior in front of the reverend. She twisted her body around to face the door and the fabric of the back of her skirt brushed James' hand.

He reached out and grasped it in his fingers. She could feel the pressure as he pulled the material close to him and the thought that they were somehow locked together ignited her passion. She stood still for a moment and allowed the emotions to surge through her body then moved away as her father ceased watching the sheriff lock the door."

"You have fifteen minutes, that's all."

"That is all we need. Thank you." Thaddeus waited until the lawman had walked away before he spoke.

"I have talked to the sheriff, James. You have not provided your lawyer with much assistance. You never mentioned the time you spent with us. We could have, at the very least, testified to the change in your character and the quality of your work habits. We did not know of your profligate ways when Sister Sarah brought you amongst us. You would have been turned away had we known you were suspected of taking another man's life.

"However, your behavior during your stay in the community was exemplary. Except," he turned to look at his daughter, "for the monogamous relationship you formed with Sister Sarah. She must carry much of the responsibility for your transgressions. She is cognizant of our ways and has sworn to follow my dictates. She should have honored her pledge."

The reverend's stern expression softened. "I have been lenient with her and am aware of her many indiscretions. I saw that you made her happy. Therefore, I, too, am to blame as I allowed your relationship to continue."

He directed his next comment to James. "So I say, '*he that is without sin among you, let him first cast a stone....*'" John Eight, verse seven.

"I, too, James, admit to being a sinner and as such, cannot condemn you. However, I will repeat the words of Jesus Christ our Savior: '*All manner of sin and blasphemy shall be forgiven unto men.*' Matthew Twelve, verse thirty-one."

"Forgiveness of your sins may not come in this world, James. Knowledge of the salvation that awaits you in the kingdom of God, however, should bring you peace as you face your trial tomorrow."

The sheriff reappeared with an undistinguished, stout man in rumpled attire.

"Sorry to cut your time short, but you folks have to leave now. Daunt's lawyer is here. He's got priority over other visitors." The sheriff found the correct key this time, opened the door and ushered them out.

As they walked past the adjoining dungeon, James' neighbor called out, "Red hair. You have red hair."

Sally cringed and then glanced at Thaddeus. He never broke stride as he followed his nose to the heavy wooden door which would lead him out of the prison.

## *Monday, February 16, 1829*

The Reverend Thaddeus Goodenough and Sister Sarah Morley attended the trial of James Daunt. They sat among the throngs of spectators who gained admission to the courtroom. They listened as the prosecution paraded their witnesses before the judge and jury. The evidence mounted against the defendant and the guilty verdict was assured when the prosecuting attorney got the boys from Hebe Balderston's tavern to admit that, on the night before the shooting, they had joined James Daunt in hypothetically planning the demise of Squire Holt.

The trial lasted three days and the jury was out for two-and-a-half hours before they delivered the guilty verdict.

# *Thursday, February 19, 1829*

For the second time in less than a week, Sally and Thaddeus rose before dawn to travel the north-south road which led between the county seat and Pleasant Valley Farm. They left before breakfast and both were hungry. Sally did not protest when Thaddeus suggested they stop at Hebe Balderston's for an early midday meal.

She lowered her head and kept her eyes on the floor as she entered the tavern. She was able, however, to scan the room before she sat down. There were few diners, two of whom were familiar. The young men never wasted a second glance on the plainly garbed woman who accompanied the stern man with the righteous demeanor. The patrons also failed to notice when the proprietress approached the table and spoke to the man. She then bade the woman to follow her.

"You have need of the advice of a woman?" Sally laughed as she repeated the statement Hebe had made to Thaddeus. "Do you think the reverend is that naïve?"

"I recognized you by your clothing, Sally, although your guise as a meek country farm woman fooled the others. They have been worried about you. I told them you only came to us in good weather and you would return in the spring."

Uncharacteristically, Hebe reached over and took Sally's hand. She was determined to avoid personal involvement with her customers; however, her interest in James Daunt and Sally Morley transcended her formerly unbroken rule. She identified with their carefree natures and recognized the underlying intelligence each sought to conceal. She was aware that she, herself, had assiduously avoided responsibility before she inherited the tavern and been forced to grow up. She was certain the carefully preserved immaturity of these two adults was now a thing of the past and that they had come face-to-face with the reality of their actions.

"How are you? Did you solve your problem?"

"Yes, thank you." Sally declined to discuss her encounter with the Indian witch doctor. "We have come from seeing James in the county jail."

Hebe's eyebrows shot up as she asked, "The man with you? James Daunt is known to him?"

"The Reverend Thaddeus Goodenough is James' spiritual counselor. He is trying to bring James to the word of the Lord."

Hebe was astounded. "Sally. Your clothes? Your manner? You...." She pointed to the bonneted young woman standing by her desk. "You are a disciple of the Lord?" Disbelief contorted her face and sharpened her words.

"No, Hebe. In fact, I am the opposite; a doubter at best." Sally considered telling Hebe of her relationship to Thaddeus but decided against it. "The reverend is a student of the Bible and a proselytizer of a society based on his interpretation of the word of God. I am travelling with him as it was my only way to see James."

"Did you tell James of your...?"

"Oh no," Sally gasped. She regained her composure and stated flatly. "His wife is with child. That is enough for him to know. He...," she could barely go on. "He," again she hesitated, "was found guilty and has been sentenced to hang on Saturday, the fourth of April."

She could not help herself. The tears started and Hebe, again, reached to comfort her.

"No. I am fine." She wiped her eyes. "Hebe, if you had not come for me today, I would have found a way to speak with you. I have something very important to discuss with you. I need your help, but in the event you cannot support me, I must have your word that you will keep everything I say in the strictest confidence."

Hebe frowned, thought for a moment and then answered. "Obviously I cannot agree to assist you until I know what you ask of me, but I can assure you that if you discuss it with me, I will not betray your trust."

Sally spoke quickly; Hebe nodded her assent and Sally said, "Thank you, Hebe." She put her hand on the older woman's arm. "You are a true friend."

Hebe surveyed her companion thoughtfully. "You have many friends, Sally. They just don't know it yet."

Sally teared up again, then tilted her head and grinned seductively, "We will see." She turned to leave.

"I must return to the reverend. I am sure his suspicions have been aroused enough. What reason shall I give him for your summons?"

Hebe's eyes sparkled. "Tell him I needed the counsel of a woman of faith and mistook you for a nun."

Sally burst out laughing and all signs of the tears vanished with her appreciation of Hebe's rarely exercised wit.

# *Friday, April 3, 1829*

Sally Morley stood in front of the large wooden door of the county jail in the early morning of the day before James Daunt's scheduled execution. Thaddeus had not been able to accompany her on the trip to the county seat. A local farmer had died and the reverend's presence was requested to conduct the burial service. He planned to ride in the mail coach and arrive in time for the hanging.

She tried the door. It was locked. She debated whether to knock or simply wait until there were signs of life around the prison. She chose the latter, backed away from the entry door and turned toward the street.

A row of linden trees lined the walk in front of the sheriff's house, the jail and the courthouse. She chose the one furthest from the buildings and sat down on the damp ground. She was pleased that she had chosen a plain brown dress with buttons to the neck as it would not show the dirt on which she was sitting.

Sally leaned back against the tree and watched a man come out of the court house and hurry along the path in her direction. It was obvious he had not seen her and Sally remained in place until he had passed. He knocked on the jailhouse door. She stood and walked over to join him.

"Please, sir," she spoke politely. "Is it too early to visit one of the prisoners?"

The man, a prim sort in his early thirties, with smooth, clean-shaven skin and slicked down hair, looked over at her and answered brusquely, "I don't think you want to go in this jail. The only convict here is a murderer who's scheduled to hang tomorrow. He's allowed no visitors but his lawyers, his mother, his wife and his preacher."

Sally felt some of the tension in her shoulders ease. James' mother was dead. Hebe Balderston must have honored Sally's request and come to see him.

Sally smiled up at the speaker. "Our mother has been here? That is good. I am his sister, Sarah. Please, ask him if he will see me."

The dandified man perked up. "He never mentioned a sister. Have you come forward with some last-minute information?"

Sally hesitated before answering and instead asked, "What is your relationship to Mr. Daunt?"

"I am the junior in his lawyer's office. I have come to make sure his affairs are in order."

Sally debated telling him of Esther Latch's shot but discarded the idea. She had given her word to remain silent. She also realized her chances of seeing James would be lessened if this man found out she was not a blood relative.

"Due to his depravity, we have been estranged. I have come to forgive him and to pray with him as a Christian sister should do." She bowed her head and folded her hands in simulated prayer. "He must know that I am here for him in this, his hour of need."

The novice lawyer, whose superior had been appointed by the court to defend James, was moved by the devout nature of the pretty young woman with the curly red hair. He said, "As long as the prisoner and the sheriff agree, I will accompany you to his cell."

He knocked again, this time with more authority.

The door opened and the sheriff glanced at the familiar young man and his companion.

"Who's this you have with you?"

"James Daunt's sister. She has come to pray with her brother."

"At this hour? It is just past dawn."

The junior counselor looked at Sally. She lowered her eyes. "I have travelled all night to be with James on this, his final full day before the hangman accomplishes his horrendous mission tomorrow and launches James into eternity."

Tears, which were not totally fabricated, appeared in the corners of her eyes and the sheriff looked suspiciously at Sally.

"Have I seen you before?"

"No, sir," she answered sweetly. "It may be my resemblance to James that causes you to find me familiar."

The sheriff scanned her face with his eyes, and finding no resemblance at all, looked questioningly at the naïve lawyer.

"Let her in, Sheriff. James Daunt needs all the help he can get."

Sally's stomach turned at the implications of the lawyer's words and she wrapped her arms around her waist in an attempt to calm herself.

The young man tentatively touched her shoulder blade as he guided her through the door and down the hall to James Daunt's last abode on earth.

"You've a visitor. Your sister." Startled, James looked up. Pleasure, relief, love, and finally, despair showed on the prisoner's face.

The lawyer recognized the emotional level of the reunion and said, "I'll leave you to visit with your sister and will return later. We must go over the arrangements for...."

"I understand," James cut him off as he reveled in Sally's presence.

"I didn't think you would come."

"Oh, James." She could barely speak as the enormity of what the next day would bring washed over her. When she recovered, she asked, "The sheriff. Does he like you?"

"I guess. As much as he can like a condemned murderer."

"I have to talk to him." Sally turned and walked down the hall.

She returned shortly with the sheriff and his keys. The lawman inserted one of the two large keys in the lock of James' dungeon, rotated it, withdrew it and tried the other key. It worked.

"One hour. With no interruptions."

Sally put her hand on the arm which had unlocked the door. "Thank you," she said softly, and brushed the man's face with her fingers. The sheriff left without a word.

"How….?"

"I told him your friends had arranged for me to come." She put her left hand to the neck of her dress and began to slowly undo the buttons to her waist. Then she grinned wickedly as she continued her explanation.

"As a parting gift. It has been done before, James." She did not tell him that a considerable amount of Hebe's money had passed into the hands of the sheriff before he had agreed to her proposition.

"Now." Sally put her hands on her hips and slowly raised her skirt with her finger tips. She grimaced as she surveyed the shackles on his wrists and ankles.

"This is going to take some doing." She smiled. "We have one hour to forget what tomorrow will bring." He stood next to his cot as she came close to him and pressed her body to his.

James had spent many hours of his incarceration reliving the pleasures Sally brought to him. He could not believe she was here, steering his hand past the open fabric of her dress to the smooth, warm skin of her breast, touching him, pleasuring him, bringing him such joy that the horrors of the future faded for the moment.

Sally, the woman who had spent the early years of her sexual maturity seeking gratification from many, could not believe she had wanted no other man since she and James had come together on the ledge. Her desperate need to know him again before she lost him fanned her longing. In spite of James' limited mobility, their passion was boundless and insatiable.

The allotted hour passed quickly, and so too, did the second hour. Half way through the third, there was a knock on the entry door and the sheriff backed away from the peephole opposite James Daunt's cell. He staved off the visitor with a shouted acknowledgement while he tidied himself. Then he called a warning to the couple on the cot at the end of the hall.

He admitted a woman and bade her rest until, he said, he readied the prisoner. After a decent interval, he walked back to the cell and waited as Sally leaned close to James and whispered, "Go out kicking, James Daunt. Give them a show." She grinned. "It does not have to be long," she paused for emphasis. "Just memorable."

As Sally followed the sheriff away from James' cubicle, she asked sweetly, "My mother has been here?"

The sheriff snorted, "Your mother? You share no blood with James Daunt, girl. Don't forget, you told me his friends sent you. Besides, I seen you in there. You gave him a fine farewell, but not one any sister would deliver."

Sally stifled the urge to lash out at him for spying on them. She curbed her temper and laughed instead.

"Jealous, sheriff? If you ever find yourself facing the gallows, I will be glad to sweeten the path to eternity for you, too." She put her hand on his arm and moved close enough for him to sense the nearness of her body.

"His mother, what did she want?" Sally pressed a little closer.

"Guess it's all right to tell you." He was visibly affected by her proximity but did not retreat.

"She wanted him to ride to the gallows on the back of a horse. She...," perspiration stood out on his forehead as Sally began stroking his arm. "She said it would be more dignified that way." He swallowed hard. "She was a nice lady and the Mayor agreed the procession would be more impressive if he rode to his death."

Sally fought the impulse to cry as she heard the words "to his death".

The sheriff ramped up his nerve and pressed his arm against her breast.

She broke loose and laughingly said, "Don't forget to let me know if you ever find yourself about to swing from a noose."

"Might be worth it." He leered at her and then said, "I'm sorry about your friend, James Daunt. He's not such a bad sort."

"No," she repeated quietly, "he is not such a bad sort."

Sally smiled her seductive smile and slowly dragged her fingers down the sheriff's arm. She left through a side door, content in the knowledge that Mother Hebe had done her job. There would be pageantry and James' execution would, indeed, be a memorable one.

Shortly after he led Sally out the back door of the prison, the sheriff brought Margaret to stand in front of the condemned man's cell. James cringed as he thought of the stigma she and his child would carry forever due to his ignominious death.

The afterglow of his reunion with Sally remained, however, and overshadowed his guilt. He clung to the memories of their passion even as he faced his wife through the bars. Their exchanges were perfunctory, and although Margaret shed a few tears, their behavior was appropriately reserved. The sheriff never bothered to check the peephole before he admitted the lawyer who had returned with Reverend Godfrey. James Daunt's wife had visited him monthly since his arrest and had never asked to be allowed into his prison quarters.

Sally left the jailhouse and glanced at the inn where she and Thaddeus had stayed during their last visit to the county seat. Groups of hopeful lodgers crowded close to the building. The innkeeper opened the door, announced there was no available space, and closed it before people could force their way inside.

Every hostelry in the town was filled to overflowing. The spectacle of a public hanging was entertainment for folks who toiled for a living and had little time or money for amusement. Spectators had started arriving the day before the event and rooms had been filled by the evening meal. People were sleeping four to a bed, on floors and in barns. Sally heard that many had cleared spaces in the meadow where construction of the gallows was taking place. It was said there was a run nearby so water was plentiful, and with the ground gently rising on either side of the narrow valley, there were choice viewing spots to be staked out ahead of the hanging.

Sally had spent the previous night as a guest at Hebe Balderston's tavern where she and four of James' friends had dined with the proprietress in her private quarters. The lads, who had initially been taken aback by the change in their former playmate's demeanor, spent much of the evening reminiscing about the good times they had shared with their doomed comrade. Sally, who had taken charge of the conversation early in the evening, remained uncharacteristically quiet and kept her memories to herself.

This morning, she had risen well before dawn in order to make the long ride to town and arrive at an early hour. And now, although it was not yet noon, she wanted to return to Hebe's as quickly as possible. There were unresolved details which required her attention.

Crowds had gathered outside the jail hoping for a look at those associated with the prisoner: his wife, his lawyer, the sheriff. No one noticed the red-haired woman who came around the side of the adjacent stone house to join them. They were too busy watching for activity around the heavy wooden door.

Sally passed through the crowd on her way to the stable to collect Pleasant Valley's horse and cart. She drove north on the Great Road and headed for Hebe's and her final reunion with James' friends. She was sure she would never see any of the lads again after tomorrow's hanging.

# Saturday, April 4, 1829

"James?" The sound of Margaret's voice broke into the semi-conscious state in which James Daunt had suspended himself. Ephemeral visions of Sally, Thaddeus Goodenough, Hebe, the boys, Margaret, Elias and Esther collided with one another as he worked his way back to reality. He pulled himself up to a sitting position.

"James, are you all right? Reverend Goodenough is here with me. We have come to pray with you, James."

"Let me through and I'll open the door." The sheriff stepped from behind Thaddeus and inserted his key in the lock. It balked; he withdrew it and exchanged it for the second one on his ring. This time the latch clicked and the door swung into the cell.

"No chairs," he observed brusquely. "Don't want my prisoner hangin' himself ahead of schedule." He signaled for Margaret and the reverend to pass in front of him and then he closed and locked the door behind them.

"James, have you thought of what you will say today?" The reverend carried his Bible and spoke in an authoritative voice. James looked behind him and saw no sign of Sally in the doorway.

"There are at least five thousand people gathered at the gallows," Thaddeus continued. "A condemned man is expected to publicly pray to the Lord God, our Father, for forgiveness. '*And the prayer of faith shall save the sick, and the Lord shall raise him up; and if he have committed sins, they shall be forgiven him.*' James Five, verse fifteen."

"Public confession, James, is but one step, admittedly a very large step, toward achieving temporal as well as divine, absolution for the mortal sin you committed against your fellow man. *'Confess your faults one to another, and pray one for another, that ye may be healed. The effectual fervent prayer of a righteous man availeth much.'* James Five, verse sixteen."

"I prefer to leave this world without speaking." James stood and faced his visitors. Remembering Sally's revelation about Esther's shot, he said, "I cannot deny or confirm that my ball killed the squire that day. I recall nothing that happened between the time I started drinking with Esther Latch and the time I loaded Elias' gun and pulled the trigger. Those memories, in themselves, are only random flashes of recollection. I do not know why I chose to aim a gun at Squire Holt. I only know that I was not myself. I was desperate, Reverend. I had lost everything: my home; my wife...."

"No, James, you had not lost me." Margaret put her hand on his and James realized this was the first physical contact they'd had since his capture. He looked at her stomach. The cape she wore was large and hung loose. There was no visible sign of the child she carried.

James covered her hand with his. He was well aware he had been seduced by her physical appearance when he had desired the pretty Margaret. Now, hearing her words of support, he experienced a brief flash of remorse for his insatiable sexual attraction to Sally Morley and the physical, mental and emotional need he had for his red-headed muse.

Sadly, he smiled and continued his reply to Thaddeus' suggestion. "I held no personal malice towards Richard Holt and never, other than in jest, considered doing him harm. In truth, I was certain Maris was behind the scheme to deprive Margaret and her sisters of their inheritances and I supported their only recourse, which was to band with Elias in challenging the will in court.

"I was desperate for money and well full of drink when I fired on the squire." James shook his head

"However, I cannot, in good conscience, admit to harboring malice toward him. On the other hand, I can attest to the extreme sorrow I feel for his death and overwhelming regret for any part I may have played in it."

The reverend lowered his lanky frame to the floor and knelt by James' bed.

"Unite with me in prayer for your soul. It can do no harm."

"Please James," Margaret pleaded as she dropped to her knees, "You must join Reverend Goodenough as he prays for the eternal salvation of your soul."

James, who had long since abandoned any hope of heavenly reprieve, hesitated as he contemplated the hypocrisy of complying with their request. Then, honoring their wishes, he turned around to face his cot and knelt between the two celebrants as they begged for his redemption.

After the reverend had spoken his inspired words and Margaret had quietly shed her tears, James watched them walk side-by-side down the hall which led from his cell to the jailhouse door. They spoke in soft tones which blurred into an indistinguishable hum by the time their words travelled back to James' ears. The irony of his wife conversing with the father of his mistress was not lost on the condemned man they left behind.

James backed up and sat on the edge of the straw-filled cot. He had but a short time to live and was surprised, and relieved, to realize he was without fear. He had come to terms with his fate and was aware that he had no interest in a future without Sally.

Even if the jury had declared him not guilty due to his alcohol consumption, the prospect of a child changed everything and Margaret's condition obligated him to honor his marriage vows. Knowing his only alternative was a return to his past mundane existence, he felt he had nothing to live for, and therefore, nothing to fear from death.

James heard the key turn in the lock. He raised his head and was surprised to see Thaddeus Goodenough reenter his cell.

"I must speak with you, James," the preacher said, "in private."

The sheriff, hearing the visitor's words, closed the door, turned the key in the lock and walked away.

Thaddeus pushed aside the shackles and seated himself next to James.

"I have given much thought to the brief conversation we had on the day before your trial. You spoke of your inability to accept the concept of an all-powerful God," he stared at James. "I am quite sure those were your words." He looked down at his hands which were opening and closing as he spoke.

"My greatest parting gift to you, James, would be the restoration of your faith before...."

Thaddeus chose not to finish the sentence. He rose and walked to the small window at the rear of the cell. He stared through the bars before continuing.

"During the time you spent with us, I came to respect you despite your irregular relationship with Sister Sarah. You are a good worker, an eager student and a fledgling leader. The younger men gravitated to you even though you were new to the community.

"Learning of your heinous crime against a fellow man came as a shock to me. I initially took your deceit personally as I consider myself to be an excellent judge of character. My acceptance of you appeared to be a serious error on my part. Upon reflection, I have come to recognize that you were, at the time of your transgression, a victim of unfortunate circumstances, poor judgment and a weakness for rum, which, to your credit, you seem to have overcome.

"As a result of my reevaluation of your situation, it became important to me that I find the proper words to guide you on your way to salvation. To that end, I spent many hours reading the Bible and in prayer." He took a deep breath and returned to stand next to James. He put his hand on the younger man's shoulder and said, "I did not find the words I sought.

"Instead," he paused, "I had to face the truth about myself.

"As a very young boy," Thaddeus' voice was low. "I read the first words in the Bible: '*In the beginning God created the heaven and the earth*,' Genesis One, verse one.

"Throughout my life, I have blindly accepted those words as truth. It was easier than asking the obvious questions: 'Where did God come from?' 'Who or what created God?'

"I have never allowed myself to consciously question the existence of the Almighty or the veracity of his word. In the past, I have swallowed all doubt in my desperate pursuit of personal salvation and I have covered my inadequacies with verbatim quotations from the Holy Book." Thaddeus shook his head.

"Since I last visited you, I have come to realize I frequently quote the Bible to reinforce my credibility as a religious leader. I do this because I have no words of my own. I have nothing profound to say. And that is because," Thaddeus' voice was choked with emotion, "I," he had trouble speaking, "do not believe.

"I do not believe in God" He enunciated each word of his confession. "I do not believe in his omnipresence, his omnipotence, his omniscience."

There were tears in the reverend's eyes. "I must accept the ultimate truth about myself. I have suppressed a lifelong skepticism. There have been times, when my meditations have been interrupted by profane thoughts which have tempted me to see God as the creation of man rather than the other way around." Thaddeus Goodenough lowered his head.

"It is only now I understand that I have spent my life challenging God, daring him to strike me down as retribution for my doubts, as well as for my sins, and by doing so, to prove his existence. My transgressions have been prodigious and unforgiveable." He dabbed at his eyes before the tears fell.

"I took advantage of, and then thrust out, the only woman I ever loved. I denied the fruit of my seed and then violated her trust. I led my flock into debauchery and disillusionment.

"I convinced myself that intense study of the Bible and personal reinterpretation of the word of God would buttress my designation as an anointed disciple of the Lord and support my views of a new society. I now know," he paused, "that I am a sham, a charlatan, and," he faltered, "an atheist.

"I have failed myself, my...," again, he choked on his words, "my family, my followers and you, James. My prayers for you have fallen on deaf ears and you go to the gallows alone with only the worthless intervention of a self-deluded, self-invented pious man."

James touched the shaking hands of the repentant pretender.

"I have no false hopes, Thaddeus," James said, speaking the familiar birth name for the first time. "I face the gallows without fear. I know that, when my time on earth is over, there will be nothing. No judgment, no salvation, no damnation. My life will simply end."

James patted the reverend's hand and wondered if Thaddeus Goodenough, absorbed in his personal grief, had grasped his words. After a moment, the reverend raised his head and spoke.

"I am relieved to hear what you say, James, because I returned to say to you: do not fear the afterlife, it does not exist. You will not burn in Hell for your sins or endure eternal suffering in Purgatory.

"Your flame of life will, indeed, be extinguished today and you will be freed from the torments of your shackles. You will rest in peace, not in heaven, but quietly, alone, and unaware." He rose from the cot and called out for the sheriff.

"I misspoke, James, when I counseled you to confess your sins, and again, when I prayed for your soul. I apologize for giving you false solace."

With a nod of his head, James accepted Thaddeus' request for forgiveness. He paused and considered his question before asking, "What will you do about Pleasant Valley?"

"I do not know. I simply do not know."

The sheriff appeared, and on the second try, opened the door. Thaddeus turned and raised his right hand.

"God bless you, my son," he said. "Who knows? Was I wrong when I blindly accepted the myth of God as the all-mighty being or am I wrong now that I, as a man of the cloth, have forsaken the pretence of acceptance? I will not know until I face my final fate. And...." A rare smile crossed the face of the Reverend Thaddeus Goodenough. "Perhaps my heartfelt, albeit heretical, blessings will come in handy today." He left the cell and walked to the end of the hall where he joined the wife of his daughter's lover.

"Almost eleven o'clock." The sheriff spoke as he, Thaddeus and Margaret approached James' cell. He inserted the key and it turned on the first try.

James rubbed his skin and shook his hands and feet as the sheriff removed the shackles from his wrists and ankles. The lawman handed him the black shirt and community pants he had been wearing on the day he was captured. They were freshly laundered. James thought the effort frivolous as he considered his unkempt prison garb more appropriate for a hanging. Then he realized these were his burial clothes as well and he was oddly comforted to know they were clean.

James pulled his well-worn work shirt over his head and Margaret averted her eyes as she and Thaddeus waited outside the cell. The sheriff remained on guard as James stepped into the familiar gray trousers. He picked up the washerwoman's contribution to his escape, put his arms in the sleeves and dropped the somber black shirt over his head.

James was dressed and standing by his cot when the sheriff opened the door for his prisoner.

"It's time to go." James took a first step and staggered slightly as he adjusted to moving around without the heavy load of cast-iron restraints. The unfamiliar weightlessness caused him to have vertigo, and as he reached the door, he misjudged the distance between his foot and the floor. Thaddeus and Margaret reached for his arms and held him between them as he exited his cell.

His companions dropped back as six armed men, all unknown to James, appeared and came toward him. The sheriff indicated their allotted stations: two on each side of the prisoner, one in front, another in the rear. They covered all possibilities for escape.

The Reverend Thaddeus Goodenough placed his hand on James' shoulder and intoned *"The Lord is my Shepherd…."*

James recognized the twenty-third psalm from his youth and shuddered as he listened to the words of the fourth verse: *" 'Yea, though I walk through the valley of the shadow of death, I will fear no evil: for thou art with me; thy rod and thy staff they comfort me'."* He hoped he was right about the nonexistence of a higher being as he was certain that, if God existed, he would not be allowed to rest in peace.

The sheriff ordered James to hold his hands in front of him while he bound his wrists with a leather thong. The members of the armed guard smoothed their clothes, tightened ranks and prepared themselves to be among the first of the featured participants in the day's spectacle.

The sheriff opened the outside door and Margaret, her head covered by a black shawl and bowed in grief and humiliation, touched her husband's hands and whispered, "I will always love you, James." She walked to her place behind his official attendants.

"God be with you, my son." Thaddeus joined her after giving James his perfunctory blessing.

The sheriff preceded the prisoner, his guards, his wife and his spiritual counselor as they left the prison which had been his home for almost six months.

James had not seen the light of day since his trips to the adjacent courthouse on the three gray days of his trial in February. He stepped from the jail and stopped. He stood still while his eyes adjusted to the April sun. It was bright and warm on his face. He looked up and was startled by the contrast of its brilliant white-gold radiance against the intense blue of the cloudless sky.

Tree branches, hinting of spring with their haze of green fuzz, moved slowly in the soft breeze. A few small flowers had survived the foot traffic which packed the earth hard and arbitrarily dotted the desecrated ground with their early blooms.

James took a deep breath, and for the first time in his life, he acknowledged the transient beauty of the world he was about to leave. He experienced an epiphany and decided to speak when he reached the gallows. His enthusiasm vanished when he noticed the black-draped wagon and simple pine coffin which stood in the center of the road ahead of him. He abandoned all thought of a public confession.

"It's him. The assassin."

James had been spotted and a roar of muddled words assaulted his ears. He looked past the guards in front of him. Crowds of people were gathered on the lawn in front of the jail and courthouse. They lined both sides of the main street, hung out of the windows of the inn and filled wagon beds in an attempt to catch a glimpse of the condemned man.

"'Angin's too good for the likes of 'im."

"You'll go to hell, James Daunt. That's where you belong."

"Poor fellow. I hear he was too drunk to have pulled the trigger."

"Guilty as charged, I say."

Although James tried to shut out the jeers, they kept coming until his escorts parted the crowd and they began their walk to the street. Oddly, the onlookers fell silent.

James surveyed the mob which lined the road and was struck by the orderly conduct of so diverse and opinionated a congregation. The crowd consisted primarily of men: farmers from neighboring communities; tradesmen and shopkeepers who lived and worked in town; hawkers who haunted public outings in search of buyers for their wares.

Scattered throughout the spectators were those who knew James Daunt as a fun-loving, amiable drinking companion who, under the oppression of overwhelming debt, and an abundance of drink, had committed a desperate, but unforgiveable, act. They sympathized with the prisoner as, at times, they, too, had been laid senseless by the siren call of the bottle.

There were women as well, although far fewer in number. Some were wives who accompanied their husbands; others, nosy spinsters and flagrant ladies of ill repute. If any one of the latter was acquainted with the condemned man, she had the decency, in deference to the grieving woman and straight-backed divine who walked behind James, to keep it to herself.

Twelve armed men on horseback rode cautiously through the crowd and encircled a single horse that waited behind the funeral cart. James had forgotten Hebe Balderston's proposal that he ride to his death rather than walk. It seemed a useless and vain pretension but he had agreed. The sheriff, himself, helped James climb into the saddle. There were no stirrups and his hands were still bound in front of him. It was difficult for him to find his seat.

The horsemen, five on each side, one in front, one in back, replaced James' six footmen. The sheriff commandeered the reins, and with his prisoner perched precariously on its back, he led the horse forward on the mile-long journey from the jail to the meadow where the gallows had been raised.

At the same time, the Reverend Solomon Godfrey left the crowd and fell in step with Margaret and the Reverend Goodenough. To the latter's dismay, the young cleric began singing "Amazing Grace".

In defense of his position as James' primary confessor, Thaddeus Goodenough theatrically moved his hands to the rhythm of the hymn and used his rich baritone voice to drown out his challenger. Sensing the drama of the moment, the two divines moved forward to serenade the condemned man and left Margaret to forge on alone.

The sight of the solitary, black-garbed widow-to-be, loyally walking alone in support of her convicted husband, brought tears to the eyes of the decent, law-abiding women who lined the street.

One stepped forward and joined her, then two, then three more. Soon, Margaret was surrounded by at least twenty-five complete strangers, all sympathetically bearing a heavy heart while they secretly thanked God that it was she, not they, who must carry the cross of being a murderer's widow.

Those who had remained in town to view the prisoner as he began the solemn ride to his just reward, dropped in behind the cavalcade as it passed their viewing spots. The crowd grew to one hundred, two hundred, five hundred bodies. The parade came in view of James Daunt's valley of death and those who accompanied the prisoner found they had been preceded by several thousand spectators who covered the hills around the temporary site of execution.

As James and his horse were led into an open area surrounded by gently sloping hills, he could see the gallows standing ahead of him in the middle of a meadow. A simple post with a horizontal crossbeam attached at a right angle and reinforced by a diagonal board, its purpose was clear. The crossbeam supported a dangling rope which ended in an ample loop topped with six or eight coils wrapped around its terminus. It twisted gently in the light breeze.

The gallows stood on a raised platform which was large enough to hold the official observers. The governor, mayor, councilmen, several lawyers and other worthy citizens waited to witness and validate the execution. Twenty constables, all armed with white rods, muskets and flintlocks, ringed the platform. James knew their mission was to keep the crowd under control and prevent any disruption of the proceedings. He also knew that the guards were not worried about him; there was no chance that he could escape.

The horse-drawn wagon with his coffin, which preceded James in the procession, was pulled over to the side as he passed. A young man dressed in the clothes of a farm hand sat alone on a crude board which spanned the width of the black-shrouded cart. Three similarly dressed young men sat on the coffin in the bed of the wagon. The four figures seemed familiar but James averted his eyes and did not try to identify them. They represented what he had been, and what he would still be, if he had not pulled the trigger on that August day in the woods.

For the first time, the implications of the presence of the coffin overturned James' false complacency. The plain pine box and the proximity of the gallows in front of him forced him to accept the reality of the consequences which lay ahead of him. A wry smile crossed his face as he admitted that he had literally come to the end of his rope. James listened as the wagon rolled into place behind him and he could feel the warm breath of its horses on his neck.

Ten years ago, James had watched a hanging on this very spot and was well aware that most of the spectators in the huge crowd which swirled around him were here for the entertainment. He hoped there were some who had come to support him in his last minutes on earth. However, as he listened to the catcalls and jeers, he accepted the reality that the spectacle of his demise was the only attraction for the thousands who lined the hills and the hundreds who had followed behind him as he rode the mile from the jail to the site of his death.

James took a deep breath and prayed to a God he did not believe in that he would keep his composure, that he would die without humiliation. He wanted to depart this world leaving the legacy of a brave, if foolish, man rather than one of a cowardly, depraved murderer.

He thought of Margaret and her spoken words of love which faded when he remembered her ill-concealed aversion to his touch. He recalled the lads from Hebe's who had come to the prison, caps in hand, to commiserate with him. And finally, he thought of Sally.

James was amazed by his physical response to the fleeting thought of her as he awaited his doom. The sly glances and mischievous grin of Sally of the Alley flashed before his eyes. He remembered the serious intelligence of Sister Sarah. He heard her last words to him: "Go out kicking, James Daunt. Give them a show. It does not have to be long, just memorable." He was still surprised by her cold suggestion that he could even think of putting on an exhibition as the air was cut off from his lungs and his neck twisted and broken by the hangman's rope.

James looked over the crowd. He was expected to make a speech; a confession of guilt, a plea for understanding and redemption. He straightened himself in the saddle, squared his shoulders, and faced the crowd. He had no idea what he would say and did not want to admit to a crime he wasn't certain he had committed. He was about to speak when he heard a familiar voice shout, "Stop!"

James turned his head and watched the Reverend Thaddeus Goodenough climb the steps to the platform and stand next to the dreaded noose. The preacher raised his arms to shoulder height and held them straight out from the sides of his body. He threw his head back and gazed silently into space before dropping it and allowing it to hang limp on his chest. His broad-brimmed hat of soft, black felt fell forward and landed at his feet.

The rumbling of the masses subsided as they absorbed the tableau of a man in black standing motionless in an approximation of Christ on the Cross. Slowly, the preacher relaxed his arms, raised his head and looked out over the expectant crowd. He began to speak in the rich tones of an experienced orator.

"Hear me, ye followers of the word of the Lord, ye disciples of his son, Jesus Christ. I stand before you, looking up...," Thaddeus raised his face to the heavens. "Looking up," he paused again, "to plead for justice from a merciful God, our Father, and looking down...," his countenance softened as he lowered his gaze to concentrate on James, "upon the sinner, James Daunt, who is about to travel to his final destination at the end of this rope." Thaddeus swung his arm in the direction of the noose, and with a flourish, dropped his hand down as he pointed his forefinger to the earth below.

"It is said that James Daunt has sinned. That he has taken the life of another man. We believe it is God's will, that if that is so, he must pay with his own. However, we must, in good conscience, ask ourselves if it is the God-given right of ordinary men to condemn a murderer, a traitor or a horse thief to die by a mortal's hand. Let us say, that, on a later day, a stranger were to come forward and prove James Daunt innocent, it would be for naught, as the condemned man will no longer walk among us.

"We will have already followed the part of the law that the Lord stated to Moses in Numbers Thirty-five, verse thirty: '*Whoso killeth any person, the murderer shall be put to death by the mouth of witnesses:*' There is, however, a qualifying addendum. '*...but one witness shall not testify against any person to cause him to die.*'

"We, his peers, have accepted the squire's nieces as reliable witnesses, and their words as truth, and therefore, we believe James Daunt to be an assassin. But they are children and they could be wrong. It is said in Proverbs Twenty-two, verse fifteen: '*Foolishness is bound in the heart of a child....*' It is possible that they were mistaken.

"However, it is too late for debate. We mortals have already usurped the divine power of our Lord to give and take away life. In a few moments, James Daunt will pay for our arrogance with the loss of his earthly existence and we, the so-called righteous, will go on living as we did before today." Thaddeus stared over the heads of the restless crowd and then changed the direction of his exhortation.

"To our credit, we are an understanding people. We must show this by refusing to let him speak of his transgression even though it is expected by our virtuous citizenry. We must accept that, if he did commit the heinous crime, he was, at the time, under the influence of Satan's disciple, that treacherous provocateur, demon rum, and he knew not what he was doing.

"Today, James Daunt is a changed man; a man who is filled with guilt, remorse and regret, not only for his crime against another human being, but for the depravity he embraced during his lifetime.

We, the children of God, must accept his reluctance to confess to a crime of which he doubts his guilt. We must show him mercy and ensure that, in the future, we make no mistakes when we condemn a man to hang."

Thaddeus looked directly at James who was shaken by the reverend's suggested possibility of his innocence. His immediate gratitude for being saved from the final disgrace of a public confession was overshadowed by the relief he experienced knowing that his guilt had been publicly challenged and uncertainty had been planted in the minds of those who awaited his execution. His child might possibly escape the stigma of being conceived of a murderer's seed.

"Now, I will say the fifty-first Psalm." Thaddeus Goodenough turned once again to address the crowd. "As I recite these words, I implore you all to repeat them along with the condemned man. We will all admit our sins as we support him in the admission of his."

Those spectators who had been to a hanging in the past shuffled their feet nervously. They looked to one another for an explanation. They wondered if it was proper for a crowd of thousands to participate in a Biblical reading on behalf of a condemned man. Were they paving the way to heaven for an undeserving reprobate? Or was he innocent and in need of their support as he pays for a crime he did not commit.

Thaddeus began: "*'Have mercy upon me, O God, according to thy loving kindness:'*" He signaled those closest to the gallows to begin their repetition of his words.

There was silence. Then one woman began the recitation. She was joined by her husband and others who stood nearby, "*...'according unto the multitude of thy tender mercies blot out my transgressions.'*" The sound of the respondents increased as more and more voices could be heard.

"*'Wash me thoroughly from mine iniquity, and cleanse me from my sin.'*" The words rose to encompass James Daunt. He joined in, repeating thoughts he had never believed but the solidarity of the chant moved him to embrace the supplication.

"*'For I acknowledge my transgressions; and my sin is ever before me'.*" Thousands of voices, united in a communal admission of wrongdoing, reverberated in James' head. The words repeated themselves until they were permanently embedded in his consciousness.

In spite of the doubts Sally and Thaddeus had planted in his mind, it was a fact that he had taken a shot at Squire Holt. Rum induced or not, there had been malice in his heart and he was, at the very least, guilty of attempting to kill a man. He was a sinner in need of redemption.

"*Amen.*" Thaddeus Goodenough, with his powers of oratory and his innate ability to read his audience, had eased the way for James to face his fate with grace. And in the process, the preacher had successfully convinced himself that he was, indeed, a man of God and worthy to spread the word of the Lord. Head bowed, hands clasped in front of him in devotion, the Reverend Goodenough walked to the back of the platform.

James' momentary euphoria vanished as the sheriff and his deputy approached. He swung his right leg over the saddle and the two men helped him down from the horse. The sheriff untied his wrists, put his hand on James' elbow and spoke softly. "It's time." He helped him up the steps and guided him to his place under the noose.

James turned his back on the lethal rope and came face-to-face with his executioner. The man had moved into the spot where Thaddeus had previously stationed himself. He wore a faded black wool sweater and ragged black trousers on this unseasonably warm, early spring day. His clothes were stained with perspiration and his sweat soaked the black woolen hood which covered his face. James looked into the eyes of his executioner and then he glanced down at his hands. He was a black man. Ludicrously, James wondered if he had heard of the American Colonization Society.

The governor, mayor and other official witnesses jostled each other as they gathered next to the hangman, each vying for a front-row view. Without speaking, the hooded man motioned them to step back. They obliged and watched as he adjusted James' stance.

Then, in a voice tinged with the exaggerated dialect and cadence of the Southern-born Negro, he said, "Stretch, Massah, Ah got to make sho' y'all is tall nuff fo' the noose to do its job."

As James straightened and raised his chin, he glimpsed a black hood in the hangman's hand. It hung open and he could see what looked like a reinforced section running around the inside. He suspected it was destined to land somewhere around his neck. James ducked slightly as the executioner slipped the hood over his head. He smelled the familiar odor of freshly tanned leather and was certain that the covering had been made especially for his execution. The fortified area lay heavy on his neck and fit up under his chin. It seemed more like a thick, wide, leather belt, and from the weight of it, James thought it might even cover a ring of steel. His initial confusion about the design of the hood evaporated as a bitter tasting fluid rose in his throat and erupted in his mouth. It was time.

The man in black made sure James was directly beneath the noose before he dropped it over his head. "Ah do mah bes' t' make this easy fo' y'all," he said. "Hold yo' chin firm, if'n y'all can. May Gawd guide y'all safely t' yo' nex' lahfe, Massah."

James steadied himself as he waited for the trap door to drop from under him.

Suddenly, there was a scuffle. Men were shouting.

"Stop or I'll shoot!"

Others cried out, "Don't shoot! You'll hit innocent people."

Raucous voices roared, "Death to the villain."

"Slay the killer."

"Avenge the wrongful death."

More shouting voices and the sounds of a nearby brawl penetrated his leather hood. James envisioned men with muskets standing firm, ready to repel the agitators, while the city fathers barked contradictory instructions to those who could not hear them. Footsteps pounded on the platform behind him. They were accompanied by the slap of hands and thud of fists colliding with human flesh. The noise surrounded and bewildered James. He swiveled his head and tried to determine the source of the fracas. The hangman swore, roughly shoved his head back to center and pushed it down. James staggered, and before he could regain his balance, he felt the trap door fall from under his feet. He knew that, in spite of the last minute disruption, the deed had been done.

Suddenly, two hands slipped under his arms, grasped the sides of his torso, raised and supported him before the weight of his body stretched the rope to its limit. Just as quickly as he had broken James' fall, the unknown savior released his grip and James hung loose in space. The crowd roared its approval and much of the scrapping ceased as the participants joined in the celebration.

James was immediately aware of the pain caused by the pressure on his neck and under his chin even though it was partially alleviated by the heavy hood. In a flash, he realized the weight of his body was borne, not by the noose, but by the wide reinforced area of the hood. To be sure, his neck had been wrenched by the jolt of his short free fall, but it was not broken. The pressure against his throat was painful and made it difficult to swallow; however, he was alive and hoped to remain so if he could just hold on until he was released from this contraption.

"Go out kicking, James Daunt. Give them a show. It doesn't have to be long, just memorable." Again, Sally's words came to him. She must have known about this possible reprieve. He started kicking but the action caused his body to swing and the pressure on his neck increased. He gave one final kick and relaxed his arms and legs as his lungs constricted. A brilliant light dazzled his eyelids. The lightheadedness that comes from insufficient oxygen deadened his brain. The strain on his neck became unbearable. He lost consciousness. His limp body involuntarily twitched, then, to all appearances, hung lifeless in his sacrificial sling.

Doubts about James' guilt were forgotten as the crowd continued to cheer. Assuming he had passed on, the masses surged forward for a better look at the corpse. Those few who had noticed the hangman's hands on James' body rationalized that he was somehow ensuring the successful end of James Daunt's worldly existence.

A smug Maris Evans Hicks had chosen to view the end of his brother-in-law's time on earth anonymously, buried in the hordes of voyeurs who delighted in the spectacle of another's misfortune. Bodies had pressed close and tempers had risen when unruly combatants had stormed up the stairs to the platform and blocked the condemned man and his executioner from their sight. The observers randomly muscled each other for a glimpse of the action.

"What's happening? People are climbing on the platform."

"They're fighting. Why are they fighting?"

"Get 'em out of there. We can't see."

"Look! The rope is taut. He must be dead."

"Get outta my way. I want to see the scoundrel swing."

When the onlookers realized the trap door had fallen and they had missed the excitement, they rushed forward as one in search of better vantage points from which to view the body in its death throes. Maris tried to work his way out of the throng but was locked between a burly farmer who stank of manure, a fish monger who smelled of the sea, and in front and back, a pair of exhausted dock workers.

"Let me through," Maris yelled, as he attempted to squeeze past the man in front of him.

The brawny stevedore threw out his arm, punched him in the ribs and shouted, "Stop pushin' me, I got no place to go."

The blow knocked the wind out of Maris and he doubled over.

The dock worker's friend to the rear responded with, "E's a gentleman, 'Arry. Mind yer manners." He followed his comments with a chop to the back of Maris' right knee.

Maris' leg buckled under him, and as he fell to the ground, he grabbed hold of his assailant's pant leg. For a moment, the two men were locked together and bypassed by the crowd. Maris tried to pull himself up but the dock worker pried loose his fingers and pushed him away. He lashed out with a final kick which landed on the side of Maris' head and James' brother-in-law fell, face forward, back into the dirt. The uncontrollable crush of human bodies now possessed, not only of curiosity but of an underlying dedication to self-preservation, swarmed over him. Untold numbers of feet stumbled into, stomped on and trampled the helpless man.

When the life force finally left the body of the surviving son of Jacob and Margaretmaris Hicks, it was an undeserved blessing.

The rowdy crowd on the platform stopped brawling long enough to cheer James' body as it swung from the end of its rope.

Two of the participants pushed their way to the foot of the gallows for a better look at the corpse, and in the process, jostled several other young men. They began to scuffle and the constables, determined to prevent a repeat of the earlier confrontation, rushed forward brandishing their white rods and firearms. Drawn back to the melee, the original combatants tried to rejoin the fighting while the constables attempted to restore order.

The executioner, who had one eye on the dangling body and the other on the growing struggle, motioned to the driver of the shroud-covered wagon. Two of the farm boys jumped over the side and guided the horses' heads as the driver maneuvered the cart forward. They signaled him to stop when it was under the suspended body

The driver left his seat and joined the remaining farm hand on the bed of the draped cart. He and his companion positioned themselves on opposite sides of the coffin so it rested between them. They removed the lid and centered the crude pine box under the condemned man. They raised their hands as the hangman cut the rope and the limp body fell into their arms. They carefully placed it in the casket.

Some onlookers shouted angry protestations at the speedy removal of the corpse. Seemingly unaware of the hecklers, the hangman descended the crude steps of the platform, paused and surveyed the complaining spectators. He climbed onto the wagon, moved into the back and stood next to the coffin. His hood still covering his face, he leaned down and with one quick motion, freed the rope from its knot and pulled the noose from the body. Before he stood up, he peeled back the lower part of James' hood.

Then he faced the crowd, swung the hanging rope over his head, pulled back his arm and threw it as far as he could. The crowd roared and the lucky folk standing near its landing place fought to possess the souvenir.

Tradition dictated that it would be taken to the green in front of the nearby tavern, cut into small pieces and auctioned off to the boisterous crowd as they filtered in and out of the establishment. It was a time of celebration, and libations would fuel the bidding.

Many in the crowd followed the noose as the hangman climbed onto the driver's seat and picked up the reins. The original driver and his companion jumped down and joined their friends who continued to hold the horses. The driver took off his cap and one by one the young men dropped some coins in the hat which was then passed to the executioner. Those who observed the ritual nodded sympathetically as they acknowledged this last act of kindness. Although the condemned man's wife had followed him to the gallows, no family member had come forth to claim the body of the murderer. It was assumed that, in lieu of a respectable Christian burial, his friends had taken a collection and hired the hangman to bury the corpse.

The executioner softly flicked the reins and the young men parted the remaining onlookers as they slowly led the wagon away from the meadow and out toward the Post Road. Several boys, filled with the excitement of their first hanging, ran beside the farm cart shouting insensitive epitaphs and banging on the sides of the wagon. The four men did nothing to stop them.

Once the coffin had passed from the eyes of the crowd, the farm hands drove off the boisterous boys, dropped back and followed behind the wagon as it turned onto the Post Road and left the town behind. They continued for a short distance then pulled into some trees which stood at a crossroad.

A second wagon, draped in black shrouds and carrying a coffin, waited off to the side. The man holding the reins was also wearing black trousers, a worn black sweater and a black hood. The color of his hands attested to the fact that he, too, was a Negro. He raised his hand to greet the men on foot before saluting his mirror image who sat on the seat of James Daunt's original funeral carriage.

The hangman raised his whip in return as the four men quickly stripped his wagon of its black draperies. He exchanged his worn sweater for a clean brown shirt and added it and his executioner's hood to the pile of funereal trappings. He carefully slid the coins the lads had collected into the band of the cap which had held them. He placed it on his head as the evidence of the hanging hoax was carried to the surrogate wagon and stashed in the empty coffin.

Then, with a flourish, James Daunt's driver snaked his whip through the air and urged his horses into a gallop leaving his companions behind. This stretch of the Post Road was worn smooth and he allowed his horses to run free.

In contrast, the second wagon, with its grieving entourage, moved decorously on its way to the cemetery where the pseudo hangman and his compatriots planned to lay the substitute coffin to rest.

The road was clear of traffic and James Daunt's savior was able to maintain his rapid pace. The hanging had precipitated a holiday and the local populace was celebrating the righteous death of a hapless murderer. The executioner was well clear of the town before he had to slow for an approaching vehicle.

Hopeful that the ruse would not be detected, and that those who had gone to the cemetery to mourn the deceased would be satisfied by the somber lowering of the coffin into the freshly-dug grave, the hangman, nonetheless, kept his horses running at full speed until the road deteriorated and he had to drop his horses to a walk.

Weeping softly, Margaret stood by the open grave which had been dug for her husband's remains. The elders had refused to allow her to bury James in the family plot so Hannah and Bettina had driven their grieving sister to Boot Hill where they waited on either side of her as she paid her last respects. They had begrudgingly agreed that Margaret could continue to live in their household; however, the two maiden ladies made no secret of the fact they were pleased to be rid of the man who had brought them such disgrace.

James' four friends lowered the coffin into the grave then stood by, their heads bowed, as the substitute hangman shoveled dirt into the hole and forever covered the corpseless coffin.

Thaddeus Goodenough and Reverend Godfrey, each individually determined to be the ultimate savior of the sinner's soul, spoke movingly over the closed grave. After their eulogies, each clasped the widow's hand, offered his personal condolences and spoke of his willingness to be of service in the future. For Thaddeus, it was an insincere offer as he fervently hoped he would have no other occasion to return to the area. Finding few in attendance who would listen to further orations, the self-fulfilled divines climbed into their shared wagon and returned to town.

Following their departure, Margaret knelt in the dirt and prayed for the soul of the man she loved. And she did love James. She even loved having him stroke her arm, caress her hair, fondle her breast. What she did not like was that which came next, but as a wife, she had known it was unavoidable.

As she stared down at the patch of earth that covered her husband's coffin, the bereaved woman began to think of her future. She had already laid the groundwork, and now that James was gone, it was time to put her plan into action.

James Daunt's first thought upon regaining consciousness was that he was definitely in his coffin. Lying on his back, the smell of fresh pine wood filled his nostrils. His head and neck hurt and the skin under his chin had been rubbed raw. Although he was able to breathe, the leather hood was uncomfortable and he struggled to remove it. Once free, he opened his eyes but it was too dark to see anything.

The discomfort caused by the rigid wooden floor of his final resting place was accentuated by the rough ride in the cart. He could hear the horses' hooves on the hard-packed dirt of the road and feel the uneven rotations of the wooden wheels. He sensed that the cart was traveling slowly on a deeply rutted road. He reached up and pushed on the lid of the casket. He raised it high enough for light to filter in at the edge. He noticed air holes around the perimeter of the box and took a deep breath. There was plenty of air to fill his lungs.

James thought about opening the lid so he could sit up and look around but decided against it. He remained quietly in his hiding place, hoping he was with friends and not on the way to his final burial place. He became increasingly aware of the pain in his neck and shoulders and welcomed it as verification that he was alive.

He tried to relive the circumstances which allowed him to survive the hanging but could not recall anything after the shock of the fall. Accepting the lack of informative memories, he tried to allay the pain by counting the rotations of the wagon wheels. As he lost himself in the rhythmic repetition of the turnings, he fantasized about Pleasant Valley Farm and his short life there with Sally. His present situation did not contaminate his reverie. He closed his eyes, replaced the present with the past, and slept.

The driver kept the wagon on a straight course to the south and held the horses to a walk. He eventually reached a designated crossroad and slowed the wagon as he made a sharp turn to the left. A grove of trees stood on the far side of the road and he pulled onto an unused country lane. He turned and looked over his shoulder to see if the wagon could be observed from the road. Satisfied he was safe, he pulled the horses up short, left the seat and climbed into the back of the wagon. Again, he glanced toward the road and then reached down and lifted the lid from the coffin.

James awoke with a start and tried to rise but was too stiff to move. He lay back and stared up at the figure towering over him. A black man. He looked familiar but a moment passed before James recognized him.

"Conshy Joe," he gasped in disbelief. "Wha…why…how…?" He was so shocked by the presence of the downtrodden boy from Hebe's that he could not formulate a coherent question. The boy looked older and stood straighter as James viewed him from the bottom of his coffin. Instead of the servile odd jobber James had seen working at Hebe Balderston's, a proud man with a classically-molded face looked down at him. How could he have looked at the young boy without noticing his high forehead, his sculpted nose with its fine bridge and gracefully flaring nostrils, the wide smile which exposed large, even white teeth and his dark eyes? It was his eyes that captivated James. The eyes of the boy at Hebe's had been downcast and wary, but the man above him had a steady, knowing gaze which revealed a confident intellect.

Conshy Joe extended his hand, "Let me help you up, James."

James bristled at the black man's familiarity. Immediately embarrassed by his involuntary reaction, he firmly accepted the hand of his liberator and allowed himself to be pulled to a standing position. James grimaced and then flinched as his tortured muscles rebelled against the movement.

Conshy Joe helped him from the casket, replaced the lid and motioned for him to sit on the flat surface.

"How do you feel? I am sorry I couldn't stop sooner but I had no way of knowing whether we were being pursued."

"I am sore but alive." James looked closely at his rescuer. "I don't understand...." He realized he did not understand anything about what had just transpired.

"I don't understand how or why you saved me, Conshy Joe." He looked at the seemingly self-assured black man who stood in front of him. "And I do not understand how you have changed so much in the few months I have been away from Hebe's."

"I haven't changed, James. I was forced to hide behind the façade of a simpleton. I am a runaway. I look younger than my years so it was relatively safe for me to assume the guise of a submissive, uneducated boy."

The young man sat down next to James. "As to your first question: the reason I'm here is because of Sister Sarah...."

"Sally?" Again, James was astonished.

"She was the first one to take me in. She found me foraging in the Pleasant Valley fields one night and hid me in her room. Early the next morning, she took me to Mrs. Balderston's tavern. In spite of her...," he paused as he looked away, "unconventional ways, she convinced Mrs. Balderston to use me in the tavern."

James was horrified by what he had just heard. "You would have been killed if anyone had found you in a white woman's room. And Sally, she would have been...." James shuddered at the prospects of Sally's treatment.

"Sister Sarah is an unusual woman, James. And a very smart one, too. She listened to the rumors and was afraid you would be found guilty. Then she remembered that I had been forced to serve as a hangman back in Virginia." Conshy Joe rubbed his eyes. "No white man wanted to dirty his hands so they made me, a slave, do their nasty work for them." The look on his face told of the pain associated with taking another man's life.

"It was then that she realized she had a chance to save you if she could get me to help her. I did not want to do it. I was afraid I would make a mistake and you would actually hang. She is very convincing and she talked me into being part of the plan." He smiled, "The fact that the sheriff could not find anyone else to serve as hangman made it all possible.

"Sister Sarah came up with the idea for the hood and the heavy leather strap that saved your neck. And she is the one who thought of sending a second wagon with a duplicate coffin for burial in the cemetery. She arranged for Nathaniel Holmes, John Heep, Solomon Davis and Elijah Thomas to drive the cart and help me bring you down from the gallows. She is also the one who suggested I bring you with me to Norfolk, Virginia." James was startled by the possibility that he would be traveling further with Conshy Joe.

"I slipped up with Sister Sarah that night in the field," the black man continued, "and she immediately recognized that I was not an ordinary runaway slave. She confronted me and I told her about my past, and also, that I escaped after the last hanging and have been on the run ever since.

"I am a valuable piece of property, James. I can read and write. I am good with numbers and I am an excellent trader. A large reward has been offered for my return as these skills are worth money to the master who is running a plantation. My dreams, however, are for a future far removed from that of a white man's slave."

Conshy Joe looked straight at James. "You were always decent to me, James Daunt. I hope Sister Sarah is right and that I can convince you to help me achieve them."

The sound of wooden wheels on the dirt path interrupted the fugitive slave's discourse. James jumped off the coffin and started to climb over the side of the farm cart.

"Stay, James Daunt," Conshy Joe looked toward the road. "This should be Sister Sarah. We are waiting for her."

James' heart was pounding so hard he could feel the blood pulsing against his eardrums. Sally? Here? Was she to be part of his new life? Was there a plan for that new life? One with a safe destination?

His stomach churned as he faced Conshy Joe. "I have to ask you…."

"No, James Daunt." The black man interrupted him. "I am aware of Sister Sarah's needs and her attractions, but in spite of the obvious temptations, we have never come together."

He smiled, then stood and assumed the bent-over stance of Hebe's lackey.

"Ah be a good black boy, Massah, and she be a prahpah white lady. Besides which," he straightened up and became serious. "I am no fool, James. I have not come this far to swing at the end of a lynch mob's rope in payment for a moment's pleasure with a white woman."

James was relieved, and again, angry with himself for the revulsion he had felt at the thought of Sally and Conshy Joe together. He knew she had experienced many men, and at first, it had not bothered him as it had been her way as long as he had known her. However, she was a different person in his eyes now, as was Conshy Joe. As was he. He was beginning to view his instincts and reactions from a different perspective. Two people he had thought simple and insignificant had turned into intelligent individuals who had saved his life, and hopefully, would help him determine the way to change the course of his future.

And he, himself, was a different person. No longer dissolute, he was now a man with a working brain. He wondered if it was possible for him, in his reincarnation, to have a second chance, to rechart his life.

James watched as a single horse pulled the community farm cart around the corner and approached them. He felt the familiar thrill race through his body when he glimpsed the female figure at the reins. As the cart drew near, he saw Sally's red hair trailing from under her bonnet. She pulled up close to the two men, smiled and surveyed James.

"You survived," she sounded relieved.

She looked closely at James to assure herself he was, indeed, unharmed, and then she stepped from the wagon and hitched her horse to a tree.

"We never knew whether the leather strap would actually prevent your neck from being broken or whether it would offer sufficient support to keep the noose from strangling you." She smiled again. "Joseph Baughman made it for us even though he has never forgiven you for leaving his shop without a word of warning the day you shot Squire Holt." She laughed. "In spite of your misdeeds, you still have friends, James Daunt."

She became serious. "Are you really fine?"

James jumped down from the wagon and moved quickly to stand in front of her. He took her hands in his and said, "I think so. My neck has taken a beating, my shoulders are sore and my head aches, but I am alive, thanks to you and Conshy Joe."

He wanted to grab her and hold her close, but unlike the old Sally, she stood erect and apart from him. He was used to having her tease him with her body, to having her lean against him, to feeling her brazen touch on pleasurable places.

Instead, her hands lay quietly in his even as he suggestively stroked her palms with his fingers. She gave no response and he dropped her hands and moved back a step.

"What's wrong, Sally?" He spoke the question almost as an admission that he knew something had changed between them.

"You must leave immediately, James. There may be questions. We do not know whether there are suspicions about the hanging or if anyone saw the second wagon. There were grumblings about the swift removal of your body from the gallows."

"Where am I to go, Sally? What am I to do?" James realized he was adrift in a world of unknowns. Unaware that he had a chance for a new future, he had allowed himself no delusions, no dreams, no plans.

Quite sure he knew the answer before speaking, he asked hesitantly, "Are you coming with me, Sally?" Then, as emotion welled up in him, he added, "You must know how much I need you, and," his voice broke, "how much I love you."

He saw her expression soften and she moved close to him. She pressed her body to his and stroked his face. She laid her head on his chest and accepted his arms as he pressed her to him. They stood, the feelings mounting between them until James could bear it no longer.

"Sally, you must come with me. I found a new life with you when we were at Pleasant Valley. My mind is clear and it remained so even when I was in prison. I have no interest in revisiting my past vices. I have changed Sally, and so have you. You know you care for me and," he laughed, "we certainly are emotionally well-suited." He held her shoulders and looked into her eyes. "Sally, I need you. Please, tell me you are coming with me."

She reached up and touched his cheek.

"No, James, I have other plans." She twisted her forefinger in his beard the way she used to do when they lay facing each other on the small bed in his room at Pleasant Valley. He felt himself respond to her intimacy.

"You are the first man I have allowed myself to truly love, but...," she removed her finger and patted the stray strands of his beard. "You have a wife and a child on the way. You are starting a new life and you should live it with them."

"Sally, you forget. I am a dead man. I cannot go home to Margaret. I would be arrested and all of this would have been for naught."

"Margaret loves you, James. She will be happy to find you alive and well. You will have to exercise caution, but she will come." Sadness tinged Sally's voice. "I know she will come."

She touched his arm and smiled. "We had a wonderful time, James, but it would never last. I would tire of being with one person. I would return to being 'Sally of the Alley'."

She laughed. "I know that is what the boys call me. And, James, that is who I am. I have many needs and I require many men, not just one, to fulfill them. No, James, I cannot come with you. I love you too much to subject you to the pain of my infidelity."

Embarrassed by her admission, Sally covered her discomfort by flicking her skirt at James and moving between him and Conshy Joe. The black man turned away as Sally tossed her hair, cupped her breasts in the old familiar way and thrust her pelvis in James' direction.

"Do not forget me, James Daunt. Do not forget me."

Just as quickly, she dropped her hands, straightened and turned back to her friend, the man who had made her lover's escape possible.

"Have you spoken to James about your plans, Joseph?"

"I had just begun, Sister Sarah."

Conshy Joe addressed James. "I am going to Virginia with you, James, ostensibly as your freed manservant. Sometime in the late fall, when I learn of the actual departure date, I will be sailing for Monrovia, in Liberia, with the American Colonization Society."

James remembered his casual thoughts of the bent-over black boy and his questioning whether Hebe's humble servant would want to be transported to a strange land. Now, having seen the man who replaced the boy, he was not surprised that Conshy Joe would eagerly pursue an opportunity for a productive life in a new world.

"I have some money, James, and I am going to set up a trading venture. Sister Sarah assures me that you would make a good partner. I need someone to handle the transactions here in America and I agree with her judgment."

As Conshy Joe spoke of his plans and of his hopes that James would join him, Sally stepped back from the two men. She turned, hurried to her horse and freed him from the tree. She climbed onto the seat of the cart and picked up the reins. James heard the wheels roll on the rough surface of the lane as she steered the horse back to the road. He started to run.

"I am going, James," she said, holding her hand up to stop him. "Joseph, you take good care of him for me." She did not smile as she flicked a command to her horse and he began to move.

"Sally," James cried. "Stop. At least say goodbye."

She urged her horse to a trot. Her red hair broke loose in the wind as her bonnet slipped off and hung uselessly down her back. James watched her turn off the lane and head north, back to the county seat, to her father and then to Pleasant Valley Farm, the place he ardently wished was his next destination.

An overwhelming feeling of loss enveloped James as he stood in that foreign grove of trees.

Conshy Joe put his hand on his shoulder and said, "I'll bury your hood while you chop this casket to kindling. Anyone sees us with it is going to wonder what a white man from up north is doing heading south with an empty coffin and a colored man in tow."

He reached under the wagon seat and pulled out an axe. He laid it on the ground, and yanked the coffin from the wagon.

James stood over the axe and stared at it. He picked it up and started to swing. He swung and swung that long-handled instrument of destruction. He felt his body strain from the effort and willingly suffered the pain in his neck, his shoulders, his back.

His head throbbed, his chest felt as if it would burst and the tears started to flow. He cried for the loss of Sally, for the fear he had felt when the noose dropped over his neck, for the wrongs he had done to Richard Holt and Margaret, for the wrongs that had been done to him. He sobbed and swung, sobbed and swung until the large box had been reduced to shreds.

He did not stop until Conshy Joe grabbed the axe handle in mid-air and said, "Enough. You have had enough. We must move on. You have exorcised as much as you can through physical labor. Now we start anew."

Ridiculous as James found his words at first, he came to know that this was, indeed, a new beginning. He had been brought back from the dead, resurrected and given a new life. He would have to choose a new name, a new life history. Time enough for that.

A brief memory of Ethan's account of the British civilian whose reprieve was capriciously overturned by Andrew Jackson passed through his mind. James shivered when he thought of how that man had been legally saved from a death sentence one day and executed by a vindictive general's firing squad on the next. Fear of experiencing the same fate motivated him to turn his back on the mutilated coffin and take his place on the wagon seat. Instead of sitting next to him, Conshy Joe climbed into the bed of the wagon.

"What are you doing back there?" James asked.

"We be in slave territory, Massah. I be in my place." James stared unbelievingly at his savior then accepted the reality of the situation. The self-educated, brave and handsome man sitting behind him was taking another chance. He was returning to the world of his beginnings where there was little hope for a man with black skin who had been born the property of a white-skinned owner.

James drove steadily until he was sure they had crossed into the next state. The sun was sinking below the horizon when he looked over his shoulder at Conshy Joe.

"Can you take the reins? I did not sleep last night and my stint at the end of a rope has become a reality. My body is trembling from head to toe. I must get some rest before I fall off this seat."

"It's not safe to stop here," Conshy Joe said, as he surveyed the flat landscape on both sides of the road. "Drive on until we find a protected place where we can spend the night."

James struggled to keep his eyes open and his hands steady until he heard, "Over there, James."

Conshy Joe pointed to the remains of a barn. A partial stone wall faced the road; rubble remained where a side wall had collapsed. "We can park the wagon there, where it cannot be seen."

Once inside their shelter, Conshy Joe released the horse from its traces. Relieved of its burden, a shiver ran down the back of the animal as it was led away from the wagon. Conshy Joe tied it to a beam which ran crosswise along the side of a deteriorating stall. Someone had stored hay under a remaining portion of the roof. He gathered some for the horse and James began carrying armfuls to use as protection against the cold of the night.

The two men cleared spots on the earthen floor and laid down the hay. "I could do with some food," James said as he stretched out on his makeshift bed.

"Don't complain," his companion countered. "At least you had a meal before they took you to the gallows. I was too nervous to eat."

"You are right. I got to eat my last meal." James laughed out loud. "One that was intended to hold me for eternity." He turned onto his side and thought of Sally as he fell into a deep sleep.

Conshy Joe was not as lucky. He had grave doubts about this part of the plan. They still had many miles to cover before they reached their destination in Virginia. Once there, he knew he would be safe with the American Colonization Society. The organization sheltered its passengers until the ships were ready to sail. He could not allow himself to relax until he reached the port and was registered to emigrate to Liberia.

After Sally turned north, she forced her horse into a gallop and kept him at that pace in spite of the burden of the bouncing cart on the uneven road. She had to get far away from James Daunt, to outrun the temptation to turn back to him. She knew it was reckless to drive her horse this way. The ruts and holes were almost certain to trip him and a horse with a broken leg would do her no good. She slowed to a stop and let her tears run freely down her cheeks and onto the skirt which covered her community trousers. Then, refusing to wallow in her unhappiness, she wiped her eyes, clicked the reins and let her horse set his own pace as she headed back to town where her father waited.

Elongated shadows created by a fading sun patterned the ground when Sally reached the meadow. She turned to the right and drove off the road as she entered the valley. The gallows had been dismantled; the officials, the ceremonial mounted escort, the deputies and the gawkers had gone home. In the distance she could see a few stragglers standing in front of the tavern where the revelers had bid on pieces of the notorious noose.

Sally pulled over and halted her horse. She thought of how she had changed since James had come into her life. Acceptance of the fact that she would never see him again brought her as much sorrow as if he had died at the end of a rope. She let her sadness linger for a moment. Then, shaking it off, she steered her horse across the crushed weeds and scuffed patches of soil where thousands of folks had stood and cheered as James Daunt's body dangled from the gibbet. No longer noticeable, particles of blood mingled with the earth where, a few hours ago, Maris Hicks had reveled in anticipation of the imminent annihilation of his detested brother-in-law.

Oblivious to the physical remnants of the day's activities, Sally left the meadow. She drove without stopping and reached the inn at suppertime. The multitudes had returned home and only she, her father, and two spinster ladies were in residence.

Thaddeus Goodenough was at the dining table when Sally entered the main room. Disapproval marked his face as he said, "I did not see you this afternoon, Sister Sarah."

"I could not watch," Sally answered truthfully. "I took the horse and cart and left town until it was over."

"He died quickly." Her father put his hand on her shoulder in an attempt to console her. "There was a scuffle and the hangman, fearing a riot, cut his body down too soon for those who had hoped to see him hang there longer.

"His premature act disappointed those who cursed the executioner and threatened to confiscate the coffin but I knew it was the will of the Lord. '*And if a man have committed a sin worthy of death, and is be to be put to death, and thou hang him on a tree:*

"'*His body shall not remain all night upon the tree, but thou shalt in any wise bury him that day....*' Deuteronomy Twenty-one, verses twenty-two and twenty-three."

The reverend put his hand to his forehead and said, "I prayed most sincerely for James' agony to end and the Lord came to me and answered my prayers. It was over quickly. The executioner escaped the wrath of the rabble and arrived at the cemetery without incident. I was there to deliver the final plea for salvation over his grave."

Thaddeus Goodenough was genuinely sorry about the death of James Daunt; however, he had to admit he was relieved to know James would never be able to reveal his reckless admission of heresy.

Sally was momentarily tempted to tell him of James' worldly redemption. She chose, however, to leave the reverend content in his belief that it was his intervention with God that had saved the condemned man from the torture of the damned.

There was little conversation between father and daughter until they rose to go to their rooms. Sally put her hand on Thaddeus' arm and said, "I do not want to stay here any longer. It is too painful. I would like to leave tonight."

Thaddeus hesitated as he thought of undertaking a second long trip on this day. He looked at his daughter and noted the strain on her face.

"I am tired but I think I can make the journey. Are you all right?"

"Yes," Sally said with relief. "Thank you, Thaddeus, for understanding."

It was after dark when they left the county seat. Sally handled the reins while the exhausted cleric slept on the hard floor of the cart. As they passed Hebe Balderston's tavern, Sally thought of the debt she owed to Hebe and the lads and acknowledged that, in all

270

probability, she would never see them, or James Daunt, again. Her chest constricted as a deep sense of loss cut off her wind and caused her to gasp for breath.

She wanted to turn around, to return to the tavern and join the lighthearted camaraderie that she knew existed inside the familiar building. Instead, she continued on. The reverend was sure to recognize at least one of the celebrants and become suspicious about the goings-on at the hanging. While she knew her father inherently opposed the death sentence, she was not sure how he would react to the knowledge that his daughter had arranged the escape of a convicted murderer.

She also feared that the boys would want to share their celebratory good times with their willing partner of the past. They were good and loyal lads but the thought of their clumsy hands clutching at her body, even in jest, repulsed her. She had grown past Sally of the Alley and was ready to fully embrace the sequestered life her father had created at Pleasant Valley Farm.

# *Sunday, April 5, 1829*

James and Conshy Joe arose before dawn and resumed their journey south.

"We must get something to eat," James said, as his stomach grumbled its discontent.

"Too early to find crops growing in the fields." Conshy Joe had been looking for a source of sustenance since they left the barn. He had seen nothing. A building appeared on the horizon and he pointed to it. "James, ahead. That looks like an inn."

"We have no money. If there is work to be done in exchange, it will take all day. I don't think we can take the chance in case there have been questions about my death. A posse could be close behind."

"I have a small amount of money which your friends collected for our escape."

Surprised, James silently thanked Conshy Joe for his foresight and the lads from Hebe's for their support.

"Good. We can stop and have a real meal." James flicked the reins and hurried the horse in anticipation of filling his belly.

"I cannot go in with you," the black man announced and James was embarrassed by his thoughtless comment.

"You're right, Conshy Joe. I'll get the food and bring it out. We can eat while we travel."

"You might arouse suspicion if you do that, James. The safest thing would be for you to go in, eat at the table and I will go to the kitchen and see what the cook will throw at me."

James had never paid much attention to the way the black slaves were treated. Now, he had to accept the fact that the man who had risked his life to save him was forced to eat kitchen scraps like an animal, while that same man's money paid for James to eat a hearty meal in a dining room.

"I will not do it. I'll come with you to the kitchen and we will share the scraps."

"No, James. That would not be acceptable and we both need to eat. We will behave in the accepted way so no one will suspect anything is amiss."

Faced with no other alternative, James consented. When they reached the inn, he pulled up in front, jumped down from the wagon seat, left the reins dangling and entered the inn. He could hear Conshy Joe speaking in the sing-song dialect of the Southern slave as he led the horse to the stable behind the inn.

James ate quickly, wrapped part of his dinner in a frayed napkin and secreted it under his shirt. He retrieved the horse and wagon and loudly ordered Conshy Joe into the back. After they had left the inn and were far from the possibility of curious eyes observing them, James pulled out the pilfered napkin with the cold remains of his meal and handed them to his hungry companion.

Conshy Joe laughed and said, "Not a very attractive parcel, James, but a far sight better than anything they shared with me in the kitchen. Thank you." His voice turned serious. "I hope they don't come after us for the napkin." They both laughed but realized that something as simple as the possession of a stolen napkin could put them in danger.

James urged the horse forward, this time out of caution rather than anticipation. When they had put a fair amount of distance between them and the inn, he pulled over to the side of the road, found a half-buried rock and took the soiled piece of linen from Conshy Joe. He carefully folded it into a small square, lifted the stone and placed the napkin in the hole. He replaced the rock and tamped down the dirt around it. On the off chance that they were stopped, no one would suspect he had taken anything from the inn as they now carried nothing with them but the clothes on their backs. And of course, they had Conshy's small stash of money which remained concealed in the band of the cap he wore.

As she had driven through the night, Sally's thoughts had been dominated by concern for James, the possible discovery of his escape, and his perilous trip to Virginia. She was aware of the dangers he and Conshy Joe might encounter: James, a convicted murderer; his companion, a runaway slave. Their chances of safely reaching the port city of Norfolk in that Southern state, and then, of finding the means to set up a trade route were sketchy at best. Contrary to her nature, she was worried.

Thaddeus had awakened with the first rays of sunlight, and shortly afterward, Sally had handed him the reins. She had remained on the seat next to him, knowing sleep would not come until she had returned to Pleasant Valley and settled into the predictability of the repetitive routines of the community.

The time had passed slowly as they travelled the north-south road. Recognizable fields had eventually appeared on her left and she saw the residents plowing furrows and preparing the soil for the seed which would be planted in mid-May.

When Thaddeus finally pulled up in front of the main building, Sally leaned over and kissed the Reverend Goodenough on the cheek.

"Thank you, Father," she said, before she climbed down from the wagon.

Thaddeus sat for a moment and then removed his hat and ran his fingers through his hair. It was time. Time for him, for Sarah, for everyone to acknowledge his paternity of the exceptional young woman he watched walk through the open door of the residence. Pride in his resolve, in her maturity, pervaded his mind and body. Pride of parentage was not enough, however, to completely mollify the recurring ache that accompanied his thoughts of his daughter.

Sally's mother watched from the window of her room. She saw Sally kiss Thaddeus on the cheek and immediately recognized the change in their relationship. She had little hope for improvement in her life but prayed that Sally would one day know normalcy. As for Thaddeus, she still cared for him, and of all his followers, she, alone, knew of the demons he carried with him and how they influenced his teachings.

She moved to open the door when she heard Sally's footsteps in the hall.

"I am sorry, Sarah. I know how much James meant to you."

"It is over and I must forget him." Sally looked at her mother. "Did you ever forget about Father? In the years before you and I came here, did you ever love another man?"

The older woman noticed her daughter's use of the word, "Father." This was the first time she had heard Sally verbally acknowledge his biological role in her lineage.

"I never loved anyone but your father. And you, of course."

"I know that," Sally continued to stare at her mother. "We are a lot alike, you know."

Her mother was silent as she considered Sally's statement and then she spoke. "We are, but our backgrounds are very different. My father was, like yours, a man of the cloth. But he was the minister of a church; a fire and brimstone preacher with traditional values and opinions. He was appalled by the ideas Thaddeus espoused. I was banished from my home as much for Thaddeus' blasphemies as I was for my own indiscretion. Where my father was a dogmatic tyrant, yours is a confused, guilt-ridden apologist seeking justification for his transgressions. You and I both suffered from the dragons our fathers were determined to slay."

"Things are different now," Sally said as she touched her fingertips to her temples. She had no energy left for conversation. "I'm tired. I would like to lie down."

"One moment." The washerwoman had interesting news for her daughter and she picked an object from the top of the chest which stood by the door.

"You have received a letter." She handed the epistle to Sally.

Surprised, Sally said, "I wonder who would be writing to me."

"I recognize the hand. It is from Lucy McDougal."

Sally frowned, "Why would she write to me. I made...."

"Yes, I know. She said goodbye to me before she left. She told me of her deception and the jeopardy in which she put you. I cannot believe I was unaware of her treachery but I was so worried about you that I only saw her as a healer."

She touched the side of Sally's face and then dropped her hand as she continued, "Lucy McDougal was most contrite when she left and grateful that you did not report her to the authorities."

"Where is she?"

"I do not know. Perhaps, she mentions her whereabouts in the letter."

Sally broke the seal on the back of the envelope and unfolded the note.

" '*Dear Sister Sarah,*' " she began to read aloud.

" '*I fear you will discard my letter before reading the contents when you discover its author so I will state my case without delay.*

" '*Knowing what you do of my descent into deceit and wickedness, you have no cause to trust my judgment. I have, however, met a remarkable woman who shares many of my philosophical ideas, and many of the same beliefs that I encountered at Valley.*' " Sally raised her eyebrows.

" '*She has published essays on matters of concern to women and now plans to speak out in public against the laws, the moral and ethical codes which allow women to be used as wives or companions for the pleasure of men. Furthermore, she advocates divorce: for personal liberation as well as for the alleviation of the detrimental effect of ill-suited parents on the welfare of their children. She is also an active advocate for public education for all children, no matter what their color or sex.*

" '*I write of my friend's accomplishments as I have joined her crusade to fight for freedom for women here and abroad. She is scheduled to speak in Philadelphia on the eighteenth of May, and knowing the liberal environment which has nurtured your intellect, I think you would be greatly moved by her words, and perhaps, inspired to join our cause.*

" '*I have a room where you can stay and would be honored to have you partake of my hospitality.*' "

Sally looked over at her mother, "It is signed, '*in friendship, Lucy McDougal*'."

"I wonder if she has read of James' fate," her mother mused.

"Knowing Lucy, I would say you are very perceptive and that she has, indeed, heard of James' sentencing, and as a result, she has anticipated my state of mind."

Sally walked over and put her arm around her mother's shoulders. Surprised, the older woman glanced sideways at her daughter and smiled.

"You have changed, Sarah." She covered Sally's hand with hers. "I am truly sorry about James. He brought new life to you and now he is gone. I hope you can preserve the memory of his days here and they will bring you solace."

"I hurt all over from the loss of him," Sally admitted.

She waved the letter in the air as she recognized the opportunity which had just presented itself. Her resolve to submerge herself in community life vanished.

"I think I will go to Philadelphia. I never believed that Thaddeus' proclamations on the equality of the sexes would eventually be accepted outside of the community. Perhaps hearing these beliefs publicly expounded by a woman will bring them widespread recognition. And," she subconsciously smiled her wicked grin, "I need something to keep me from thinking of going south."

Her mother looked puzzled but chose not to question the nonsensical statement.


Margaret was deep in thought and did not hear the soft footsteps of the visitor as he tentatively approached the open door behind her.

"I have come to pay my respects, uh…." Nehemiah Trimble, hat in hand, stood in the doorway, "Ma…, Ma…, Margaret." He stuttered as he said her given name.

Nehemiah could not remember a time when he had not been in love with the pretty Margaret Hicks. His infatuation had begun as a childish crush, ripened with his physical maturity and burst forth as full-blown, unbearable passion following her surprise visit on a cold day in January.

"Hello, Nehemiah. It was good of you to come."

Margaret, startled by his unexpected appearance, pulled herself together and smiled her welcome.

"I wanted to...."

Margaret nodded her head in acknowledgement of his sympathies.

"I know. I am pleased you have come. You have always been here for me, Nehemiah. I have counted on you in the past as I am sure I can count on you now."

It was true. The awkward farm boy had always been close by and ready to help during her growing-up years. She was certain of his support now.

"Please sit down, Nehemiah. I must talk to you." She smoothed her skirt and patted the seat of the chair next to her. He started to sit then changed his mind and stood next to her.

Margaret took a deep breath and spoke with a slight tremor in her voice.

"Nehemiah, I am with child."

Nehemiah Trimble flushed and stammered, "Ja..., Ja..., James..., James Daunt's ch...child?" He lowered himself into the chair she had indicated.

Margaret took his hand. "No, Nehemiah. The child will not come until the fall." She let the words sink in before she continued. "The child is yours, Nehemiah."

She turned away from him, remembering the day the lawyer told her James did not have a chance and was certain to hang. Margaret had realized her life as the servant of her siblings was written in stone. Aware that no one would willingly marry the widow of a convicted murderer, Margaret had conceived her plan.

Her time was right on that fateful January day; two weeks had passed since her last menses. She fixed her hair and slipped into her best day dress and cloak. Then she drove herself to Nehemiah Trimble's farm.

When the shy man hesitated to ask her into his home, she told him she was in need of his advice. Flattered, he showed her into the parlor and cleared the sofa so they could be seated. She started to speak but broke down and cried. What had begun as crocodile tears turned into genuine sobs of despair as she acknowledged the future that lay ahead of her if her plan failed.

Nehemiah moved closer to her and she put her head in his lap. Overwhelmed by the close physical contact with his lifelong love and stimulated by her cheek resting between his legs, he lost control of his senses. Encouraged by the desire she had aroused in him, Margaret raised her head to his chest and put her arms around him. Then she lay back on the sofa and gently pulled the vulnerable virgin to her.

Nehemiah's apologetic guilt after their coming together intensified Margaret's distaste for sexual bonding. The objective, however, had been achieved: she was with child. His child. She had realized her goal and ensured her future would be safe from the tentacles of her siblings.

"Mine?" Nehemiah's reactions vacillated between the joy of possibly winning the hand of his childhood sweetheart and sheer horror at the thought of having sired a child out of wedlock, of having bedded the wife of a murderer, and the unwelcome suspicion that he had, perhaps, been compromised.

"Yes, Nehemiah, yours."

As far as Nehemiah Trimble was concerned, however, it was now an indisputable fact. The child was his and its mother, his wife to be.

As for Margaret, she appreciated the absurdity of her situation. Here she was, a woman who abhorred the ultimate union of the sexes and yet she had deliberately entrapped two men by supplying her body for their erotic pleasure. She had endured James' advances because she truly loved him; Nehemiah, however, would get no such consideration after the marriage vows had been said.

As James urged the horse back onto the road, a voice called out. "Stop. Stop right there. I have you in my sight and I will shoot."

James' instincts told him to spur the horse forward, but instead, reason prevailed and he turned around to face the person who had spoken. A lone man stood with his foot on the rock where he had buried the napkin.

"A napkin," he thought. "A single stolen napkin."

"Why are you stopping me?" He called back.

"What did you hide here?" The man kicked at the rock with his foot but it remained solidly in place.

"A handkerchief. I buried a handkerchief."

"Why'd you do that?" The man kicked again with no success.

James thought quickly. "My slave used it." He gambled on the gunman's prejudice. "Wasn't any good to me after that."

The man walked toward them, his musket steady. "Let me look at that slave."

He approached the wagon and stared intently at Conshy Joe. "What's your name, boy?"

James saw his companion bristle, then hunch over in his subservient manner.

"Conshy Joe," he muttered.

"Speak up, boy. I can't hear you."

"His name is Joseph Conshohocken," James said.

"Where'd a nigrah like him get a highfalutin name like that?"

"He is the son of an Indian chief." James was astounded to hear the words come out of his mouth. He had not anticipated the need for an alibi for Conshy Joe. He had feared their real troubles would come from the discovery of his own escape.

"Hey, boys," the man shouted. "I got me a real live black-as-soot Indian chief here."

James turned to see four men on horseback emerge from the woods behind him.

"We been lookin' for your Indian chief, son. He run away yesterday. He's got a big price on his head, dead or alive, and we aim to take the two of you in dead. It's easier."

The men laughed as their leader climbed aboard the wagon, seated himself next to James and placed his musket on his temple.

"Sam," he shouted, "you go to town and get Squire Calvert and his reward money. I'll get this no'thern boy to drive us up the hill."

One of the men spurred his horse and rode off at a gallop. The other three whooped and hollered like drunken Indians as they came abreast of the wagon.

"How you like them sounds, chief? Remind you of home?"

The leader laughed as he increased the pressure on the end of his gun and ordered, "Drive, boy. Just follow that road to the top of the hill there. Ain't got far to go."

James did as he was told. He drove a short distance until the man pointed to a little used cart path off to the left. He followed the path to the top of the hill.

"Stop here." The three men on horseback closed in as their companion lowered his gun and took the reins from James. He deftly maneuvered the wagon under a large tree. He jumped down as one of the other riders dismounted and steadied the horse.

"All right, boys. Stand up on that seat." His comrades leveled their guns at James and Conshy Joe as the leader uncoiled two heavy ropes. He created a simple slip knot and produced a primitive noose. He repeated the process on the second rope as the two remaining riders kept their horses circling the wagon.

"I am sorry, I never should have stopped." James spoke quietly to his friend.

"Someone would have gotten us, James." Conshy Joe stepped onto the seat. James stood and looked at the men.

"Do you think we could get one of their guns?"

"Stop whisperin'." The leader spoke harshly as the men halted their horses and kept their weapons sighted on the prisoners.

"I told you to get up on the seat," The leader climbed into the back of the wagon as James complied. The vigilante swung the free end of the first noose over a thick branch of the tree and then tossed the second in the same direction.

"James," Conshy Joe abandoned his subservient persona and stood straight. "James, I like it."

"Like what?" James asked incredulously.

"Joseph Conshohocken. It's a fine name."

James managed a wry smile. "You are a phenomenal human being, Joseph. I have been very fortunate to know you."

"I feel the same way about you, James. Unfortunately, I fear our friendship is doomed to be quite short-lived."

James looked past the newly-minted Joseph Conshohocken and thought about the irony of his current situation: Here he was, standing on a wagon seat, under a tree, on the top of a high hill with a view that went on for miles; and he was about to be hung for aiding and abetting the recent flight of a runaway slave when, in fact, the suspected slave had been far away, facilitating the escape of a convicted white murderer from death by hanging.

That was the last concrete thought James Daunt had before a noose, for the second time in two days, dropped over his head and encircled his neck.

# *Epilogue*

The man on a white horse looked at the two males in front of him. One was black as coal, the other, pale as a jailbird. They stood next to each other on a wagon seat. Each had a noose around his neck.

"Good work, men," he said, smiling at the vigilantes standing around the makeshift gallows.

"Only problem is he," he pointed to the hunched-over black man, "he ain't my black boy."

The members of the posse shifted uncomfortably as they saw the reward money slipping away.

"May as well hang him anyway," the good-natured slave owner said as he continued to point his finger at Conshy Joe. "Only good nigra is a dead nigra."

He turned away. "Keep lookin', boys. Reward just went up ten dollars." He spurred his horse and headed back towards town.

"Easiest thing to do is hang 'em," the leader said. "Ropes are up and we're in the mood for a party."

"Don't seem right. He," a second speaker pointed to James Daunt, "ain't done nothin' wrong, if as he says, this one," he moved his finger to point to Conshy Joe, "really is his slave and not a runaway...."

"Yankee stranger. You heard him talk. Up north abolitionist, if you ask me."

"Wait a minute." James spoke up. "You have nothing to gain by hanging us. There are people who'll come looking for me."

"You scare us, white man," one of the captors sneered.

"Quiet, Tom." The leader took charge. "We could let him go and sell the black one. Gotta get something out of this."

James Daunt, the rope still around his neck, said, "Conshy Joe, here, he won't bring anything on the auction block. Look at him. Nothing but skin and bones and bent over, too."

His companion was, indeed, a sorry sight. The man who had momentarily stood tall as the noose dropped over his head, now appeared slight of build with rounded shoulders and a hangdog carriage. He was the image of an unmotivated, worthless parasite.

"What you got to trade for your freedom?

"Horse and wagon we came in," James replied.

"No money?"

"No."

"How you get down here without any money?"

"I have a job waiting in Virginia."

"Doing what?"

James paraphrased Joseph's words: "I'm good with figures."

"Oh." The leader of the group thought for a moment. "We'll take the horse and wagon. No need to bargain with them, boys, they ain't got a choice." He shook his head. "They're no good to us alive and no good dead. No sense worrying the sheriff over two strangers decorating the hanging tree."

The leader pointed to James Daunt. "Let's see if the man who's so good at figures is as good at walking. Long way from here to Virginia with no horse and no money." He laughed.

"Free 'em, boys, and get them off the wagon." Reluctantly, two of the men lifted the ropes over the heads of the previously doomed men. Then, as a last gesture, they pushed the two former prisoners off the wagon. James fell in the dirt but Conshy Joe momentarily forgot his submissive facade and landed effortlessly on his feet. He quickly resumed his survival role and shuffled over to stand by James. Only one of the mounted men noticed the bent-over boy's agility. He raised his eyebrows but decided to keep quiet.

The leader tied his horse to the back of the wagon and mounted the seat. He flicked the reins, and without a backward glance, turned the horse around and headed down the hill. His posse followed behind.

James looked off into the distance and grinned. "I think we should avoid the town, Joseph, what do you think?"

The black man laughed. "I think that's a very good idea, James." Joseph pointed straight ahead. "I suggest we go south, across that field." He grimaced. "Another day with meager pickings for our stomachs. But...," he put his hand on James' shoulder. "The sun is shining. We have money in my hat, shoes on our feet, and a bright future ahead of us once we reach Virginia."

James looked at his companion. "Two days ago, I would have scoffed at anyone who said Conshy Joe was a positive person. You, Joseph, are a constant amazement to me."

As James walked away from the hanging tree he realized his friend was lagging several paces behind.

"Just being safe, James," Joseph said as he bent over and dragged his feet. "We have a long trip ahead of us and a servile Conshy Joe has a much better chance of making it to Norfolk than a cocky Joseph Conshohocken.

"By the way," he stopped and stood straight. "I think 'The Chatsworth and Conshohocken Liberian Trading Company' would be a good name for our venture."

The future entrepreneur noticed James' puzzled expression and said, "You gave me a new identity, the least I can do is return the favor."

"Chatsworth," James spoke the name softly, "James Chatsworth." Images of Sally and Pleasant Valley, Margaret and his unborn child interrupted his contemplation. Sadly, he pushed them from his mind. They belonged to the world of James Daunt and James Daunt was dead. However, James Chatsworth was alive and standing free under a bright southern sky.

"The Chatsworth and Conshohocken Liberian Trading Company." James said the words slowly, reverently. Then James Chatsworth extended his hand and Joseph Conshohocken shook it.

"I like it, Joseph," James said. "It's a fine name. A fine name indeed."

# *Questions*

1. The word "reverberation" means an extended or continuing effect resulting from an action or event. Beginning with the two shots fired at Squire Holt, there are a number of instances in *Reverberation, The Novel,* where actions precipitate subsequent actions and/or consequences. Which do you consider the most important to plot and character development?

2. Abuse of power by religious father figures, slanderous political campaigning, abortion, torture, and racial discrimination are touched on in the book. These same subjects are extensively covered by our news media today. What are the similarities, and differences, between events in *Reverberation, The Novel,* and those which are happening now?

3. Inheritance. The word itself conjures up material goods and wealth, social standing, DNA, personality traits, and a slew of other good and bad built-ins. Inheritance can also be the panacea for the need, or greed, for money. How does the prospect of an inheritance motivate members of the Hicks family? Would the schism between Maris and his sisters have occurred if Richard Holt hadn't testified to the existence of a deathbed will? Are the Hicks siblings dysfunctional and, if so, how? Was the family, as a unit, already in crisis before the death of Jacob Hicks?

4. Which do you think came first: Thaddeus Goodenough's radical religious ideas or his sexual activities? Can you accept any of his proselytizations? If so, how would they change your way of life?

5. The utopian socialist communities of the nineteenth century were reborn in the second half of the twentieth century with the establishment of hippie communes. Using Pleasant Valley Farm as an example, do you think the utopian and hippie communes share similar roots, philosophies, and living conditions? How are they the same? How do they differ? Are these factions lifestyle advocates or protest groups?

6. The presidential contest between John Quincy Adams and Andrew Jackson is the first in which political parties play a major role. How does the 1828 campaign compare with our current presidential race? Which do you think plays a larger role in determining the outcome of an election: the exaggerations, untruths and rumors of the candidates' representatives or the candidates' avowed stands on the issues? Are you in favor of campaign reform and what are your suggestions?

7. How does James Daunt impact the lives of Jacob Hicks' four daughters? Is his influence life-altering in each case?

8. The American Colonization Society supported the settlement of free blacks in the colony of Liberia. Why would these men and women choose to uproot themselves and their families and move to an unknown, primitive land? Do you think similar repatriation efforts would help to solve our country's current illegal immigrant problem?

9. The forms of torture described in *Reverberation, The Novel,* were actually used as psychiatric therapies in the early nineteenth century. Is the horror of torture less when it is employed as a medical "cure" or in a religious ritual than when it is used as punishment or for information-gathering? Can you think of any contemporary medical treatments which can be described as torture? How do you feel about the Guantanamo Bay water-boarding controversy?

10. Do you equate Thaddeus Goodenough's initiation of Sally with the abuse of today's religious father figures? Do you think Sally's resulting promiscuity is an understandable aftereffect of the violation by a trusted adult? Does Sally's anticipation of Thaddeus's initiation make the preacher's act any less perverse?

11. Under certain circumstances, James, Sally and Conshy Joe minimalize their innate intelligence. What are their reasons? Do Sally and James seek to avoid responsibility for their actions by hiding behind carefree façades?

12. Sally goes to an Indian shaman first, and then to an herbalist when she seeks to abort James' baby. Can you sympathize with women who turn to untrained abortionists for help with unwanted pregnancies? Some women bond with their babies at the time they become aware of their pregnancies, other women never form that bond. Do you think the latter situation is due to circumstances or the nature of the mother-to-be? Do you think abortion should be the political issue it is today?

13. Why does Sally choose to return to Pleasant Valley Farm instead of joining James in his new life? Why does she then decide to follow Lucy MacDougal? What would early suffragettes think about the lifestyle, appearance and behavior of today's women? In your opinion, have things "gone too far" or not far enough?

14. Do you think a convicted white murderer and a runaway black slave will find financial success as international traders working in primitive Liberia and antebellum Virginia?

Go to <u>www.reverberationthenovel.com</u> for additional questions.

# *Acknowledgements*

My eternal gratitude to Hillary Wittich, Nickie Smith, Lucy Cherry and Ed Guenther for their constructive criticisms, insightful comments and much needed encouragement.

*Merci beaucoup, mes amis.*